## Praise for *Starting fro*

"In *Starting from Scratch*, Kate Lloyd creates a delightful cast of characters with flaws to which we can all relate. This is a story rich with details from the Lancaster County Amish countryside. You'll want to keep turning the pages through the twists and turns to discover if Eva makes the right choices in love and faith."

**Kelly Irvin,** author of the Amish of Bee County series

"From the whirlwind beginning to the delightfully unexpected ending, *Starting from Scratch* is an adventurous tale of life as you rarely see it."

**Naomi Miller,** author of the Amish Sweet Shop Mystery series

"Love, forgiveness, and a reminder of the devastating power of words—*Starting from Scratch* will tug at your heartstrings, tickle your funny bone, and leave you breathless for more."

**Amy Lillard,** author of the Wells Landing Series

"You will enjoy every minute you spend with *Starting from Scratch*, and you will come away at the end with new life in your heart. That's simply the way it is with Kate Lloyd's novels. They're hours and days of reading wonder."

**Murray Pura,** author of *An Amish Family Christmas*

## What Others Are Saying About *A Letter from Lancaster County*

"*A Letter from Lancaster County* is a touching story that explores the way relationships intertwine and the varying ways people interpret the same truths. This book drew me in from the beginning, kept me guessing, and touched my heart—everything I want in a book. Highly recommended."

**Beth Wiseman,** bestselling author of the Daughters of the Promise series

"Two sisters, one man, and a Mennonite farm are at the heart of Kate Lloyd's new novel about family ties. When Angela and Rose, sisters who are opposite in every way, return to their mother's childhood home, they come to grips with issues long neglected...and emerge from the visit transformed. Lloyd's fine storytelling in *A Letter from Lancaster County* will captivate and delight fans."

**Suzanne Woods Fisher,** bestselling author of *The Quieting*

"Kate Lloyd's *A Letter from Lancaster County* is a wonderful read. I was wrapped up in Angela and Rose's story from the first page and couldn't read it fast enough. Kate has a way of writing that feels fresh and new. It was descriptive, meaningful, at times humorous, and always gripping. Anyone who picks up a novel by Kate Lloyd is in for a treat."

**Shelley Shephard Gray,** *New York Times* and *USA Today* bestselling author

"From the first page, I was drawn into this lovely story and felt as if I were walking with the characters through the plain and simple community in Lancaster County. This book will touch your heart."

**Vannetta Chapman,** author of *Anna's Healing*

"Fans of Kate Lloyd will adore this new women's fiction set in Amish country. Dynamic protagonists and an increasingly tense narrative set the scene for a heart-wrenching and engaging story."

**Laura V. Hilton,** author of *The Amish Wanderer*

"Kate Lloyd's newest novel offers an insightful look into the lives and loves of two very different sisters. While dealing sensitively with the very real issues of temptation, brokenness, and unforgiveness, Lloyd manages to avoid pat answers while still offering the hope of redemption. *A Letter from Lancaster County* is a thoroughly engaging read."

**Ann Tatlock,** award-winning author of *Once Beyond a Time*

"In *A Letter from Lancaster County*, Kate Lloyd tells a thoughtful and compelling story of two sisters and their life-changing journey. Kate's sense of setting (lovely!) and her depiction of realistic characters quickly draws readers into the drama. As the story unfolds, themes of reconciliation and redemption are explored in a heartfelt and gracious manner."

**Leslie Gould,** bestselling and Christy Award–winning author

"Beautifully written, *A Letter From Lancaster County* is a truly mesmerizing tale."

**Patrick Craig,** author of the Apple Creek Dreams series

# Starting from Scratch

## Books by Kate Lloyd

**LANCASTER DISCOVERIES**

*A Letter from Lancaster County*

*Starting from Scratch*

# Starting from Scratch

KATE LLOYD

HARVEST HOUSE PUBLISHERS
EUGENE, OREGON

All Scripture quotations are taken from the King James Version of the Bible.

Cover by Garborg Design Works

Cover images © Phonlamaiphoto, Milkos, Yastremska / Bigstock

The author is represented by MacGregor Literary, Inc.

This is a work of fiction. Names, characters, places, and incidents are products of the author's imagination or are used fictitiously. Any resemblance to actual persons, living or dead, is entirely coincidental.

**STARTING FROM SCRATCH**



Published by Harvest House Publishers
Eugene, Oregon 97408
www.harvesthousepublishers.com

ISBN 978-0-7369-7023-5 (pbk.)
ISBN 978-0-7369-7024-2 (eBook)

Library of Congress Cataloging-in-Publication Date

Names: Lloyd, Kate (Novelist)
Title: Starting from scratch / Kate Lloyd.
Description: Eugene, Oregon : Harvest House Publishers, [2018]
Identifiers: LCCN 2017035965 (print) | LCCN 2017040450 (ebook) | ISBN 9780736970242 (ebook) | ISBN 9780736970235 (paperback)
Subjects: LCSH: Amish—Fiction. | Lancaster County (Pa.)—Fiction. | BISAC: FICTION / Christian / Romance. | GSAFD: Christian fiction.
Classification: LCC PS3612.L58 (ebook) | LCC PS3612.L58 S73 2018 (print) | DDC 813/.6—dc23
LC recond available at https://lccn.loc.gov/2017035965



**Printed in the United States of America**

18 19 20 21 22 23 24 25 26 / LB-GL / 10 9 8 7 6 5 4 3 2 1

*To my cousin*

*Alex McBrien*

# One

*Mamm* peered out my bedroom window as buggy wheels crunched to a halt in the barnyard.

"*Ach*, Evie." She spoke over her shoulder. "Reuben and Marta are here. Two days early."

I wasn't packed yet, but I plastered on a smile and said, "*Wunderbaar*," as if my whole world weren't being turned upside down.

I flew to the window to see my brother's boisterous family of five gathering boxes from their buggy and making their way up the porch steps to the back door.

Minutes later, Marta, my tall and angular sister-in-law, marched into my bedroom and gave me a one-armed embrace. "Almost finished packing?"

"Uh, not yet. We thought you were coming the day after tomorrow."

Marta straightened my prayer *kapp* and tied the strings under my chin as if I were one of her daughters. "Well, now I can help ya, but you should have already started." Marta's gaze landed on my unmade bed. "Where's your suitcase?" She shouted to her twin daughters. "*Kumm rei*, Nancy and Mary Lou. Help your *aendi* move out."

"I'm the one who needs help," *Mamm* said, I figured for my benefit. "Want to see the *daadi haus*, girls?" She called to them as she started down the stairs to the kitchen. My prudent mother had already thoroughly cleaned and moved my father's and her clothing into the small house attached to a corner of the larger home. My grandparents had resided there before their deaths.

"*Ach*, we packed our belongings yesterday and rose at dawn to get here." Marta let out a weary yawn. "Our landlord was badgering us to leave or he'd charge us another month's rent. And your *bruder* was determined we get here today. He's so excited. But we should have called you first."

My brother Reuben now owned the property and would run the farm so *Dat* could retire.

"Not a problem," I said. "It's fine."

"You do want my help packing, don't ya?" Marta asked. "Our *dochders* are dying to sleep in here tonight."

"They could sleep with me." I straightened my sheets, blanket, and the Lone Star quilt my grandmother made for me when I was a girl. "We can have a slumber party."

"*Nee*, they need to turn in early. We all stayed up too late last night." Her eyes squinted above her beaky nose. "I regret having to say this, but if you'd found yourself a *gut* husband, we wouldn't be in this awkward predicament."

Her words harpooned into my chest. "You may be right." I recalled the sermon one of our ministers expounded in church last Sunday: Turn the other cheek. "Okay, I'll get ready right now. I'm sure *Dat* won't mind taking me today instead."

"I hope you know I'm speaking the truth in love, Evie." She gave me a quick, unexpected one-armed hug. "You may have made mistakes, but I never bought into those rumors."

*Ach*. I didn't want to rehash them. "*Denki*."

Marta called down the stairway. "Reuben, will you please bring up an empty suitcase for your *schweschder*?" Then she sashayed over to my solid-colored dresses and black aprons hanging on hooks on the wall. Her long arms scooped up the clothes as if they were sheaves of harvested wheat. Before I could open my mouth to ask her to stop, she tossed them on the bed atop the quilt. I hoped my new bed would be big enough to accommodate it. Well, of course it would. Yet I'd neglected to inquire how my future abode was furnished. I should have asked a myriad of questions before accepting the job working in the nursery. But my favorite cousin, Olivia, insisted I pounce on the job before someone else did. For some reason, she'd recently given up her position managing the café there, but she insisted the nursery was a good place to work.

As I gathered my toiletries, my mind spun like a windmill during a tempest. I'd planned to drive *Dat*'s buggy to the nursery today to meet the owner and survey my new home, described as a cute cottage by Olivia. Sometimes she embellished her descriptions, but I'd be happy with a storage shed now that Marta was here.

Olivia told me the place had been recently vacated by an aged housekeeper who'd lived there until she moved to Indiana to reside with a niece. The dwelling was strictly Amish, meaning no electrical wires or telephone. Propane lights illuminated the interior, and a small refrigerator and gas stove provided cooking options. But I'd forgotten to ask if it had an indoor bathroom or an outhouse.

Reuben lumbered up the stairs and opened a suitcase on my bed. Marta gave him a look of appreciation—an outward show of affection was *verboten* in our Amish community. I figured she rarely showed him affection even in private. Yet they had three children, so who was I to look down on her? She and my brother shared a harmonious marriage, while I seemed doomed to be single the rest of my life.

A few minutes later I sat on the suitcase's lid while Marta fastened the metal latches with gusto. I'd known this day would come, so why was I discombobulated? For one thing, I'd hoped to leave with dignity and leisure, not feel as though I was being booted out of the house like a stray cat.

"There. Now you're all packed." Marta grabbed hold of the handle and lugged the suitcase down the stairs. Following her into the kitchen, I scanned the only home I'd ever known. I recalled an abundance of fond memories, sitting at the kitchen table with my parents and brother, helping *Mamm* wash the dishes after meals. I hadn't wanted to live here forever, but I felt the weight of defeat. I'd expected to be married by now, with children of my own.

"Darling *dochder*, you don't have to leave us." *Dat* stepped toward me from the utility room. "We have that spare bedroom used for sewing." My father and I had always shared a special bond.

I wouldn't mention how difficult living with my sister-in-law would be, particularly if she kept reminding me of my past. Yet I had no right to complain after the embarrassment I'd caused the family by pining away for Jake Miller for seven years. Not to mention the troubling rumors about me. Even though I was innocent, at times I'd been tempted to confess guilt before our whole congregation just to put an end to the whispers.

"I'd better follow through as planned, *Dat*. I don't want to be labeled a quitter before I even start." Besides not wanting to live with Marta, I couldn't imagine myself in the cramped room that housed a treadle sewing machine and piles and piles of fabric. I'd amassed most of it while working at the fabric store in Intercourse. "You know it's full of material. Though that's my own fault for not resisting sales, plus my employee discount at Zook's. I'd assumed someday I'd need all that fabric to sew clothes for my own family."

He stared at the oval rag rug on the floor at his feet. "Did ya have to quit that job for some reason? Your boss was *Englisch*, but he's a fine man."

"I loved that job, but only women shop in there. I'm hoping to meet someone. Someday."

*Dat* winked. "*Yah*, I suppose not many single men come in for quilting fabric. But you could go to singings."

"At age twenty-nine, I'd be the oldest woman there." And not yet baptized.

"If only you hadn't gotten mixed up with that miscreant Jake Miller."

My jaw clenched at the sound of his name. "*Dat*, that's ancient history. And he didn't do it."

"How do you know for sure? Were you there?" He wagged his callused finger. "Few acts are worse than arson. A terrible thing, burning down a farmer's barn, even if it was ramshackle."

"But I'm sure Jake is innocent."

"Because he told you so? If he's so upstanding, where is he? His parents need him. He's their only son now."

"I'm not exactly sure where he is." That wasn't entirely true. I knew he went to New York State when he left Lancaster County.

"Maybe that's for the best."

"*Yah.*" I might go looking for him if I knew where he was. A scandalous mistake.

Half an hour later, while *Dat* hitched up our mare, *Mamm* left the *daadi haus* and moved to my side. She took my hand.

"I notice you're not bringing your hope chest, Evie. Does this mean you've given up on finding a husband?"

"*Mamm*—" I couldn't bear to have this conversation yet again.

She must have sensed my discomfort. "No matter. We'll keep it here."

With *Mamm* on my heels, I dragged my bulky suitcase off the porch and down the back steps. *Dat* had already loaded the buggy with several cardboard boxes filled with items I might need: a pot, a pan, mismatched plates and flatware, and a coffee mug I'd picked up at rummage sales. He also put my boots into the buggy. He lifted my suitcase and wedged it in. I felt rushed, sure I was leaving something important behind.

*Mamm* placed a wicker basket of food items on the front seat. I noticed a tear at the corner of her eye and guessed her sadness stemmed from the fact that she'd missed the opportunity to see me wed. She'd dreamed of hosting a huge wedding in our home, as was customary. Her guest list and menu had been planned for years, as well as her intention to plant copious amounts of celery. I'd let her and the whole family down.

"Wait!" Marta charged down the porch steps, carrying my quilt. "You forgot this." She shoved it in the back and shut the door. "Goodbye."

Without further farewells or well wishes, Marta flew to her family's buggy to gather more of their possessions and trotted an armful inside.

Minutes later, *Dat* steered the buggy out of the barnyard. The mare transported us past familiar farms, outbuildings, and fields soon to be dotted with the chartreuse of corn bursting through the spring soil. I spotted an Amish woman collecting her dry laundry, the rainbow of garments sorted by size and colors. Her youngsters danced around her playing keep-away with clothespins. The woman looked about my age. I felt like an over-the-hill has-been.

Coveting the scene, I remembered another minister expounding last year about overcoming envy—how it served to embitter a person and angered the Lord. I knew I should focus on my blessings.

An hour later, from way down the road, I spied the Yoder's Nursery sign. The name was inscribed in tall letters. I'd driven by the nursery many times, but I had never entered because my parents either ordered their seeds by mail or insisted we shop locally at an uncle's small establishment. And I steered clear of the barn across the road. My Jake had been accused of burning down the barn that stood there before. This new barn had been promptly built, but I couldn't bear to look at it. I was thankful *Dat* made no further mention of the appalling incident that still haunted me—the beginning of the end of my world.

As we neared the nursery's front driveway, I sat forward and gawked out the window. *Dat* piloted the buggy onto the gravel parking lot large enough to accommodate fifty or more vehicles, although only a half-dozen automobiles were present today. Several horses and buggies were stationed at a railing. I canvassed a retail shop's exterior—a smallish structure made of gray stone—and four large-scale greenhouses. Behind them spread acres of deciduous and evergreen trees planted in neat rows.

Despite the marvelous surroundings, my stomach clenched. I felt like a child might on her first day of school in a different district where she knew no one.

*Dat* slowed us to a halt. "Look at all those fine Amish men working here." He stroked his graying beard. "Most are single."

"*Yah*, I see they're clean-shaven. But they're too young for me."

"You look youthful for your age, Evie."

"*Denki*, but you know age is not my only problem."

"I thought that whole misunderstanding got cleared up. If the deacon and a minister thought you were guilty of any indiscretion, they would have stopped by to speak to us years ago." He patted my knee. "Although your *mamm* and I prayed for you many a time, that you wouldn't run off and do something foolish."

"*Yah*, I know, but—"

"Now, now. Most everyone in the county has forgotten those rumors."

"I wish that were true, but last month in the fabric store I noticed two women staring at me and whispering."

"Is it possible you overreacted? Were they one of us or *Englisch* tourists?"

"Probably tourists, but—"

"There's your answer. Are you not used to *Englischers* gawking at you by now?"

"*Denki, Dat.*" My father was the kindest man on earth.

"We've been taught that the Lord abhors malicious gossip. 'Death and life are in the power of the tongue.'" He jiggled the reins and steered the mare away from the greenhouses toward the far end of the parking lot. A three-story white house with black shutters framing the windows grabbed my attention. Even under the grayish sky the structure's brightness made me stare. Next to the house, a colossal maple tree spread mammoth limbs not yet bearing unfurling leaves.

"Is that the owner's house?"

"Sure is. And his new *Englisch* wife's." *Dat* turned to me, his eyes sympathetic. "They both married later in life. He's in his early forties and she's in her late thirties. They already have a child."

His heart was in the right place. He was trying to make me believe I could still bear children at my age. I'd let my parents down by not giving them grandchildren.

*Dat* seemed oblivious to my musings. "The owner did a fine job fixing up this old house. It was run-down when he purchased it."

"*Yah*, it's a beautiful home. But where's the cottage where I'll live?"

"Hold on." He brought the mare to a halt and waved an arm to an Amish worker, who strode over to us.

"Can you help?" *Dat* asked. "We wish to speak to the owner, Glenn Yoder."

"Glenn's out of town." The young man's gaze wandered over to me before returning to *Dat*. "And our manager, Stephen, is running an errand." He gave me another looking over. "Is this the new girl? We weren't expecting her yet."

He'd called me a girl? I sighed. I was ten years this lad's senior. But I was used to being called a girl by *Englisch* customers in the fabric store.

"*Yah*, this is my *dochder*." *Dat*'s tone was friendly. "We're looking for the place where she'll live, if that's all right."

"Of course. Stephen said you could move right in. The cabin is around back of the big house. The Yoders' housekeeper is in the main house, and she has a key if it's locked."

"*Denki*." *Dat* clucked to the mare, and she rolled us forward, skirting the house.

"A cabin? Olivia said it was a cottage."

He fingered the reins. "What's the difference?"

"Nothing, I suppose." Men and women each saw the world from a different perspective, I reminded myself.

Not far from the house stood a sturdy cream-colored structure with a hunter-green door. A rocking chair rested on its narrow porch. In a couple of front windows, forest-green shades were rolled partway down.

*Dat* hauled back on the reins and jumped out of the buggy. He tied the mare to a hitching post, mounted the porch's three wooden steps, and strode to the front door.

I sat, paralyzed. I couldn't recall ever being so anxious.

"Evie, you look like you saw a ghost. Are you okay?"

"Guess I'm a little *naerfich*." To put it mildly.

"No need to be nervous." He knocked, waited a moment, and then turned the knob. The door opened. "Guess they don't keep it locked."

I climbed out, landing hard. The earth beneath my feet seemed to undulate, but I steadied myself as I grabbed the handle of the wicker basket.

I walked up the steps. "Maybe you'd better go in first." I motioned to *Dat*. "What if someone's in there and just didn't hear your knock?" I often pretended I was fearless, but I was barely strong enough to carry the basket.

*Dat* chuckled as he stepped inside. "Come on, *dochder*. It's nice in here."

I peeked around him to see a tidy room with a single bed against the far wall, and a small couch and a propane lamp—its tank housed in a wooden base—near a fireplace. I could tell a woman or two had spent time cleaning this cabin. The white porcelain sink under a paned window and the kitchen counter were spotless. On either side of the counter stood a gas stove and a small propane refrigerator. Through a partially opened door I saw a bathroom—a white-tiled cubicle with a shower and a sink with a mirror above it. Nice!

The walls were painted a buttermilky cream, and the varnished solid wood kitchen cabinets, trim, and bathroom door were honey-colored. The taupe linoleum floor begged for some throw rugs, but all in good time.

*Dat* hauled my suitcase inside, and then we brought in the rest of my belongings. I strolled over to the bed and pulled back the blanket to see clean white sheets. Good. I'd forgotten to bring my own linens. "My quilt will fit on this nicely."

"You're all set." He kissed my cheek. "I best be getting back to see how your *bruder* and his family are doing, not to mention helping your *mamm* get settled in the *daadi haus*."

"Leaving already?" I had a panicky feeling in the back of my throat. "If only the owner were here to greet me. I'd planned to come meet him in person before moving in."

"He'll no doubt be back soon and you'll have your chance."

"Wait. Are you sure this is all right?" My voice came out with a quaver, sounding so timid I barely recognized it.

"Glenn Yoder is a fine man, even if he broke his parents' hearts by not joining the Amish church. He married an *Englisch* woman older than you are. And like I said, she gave birth to their first child several months ago."

Maybe there was still hope for me.

# Two

As I listened to *Dat's* buggy roll away, I second-guessed my decision to move here. I'd been hired on Olivia's recommendation without a proper interview. If I hurried, I could catch up with him and return home.

Hold on. That was downright silly, immature thinking. I was a grown woman and needed to take care of myself. Why wouldn't they like me as much as Zook's owner had?

First things first. I stowed *Mamm's* food in the pint-sized refrigerator. I'd rarely seen an empty refrigerator, and it was so clean inside too. Our refrigerator at home was always jam-packed with meats, cheeses, and yummy leftovers. Well, I doubted I'd starve working near a café, which must stand behind the greenhouses. I supposed it depended on when they served food. I knew Olivia's baked goods would be available if employees were allowed to eat meals there. Still, after laboring in the soil all day, they might not be permitted to dine with the café's patrons.

Deciding I'd have a snack later, I unclasped and opened the suitcase and then spread an armload of clothes across the bed. A tall bureau stood ready and welcoming. Above it hung an oval wood-framed mirror with a bedraggled woman gawking into it.

*Ach*, my heart-shaped *kapp* had collapsed like a failed soufflé. Clumps of my hair *Mamm* thought was the color of caramel straggled out from under it. I untied my *kapp's* strings. My beige dress and black apron did nothing to improve my appearance, but I'd fix my hair later.

I knelt on the floor and pulled open the bottom drawer of the bureau. I was pleased to see plenty of room for my black socks. As I arranged them neatly, I imagined moving into my future husband's home someday. Always his face looked like blond and striking Jake's, my first love, whom I hadn't seen for seven years. Silly musings. I was determined to replace his face with another man's. Soon, I hoped.

Without warning, the door blew open, and I let out a surprised yelp.

"Sorry I startled you." A tall man dressed in jeans and a yellow collared work shirt stepped into the room carrying an LED lamp—not Amish, judging by his clothing and *Englisch* haircut. "Are you the new employee?" he asked.

I got to my feet and put out my hand to shake his. "Yes. Hello. I'm Eva Lapp." I scanned the bed and felt heat flushing my face when I saw my nightgown draped across it. I bundled it up and stuffed it in another bureau drawer.

He tilted his head. "We weren't expecting you for a couple of days."

"I'm sorry. I should have called ahead to warn you I was coming early." I'd spare him the details of my mad dash to get packed and leave home.

"No matter. I'm Stephen Troyer, in charge of the nursery while the boss is out of town for a couple of weeks. I was just stopping by to make sure everything is okay." He set the lantern on the small table next to the bed. "We're happy to have you, Eva. The café has practically had to run on its own since Olivia left."

"Café? I thought I'd be working in the nursery with plants. And perhaps maintaining a vegetable garden." Gardening was my passion.

"No, we need a replacement for Olivia in the café. We have plenty of staff in the nursery. Although the little herb garden behind the main house might need tending now that Edna's gone. She's the Amish woman who used to live here and was my boss's housekeeper for many years. But she had a stroke, and her family moved her to Indiana to live with one of her nieces."

My mind spun with the impossibility of the situation. Why hadn't Olivia been clear about this? "But I know nothing about running a restaurant." Or much about cooking.

The corners of his mouth dragged down. "Can you manage a cash register and credit cards?"

"*Yah*, I did that in the fabric store, my last place of employment."

"And can you brew a decent pot of coffee?"

"I'm used to making it for large crowds after church services and such. Nobody has ever complained."

"Anything will taste better than the coffee made by the two girls we have now." He raked a hand through his nutmeg-brown hair. "Olivia said you could accomplish anything if we give you directions. We were so relieved when she suggested you and said you needed a place to live."

"I'm afraid my cousin might have stretched the truth a little." I scanned the cabin and reminded myself she was doing me a favor. "I don't possess half of Olivia's culinary skills. Only what I've done at home. I always favored the garden and helping *Dat* with the milking when he needed me."

"No cows to be milked around here. But we do have chickens and fresh eggs you're welcome to gather and eat for breakfast." His hazel-brown eyes probed mine. "Should I find someone else for the job?"

I canvassed my cozy new abode. "*Nee.* I'm used to working with the public. I'm sure I can learn what's needed." I hoped.

"It's still early in the year, but we expect to get busy once the flowers are in bloom. Our goal is to have the café cover its overhead and make a profit. My boss was determined to build the place. It was his dream, so there you go. The nursery's a bustling place spring through autumn. In winter, we sell Christmas trees. Glenn plans to have the café open all year."

"I'm used to waiting on impatient customers. We would get buried at the fabric store during a sale. And I'm here now." My being here must be God's will. Wasn't it?

"Come on. Let me walk you over there before you settle in." I understood him to mean, *before I have to kick you out in favor of someone more suitable for the job.*

He glanced down at me. "I feel as if I know you, Eva. Have we met before? Wait. Didn't you date Jake Miller?"

I cringed. "Many years ago."

"I heard he still lives in New York." Again he gave me an inquisitive look, waiting for my response.

"I heard that too." Jake had sent me only two letters—both without a return address—and left me one voice message on the phone shanty recorder, just to say hello. But he never explained why he left or what was to become of our relationship. He just told me he was fine, all in the vaguest of terms. And then I never heard from him again.

"Someone said Jake was working for a construction company in the Conewango Valley." Stephen's tone was somber. "He and I lost touch shortly after his older brother died." He tugged his earlobe. "You must know his father always favored his older son over Jake."

"Yes, Jake's dad treated Jake unfairly. Finding fault in everything he did."

"I figured that's why Jake took off." Stephen's statement sounded like a question, the way it went up at the end.

"I'm still not sure. I was away then." I didn't want to bring up the rumors circulated about me, but I did wish to continue our conversation. "Is Jake… Is he married?"

"I don't know. Possibly, after all this time."

I expelled an audible sigh and felt my shoulders droop. Well, of course he'd be married by now and probably have several children. But if so, that news had never reached my ears.

"You know about that barn fire?" Stephen's mouth grew hard.

"I'll never forget it as long as I live. Praise the Lord no one was killed or even hurt. But I felt sorry for the calves." I snuck a peek at his ruggedly handsome face. "Still an unsolved mystery?"

"Yes, but I do know Jake wasn't guilty. He was with me that night, not that he was following the *Ordnung*. I was and still am Mennonite and not under the same restrictions. But I was acting like a knucklehead."

"I've always wondered why Jake didn't defend himself." Finally, I might get a straight answer to the questions that had plagued me about that fire.

"Well, like I said, we were both up to no good. On a lamebrain lark, Jake bought his wreck of a Toyota sedan and hid it from his folks. As I recall, he was twenty-two and still in *rumspringa*. Fact is, he and I and some buddies were in that old barn that evening, drinking beer, playing cards, and joking around, but nothing more. We were using a battery-powered lantern and knew better than to smoke in there. When we left the barn, it was standing. None of us would've been foolish enough to do anything to start a fire. We knew the value of barns. Someone must have seen his car and reported it to the police."

"Why didn't you tell the police all that?" A better question would have been to ask why Jake hadn't defended himself.

"The barn's owner was and still is Amish. He didn't press charges. I never have understood that way of thinking. But the whole community pitched in, including Jake and me. Our heads hanging low, we all helped rebuild that barn better than new. Tongues were wagging the whole time, but no one came out and accused us."

"But still, you could have spoken up. You both should've come out and confessed to being in the barn."

"You're right, but that would have meant telling everyone Jake owned a car. His father was already angry with him. Jake sold that ill-fated Toyota a week later. I still feel as if it were my fault. I was two years older and should have set a better example for him."

Stephen must have seen an expression of worry on my face. "A year later—I guess you were out of state—I heard Jake left. He's only returned to Lancaster County a couple of times that I know of."

"And you never hear from him?" What was I doing speaking of a subject so personal with a stranger? Yet for years I'd ached to have this conversation with someone who'd not only known Jake, but was willing to talk to me about him. A gravitational pull still drew me to him.

"I was surprised he did, but he made a couple of calls to my cell phone." Stephen shifted his weight. "He asked about you."

I held my breath and waited for him to continue.

"Jake said he'd heard you had a new boyfriend."

"Did you tell him I didn't?" My mouth was so dry I could barely get out the words.

"I'm sorry, Eva, but I had no way of knowing. I'd heard you were seeing someone in Ohio, but I didn't know if that was true."

"None of the stories about me are true." I shuddered to think of what Jake and Stephen had heard. Rumors that I'd run off to Ohio to give birth to either Jake's or another man's child had swirled like a flock of crows throughout the county. But I'd been in Ohio taking care of premature newborn twins for an ailing cousin.

Rubbing his chin with his knuckles, Stephen appeared uncomfortable. "Shall I show you the café now?"

"*Yah*, sure." I tried to insert a ring of enthusiasm into my voice. For an *Englischer*, Stephen seemed to know the Amish well.

He moved toward the door just as a young Amish woman carrying towels glided onto the porch. I had a multitude of questions I still wanted to ask Stephen, but our conversation would have to wait.

"Oh." Her eyes widened. I was glad the door was open. The last thing I needed was to be seen as a loose woman, something I wasn't and never had been. But shaking a bad reputation was like pulling your foot out of a wasp's nest without getting stung.

"Eva, this is Susie."

"Nice ta meetcha," we said in unison and then both chuckled.

Susie seemed around seventeen. Maybe younger. "I brought ya clean towels."

"I wasn't expecting to be waited on, but I'm delighted. I neglected to bring towels and a washcloth." What else had I forgotten?

"Edna left them. They're nice and soft. So are the bed linens she left." Susie stepped into the bathroom and spoke to us through the open door. "I do several loads of laundry for the nursery every day anyway, so it's no trouble to do whatever washing you need done. Really." She hung the pale pink towels on a rack.

"*Denki.*"

"My *bruder* Mark works here too."

"He's quite popular with the young ladies," Stephen said.

"*Yah*, he is." Susie sent me a grin.

"But no time to chitchat right now," Stephen informed her in a no-nonsense manner, as if he wanted her to get back to work. "We're off to the café."

As I followed Stephen down the steps, a black cat streaked across our path. I inhaled the heavenly aromas of sarcococca and daphne. The early-blooming flowers must be nearby. On either side of the pathway, pansies, bleeding hearts, and blooming hellebore grabbed my attention, along with many species I didn't recognize. Clumps of miniature daffodils and tulips pressed their way through the earth. But there wasn't time to investigate now.

I increased my speed to keep up with Stephen's long legs. We strode by the main house and the enormous glass greenhouses I was dying to explore.

We passed several young, clean-shaven Amish men wearing straw hats. They spoke to Stephen in *Deitsch*, asking questions and listening to his instructions. I was surprised to hear him speaking to them in fluent Pennsylvania Dutch.

One of the young men tipped his hat at me and sent me a goofy grin that seemed flirtatious. But he was too young for me.

# Three

The nursery was magnificent, but nothing prepared me for the charm and eloquence of the café, which stood behind the last greenhouse. As I entered, I inhaled the fragrance of the tropical plants embellishing it. Near the entrance to the right-hand side was a raised fishpond with a small waterfall. About eight orange and speckled fish swam toward us as if without fear.

"Want a snack, fellas?" Stephen reached into a can, gathered a portion of pellets, and sprinkled them onto the water. The bold fish swished to the surface to gobble them up, causing the water to ripple. "These are Japanese koi," he told me. "They're consummate beggars, so don't overfeed them."

The spacious room was high ceilinged, and two of the walls were glass, allowing me to watch workers carrying plants or pushing wheelbarrows. Oak chairs clustered around a dozen tables. Ahead, an expansive glass case stood by a cash register. Half of the case was dedicated to salads, such as beet, coleslaw, and fruit, and the other half was filled with what could only be Olivia's baked goods: whoopie pies stuffed with fluffy, whipped filling; fruit tarts; slices of zucchini bread; muffins; and carrot cake. My mouth watered as I stared into the case to admire the display of delectable items I'd never be able to make. I gulped. What had I gotten myself into?

Stephen stood at my side. "Olivia is still sending baked goods. Her brother delivers them on his way to work."

"Wonderful." I could hear too much enthusiasm and relief in my declaration. I steadied myself. "What other foods do you serve?"

"A soup of the day and cold sandwiches. See the chalkboard sign up there?"

I lifted my chin and caught sight of the framed board and the words *Potato Soup* in neat cursive writing. Below that was written *Ham and Swiss on Rye*. "Sounds *gut*."

Stephen scanned the room. Two couples sat chatting at a table, and one man read a newspaper while sipping coffee. "Not many people in here right now," he said, "but some days we get swamped."

I noticed a low table off to the left with flatware, napkins, mugs, paper cups, a water dispenser, and a large coffee urn and carafe of hot water. The place seemed to be self-service for the most part. A stack of magazines and copies of the local newspaper fanned across a stout table.

Rock music suddenly blasted from the back of the building. I assumed it was emanating from the kitchen.

"What the—" Stephen's flattened hand flew out. He ping-pinged on a low metal bell and then leaned over the counter. "Where is everyone? Sadie? Jennifer?"

The music fell silent. A moment later, two late-teen Amish girls poked their heads out from the kitchen.

"Someone must be on the floor or at the register at all times," Stephen said. "And keep that radio turned off."

Both girls tittered, their hands covering their mouths as they gulped down what appeared to be corn bread—a crumb adhered to one of the girls' lower lip.

Stephen turned to me. "You see why I need an adult working here?"

I smiled, not wanting to seem mean to the two young ladies. But I was a mature adult compared to these girls.

"Can you make soup in the morning?" he asked me.

All the years of assisting *Mamm* as she prepared meals for the family were a gift to me now. She'd told me someday I'd need to know how to cook, meaning when I got married and raised a family. Now I felt foolish for not paying scrupulous attention. I'd have to thank her if I could pull off this charade.

"*Yah*, I can make soup if I have the ingredients."

He frowned. "We have an odd problem in that area. No matter who places the food orders, we always seem to come up short. Inventorying will be part of your job. Our wholesale produce and meat man has a phone."

"Okay. I can even bake bread if required."

"No need. The bread's delivered. You'll need to inventory and put together an order to be brought in the next day." He extended his arm. "Want to come in the kitchen and have a look?" He directed me around a corner to the area behind the register and glass case.

A lidded metal vat sat on a burner. "Taste the soup, will you?" he said.

I slid my hand into a pot holder, lifted the lid, and found a clean tablespoon. I brought a spoonful of the whitish liquid to my lips and swallowed the blandest soup I'd ever tasted.

I turned to the girls. "Who made this?" Sadie raised a timid hand.

I tried to sound knowledgeable as I recalled *Mamm*'s delicious potato soup. "Just my opinion, but it needs salt and seasoning. And next time, maybe start with chicken stock and add chopped onion and fried bacon or diced ham."

Stephen sampled a mouthful. "This is blah. Can you doctor it up right now, Eva?"

I surveyed the spice rack and found basil, but not much else. "At this late stage, salt and pepper might be the best I can do, unless one of you girls will chop and sauté onion and celery and dice a little bit of ham."

But at this moment there wasn't time to do much but add the salt and pepper.

"Why, look at this darling place," came a female's brassy-toned voice with a Southern accent. "Cute as can be. And I'm starving."

I left the kitchen and saw half a dozen more *Englisch* women strolling in.

"Put in your orders up here," Stephen said, having followed me. He handed Sadie a pad of paper. "Ready to dive in, Eva?"

"But I haven't unpacked."

He shot me a dubious look. "Plenty of time for that later." He poured a mug of coffee and positioned himself at a nearby table.

"Y'all go ahead and order. I'll save us a table." One woman, pleasantly wide at the girth, draped a paisley jacket over a chair by the pond. "Look, everyone, they have koi." But the other women had flocked to the front counter and were staring into the glass case.

"Separate checks?" Sadie asked.

"Yes, if it's not too much trouble." The woman pointed to coleslaw, pasta salad, and broccoli salad. "I'll take the three-salad plate and a blueberry muffin with butter."

"And to drink?"

"Coffee." She brought out her wallet. "No, make that hot tea."

After the woman paid, Sadie handed her an empty mug and produced a basket of tea bags. "Please choose a tea bag and then serve yourself hot water. And get a napkin and flatware." She pointed out the table housing the hot water carafe. "We'll get your order right out to you."

"I'll follow you," Jennifer said to the woman.

I stood off to the side, watching Jennifer spoon mounds of salad onto a plate and then select a muffin and a pat of butter to put on a smaller plate while Sadie took the next order.

"How's your soup?" another woman asked me.

"Want to give it a taste?" I asked.

"Nah, that's okay. I'll take a bowl, and a ham and Swiss on rye, heavy on the mayonnaise and mustard. And iced tea."

"Yes, ma'am." With Sadie's assistance, I rang up her order and processed her charge card.

Within minutes all the orders were in. Sadie and I assembled sandwiches while Jennifer served salads and muffins and ladled soup.

Jennifer grinned at me. "Sure is nice having ya here."

"*Denki.*" I sighed at the prospect of spending the rest of the afternoon inside serving and preparing food.

Stephen got to his feet and moved toward me. "You're doing great, Eva."

"Thanks." I'd executed every task with ease. I'd even sprinkled grated Parmesan cheese over the soup to liven it up.

Ten minutes later, I watched Jennifer take desserts to the tables.

"Tomorrow is Jennifer's last day," Stephen said.

I couldn't disguise my look of surprise.

"Don't think you and Sadie can handle it?"

"Maybe if someone came in to bus tables and wash dishes." I glanced into the kitchen at a dishwasher and a wide metal sink stacked with soiled plates and coffee mugs.

"*Ach*," Sadie said. "We let things get behind." She got busy emptying the dishwasher.

"Can you work for a few more days?" Stephen asked Jennifer as she strode by with some cleared dishes.

"*Nee*, I'm sorry. Just tomorrow."

"I'll have to hire someone," he told me. Stephen caught me staring at the clock on the wall. Already two o'clock, and I hadn't unpacked. Or had lunch. But I wasn't hungry.

"We serve food only until three this time of year," he told me. "We leave the place open, cover the cases, and let our customers serve their own tea and coffee on the honor system. Since you're here right now, will you stick around should another group show up? You're doing great. Better than great."

"*Denki.*" So I'd nailed the job. Not the job of my dreams, but an occupation many women would adore. Maybe a single man my age would saunter into the café tomorrow and ask me out. Too bad Stephen was Mennonite…

"Sure." I shot him a grin. "It's not as if I have anywhere to go other than touring the nursery." Which I would love to do.

"I bet we can find someone to help clear and wash dishes." Stephen pivoted toward the door.

"Luke?" Sadie said. "My little *bruder*'s looking for a job after school."

Stephen turned back to her. "He's already committed to helping us plant seedlings. I'll think of someone—"

Sadie hurried over to Stephen and spoke sotto voce. "Please, not the housekeeper. She was hinting that she wants to work here until the Yoders return."

"What's wrong with her?" Stephen said. "I've known Beatrice Valenti for a long time. She's a good friend of Glenn's, and she's a widow."

"She's grumpy. And she's so old." Sadie covered her mouth. She appeared to have plenty more complaints on her mind, but she must have known it was sinful to malign others.

Sadie sent me a furtive glance. I wondered exactly how old this widow was. She had apparently read my mind. "She's at least your *mamm*'s age, Eva. She grew up around here, and she's of Italian descent. But she can speak some *Deitsch*, so beware of what you say."

"I remember her from the fabric shop where I worked," I said. When Beatrice browsed there, she'd looked right through me and chosen to work with another saleswoman. But I still would have gone to her husband's funeral if I hadn't been sick.

"And she's related to Rose Yoder's aunt," Stephen said. "My boss has been wanting to help Beatrice out since her husband died several years ago. She lives in the big house and looks after their baby girl. While they're out of town, she's house-sitting and taking care of the dogs."

"The Yoders have *hunds*?" The backs of my knees weakened.

"Yes, three of them."

Since childhood, I'd been afraid of dogs. When I was five, our neighbor's German shepherd bit my leg and sent me to the emergency room for stitches. I hadn't been able to shake the bone-deep fear—the feeling of pain and helplessness. *Dat* and *Mamm* had never owned a dog. Only a bushel of barn cats my brother and I had loved to cuddle as children.

Stephen must have recognized trepidation in my demeanor. "They're all friendly."

If I'd known dogs were running around the nursery, I wouldn't have accepted the job. But I dared not voice my concerns.

# Four

Near three o'clock, a young Amish man strolled into the café. Removing his hat, he zoomed in on me. "Are you Eva?"

"*Yah*." I recognized him as the guy with the goofy grin. Although he seemed at ease.

"I'm Mark." He extended his hand to shake mine. "Stephen asked me to give you a quick tour of the nursery before it gets dark." His face was thin, and his features were refined in a way many women would appreciate.

He glanced around at the empty tables. "Sadie and Jennifer know how to close up by themselves." They nodded and grinned at him, making me think they both found him good looking. Which I guess he was, what with those smoky-green eyes. But he must be five years my junior, and I felt no zing of attraction.

I did want to see the nursery, but I hesitated when I noticed two large, brown Labrador retrievers had accompanied him and waited by the front door of the café.

This was a day I would overcome a multitude of my fears, I told myself as I followed Mark. The dogs wagged their tails. But then one barked, startling me and sending spikes of adrenaline down my arms and legs.

"That's Missy, Heath's *muder*. Heath's large but still a pup inside." Mark must have noticed my reticence just as Stephen had. "They belong to the owner, and they're both very friendly. They even sleep in his house at night."

I put out one hand, and Missy licked my fingertips. I dried my hand on her silky coat and then pet her son, Heath, a boisterous canine who seemed to want to jump on me.

"*Nee*, no jumpin'." Mark kneed him away, saving my dress and apron from muddy paws. "He still needs a bit of training." Mark turned to me. "The customers don't appreciate it either."

I shadowed him onto a flagstone path anchored by moss and lined with decorative containers displaying original and attractive combinations of flowers. We strolled under a trellis cloaked with coral-colored climbing rosebuds intertwined with wine-colored clematis. More than ever I wanted to work out here in the nursery. The combination of aromas—newly watered plants, mulch, and fertilized soil—was intoxicating under the setting sun. Not that I'd ever been drunk. Heavens no. One time I took a sip from Jake's bottle of beer. I found the drink offensive and knew my parents and their bishop would disapprove even if I was in *rumspringa* and not yet baptized.

As I trailed Mark into the retail shop, I watched half a dozen chickadees and flashy scarlet cardinals descend on a feeder hanging from a nearby pole. They were having a dandy time, tittering and chirping and picking out the sunflower seeds. I smiled and lifted my chin, attempting to appear confident when in fact the opposite was true.

We entered the smallish building made of gray stone. One interior wall was bedecked with rakes, shovels, clippers, saws, and gloves. There was hardly a square inch of vacant space. The opposite wall displayed rubber boots, gloves, clogs, hoses, and watering cans. At the far end stood a collection of flowerpots: ceramic, metal, and cement crafted to look like stone. A rack displayed packets of seeds. It was all an orderly profusion I'd love to investigate.

An Amish woman about twenty years my senior stood at the register ringing up bags of daffodil bulbs for a customer.

"*Denki*," the salesclerk said.

"*Gem gschehne*, Bess," said the young woman, and then she departed.

The round-faced saleswoman was adjusting her white heart-shaped head covering when she noticed Mark and me.

"Bess, I'd like you to meet our new café manager, Eva Lapp."

The title still struck me as ludicrous, but I shaped my lips into a smile.

Bess smoothed the front of her black apron and then extended her small hand to shake mine. "Glad to meet ya, Eva. I hope you'll be happy here."

"I'm sure I will be."

A catalog lay on the counter with a photo of the owner's house gracing the cover. Clumps of daisies crowded the foreground, a hammock hung beneath the maple tree, and a black cat posed on the railing of the wide front porch. Behind the home, I knew, crouched my new abode.

Stephen sauntered into the shop and handed me a ring of keys. "I nearly forgot to give you these. One is for the café—both the front and back doors—and the other is for the cabin."

I handed him a slip of paper with some needed items for the café's kitchen. "I wasn't sure where to put this."

"Best to leave your list here where I'm sure to see it." He turned to Bess. "Would you call this in right now?"

"Certainly." She scanned the list and nodded her approval.

"Next week you can start calling in the food order yourself, Eva. It'll be one less thing for Bess and me to do."

"Glad to." I knew I should be pleased that he trusted me, but I still felt unsure. I must do everything I could to make myself a necessity. If this job didn't work out, then what?

After Mark excused himself and left, I glanced out the window and noticed the sky's color was draining. "If you don't mind, I'll go and unpack," I said to Stephen.

"Of course. Can you find your way?"

"Yes, as long as I can see the big house, I'm sure to find it."

He shot me a curious look I couldn't decipher.

"Is there something more I should know?" I said.

"Not that I can think of. If you need anything, ask Beatrice. She knows how everything in the cabin works."

"Thank you. I'll see you tomorrow."

I gave Bess a small farewell wave. She smiled in return. "*Gut* to meet you," she said as I headed outside.

Because it was only mid-April, the sun was setting on the early side. I'd lost track of time; I should have looked at the clock in the shop. I hadn't seen a battery-operated clock in the cabin and had forgotten to bring mine.

Up ahead, the main house glowed with radiance as the pumpkin-orange sun lowered itself into a cushion of clouds. Nothing beat the glorious sunsets in Lancaster County. I couldn't imagine living anywhere else. But, evidently, Jake never loved the area as I did. Or loved me as he'd professed. When we were together, he'd treated me as though I were a princess, always attentive to my needs and promising a lifetime of his devotion. But that didn't last.

I took a shortcut past the greenhouses and onto a path along the perimeter of the Yoders' home. A yappy terrier bolted from the back of the house and raced toward me with its ears pricked and hackles raised. My first instinct was to ball my hands under my chin, but I steadied myself and said, "*Wie geht's*?" as if I spoke to dogs every day of the week.

As I neared the main house's back porch, the screen door creaked open, and an older woman's hoarse voice called out. "Who goes there?"

"Just me. Eva Lapp." I moved toward the portly woman I'd always supposed was in her late sixties. She was wearing metal-rimmed spectacles and a mid-calf black skirt. Her salt-and-pepper hair was parted in the center and pulled severely into a bun. No head covering. And gold hoop earrings, of all things. In the past I'd had hankerings to try on earrings, but had resisted.

"I recognize you from Zook's." She stepped out onto the porch. "My name is Beatrice, in case you can't remember."

"How nice to see you again." I feigned a cheerful expression. One way or another, she was my neighbor, and I needed to find common ground with her. "I heard you're house-sitting."

"Yes. I live on the third floor. Since Edna left, I'm the housekeeper, and I help take care of the Yoders' little girl when Rose is busy making her birdhouses."

"It looks like a wonderful home."

"But too big for one person. Although Glenn Yoder lived here all by himself for years." She came down the steps and stared back at the structure with vacant eyes. "Living alone is sad and lonely. I'm a widow, you must know." She sniffed. "I've been at odds ever since my husband died."

"I was sorry to hear of your loss."

She worked her mouth. "So sorry you didn't come to his funeral?"

"I wanted to, but I had a terrible head cold. Coughing and sneezing. I was bedridden. My mother said I shouldn't spread the germs."

She humphed. "Even Jake Miller came back for the funeral."

"He did?" Obviously, Beatrice knew about my past with Jake, but I was too stunned that no one had told me he'd been at that funeral to care. Now more than ever I wished I'd been able to attend. But my nose had been red and drippy. Truth is, Jake could have visited me while he was in the area, but he never even made a call to the phone shanty. Maybe he'd brought a wife with him. I was dying to ask Beatrice, but I didn't want to give her more fuel for animosity toward me.

"His mother and I grew up next door to each other," she said, "where she still lives with her husband, Amos, and raised their family. Ruth occasionally invites me to her quilting frolics." She chortled. "You know how the Amish enjoy gossip."

I didn't appreciate her condescending remark, but I sucked in my lips. Not that her statement was false. Sometimes the Amish grapevine spread rumors faster than the Internet. Or so I'd been told, never having used a computer or a smartphone.

She pointed a gnarled finger up to a window on the third floor of the main house. "That's my bedroom. I can see your little cabin perfectly from my room, so don't expect to be entertaining men."

"I don't plan to." Other than riding home from several singings with fellows who held no interest, and then in Jake's buggy and a couple of times in his ill-fated car, I'd never been courted. "I'm not dating anyone."

She peered down her hooked nose. "Just today I spotted Stephen alone with you for the longest time."

"We were speaking strictly about business, and the door was open." I had nothing to be ashamed of and yet felt warmth in my cheeks. I remembered reading *The Scarlet Letter*, a book borrowed from the library. Did I wear a sign on my chest?

The terrier sniffed my ankles. "That's Minnie. She won't hurt you, but she's a good little watchdog."

I dropped my hand to the dog's level and forced myself to scratch the wiry fur between her ears. "*Gut.* If she barks at night, I'll know to lock my door."

Beatrice dipped her hand into a pocket and brought out a key. "Did Stephen give you a key?"

"Yes. Thanks, I'm all set."

She shrugged. "If you ever get locked out, you can come to me." I realized her comment was an act of kindness, but her face remained stony, her mouth severe. Was this a woman I wanted working in the café? I couldn't imagine asking her to do anything I couldn't do for myself. And I doubted she could run a cash register.

"I'd best go unpack." I pivoted toward the cabin. "Then I should call my parents to tell them I'm okay. Is there a phone shanty nearby?"

"No, but there's a phone in the café and in the kitchen here. I suppose you could use the owner's right now."

The thought of going into the main house with her made me nervous. "I can wait until tomorrow. I don't want to trouble you."

"It's no trouble, and I have nothing else to do. Usually I'm so busy when the owners are home, but they won't be back for a couple of weeks."

"There is one thing. I neglected to bring a book."

She fingered the small gold cross at her neck. "The Yoders have plenty of books, but perhaps not what you're used to reading."

"I like reading the classics and some contemporary books without violence or immorality."

She raised an eyebrow. "Come around tomorrow when I'm not just about to prepare my supper, all right?"

"That's very kind of you. If you think the owner won't mind."

"No, Glenn has a veritable library. And his wife, Rose, is generous too."

I felt a drop of rain on my cheek.

"Looks as though clouds have moved in." She angled her hefty torso toward the back porch. Was she afraid of melting like the witch in the *Wizard of Oz*? Not that I wanted to get drenched either.

I heard a rumble of thunder in the distance. "Good night, then," I said, but she'd already spun away. She ascended the porch steps and plunged through the back door, a black cat at her heels.

Beatrice called Minnie's name, but then she slammed the door shut when the dog didn't respond.

# Five

Seconds later I found myself standing in a deluge of rain. I dashed to the cabin and was glad to find it still unlocked. Cold and clammy air encompassed me. I lit the lamp next to the recliner and patted my face with a hand towel. I set about hanging up my dresses in the first closet I'd ever had. I used the pegs on the wall for my aprons.

I glanced in the mirror above the bureau. *Ach*, my cap was drenched and flattened. I wondered how long I'd looked disheveled. In the dim light, my face appeared creased like that of a woman twice my age. Crow's-feet at the corners of my eyes, crevices on my forehead. Vanity was a sin, I told myself, but my ghastly image made my throat shrink with sadness. If Jake ever came home for good and wasn't married, he might turn away with distaste. Yet Beatrice had landed herself a husband. No doubt at a young age, when her skin was blemish-free and her temperament charming for his sake.

I pulled out my hairpins and tossed my dripping *kapp* on the showerhead in the bathroom. With a towel I blotted my soggy hair—a pitiful, tousled mess. Next, I removed the straight pins from my black apron's waist, set them on the bureau on a small tray, and then hung up the apron and dress. I slipped on my nightgown, nestled into my fuzzy bathrobe, and found my slippers, glad I'd thought to bring them along.

I extracted my toothbrush from the suitcase. I hadn't put away most of my belongings, but I shut the suitcase and set it against the wall. Fatigue enshrouded me, but I dug through the cardboard boxes. I found a battery-powered clock I didn't recognize. Perhaps Marta had dropped one of hers in there for me—an unexpected act of kindness.

Raindrops pattering on the roof turned into a torrent of splatting. I hoped the roof was waterproof. A flash of blue-white light filled the room, followed by a blast of thunder. I was used to storms, but I recoiled, feeling exposed and frightened. I could do nothing about it except start a fire in the hearth, see what *Mamm* had prepared for me to eat, and enjoy my supper—alone.

Split wood, kindling, and crumpled newspaper sat on the hearth, and a box of matches perched on the mantel. Someone had been thoughtful. In no time, my fire sprang to life, hungry flames licking the kindling. The fire's crackling sound brought me a feeling of safety and peace until I heard a scratching at the front door. What in the world?

I cracked open the door to find the owners' scruffy terrier, her coat drenched, looking up at me with hopeful eyes.

"Shoo. Go home. What in the world do you want? Certainly not to come in and dirty the floor." But her wagging tail and whining tugged at my sense of pity.

I closed the door, hurried to the kitchen counter, and returned with a few paper towels. When I opened the door, I hoped the pooch had retreated to the main house, but she was still there.

"How could Beatrice leave you outside on such a miserable night?"

Blobs of rain bounced off the earth. Lightning shattered the sky. A deafening strike hit a tree close by, and the dog bolted into my cabin.

"Hey, *hund*, wait a minute." I blotted the animal's fur and paws. I dropped a cloth towel on the floor. "You sit on this," I told her, and I was surprised when she obeyed. What had Beatrice called her? Minnie? I supposed that was an appropriate name.

"What would your owner say if she knew you were left out in the rain?" The pup gazed up at me as if she understood how off-kilter I felt.

Minutes later, I munched on a meat loaf sandwich on wheat bread as only *Mamm* could prepare. I plopped down on the small couch. Minnie sat at my feet sniffing the air, her ears pricked. I knew I shouldn't be suckered in, but I broke off a corner and tossed it to her. She snagged the treat out of the air before it hit the floor.

As I glanced out the window, another flash of lightning slashed the sky, followed by bellowing thunder. The dog dropped to her stomach. Shivering, she nestled at my feet.

"I'm not letting you on this couch with me, so don't get any ideas."

The wind gained velocity, blasting against the cabin, making the windowpanes rattle and the timbers creak. I heard something on the roof and wondered if the shakes were flying off. Well, there was nothing I could do about it now unless I dared racing to the main house. No, I'd get soaked, and I suspected Beatrice would see it as an act of cowardice.

I recalled my bookshelf at home. "Why didn't I bring something to read?"

Minnie cocked her head. I was asking a dog for advice? That was a first. I looked out the front window to see the porch light flicker off. The nursery lights and the streetlamps on the main road were snuffed like candles. I could see a dim light on the third floor of the main house. Beatrice must have had a battery-powered light fixture or a lantern.

I scanned the room and saw a Bible sitting on a shelf in the nightstand. It wasn't the kind of reading I had in mind, but it might calm my racing thoughts. I'd never get to sleep with this raging storm even if my stomach was full. And what should I do with the dog? I guessed she would have to stay inside.

I shuffled into the bathroom to wash my face and brush my teeth. Again, I caught a glimpse of myself in the mirror and winced at my pathetic reflection. Illuminated by the battery-operated lamp, my hair looked drab and my features elongated. I'd shower in the morning and spend extra time combing and parting my hair. Thankfully, I'd brought several clean and pressed *kapps*.

I draped my Lone Star quilt from home over the bed. A perfect fit. Then I pulled back the sheet and blanket and snuggled inside my chilly cocoon. The mattress felt soft and squishy. I imagined the previous resident, Edna, had weighed quite a bit more than I did. She'd broken the springs in and left a few lumps. I propped the pillow against the headboard, all the while listening to the rain beating against the windows. A lightning strike shattered the air. Poor Beatrice. Should I go check on her? No. If she was on the third floor, she probably wouldn't hear my knocking.

With the lantern on my nightstand, I opened the worn Bible somewhere in the middle and found it written in English. Our family Bible was in German. Not knowing where to start, I opened at the bookmark and read Psalm 4:8 aloud. "I will both lay me down in peace, and sleep: for thou, Lord, only makest me dwell in safety."

I'd never been a good sleeper, and, apparently, Edna suffered from insomnia too. But I felt my lids droop. I'd endured a long day.

Knuckles rapping on the door made me jerk. Had I thought to lock it? Minnie leaped to her feet and growled. She sniffed under the doorjamb and then barked.

"Who's there?" My voice wobbled.

"Stephen Troyer. Are you okay? Is Minnie in there with you?"

Hating to leave the comfort of the bed, I jammed my feet into my slippers, plopped a scarf atop my head, and dove into my black coat. I cracked the door open.

"Sorry to bother you." Stephen stepped inside and shut the door behind him as the wind whooshed into the small space. Minnie jumped on his leg. "There you are, you scamp. Beatrice was worried sick you'd run away."

I was tempted to tell him the woman left the poor animal out in the pouring rain, but I held in my words.

"I bet you want your supper, don't you, girl?" Stephen bent down to fluff Minnie's furry head. "Although it looks like you've made yourself at home."

I clutched the front of my coat together and buttoned it. "The poor little dog was frightened and wet. Next time I'll leave her outside."

"She's a consummate beggar."

"I gave her a little something."

He scanned the cabin's interior. "I knew you'd be all set here, but did you see that the main house and nursery have lost electrical power?"

"*Yah*, I'm used to living without electricity. But what about the café tomorrow?"

"The café alone has a generator that switches on the moment electricity goes off, so no worries in the morning. And a gas stove. I should have told you."

"What about the tropical plants in the greenhouses?"

"We'll light propane heaters if needed. Who knows? The electricity might come right back on tonight. But I doubt it." He glanced out the window and sucked on his lower lip. "Beatrice called me from the house to warn me."

I peered outside, but I couldn't detect much. Just the silhouette of a woman standing in a third-floor window watching this cabin. Watching me entertain a man. Which she would no doubt report to whoever would listen.

"Is Beatrice all right?" I asked. "Should we check on her?" Not that I wanted to. Here I was with a man and the door shut, just what I told her I'd never do.

"I don't think that's necessary. She's a tough old gal. Although in the past she was used to having a husband take care of her." He grasped the doorknob. "Come on, Minnie. Let's get you home."

The dog flattened herself against the couch in front of the hearth.

"I don't mind keeping her for the night if that's okay." I didn't look forward to spending the night in solitude, but I'd never imagined myself wanting the company of a dog.

"Sure. She's nice and dry, and the walk back to the house is muddy."

When he opened the door, Minnie scrambled to her feet, darted outside, leaped off the porch, and raced to the main house.

Stephen chuckled. "She must still be hungry." He took hold of the doorknob again as he stepped out into the darkness. "You should lock this door at night" were his parting words.

# Six

I awoke to the sound of a bird trilling. The sky was bright, the room illuminated by the sun's brilliance. I glanced at my clock and was surprised to see it was already seven. After a fitful night of troublesome thoughts assaulting my brain, how had I managed to sleep in? I'd forgotten to set the clock's alarm.

My intention had been to be at the café at seven to start the soup, but in truth I had a long span of time until the café opened at nine. I showered and spent extra time combing out my hair and parting it in the center just right. I found a clean *kapp* and was thankful it didn't require pressing. But my navy-blue dress needed ironing, even if a cotton and polyester blend fabric. No time to worry about a few wrinkles that would surely come out as the morning progressed. I pinned on my black apron. In my haste, I pricked a finger. I chalked up my clumsiness to fatigue and a jittery case of the nerves. Yes, I was anxious. My hands shook, and my thoughts raced.

Outside, tree branches, twigs, and leaves lay strewn about as if they'd been swept in by a tide. Planted pots were tipped over, their flowers littering the ground. One of the chairs on the house's back porch lay on its side.

Minnie was nowhere to be seen. I assumed Beatrice had let her into the house. One of the huge Labrador retrievers galumphed toward me as I made my way to the café. I assured myself I had nothing to be afraid of and kept going, not allowing myself to succumb to my fears. After last night, I should be able to stand up to anything.

But deep inside I was still nervous as I scurried to my new job. I'd heard dogs could smell fear. I must reek of it.

I brought out my keys, but the café's front door was unlocked. Glancing through the glass wall, I saw light in the kitchen. Someone had beat me here. Or maybe Stephen had unlocked the door as a favor.

As I stepped inside, my nostrils caught the hint of split pea soup and a trace of smoked ham. I hurried to the kitchen and saw Beatrice's rounded back as she stirred the metal vat I'd set out the day before to soak the peas.

She adjusted the heat, reducing it, and placed a lid atop the vat. She wore a white chef's apron cinched around her ample waist, a patterned blouse—green with small yellow flowers—and again a calf-length black skirt. Both the blouse and skirt were nice enough to wear to an *Englisch* church service.

"What are you doing here?" My words charged out with an acerbic flair that was unwarranted. I'd wanted to prepare the soup. "Why are you cooking?"

She peered over her plump shoulder. "Stephen told me I should come in and help when needed. And, apparently, I am needed today."

I looked up at the wall clock and saw it was seven thirty. "We don't open until nine."

"Never too early to start soup." Beatrice pivoted toward me. "I couldn't fall back to sleep once I'd awakened. Not in the big house all alone without the Yoders."

I stepped around her and peered into the vat. Diced carrots, onions, and potatoes floated on the surface. "You put in carrots and potatoes?"

"Yes, I always do. Carrots sweeten the soup, and potatoes thicken it. Plus, I added a few herbs and that nice smoked ham bone."

"Which herbs?"

"It's my mama's secret recipe, so I mustn't divulge the exact ingredients."

"But this café is open to the public. Someone could have a food allergy." I doubted my declaration, but she owed me an explanation. Not only that, but she hadn't cleaned up her mess. The knife and cutting board needed a thorough washing, and carrot tops and other debris needed to be tossed into the garbage. She must have noticed my looking over the disarray because she said, "I didn't know where to put the carrot and potato peelings. I assume they're saved for a pig farmer or put into compost."

She was probably right, but I didn't have the answers. So much to learn. "I'll ask Stephen."

"He may not come into the café all morning. Such a mess outside. He and his men will be busy readying the nursery for business. Plus, there's still no electricity in the retail shop. Looks like receipts will have to be written out the old-fashioned way." One corner of her mouth lifted. "The *alte* ways are often the best, as the Amish say."

The fact she spoke a bit of Pennsylvania Dutch irked me for no good reason. "I'm glad for the generator, or the refrigerator would have shut off." I heard its steady pumping.

"Yes, the food would go bad in no time."

I was tempted to take a taste of the soup, but no steam rose from its surface. It hadn't heated thoroughly, nor were the vegetables cooked. Not a fair assessment.

She sprinkled salt into the soup. "Don't worry, Eva. It'll be the best pea soup you ever ate." She gave me a quirky wink that seemed out of character.

"I look forward to sampling it." I figured I could learn a lot from her and scolded myself to remain humble. I'd been taught to respect my elders. But I wasn't used to being talked down to as if I were a child. I guessed some of her better-than-thou attitude came from knowing about my former relationship with Jake. As his mother's neighbor and friend, she had no doubt been privy to his antics. Plus a few tall tales.

She cleared her voice. "Well? Will I receive no show of gratitude?"

"Oh, I'm sorry. Thank you very much." I tried to compose an expression of appreciation on my face with a smile.

"Those other two young girls can tidy this area. I've seen them standing around with nothing to do. Idle hands are the devil's plaything." She lowered the flame on the stove top again. "Don't let this soup burn. Nothing is worse than burned pea soup." She glanced at me. "What soup are you making tomorrow?"

"I'd planned on vegetable barley, but I don't know yet."

"You'd better make sure you have all the ingredients. Did you order barley? Food doesn't magically pop out of nowhere. But you could check the cupboards and freezer. You might get lucky if Olivia stocked it with broth and meats."

"Wonderful." I opened the freezer and was glad to see a bundle in white butcher paper marked stewing meat, which I set in the refrigerator to thaw.

"Place an order today for more," she said, "but don't expect it until late afternoon or tomorrow. After that fierce storm last night, the warehouse might be running behind."

The back door to the kitchen opened, and a deliveryman carted in loaves of wheat and white bread. Sporting a mustache, the fellow was obviously *Englisch*, in his late fifties. He smiled at me as I moved toward him. "Are you the new manager?"

"Yes, I'm Eva Lapp."

"I'm Scott McCann. Nice to see a pretty new face here."

I squirmed inside, hearing those words with Beatrice's ears. He had yet to acknowledge her. Or maybe he'd met her in the past and found her unwelcoming.

"That was quite a storm last night." He glanced around the kitchen. "I'm glad we didn't lose electricity at the bakery."

"We'll be fine at the café with our gas stove and generator," Beatrice said.

The phone rang, making me start. I reached for it before Beatrice could. "Yoder's Nursery Café."

Olivia's sparkling voice came out of the receiver. She must be calling from her phone shanty. "I haven't cooked, and my *bruder* wouldn't be able to deliver the baked goods today anyway. A tree fell across the road. Sorry. I hope you have enough left from yesterday to see you through."

"*Yah*, we'll be fine. Day-old whoopie pies and cookies at a discount. Our refrigerated case is still cold."

"When you come over someday, I'll give you baking lessons. Or I'll come there."

"That's kind of you, but as long as you're willing to bake for us, please continue."

"But not today. Last night one of my *dat*'s sheds blew over. He's out there with a team of horses pulling it upright. I haven't had time to bake. My *mamm* said, 'All things work together for good to them that love God.' Her answer for everything."

I'd certainly heard that verse a few times growing up, and I wished it were true. So far, all things were not working for good. Maybe I didn't love the Lord as I should because my prayers had not been answered.

"Evie, I have some news for you." Olivia's voice rose. "If you still care—and I know you do—I heard Jake's coming back to his parents' home tomorrow. His *dat* got kicked in the forehead by a mule last week. He's been in the trauma unit at the hospital in Lancaster and is in a coma. The doctors don't know if he'll ever wake up, but he's breathing on his own. For how long, they don't know. He's lucky to be alive, they said. Neighbors are pitching in to help Jake's *mamm*."

I wondered why *Mamm* and Beatrice hadn't mentioned this fact. They had to know. Maybe they didn't want me to be privy to the information.

"I suggest you don't stop by to see Jake at his parents'," Olivia said.

"Oh?" Because Beatrice and Scott were within earshot, I couldn't inquire further or speak what was on my mind. I also decided not to ask Olivia why she didn't tell me I was replacing her at this managerial job until I could do so in private. "No time. I'll be busy all day." My words came out in a whisper. "Anyone wanting to see me can find out where I am." But Jake obviously didn't care, a hideous truth that could make my world stop revolving. "I've got to get back to work. Please let me know about tomorrow, Liv. If we don't have your baked goodies, we might lose all our customers."

"*Nee*, you can always bake more."

"*Ach*, I don't think so." She had more faith in my culinary skills than I did. I'd been shortsighted and naive to figure I'd learn when I got married.

After saying goodbye, I clunked the phone receiver back into its cradle. While I'd been chatting with my cousin, Scott had filled the metal rack with loaves, including whole wheat, white, and rye.

Beatrice brought out a long-handled ladle. "I'll keep an eye on the soup while you make coffee, Eva."

"Okay." I was glad for the help, even if she was bossing me around.

"Goodbye and thanks." I lifted a hand to Scott as he exited.

"See you tomorrow, Eva." I listened to the back door shutting and his truck whisk away.

# Seven

"Good morning." Stephen strode into the café at nine and set several newspapers on one of the front tables. Then he pulled a reader board out onto the walkway with the word *Open* written across its surface and returned. "How are things going?"

"Fine," Beatrice answered before I could speak.

"I'm glad you're here, Bea. Jennifer just called to say she can't make it because their road is blocked. This was to be her last day anyway."

Beatrice puckered her face. "These young folks are so unreliable."

"The roads are a mess." He sent me a crooked smile. "Sadie called to say she'll be here as quickly as she can make it on her scooter. She'll probably be about an hour late."

A middle-aged *Englisch* couple trudged in. "We were hoping you'd have coffee," the tallish woman said as she neared the carafe. "No electricity on our block or maybe for miles."

I brought out two mugs and then hurried to the refrigerator to fetch the half-and-half, already in a pitcher. The woman seemed to know the drill and served herself coffee, plus another mug full for her husband, who'd already sunk into a chair and opened a newspaper.

The woman pointed at the glass-enclosed case. "How about a couple of those corn muffins and some butter?"

"Certainly, but I must warn you they're a day old."

"That's fine as long as the coffee is fresh."

"It's nice and hot." I scooted around behind the case and placed two muffins on plates, along with pats of butter. "Please take a napkin and a knife while I ring you up."

My first transaction of the morning had gone smoothly, but I looked up to see more *Englischers* entering. "Don't worry, Eva. Beatrice will help you until Sadie arrives," Stephen said.

"Sure, if you need me." Beatrice seemed tickled. "I'm glad I fed the dogs first thing. I'll let them out so they don't mess the house and then come right back." Beatrice followed Stephen out the door.

My, he was an attractive man and two years older than I was. A shame he wasn't Amish. Would I leave the Amish church if I fell in love with an *Englisch* man? No, I wouldn't break my parents' hearts the way Jake had broken his. At least I didn't think I would.

I'd often wondered if Jake had jumped the fence into the *Englisch* world. I'd have to see him to know. Or perhaps it was better if I never set eyes on him again—especially if he was married and had children. Olivia must have thought he was married to suggest I not go see him.

His poor parents. I felt the weight of sadness in my chest as I thought about his father's injury. His *dat* was a rigid, standoffish man, although maybe he'd have mellowed if he ever woke up again. No matter his personality, no one deserved a paralyzing injury. I wondered why God allowed such tragedies. For the same reason he let me remain single and lonely all these years?

"See, I told ya'll," a plump woman with fringes on her suede jacket's sleeves said to her two *Englisch* friends. "The Amish don't need electricity to make things work."

Rather than explain we were working our cash register off a generator, I smiled at the three women as they strolled to the side of the case filled with pastries. The generator was not connected to the electric grid that expanded across the world like a spider's cobweb, thus earning the bishops' approval.

I served the women tea and muffins. They were pleasant until one brought out her smartphone. "May I take your photo?"

"*Nee*." I put out my hand to block my face. "Please, it's forbidden."

"Oops, too late." Grinning, her face crinkled. "Never mind, honey. I won't show it to anyone." She held up the phone again and I spun away, retreating into the kitchen just as Sadie arrived through the back door. Her face was flushed, I assumed from the arduous trek on her scooter.

"One of those women took my picture." I grimaced. "This type of behavior seldom happened in the fabric store."

"We need to put up a sign saying no photos allowed." Sadie was ten years my junior but obviously wiser in other ways. "I'll ask Mark to make one when he comes in for his morning *kaffi*."

Ah, she was wiser in the ways of men too. No wonder she'd hurried to get to work so quickly despite roads littered with branches.

"Susie's *bruder*?" I asked.

"*Yah.*" Her eyes brightened.

A steady stream of people came in, mostly *Englisch*, who were delighted to find we had warm food. By noon, we had served the soup, which was tasty. Customers raved about it, and Beatrice beamed, but she did not claim she'd prepared it. She was helpful taking food to the tables, but not clearing them. Fortunately, most of the customers brought their used plates and bowls to a plastic tub—or Sadie did, and then she swabbed clean the tables' surfaces. Any tips left were dropped into a jar near the register. Most were coins, but I noticed a few dollar bills, which I assumed would be given to Sadie.

During a lull I served myself a cup of soup and stepped into the kitchen. Beatrice had indeed produced a delicious meal, better than mine would have been. I doubted she would ever reveal her secret ingredients, but I could ask.

Sadie stood at the washbasin, vigorously scrubbing the dirty dishes, rinsing them, and then setting them in the dishwasher or drying rack. I asked her if she wanted a break, but she shook her head. I figured she was still waiting for Mark, who had not arrived for his morning coffee.

"You step outside for a few minutes before Beatrice leaves," she said.

"Are you sure you're okay?" I asked.

"*Yah*, I can work the cash register. Well, *gut* enough."

"I was just on my way out." Beatrice untied and removed her apron. "If you two can't handle the café without me, let me know and I'll come back. But I have plenty to keep me busy in the main house." There went my chance for a short stroll and an opportunity to ask Beatrice about her soup recipe. Which reminded me I needed to make sure I had the ingredients for tomorrow's soup, plus hand in my order for vegetables and meats, not to mention fresh milk, butter, and other staples.

As Beatrice marched toward the door, Mark strode in and held it open for her. Sadie bustled over to pour him coffee. He thanked her and then turned to me. "How *ya* doing, Eva?"

Sadie stood at his elbow, but he didn't seem to notice her. Only me. His gaze honed in on my face, and his intense expression conveyed appreciation. He found me attractive?

"I was wondering if you'll start attending this church district on Sunday." He sipped his coffee. "I'd be honored to drive you there and later to our singing."

I glanced at Sadie and saw her demeanor slump. She pressed her lips together and hung her head.

"I hadn't given it much thought." Not true. I'd pondered the upcoming Sunday, a nonpreaching Sunday in my parents' district. It was a family time of socializing and visiting neighbors, who would probably riddle me with questions about my new job and maybe tell me about Jake's reappearance—if Olivia was right that he was coming.

"Let me know and I'll pick you up." Mark polished off his coffee. "I'm happy to drive you there or anywhere. If you haven't heard about my standardbred, I think you'll be pleased. Not that I should brag."

I pictured him washing and polishing his buggy to transport me for nothing. Mark was probably five years my junior and couldn't possibly choose me over Sadie. I almost suggested he take her, but I didn't wish to embarrass either one of them.

"I haven't gone to a singing for years," I said.

"I'd be happy to escort you. Plus, it's a *gut* way to meet your new neighbors. You are planning to stick around, aren't you?"

"*Yah,* if I can. When the owner comes back, I assume he'll have the final say."

Mark's eyes never left mine. "Let me know about Sunday. Service will be in Willie Fisher's barn several miles away."

He handed the empty mug to Sadie. Her face was solemn.

"I'd best get back to work." He pivoted toward the door, away from her. "We still have quite a mess to clean up, including half the parking lot."

# Eight

The day seemed to flitter by, what with all the customers, plus a produce delivery I was most happy to see. Fresh vegetables, fruit, and meat. I noticed we were running low on roast beef and ham.

"I hope you don't mind that I ordered this," Sadie said after thanking the deliveryman.

"Quite the contrary. I appreciate your help." When we had a lull with customers, I used the time to call Olivia's phone shanty and left a message asking if she could deliver pastries and muffins tomorrow. I hoped she'd get back to me before three.

"So do ya think you'll go with Mark?" Sadie opened the refrigerator door.

"Unlikely, although I do want to attend church. I haven't been to a singing for years and have no intention of starting now."

"Ya don't like to sing?"

"I used to, many years ago." I was tempted to tell her how surprised I was at Mark's attention, but I didn't want to make her sad. She obviously had a crush on him. The words *unrequited love* floated in the back of my mind. I could relate.

"Mark has never offered to take me anywhere." She tossed in several bunches of carrots.

"He might. You're pretty and smart." And she did not strike me as a woman who would allow herself to become an old maid as I had.

Perhaps I should have entertained attention from that older widower last year, but he was unappealing and had ten unruly children. "If not Mark, I have no doubt some other lucky fellow will court you."

"I'm almost eighteen."

"Plenty of time to find the right husband."

"Why did you never marry?"

I was hoping to avoid answering that question. "I wanted to... Have you never heard?"

"Only what Beatrice mentioned, that your sweetheart moved to New York years ago and was last seen wearing a beard."

"What?" Her words stunned me as if she'd slapped me in the face. If Jake wore a beard, he was married. Only married Amish men wore beards. "Are you sure?"

"That's what Beatrice said, but I don't know if it's true. Sometimes she gets her facts mixed up." Her brows knit. "I'm sorry if I said the wrong thing."

I tried to appear confident as my mind churned with shards of uncertainty. I wondered what other bits of gossip Beatrice had sprinkled. "Nothing more?" I asked.

"Only that you worked in the fabric shop and lived with your parents until yesterday." She glanced through the kitchen doorway to the front door as an *Englisch* couple entered.

The phone in the kitchen jangled. "I'll get it." I hustled to answer and heard Olivia's vivacious voice.

"How's everything going, dear cousin?"

"If you're calling to tell me you're bringing baked goods in the morning, then I'll tell you I've had a *wunderbaar* day."

"That's exactly why I'm calling, Evie. The roads are clear, and I've been baking all afternoon."

"*Gut.* That's a relief."

"Is everything okay? You sound *naerfich*."

"I'm not nervous." The words shot out of my mouth too quickly. "Sorry, Liv. I guess I am a little stressed."

"It's your first day at a new job. Of course that would be stressful."

I didn't want to bring up Jake's name. And I decided to let go of Olivia's neglecting to tell me this was a café job. It didn't matter now. "I have a few questions for you about the kitchen here."

"You should be fine with that nice generator and Sadie and Jennifer to help you."

"Jennifer didn't make it in today. And she gave me notice, so we'll need to hire someone else. Do you know of anyone looking for a job? Beatrice stepped in."

"That must have been helpful." She chuckled. "Not the sweetest woman in nature, but capable and a hard worker."

"*Yah*, she's been a tremendous help." And I hadn't properly thanked her. I was still reeling from her disclosure to Sadie that Jake might be a married man. "Have you heard any more about Amos?"

"*Ach, nee.* What a terrible injury. From what I understand, if coma victims wake up, it's not the way it's portrayed in the movies. Recovery is a slow process. They might have to learn to speak and walk again. They may lose chunks of memory."

"Liv, you go to the movies?"

"Er...just a few times. But please don't tell anyone. *Ach*, my parents would kill me." She was six years younger than I was and in her *rumspringa*, her time for experimenting with the *Englisch* world. But I knew her parents were strict.

"*Mamm* took the Millers a casserole," she said, "and neighbors are setting aside their differences with Amos and helping out in the fields. You know how ornery Jake's *dat* is, but neighbors are keeping their farm going until Jake gets home. Jake's two *schweschders* are married now and live on dairy farms in Ohio with their husbands and children. They rushed home by train to see their *dat* in the trauma unit, but since he was in a coma, they got no response. They stuck around for a few days but then returned to Ohio. Their husbands wouldn't leave their herds to see a man who was sleeping. I don't think they ever got along with Amos, and vice versa."

"Liv, Beatrice said Jake was last seen wearing a beard." My voice came out as if I were being strangled.

"So I hear. That's why I suggested you don't go see him. Please tell me you're not still pining over him. It's time to move on. You have a new job, a new life, and ample opportunity to meet a new man."

"Someone here does seem interested, but he's so young."

She guffawed. "Still a teenager?"

"*Nee*, but about five years younger than I am. His name is Mark. But—"

"Mark's a good guy. Honestly, Evie, how long are you going to cling to a dream that will never come true? Especially if Jake is married." A woman's voice spoke *Deitsch* in the background. "I have to run. Our neighbor wants to use the phone. Expect to see my whoopie pies in the morning."

"I wish you could deliver them in person so I could see you."

"I may be in *rumspringa*, but my *mamm* does everything she can to keep me in the house. That's why she insisted I leave my job at the café. She's afraid I'll run off with—well, never mind. I was ready for a change anyway."

"I wished I'd run away with Jake those many years ago."

"Now you're talking foolishness."

"*Yah*, I am. Because he never asked me to go with him."

By closing time, I was mentally and physically exhausted. My feet felt like cement blocks—as if each of them had grown two sizes. Maybe I should wear sneakers like Sadie did instead of my black-laced leather shoes. She waltzed around effortlessly and with good cheer, but then she was also more than ten years younger than I was.

She and I swiped the tables clean and put away the washed dishes so we'd start afresh in the morning. I asked her if she had a friend looking for a job. "When the owners come home, Beatrice will no longer be available to work in the café."

"Fine with me," Sadie said.

"She was a godsend today." I needed to stop by to thank her on my way to the cabin.

When I stepped into the fresh air, I was greeted with a myriad of earthy aromas. The sky was gray, but birds twittered. A few customers wandered past the greenhouses on their way out of the nursery. I saw the owners' two Labrador retrievers flouncing toward me, so I stepped inside a greenhouse and closed the glass sliding door behind me.

"How did your first day ago?" Stephen leaned on a shovel's handle.

"Perfect." A slight exaggeration.

"I hope you're planning to stay with us."

"*Yah*, absolutely."

"Tired?"

"I'd be lying if I said I wasn't. And my feet..." I glanced down at my shoes and noticed a scuff on one toe. I'd stood on my feet all day at the fabric store, but the floor had been carpeted, not painted cement.

"Want me to drive you to the mall to buy a pair of comfy shoes?" He let go of the shovel and moved closer.

I imagined Beatrice's evil eye as I got into Stephen's car. "Thanks for your kind offer, but I'd better take a bus to town. I'd adore a pair like Sadie wears if they're allowed at work."

"Sure. Wear whatever is most comfortable as long as it isn't toeless. I'd be glad to take you there right now. I was about to run out to purchase supplies at the hardware store. It's no trouble to take you by the outlet mall."

"I couldn't bother you." Yet my feet throbbed.

"No trouble, but I need to leave in the next thirty minutes." He checked his watch. "Does that give you enough time?"

Of course, I was not wearing a wristwatch. "*Yah.* I'll get my purse."

He must have understood my reticence about the dogs milling outside because he said, "I'll take those mutts with me and meet you in the parking lot. I drive a white pickup."

"Okay. I'll see you soon." I stepped outside to find the sky darkening. No glorious sunset tonight. As I hurried to the cabin, I noticed Beatrice weeding the herb garden. In another month, basil, sage, rosemary, and lavender would swell in the afternoon sunshine, but today the air hung heavily as if the clouds would open up again. I decided to take my rain jacket.

Beatrice glanced up at me. I strode over to her and said, "Thank you for helping in the café today."

"I didn't do it for you."

"I appreciate your hard work in any case. And your soup was *appeditlich*, much better than mine would've been."

The corner of her mouth lifted on one side as if she were holding in a grin. "I suppose you'll want me to make soup again tomorrow."

"I think I'm all set, thank you. But I truly appreciate your willingness to share your culinary skills with me. You are a much finer cook than I am."

Finally, her face softened, but she turned away and got back to weeding. I dashed into the cabin, checked myself in the mirror, and tucked stray hairs under my *kapp*. I grabbed my jacket and purse and headed back out the door.

I found Stephen standing by his pickup speaking to Mark, who stared when he saw me.

"You need a ride somewhere?" Mark asked. "I can take you in my buggy anywhere you wish to go."

"I don't think I have time today, but *denki*." I hoped I hadn't hurt his feelings by accepting Stephen's offer, but I expected this to be a quick trip, and I wanted to be home before nightfall.

Stephen opened the passenger door. I climbed in and he shut it behind me, and then he rounded the vehicle to his side.

"Is the electricity back on?" I asked.

"Yes. Finally. But the weatherman predicts another storm tonight." He started the engine and then looked over at me. "Are you uncomfortable being alone with me? Maybe we should invite Beatrice."

"No, I'm fine." Then why were my hands clammy?

"I often take Amish employees to help me pick up merchandise, although they are usually male." He sent me a reassuring smile. "Would you please buckle your seat belt?"

"*Ach*, sorry. I'm not used to riding in a pickup. We sure are up high. I've never even sat in the front seat of a car. Just in the back of passenger vans." I craned my head, but I couldn't locate the seat belt clip.

"Allow me." Stephen slipped his hand behind my shoulder and found the culprit, and then he tugged the belt across the front of me and attached it with a metallic click. I could imagine Mark standing outside, watching this maneuver, and I felt my face flush. My parents wouldn't have approved either. But this was not a social outing. And my feet ached.

Glancing over his shoulder, Stephen backed up and then nosed his pickup out of the parking lot onto the road. We passed several buggies, but fortunately I didn't recognize neighbors or acquaintances—until we came upon a bishop's buggy with its usual open front. The bishop—a bearded man I didn't recognize—seemed to be busy speaking to a young woman and didn't look our way.

I craned my neck in the other direction. "I can't believe how many new buildings have been built along the highway."

"Yeah, the whole area is expanding with housing developments, shopping malls, and car lots. I guess they call that progress."

When he took a right and we entered the mall, I saw a plethora of fancy storefronts. Stephen stopped in front of the Nike outlet.

"Several shoe stores are near here, but this one's popular." He set the parking brake. "What did you have in mind again?"

"Something like what Sadie wears. Lace-up and cushioned soles. If you're sure Glenn won't mind."

"Not at all. I might come in and look around for something

myself." He jumped out of the pickup as I unclipped my seat belt. In a moment he'd rounded the vehicle and opened my door, I assumed to get this trip over with so he could dash to the hardware store.

Stephen browsed through the showroom for a few minutes and selected a pair of flip-flops he called sliders. "The price is right," he said. "Eventually, summer will be here again."

On the other hand, I tried on several styles of walking or running shoes and became the new owner of my first pair of running shoes that made my feet feel as if they were treading on cushions of air. "You should buy some white socks to go with them," Stephen told me.

"I've never worn white socks in my life. Are you sure?"

Both Stephen and the shoe salesman nodded.

"But if you feel uncomfortable not wearing black socks, I don't want to be a bad influence," Stephen said.

I paid for the shoes and two pairs of soft white socks with cash. I could afford the purchase, but I felt a smidgen of guilt for buying such fancy footwear.

Five minutes later, Stephen motored us back onto the road and then swerved off and trotted into a hardware store while I stayed in the pickup. As I sat waiting, I second-guessed my purchases. Several buggies stood at a hitching post. I slumped low in my seat and hoped no one I knew would notice me.

Back behind the steering wheel ten minutes later, Stephen turned on the radio as a newsman was announcing an approaching storm, expected to be worse than the previous night's. Droplets landed on the windshield.

"Oh, great. I'd better hurry." He sped back onto the highway just as a buggy was entering. A truck barreling toward us from the other direction honked long and hard. The horse reared and then took off, galloping too close to the side of the road. Its driver was unable to control the animal, and the buggy's right front wheel slid off the road.

I covered my mouth with my hands as I watched the buggy gain momentum and then bump to the bottom of an embankment, where it tipped on its side.

Stephen slammed on the brakes and veered onto a gravel patch. "Stay here."

He leaped out and loped down to where the horse was kicking and thrashing to get up. In a flurry, an Amish man and woman climbed out of the buggy. With Stephen's help, they unhitched the horse, and the animal struggled to its feet.

I couldn't sit there, watch, and do nothing. As I shouldered open the door and got out, two cars and several buggies pulled to the side of the road, their male drivers scrambling down the hill. Eight men, both Amish and *Englisch*, stood the buggy upright, but a wheel was broken and the horse limped.

A police car lurched to a stop, and a burly officer who looked to be in his late thirties got out. "What happened, miss?"

I didn't dare say a word. I had every confidence Stephen would set things right, but I'd been wrongly accused in the past. An aid car's siren wailed, followed by another squad car, which screeched to a halt on the other side of the road. Two medics trotted over to us.

"Anyone injured, Wayne?" one medic asked.

"Doesn't look like it," the officer said. The medics picked their way down the hill and spoke to the Amish couple and Stephen. The Amish driver slapped his straw hat against his thigh and then set it on his head. Her neck bent, his wife stood looking at the horse.

A crowd gathered around me and then another policeman. A light flashed as an *Englischer* wearing a baseball cap took my picture with the officer.

"This is great," another *Englisch* fellow said. "I'm from *LNP Always Lancaster*, writing an article on buggy and car accidents for the paper." The reporter and photographer jogged down the hill. I wanted to scramble after them to beg them not to use my picture in the newspaper, but I feared the photographer might take another.

"Miss, were you in the pickup during the accident?" the policeman named Wayne asked.

"Yes, but I wasn't driving."

He chortled as he scanned my Amish attire. "I didn't think you were. But can you tell me what happened?"

"I wasn't paying much attention, only listening to the radio. I heard a truck honk, and then I saw the buggy swerving off the side of the road."

"Is that Stephen Troyer from Yoder's Nursery down there?"

"Yes."

"I know him well." He peered into my face. "Had he been drinking?"

"No. We've both been at work all day and then shopping."

"You work at the nursery too?"

"Yes. Just started today."

The officer picked his way down the hill and spoke to Stephen, the buggy's owner, and his wife. The couple seemed unscathed. I was aching to go down to help, but I worried I'd further complicate the situation.

The second officer followed him down the ravine, and then Wayne returned. "Looks like I'm giving you a ride home, miss. Stephen asked me to since he'll be here for a while." He must have noticed my jaw drop because he added, "I'm Officer Wayne Grady. Don't worry. I'll take good care of you, and I know where the nursery is. Stephen said you live in the small cabin on the property."

"Yes, I do, but I don't want to trouble you." I scanned the buggies and saw women and children climbing in as the downpour increased. No one I recognized.

"I'm headed that way anyway, miss."

"Okay, thanks." I waved at Stephen, but he was busy helping the Amish driver remove the buggy's wheel, I assumed to take it to be repaired. Stephen would need his pickup for that job and his passenger seat for the Amish couple. I'd be nothing but in the way. I reached into his pickup and grabbed my purse and my bag from the outlet mall.

Wayne opened the squad car's passenger door. "You'll be safe with me. I promised Stephen to take extra good care of you."

"Maybe I should sit in the backseat."

"No, the seat's covered with hard plastic and not clean enough."

Again, I searched the sea of faces for someone I knew, but I found no one. And a buggy ride all the way to the nursery would be a great inconvenience. As I slid into the seat, heads turned. Apparently, I still cared too much what others thought of me. I tried to appear dignified, but the moment I sat in the squad car's seat, I slid down, hoping to be out of sight.

"Stephen said your name is Eva Lapp."

"Yes." My tongue seemed to be a limp appendage. "Thank you for the ride."

"Like I said, not a problem. I know where the nursery is. I've taken my wife there plenty of times. She loves gardening."

A buggy passed us heading the other direction. I recognized the deacon from my parents' district. No doubt about it, he stared right at me. I hoped he only caught a glimpse of my *kapp*, which must be flattened by the rain.

Ten minutes later, Wayne and I rolled onto the nursery's gravel parking lot. The electricity was on, and lights illuminated the greenhouses. The shop seemed to be closed for the night, but I assumed anyone in the area could make out the squad car easily with the rain reflecting off its surface.

"Thank you, Officer. You can let me out here." I reached for the door handle.

"Hold on. I promised Stephen to take you to your doorstep. And call me Wayne." He continued driving around the side of the big house. I figured Beatrice had heard the car and was ogling at us out a window. Yes, as I exited the squad car, she opened the back door and stepped out onto the covered porch. She must have been worried about Stephen, I told myself. But I couldn't face her right now, not clutching the bag containing my new, worldly shoes.

"Thanks for the ride, Wayne." I jumped out and shut the car's door behind me. Minnie barked and scrambled to greet me. The two Labs followed. One let out a woof. The last thing I wanted was to have more attention drawn to me, but there was no getting around it. I had arrived in a police car. And I'd been alone with Stephen.

I hurried into my cabin and closed the door before the dogs could follow me inside. A minute later, knuckles rapped on my door. I opened it to find Beatrice carrying a black umbrella.

"Where's Stephen?" Her eyes surveyed my wet clothes and *kapp*. "I saw you two leaving together hours ago."

"He's helping an Amish man with his buggy wheel."

Her gazed moved to my Nike bag. "You two went shopping at the mall?"

"He needed something from the hardware store and offered to take me. I told him my feet hurt so much..."

Her white lips pressed together. "Dry off, for goodness' sake, before you get pneumonia."

I stepped out of my soggy shoes and hung my dripping jacket on a peg. I must have looked an unruly sight with the hem of my dress wet and mud-spattered. I'd wait until she left to remove my *kapp* and check my disheveled hair in the mirror.

As if anchored to the floor, she folded her arms across her matronly bulk. "I suppose you'll be needing my help with the soup again tomorrow."

"Thanks for the offer, but I have it all planned, and we have the ingredients already. Beef barley."

She lifted her pointy jaw. "Including beef stock?"

"Uh..." I reached for my copy of *Family Life*, the one periodical I'd brought from home. "I saw the recipe in a magazine recently. A reader from around here sent it in." I opened the black-and-white monthly magazine and located the recipe.

Beatrice snatched the publication out of my hand. "Are you blind? Right at the top of the list of ingredients is beef stock. Got some in the café's kitchen?"

"I don't recall seeing any, now that you mention it." I felt the way I had in second grade after I'd flubbed a spelling test because I hadn't studied. "Maybe chicken stock will do."

"Not if you want your soup to taste its best."

I let out a lengthy sigh.

"No need to fret," she said. "I have canned beef stock in the house you can use."

Disappointment blanketed me, but I knew it would be prideful and plain old silly to not accept her generosity. "Thank you for your kind offer."

# Nine

Several hours later, the rain increased and the wind gained velocity. It looked as though I would spend another lonely evening. I missed my parents, but I knew they had their hands full. I'd assured them I was a grown woman and would be fine by myself. But I wasn't. I was so lonely that I wished Beatrice had invited me to the big house for dinner.

Another electrical storm lumbered up the valley.

I filled the kettle with water to make a soothing cup of tea, set it on the stovetop, and ignited the flame. The kettle seemed to take forever to shrill. I rushed over to turn off the stove and brought down a cup and a tea bag. As I poured water over the bag, a clap of thunder sounding as loud as a stick of dynamite exploding hit a tree or building nearby. The floor shook. My hand jerked, spilling most of the hot liquid onto the counter. I wondered if the main house had been zapped and if the owner had a lightning rod, unlike *Dat*, who maintained God was in control.

I went to the window and saw the electric lights still beaming in the nursery. Beatrice came flying out the back door and beckoned me to come to her. She was waving her arms and yelling in what I thought was Italian. The last thing I wanted to do was brave the downpour as the droplets of rain bounced off the ground. I knew I must respect my elders, but this woman was making it hard for me to be polite.

Well, I was glad I'd bought the new shoes for tomorrow.

I put on my rain jacket, rubber boots, and a scarf, and then I sprinted over to the back porch and mounted the steps.

Beatrice's words came out staggered. "The maple tree—out front—got struck. What if it falls and hits the house?"

I was at a loss for words. I'd always lived at home where my *dat* took care of everything.

She wrung her hands. "If the tree dies, Glenn will be crushed. He told me it was one of the reasons he bought this place."

I saw headlights entering the parking lot and recognized Stephen's pickup. He pulled up alongside the house and jumped out. He wore a plastic rain jacket and boots. "I thought I'd better come over and check things out." He glanced my way. "I live just down the road."

Beatrice told him about the tree, and Stephen brought out a flashlight. "I'll go have a look-see. Beatrice, would you turn on the front porch light?"

I followed them into the house and to the front door, through a plush, modern kitchen with a gas stove and the latest electrical cooking devices. Beatrice flipped a switch, illuminating the porch.

Stephen swung open the door, trotted down the steps, and stood out in the clipped grass yard, shining his flashlight beam on the tree's mighty trunk. "The maple was hit. It's not smashed or missing limbs, but I can see a gash down the side." He shone the beam up and down the tree's lengthy torso. "Nothing to be done about it tonight, and it sounds as though the storm is moving on."

"It's an ill omen." Beatrice turned to glare at me. "*Un cattivo presagio.*"

Stephen flicked his flashlight on and off. "Now, now, Beatrice, we have electrical storms every so often. The weatherman predicted this one."

"Well, we've had two since Eva arrived. And now Glenn's beautiful maple tree..."

I felt compelled to defend myself. "My *dat* has lost many trees during storms." But I'd never seen damage like this.

"It looks as though a giant hand ripped off a strip of bark and tossed it across the yard," Beatrice said.

"I'm glad I wasn't standing near it." Stephen stroked his jawline "It's been a long day, and I'd better get home." He turned to leave.

"Wait." I moved further out onto the porch. "What happened with the Amish couple and the buggy?"

"I drove the driver and the damaged wheel to a repair shop. The owner gave him a loaner until he fixes the wheel. Then I returned the man and the extra wheel and dropped him off. He assured me he was fine and didn't need additional help. Several of his Amish neighbors had waited and would assist him. One brought him a fresh horse. I have to give it to the Amish. They take care of each other."

"That they do," Beatrice said. "They obey the Bible as we all should. 'Thou shalt love thy neighbour as thyself.'"

"Indeed." Stephen sent her a smile, but his eyes remained sapped of energy. "See you in the morning." He trotted down the steps and into his pickup. Moments later, his vehicle exited the parking lot.

"I hope this has taught you a lesson." Beatrice ushered me into the house and secured the front door. "Stephen is a fine man, but he's not one of you. What would your parents think? You should never have accepted a ride from him. And then you return in a patrol car?"

"He's my boss until Glenn returns."

She scowled. "Don't you wish to find a good Amish husband?"

I lowered my chin and resisted answering. Then a thought occurred to me. "Since I'm here, may I take the soup stock with me?"

"I suppose, if you promise not to drop it."

"I'll guard it with my life."

Her face bunched up as though she'd eaten a slice of lemon. It was unlikely she believed anything I said.

# Ten

The next morning sunlight streamed into the cabin, sneaking past the crack between the window and the roller shades. A wren's melodic trilling from outside my bedside window announced it was time to rise. Good. I hadn't overslept. Plus, I possessed two jars of beef stock. Today my soup would be superb. I felt foolish for not reading the recipe with more care.

Oh, dear. Had I thanked Beatrice for her generosity? I owed her my gratitude.

I showered and dressed hurriedly, but then I spent extra time parting my hair in the middle, putting on a clean *kapp*, and checking for miscreant hairs.

I glanced at my new shoes sitting by the door on a mat. My black leather shoes were coated with mud and needed a thorough shining. No time. I would wear my Nikes. I looked forward to a day without foot pain in my spiffy new shoes. Perhaps a day without pain at all. I needed to be optimistic, anxious for nothing.

I envisioned my parents sitting in our kitchen, *Dat* bowing his head as he led silent prayer. But chances were my parents would choose to eat breakfast in the *daadi haus*, which contained a small kitchen. Waking up to find Marta orchestrating her home would be difficult for *Mamm*. My brother's children would be chattering as they finished their chores and got ready for school. According to Reuben, Marta was a quintessential cook.

Once I was ready to leave, I slid my feet into my new cushy socks and then my new shoes. I tied them and stood. Ah, comfort. Many younger Amish women wore them. Maybe one reason few single men ever noticed me was they thought I was too old fashioned. Even if I were almost thirty, today I would make a gigantic effort to be outgoing and fun, like Olivia and Sadie, who wore athletic shoes when not in church. Most of our customers at the fabric store had found me personable. But then again, they were female, and we had a common bond: sewing and quilting.

I checked out the door and was glad not to see Beatrice already sweeping the back porch or tending the herb garden. I carried the jars of beef stock in my Nike bag so I couldn't possibly drop them.

The sky stretched blue, like a vast ocean blushing with pink. I should check the weather report later in case another storm was predicted. I prayed silently for clear skies. Then a tumble of requests came to mind. One was to see Jake. A foolish request, but I needed my questions answered. Was he indeed married? If so, maybe that fact would set me free. I could move on and quit circling back to the past. *Mamm* had assured me it wasn't too late to find a spouse. She'd hinted that marrying a widower might be a good solution. With Jake out of the picture, I might consider it. And then there was young Mark, who made me feel old. Although I didn't experience a tingle of attraction, in the long run what would that initial magnetism matter? My parents had aged like a pair of comfy slippers.

Outside, I was tempted to inspect the maple tree's damage, but I didn't want Beatrice to catch sight of me. She'd be sure to accompany me to the café and take over my soup preparation.

As I neared the café, Missy and her enormous pup galumphed toward me and sniffed the bag.

"This isn't for you." I noticed my dread for them was diminishing by increments. Good. I would overcome my fears one at a time.

I found the door locked and used my key to open it. Once in the kitchen, I heated up the beef broth and eight cups of water, and then

I added the barley, tomato juice, peas, and beans. I chopped onions and celery to add in an hour. I remembered the stewing beef in the refrigerator. Thankfully, it was partially thawed. I tossed it in and hoped it wasn't too early, that all these ingredients wouldn't turn to mush by the time customers wanted lunch.

"Have you put in salt and pepper?" Beatrice's voice startled me.

My hand moved to the salt. "I was just about to." What? I was starting the day off with a lie? "That's not true. The recipe said add salt and pepper to taste, so I was waiting." I looked into her sleep-creased face and added, "Maybe you could help me with that later if you have the time."

Her features softened, a grin widening her thin lips. "Yes, I'd be glad to help. Happy to. *Con piacere.*"

Her expression transformed when she noticed my feet. "Have you checked to see if those running shoes comply with your *Ordnung*?"

"I should've thought to do that before I purchased them." I wanted to ask her why she cared, but I didn't want to hear her opinions.

"Bishop Harvey comes in once a week. Perhaps today. He can assess your footwear. Surely by now he knows you came back yesterday in a police car and will wish to speak to you. Or he might send Deacon Benjamin and a minister to gather facts."

An *Englisch* woman was meddling in my personal affairs. To change the subject, and also because I needed to voice my thanks, I said, "Beatrice, I'm very grateful for the beef stock. Please forgive me if I didn't thank you properly last night."

Her plump face veritably beamed, her cheeks turning rosy. "No problem. The lightning had us all on edge." She stirred my warming vat. "Let me know anytime I can help you. There's not enough to keep an old woman busy all the time in the big house by herself. Maybe you'd like to join me for supper tonight."

I hesitated as I envisioned an awkward encounter, but I couldn't refuse her hospitality. "Thank you very much. I'd love a home-cooked meal." I couldn't imagine what we'd converse about.

"Unless you were planning to meet someone?" she said.

"You mean a man? No."

"We need to find you a husband—unless you're holding out for Jake Miller, a foolish endeavor. *Presenza di acqua sotto il ponte.* I mean, water under the bridge."

"Do you know anything about him? I mean, recent news?" My voice rose in pitch like a plaintive plea.

Instead of answering me, she perused the recipe. "Did you remember to add the oregano?"

"Not yet. Are you sure that's in the recipe?"

"Maybe you need reading glasses. Have you considered them?"

I scanned her homely metal-rim spectacles. "Not yet."

"They're inevitable." She polished her glasses on her skirt. "But let's find you a husband first."

"You make it sound easy."

She placed the glasses on the bridge of her nose. "We have several single Amish men working here. Mark seems to have noticed you. His father owns a spacious and prosperous farm Mark is sure to inherit, as he has only sisters."

"Why isn't he working on his father's farm instead of coming here?"

"I'm sure he gets up early and does his chores before he leaves the farm. He probably works here to earn extra spending money. Glenn and Stephen are glad to have him. Mark is one of their best employees. And good looking, too, don't you think?"

"*Yah*, and young."

"And you hold that against him? You want to end up marrying an elderly codger?"

I chewed at the side of my thumbnail as her queries bombarded me. These were questions I'd asked myself a hundred times.

"I hope you've not become infatuated with Stephen. As I said last night, he's a fine man, but he's not one of you. He regularly attends his Mennonite church. And I hear tell he used to have a drinking problem."

What right did she have to discuss him behind his back? I felt like asking her what business it was of hers. Talk about nosy. I could feel heat traveling up my neck, but I remained silent.

"I can't imagine he'd ever turn Amish and give up driving his pickup just to be with you, Eva." Her eyes fastened onto mine. "You'll have no future with him if you're an Amish church member."

"I haven't joined yet, but I plan to." I'd told my parents I'd take the mandatory classes when I turned thirty. Yet given the right circumstances, I might change my mind. No wonder they fretted over me. If I were honest with myself, I'd have to wonder if I could develop a crush on Stephen.

More than anything, I longed to be married to a man I adored and hold our baby in my arms. My biological clock was ticking. But Jake still owned my heart, paralyzing me, keeping me from moving forward.

"Good morning, ladies." Stephen strode into the café, folded newspapers under his elbow. "I need to speak to Eva—alone," he told Beatrice.

Her eyebrows shot up with a look of surprise and confusion. "I'll come back at opening time. That is, if you still want me to."

"Absolutely. You were a blessing yesterday. What would we have done without you?" His words initiated a grin on her face.

She untied her apron and draped it across a chair.

"Thanks for your help with the soup this morning," I told her departing form. She exited and closed the door without looking back.

"Is something wrong?" I kept my distance from Stephen, who seemed agitated.

"I wanted to show you the newspaper before anyone else did." He unfolded it to expose the front page. "Check this out."

"*Ach.*" I drew near to see my image in black-and-white. I was standing alongside two police officers in front of a squad car. The photographer had taken the photo at an angle, so my features were not readily identifiable. Yet anyone who knew me would recognize my profile.

"Say it isn't so." My hand moved to my throat.

"The reporter had his heart in the right place." Stephen shifted his weight back and forth. "This article admonishes drivers to pay more heed to buggies and describes the needless accident and the horse's injury."

With a shaky hand, I took the paper from him and examined the photo. "Thank the Lord my parents don't read this paper." But I knew it had an expansive circulation in Lancaster County.

"Does the article mention what happened to the horse?" I felt compassion for the poor animal. "Will it be all right?"

"Didn't say. And the honking truck is long gone." He refolded the paper and tucked it under his elbow. "I don't think our customers need to see this issue. Especially if the bishop comes in later."

Despite my trepidation, the morning hummed along smoothly. Joe, Olivia's lanky older brother, delivered her baked goods, Sadie arrived in a cheerful mood, and Beatrice came back with a smile on her face. I banished all thoughts of the horrendous newspaper photo from my mind and concentrated on running a tight ship as customers straggled in at nine.

I watched Sadie's face brim with gladness as Mark arrived for coffee. I had to admit he was a fine-looking young man—his jawline rectangular and smooth. No wonder she hoped to attract his attention.

"Good morning, Eva." Was he intentionally ignoring Sadie as she brought him a mug of coffee? He finally mumbled a meager "*Denki*" to her.

"Hello, Mark." Beatrice bustled to his side. "I invited Eva for supper tonight. Would you care to join us?"

"Uh, I don't know if I can come," I said before he could answer. "I might grab a snack from the café."

"Why, of course you can come. You said you would." Beatrice patted my arm in a matronly fashion. "I've already purchased the fixings for spaghetti and meatballs. Wait until you taste my marinara sauce—a family recipe brought over by my grandparents from Tuscany."

"That sounds tasty, but—"

"I won't take no for an answer." She turned to Mark. "Can I count on you?"

"*Yah*, sounds *gut*. I'll have to go home first to help with chores, but then I'll come right back. I don't live too far away."

"*Perfetto.* We'll wait for your return." Beatrice seemed pleased with herself, her mouth widening and her eyes sparkling.

How could she put me in this awkward position without consulting me first? She was playing matchmaker and not considering my wishes. Or Sadie's.

As Mark stood sipping his coffee, his green eyes stole a glance at me. I didn't want him getting the wrong idea, and yet I'd told *Dat* I was on the lookout for a beau.

I wondered if Mark knew how old I was or anything about my dicey past, or if he'd seen the newspaper today. Not that I'd done anything wrong. Yet if I hadn't accepted a ride from Stephen, I never would have ended up standing at the side of the road with policemen for all the world to see.

"Then it's settled." Beatrice glanced down at my Nikes. "Unless you have other plans, Eva. Such as going jogging or shopping?"

"*Nee.* No more shopping sprees."

Mark scanned my feet. "Hey, I like your new shoes."

"This is their first day, and they're already comfortable. I hope women are allowed to wear them in this district."

"As far as I know. You can ask Bishop Harvey when he comes into the café," Mark said. "He's a godly man and fair."

"If he says no, then of course I won't wear them."

"I can't imagine he wants your feet to hurt. Harvey's not as conservative as your parents' bishop, but I've heard Jonathon Stoltzfus is so old he rarely leaves his house, so he'll never see them." Mark moved toward the door. "I'd better get back to work." He tossed Beatrice a grin. "Thanks for your invitation. Can I bring anything?"

"Just yourself." Her face showed satisfaction, her gray eyes animated as if she'd just pulled off an incredible feat. I glanced over her shoulder and saw Sadie looking despondent, her arms slack and hanging at her sides. Poor thing. No matter. After tonight Mark would understand he and I were not a good match. Or was I turning judgmental? In my mind, I prayed the Lord would steer me in the right direction and not allow Beatrice to orchestrate my world.

The café's lunch rush kept me too occupied to worry about my social life. I was gratified when customers commented that they liked the soup, and I mentioned that Beatrice had helped me.

"No, Eva did most of the work." Once again, Beatrice showed more humility than I'd expected. Maybe I'd misjudged her, but I cringed when I thought about dining in Glenn Yoder's house with her and Mark.

When a tall, older man with spectacles and a voluminous salt-and-pepper beard sauntered in, Beatrice introduced us by first names, as was common. "Eva, come meet Bishop Harvey."

He shook my hand, his grasp firm. "I heard you're working here, Eva." His stare probed into me. "How's the new job going?"

"Couldn't be better, thanks to Beatrice and Sadie."

"That's *gut*. I think you'll find Glenn Yoder an excellent man to work for. Of course, we're disappointed he didn't join the church." He glanced down at my feet but didn't seem disturbed by my shoes. I was glad I'd chosen the black ones instead of the neon green.

"Eva, I hear you've not been baptized yet." He was old enough to be my grandfather, and his crusty voice was deeper, more forceful than mine.

"Not yet, but I intend to." I had just lied to a bishop. In fact, I wasn't sure I would ever become baptized. Would God punish me if I didn't follow through?

"Excellent," he said. "Classes for new members in this district are starting soon."

When Beatrice moved out of earshot to help a customer, I asked him, "Is it all right for me to eat supper in the main house?"

"*Yah.* I'm not concerned that Beatrice will lead you astray. She's Catholic, but you're safe with her as long as you don't start attending her church."

"*Nee,* I never would." I lowered my volume. "About supper tonight. What if she has also invited a single man to join us?" I hoped he'd nix the whole idea.

"Is he Amish?"

I nodded.

"I foresee no problem as long as Beatrice is there. She's not such a bad matchmaker. She's introduced several Amish couples who later married."

"Harvey, do you know I'm almost thirty?"

"Are you afraid you're too old to start a family?"

My tongue felt as if it held a mouthful of peanut butter. I shrugged.

"I don't think *mei frau* would have minded me telling ya that she didn't give birth to our first child until age thirty-one. We prayed and waited like Abraham and Sarah until the Lord blessed us with children. Five of them." His voice was kind and reassuring, but I couldn't bring myself to look into his eyes.

He stroked his capacious beard. "'Wait on the Lord; be of good courage.'"

I was saved from having to reply when a bevy of *Englisch* women bustled into the café and zeroed in on the glass case.

"I best be getting back to work." I checked my *kapp*. *Ach*, I'd tossed its strings over my back in a casual manner. "Beatrice and Sadie need me at the cash register."

"*Yah*, of course. Anytime you wish to speak further on this or any subject in private, please let me know."

"*Denki.*" I spun on my heel and hurried away.

# Eleven

Dread encompassed me as I primped for supper. I asked myself why I'd changed into my favorite sky-blue dress that matched my eyes, and why I'd spent an inordinate amount of time arranging my hair and positioning my *kapp*.

As I assessed myself in the mirror, I recalled Sadie's forlorn expression when she left the café. She was a far better match for Mark than I was, but, apparently, he didn't think so or he would have driven her home from a singing by now.

I stepped out onto my porch and was flabbergasted to see Mark standing at the bottom of the steps.

"Sorry. I didn't mean to startle you." He tipped his straw hat.

"Um—I didn't hear your buggy pull up or the dogs barking." I tried to regain my composure while flattening my apron.

"Look, Eva, if you'd rather I didn't stay for supper, I don't need to." He ran his thumbs up and down his suspenders.

"And disappoint Beatrice?"

"Well, now, it's you I came to see. You must know that."

I paused, trying to find the right words. "Perhaps we should speak before we go inside." I glanced toward the back door of the house and was happy not to see Beatrice spying through the paned window. "Mark, you will no doubt hear rumors about me."

"I already have, and I couldn't care less. You know how wagging tongues pollute the air. We are admonished not to gossip, but that doesn't stop some people from poking their noses where they don't belong. We're all sinners, *yah*?"

"Most of the gossip isn't true, but not everything said about me is a lie. For instance, I'm almost thirty years old."

He appeared unruffled. "You look much younger, and you're beautiful." He gazed into my face until I looked away. "I'm twenty-four," he said. "A mature adult."

*Ach*, I didn't wish to say something callous and hurt his feelings. "Well, you're far younger than I am." I couldn't believe we were having this conversation. "How about Sadie? I think she's sweet on you."

"She's not my type. Too skittish, like a colt." He stepped forward until I had to look into his eyes. "Please forgive me if I'm coming on too strong. Maybe you don't find me attractive, but I'm determined to win your affections."

The lowering sun cast a salmon glow across his face. He had a fine-looking face, I had to admit. But I couldn't help comparing him to Jake, who would always hold a place in my heart. I wondered if Mark knew Jake. Growing up in the area, the two of them might have crossed paths.

I descended the steps, and we strolled toward the house's back porch. The door swung open with a flourish as if Beatrice had been waiting just inside. A cloud of scrumptious warm air floated out, making my mouth water.

"Don't be shy." Beatrice's mouth curved up into an impish grin. "Come inside, you two."

The black cat flew into the kitchen as Beatrice shook her finger and scolded the dogs in a flurry of Italian.

Mark and I ascended the steps. "After you." He waited for me to enter the house first. He was a gentleman too. Why was I being so standoffish?

"Wait until you taste my spaghetti and meatballs," Beatrice called out from inside. "Mama's recipe from the old country is *deliziosa*." Which I assumed meant "delicious" in Italian. "You won't find this at the Olive Garden."

I scuffed my shoes on the welcome mat before stepping inside. The kitchen was stylishly updated with frosted-glass-faced cupboards, granite counters, and brushed aluminum appliances. Above the stove hung an impressive assortment of pans. A panini maker also resided on the counter.

"This house is mighty fancy," Mark said. He scanned the counter with its Cuisinart and electric toaster.

I inhaled the savory aroma of simmering tomato sauce, garlic, basil, and ground beef. The round table was set for three. Flowered cloth napkins and decorative plates—from Orvieto in Tuscany, Beatrice said—looked festive. A block of Parmesan cheese sat on a wooden cutting board next to a grater. A chunky loaf of Italian bread waited on a wooden board alongside a serrated knife. Water in a large metal pot simmered, sending a steamy cloud to the ceiling.

"We'll eat right here in the kitchen if you don't mind." Beatrice took Mark's straw hat and hung it on a hook next to several baseball caps that must have belonged to Glenn. "Make yourself comfortable while I put in the pasta." She glided to the stove and slid straight noodles into the pot of bubbling water.

I scanned the room. A pie on the counter emitted a fruity aroma with browned-to-perfection dough.

"Glenn and his wife received fancy china and silverware as wedding presents, but we'll use their everyday plates and flatware." I had imagined a stilted conversation, but Beatrice acted lively, chattering about how much she'd enjoyed working in the café even though she missed Glenn and Rose's wee *ragazza*, whom she described as *bellissima,* I assumed to mean "beautiful."

"The little girl's name is Emmy. She was born a month early, and the doctor insisted she stay in the hospital for a week. Poor Glenn and Rose were frantic. That's when they hired me to live on the third floor to keep an eye on her. She's like a grandchild to me now."

I was glad Beatrice was in such a loquacious mood. It saved me from having to fabricate a subject when all I wanted to do was eat and then retreat to my cabin.

Beatrice was a gracious hostess and would not let me help serve or clear the table. After we all consumed her marvelous spaghetti, she sliced into the pie. Its crust was so flaky I was tempted to take a second piece when she offered it, but I'd promised myself not to gain weight while working in the café.

She dabbed at the corners of her mouth with her napkin. "Eva, now that you're living in a new district, you simply must attend a singing."

"What?" I felt like an opossum stuck in the middle of a road. "I haven't been to one of those for years."

"All the more reason to go. Don't you want to lift up your voice in song and praise the Lord?" She turned to Mark. "You could drive her home, couldn't you?"

He seemed to grow taller in his chair. "*Yah*, absolutely. And give her a ride there too, unless she has other plans."

I tried to think up excuses. "People might think we're dating."

"Would that be so terrible, Eva?" Beatrice said.

"I might go to my parents' this Sunday. This will be their district's nonpreaching week. They'll be entertaining or visiting neighbors."

"Please reconsider, Eva." Mark's eyes pleaded. "If you like, I can tell everyone I'm just giving you a ride out of convenience because you're living here."

Did he not understand the word *no*?

Beatrice pushed her chair away from the table. "Then it's all settled. Mark will drive you, Eva."

"Nothing's settled yet, thank you." I stood to clear the dessert dishes. To change the subject, I asked, "Are the Yoders coming home this Saturday?"

"No, a week from Saturday."

"I'm happy for them," Mark said. "Glenn finally met his soul mate, even if she isn't Amish."

"You should be married by now too, young man." Beatrice sank back into her chair.

Mark's cheeks blushed. "Sometimes *Gott* puts people together..."

It seemed to me Beatrice was doing all the putting, but maybe she had a good idea after all. It was about time I got realistic.

When Mark and I bid Beatrice good night, Mark switched on his small flashlight and escorted me past the herb garden to my cabin.

"See you tomorrow." I certainly wasn't going to invite him inside for a multitude of reasons, so I dallied at the bottom of my steps.

The evening sky had turned from aquamarine to sapphire blue. I adored Lancaster County's sky at dusk. The air was laced with a myriad of farmland scents. Amid a fusion of distant sounds—horses clopping and wagon wheels churning on the road, an owl hooting in the forested area out back—an automobile's engine groaned, but it didn't turn into the nursery's parking lot. Not that I was expecting to see Stephen again tonight. *Ach*, what made me think of him?

I climbed my stairs and turned the doorknob to make sure I hadn't locked myself out. I pivoted to Mark. "Good night."

"Good night, Eva." He must have known I wouldn't open my door until he was gone. "I enjoyed getting to know you better." He made no move to approach me. "If you'd rather not go to the singing with me, I won't hold it against ya."

"I hope you understand my reluctance. I do love to sing—"

"But you're holding out for a better offer? Like for Jake to show up and sweep you off your feet?"

"So you know the whole story?"

"*Yah*, I have relatives in your parents' district. I know Jake's back, living with his parents again. And his *dat* came out of the coma and came home from the hospital this morning. His doctors preferred he remain in the trauma unit longer, but without insurance, even one day in the hospital was too expensive. Plus, Jake's *mamm* said she could look after him."

"Then he must be doing better than a lot of coma patients do when thcy first wake up."

Mark massaged the back of his neck. "Well, Amos can't speak or walk, but he's able to drink from a straw and eat if someone holds a spoonful of strained food for him. Poor man."

"I've heard it takes weeks or even months to recover once the person wakes up. Each experience is unique, like a snowflake, and some need to relearn everything." I recalled Olivia's description, which had coincided with a magazine article I'd once read.

"Are you hoping to see Jake?"

"What?" I sputtered. I hadn't expected his abrupt, personal question. "*Nee.* And I heard he might have gotten married."

"Not that I know of. But I haven't seen Jake for years, and my relatives don't talk about him much anymore." He removed his hat and raked his fingers through his thick hair. "I do know one thing. If you fell in love with me, I'd never leave you."

"Hold on, there. You don't even know me."

"I know enough, Eva. May I call you Evie, the way your friends do?"

"*Yah*, if you like."

"Bishop Harvey told me friendship can lead to love."

"I suppose." *Mamm* had said the same thing, although she added that she and *Dat* became enamored at first sight and could hardly wait for their wedding day.

Mark surveyed the star-studded heavens. "It's a beautiful evening. Perhaps you'd like a buggy ride right now."

His persistence was beginning to vex me. "*Nee, denki.* After working all day and eating a huge meal, I'm ready for bed."

"I figured you'd say that, but I thought I'd give it a try."

Moments later, I entered the cabin and realized my feet didn't hurt. A small victory. And not one person had commented on my footwear other than Beatrice and Mark.

As I envisioned myself flopping into bed, I recalled I'd forgotten to ask Beatrice to borrow reading material. I glanced out the window and saw the main house was still illuminated.

I dove into a sweater and dashed over there. When I knocked, the dogs barked ferociously, but fear didn't invade me as it had before.

"Coming," I heard Beatrice calling above the commotion. She gave me a double look through the glass-paned door and then pulled the door open. "Back for more pie already?"

I patted my tummy. "No. I'm so stuffed I couldn't eat another morsel. But I do have a request if you still think it's okay. You seemed to when I asked before. May I borrow a book?"

"Depends on what kind you want."

"Something to help me fall asleep. Or a magazine like the *Connection*."

"You should have borrowed one from the café."

"I didn't know if that would be okay. I could run over there and get one right now."

"No, Glenn and Rose have plenty of reading material. Come in."

With the three dogs dancing at my feet, I stepped across the threshold. "Outside, all of you." Beatrice swooshed the dogs out. "Come back when you can behave." She turned to me and asked, "So did you really enjoy your meal?"

"Yes, absolutely. It was delicious. Couldn't have been better."

"I'm glad you enjoyed the food. And what about Mark? Isn't he a fine man?"

"Yes, he seems to be."

"And handsome, don't you agree?"

I lowered my eyes and fixed them on the pepper grinder. "I can't deny he's good looking." But I knew from experience that appearance wasn't everything.

"Why are you hesitating, Eva? At your age you should be thrilled to have the attention of an eligible bachelor. Many Amish women in this county would do anything to catch his eye."

I needed to stop this roller-coaster conversation about my personal life with an *Englisch* woman I hardly knew. I peeked toward the living room, where I'd noticed bookshelves earlier. I asked again. "May I borrow a book?"

"Go in and have a look."

She led me to the grand living room with a shoulder-high hearth, a leather couch, and a corduroy-covered recliner pulled close to the fireplace. I imagined Rose cradling their baby and cozying up to the fire's warmth on wintry evenings and felt a yearning in my heart for a baby of my own.

Over the mantel hung a large painting of a fisherman wading in a mountain stream, and next to the fireplace stretched a floor-to-ceiling bookcase chock-full of books.

I ran my fingertips across the books' spines. "They certainly own a lot of books about fly fishing, carpentry, and how to raise children."

Beatrice sidled up next to me. "Many people don't have large families the way we Catholics and Amish do. Some grow up knowing little about rearing children."

I caught sight of the name Jane Austen on a book spine. I'd read it before, but I wouldn't mind reading it again if I found nothing else. I pulled the book out to inspect the cover of *Pride and Prejudice*.

"That's Rose's section. I'm sure she wouldn't mind if you read any of them as long as you returned the book in one piece."

I slipped it back in next to *The Scarlet Letter* by Nathaniel Hawthorne. When I saw the title, my lungs refused to inhale. I felt light headed.

Beatrice said, "That's the story of a wretched young woman who must wear an embroidered *A* on her chest because she was found guilty of adultery."

I swallowed. "Yes. I read it years ago. I checked it out of the library without asking the librarian what it was about." The novel had been on the public high school's summer reading list tacked to the bulletin board.

"Then no need to read it again. I'm sure if there were a lesson to be learned, you've gleaned it." *Ach*, she categorized me an adulteress?

My fingers found *Wuthering Heights* and *Jane Eyre*.

"Rose named their dog Heath after Heathcliff, one of the characters in *Wuthering Heights*. Those two books might be a bit dark for a young lady living by herself, although Rose loves them." I was surprised Beatrice had read so much, but I wouldn't voice my opinion, which she might find judgmental. Because it was.

"How about *Rebecca*?" I pulled out another hardback.

"Rose told me that's her favorite book, so I'd better not lend it out. But I'm sure all the rest would be fine."

Beatrice brought out *A Room with a View*, a novel I'd never heard of. "There's only one mildly violent scene in this delightful story by E. M. Forster. Parts of it take place in Florence, Italy, one of the most charming cities in the world." She handed me the book.

I turned it over, hoping to scan a blurb on the back cover, but it was hardbound. "What's the book about?" I asked.

"In short, it's a romance set in Italy and England. And much more." Her hand patted her heart. "I wish you could visit Tuscany. Every few years *mio marito*—my husband—and I would travel there for a week. But not anymore, now that he has passed on." She blinked. "You'd better scoot off to bed, and don't read too late."

"Okay, thanks." I covered my yawning mouth. "I can't wait to climb into bed, put my feet up, and read."

# Twelve

A rooster crowed, rousing me from slumber. For a moment I thought I was back in my childhood home, but I would have recognized our rooster's unique crowing, the way it dipped at the end.

I'd slept fitfully after reading *A Room with a View* for an hour. I'd extinguished the lantern, lain in the darkness, and contemplated visiting Florence, where everyone spoke Italian and no one knew about me or my past. Of course, I never could. Not by jet, anyway. Flying was forbidden by the *Ordnung*. On an ocean liner, then? No. What was I thinking?

I'd finally turned the lantern back on, opened my Bible, and searched for words of comfort in the book of Psalms until my eyes grew dry. After turning out the light, I repeated Psalm 4:8. "I will both lay me down in peace, and sleep: for thou, Lord, only makest me dwell in safety."

But I had not felt safe because I'd tossed for hours. Proof positive was my sheets and quilt askew and half off the bed in the morning.

A never-ending volley of worries had tangled through my mind as it attempted to come to grips with the fact I was living alone and managing a café. I was in over my head, like walking at the bottom of a pond. My future blurred. I'd pictured Jake's father lying helpless after his comatose state, imagined the possibility of seeing Jake and being rejected again, and considered Mark's invitation to the upcoming singing. Somewhere around two o'clock a dog barked. Or was it a coyote yapping or a bad dream? I still didn't feel completely at ease with the dogs.

I must have eventually fallen asleep because sunlight filtered into the room and the clock by the bed pronounced it was already six thirty. I sat up with the feeling of dismay. Why hadn't I prepared for today's soup ahead of time? I should have humbled myself and asked for Beatrice's input. But last night I couldn't wait to flee the house, book in hand. She would no doubt mention my reading an *Englisch* romance to everyone she ran into and continue her mission to couple me with Mark. I had to ask myself why I was resisting his invitations. In a few hours I'd see him again in the café, along with Stephen and Sadie.

If I didn't know better, I would've thought someone was pounding a nail into my forehead. *Ach*, a headache, probably caused by lack of sleep or a sinus infection. I knew from experience that the best way to rid myself of the pain was to elevate my head. I forced myself to a sitting position. If *Mamm* were here, she'd offer me essential oils in steamy water to breathe. I sighed as I told myself those days were over. I was on my own. All the more reason to find myself a husband. More than ever, I didn't want to die an old maid, even if it meant marrying a man I didn't love.

The image of sunlight glinting off Jake's blond hair dominated my musings. Somehow, I must find a way to see him.

The ticking clock prodded me to hurry. I splashed water on my face and then chose a chestnut-brown dress. I pinned on my black apron with care. I parted my hair and yanked it back, increasing the throbbing in my forehead. I planted the *kapp* I wore yesterday atop my head.

I glanced down at my new shoes and grinned at the evidence I was venturing out of my rut. I didn't need to cross an ocean to do that.

As I exited the cabin, Missy frolicked over and jumped on me, leaving muddy paw prints on my apron and one shoe. "*Nee*, Missy." No time to change my clothes now.

As I shambled past the big house, Beatrice poked her head out the back door. "Don't leave yet."

Expecting a lecture, I froze.

"Wait up, Eva. I made stock for the café out of the leftover chicken and bones from my supper the day before yesterday. I hope you don't mind."

I did mind not being consulted first, but I was also grateful.

"You're an angel." I heard a ring in my voice. "I'm making vegetable soup this morning, and your stock will improve it greatly."

She looked me up and down. "I like that color dress on you, Eva. I wonder why some young women wear unsightly colors. But Bishop Harvey doesn't seem to care. Never mind. God didn't make me a man, so I'll never be a priest, minister, or bishop."

I had no answer for her and only wanted to be on my way to work. "How will I get the soup stock to the café?"

She laughed, her plump belly jiggling. "Are you strong enough to carry it without spilling?" She beckoned me into the kitchen and tipped her head to a lidded pot. "If need be, you can use one of the low wagons customers use for collecting plants. Or maybe Mark's already come in. He's so smitten with you that he might have arrived early."

My head throbbed again. "I'll see if I can manage." I moved to the stove and tried to lift the pot. Its contents sloshed from side to side, warning me. "Well, maybe not. The wagon sounds like a *gut* idea."

"Another good idea would be to ask Mark to pull the wagon."

"No, I'll try by myself."

Beatrice shook her head. "Did you ever consider how much easier your life would be if you'd take other people's advice more often?"

My headache amplifying her voice, snarly words danced on the tip of my tongue. But I swallowed them down. "You may be right. I'd best be concentrating on the soup. Can you tell me where a wagon is?"

"There's one at the side of the house."

"Thanks." I grabbed hold of the pot's handles and shuffled out the door before she could give me any more advice. I found myself at the bottom of the steps surrounded by Missy and Minnie, both dogs sniffing at the pot.

"Go away." The dogs paid me no attention. They followed me around to the side of the house, where I located the wagon, and then all the way to the café.

When I reached the door, reality struck like an alarm clock chiming. I'd forgotten the key. It was sitting in the cabin on the counter next to the sink. But I couldn't leave the soup stock unattended. Missy was large enough to tip the vat over.

"Locked out?" Stephen was headed in my direction.

"*Yah.*" I couldn't bring myself to look at his face. "In my rush, I forgot my keys. I'm so sorry." And embarrassed.

"No problem. Perfection is not required."

"That's good news." I'd seldom felt more imperfect.

Stephen shooed the two dogs away. "I wonder where Heath is."

"I haven't seen him this morning, but I thought I heard barking in the night. I could've been dreaming."

He glanced down at the soup stock. "Has Beatrice been helping you out?"

"*Yah*, and I'm most appreciative."

"Let me carry that." But before he lifted the pot, Stephen tried the handle and the door swung open without protest. "Huh? Did you lock up last night?"

"*Yah.*" I pictured myself inserting the key and then testing the door to make sure it was closed properly. "I'm certain I locked both doors and then took the key with me."

"No broken windows. We keep a spare key in the retail shop, but I can't imagine any of our employees using it. And Olivia used to have one. I hope she didn't make a spare."

Stephen lifted the pot, carried it through the dining area, and brought it into the kitchen, where he placed it on a counter. Then he canvassed the dining area. "Everything looks okay."

I pushed a chair back into position. "I recall giving this room a thorough looking over. Including this chair. It was snug against the table."

The corners of Stephen's mouth angled down. "Do you think someone was in here?"

I strode to the cash register and detected a subtle residual scent of cigarette smoke. "*Yah.* I'm glad I took the money out and gave it to Bess."

"And you're sure you locked the doors?" Stephen asked.

"Positive. More than anything, I hope you don't think I'm lying."

"No, not for a moment." He touched my elbow. "I thought these shenanigans were behind us. In the past we've had minor vandalism we attributed to Olivia's boyfriend—if they're even still dating. I hope not. His name's Butch, and he's a bad seed, but we have no proof."

"But they're in *rumspringa*, aren't they?"

"Even so, her deacon and a minister paid a call to her parents and complained about him. That's one reason her parents told her she couldn't work here anymore." He surveyed the café's interior. "I hope there's no damage, whoever the culprit was. In the past, we've had planted pots tipped over, but no one has ever broken into the café. Not that it was technically broken into because the person must have had a key."

Back in the kitchen, he lifted the pot and put it on a burner. "I'd better let you take it from here. I'm a terrible cook."

With his broad shoulders and muscled arms, Stephen seemed capable of doing anything. But I let his comment go. I didn't want him to think I was a flirt. I figured Beatrice would fill him in on our supper last night and make it seem as though I was leading Mark on.

"Still like your new shoes?" He gave them a looking over.

"Very much. I'm sorry I forgot to thank you for the ride."

"And I'm sorry your photo ended up in the newspaper." Stephen stepped back into the dining area. "Between tourists and newspaper photographers, it's hard for Amish to keep out of camera lenses."

"I've grown up with it and should know better than to stand next to a policeman at the side of the road. But your friend Wayne was very nice. Nevertheless, I hope to never ride in a squad car again."

"I can empathize. I've had a few minor scrapes with the law, but that's all behind me now."

"You were in jail?"

"No, but if I hadn't gone to AA and gotten sober, I could be right now. I got one too many DWIs and was spiraling to the bottom of a pit. Alcohol can sneak up on you that way." He paused as if replaying his past in his mind. "I got turned around, and I've never had another drop since."

"I'm glad."

"Thanks. I feel free and will never go back. But just in case, I avoid situations that could tempt me. I never want to get hooked again by convincing myself I have enough strength to battle alcoholism by myself."

"You seem the least likely of men to be helpless."

"Without God, I'm as helpless as anyone else. Too many people fool themselves into thinking they're in control."

After Stephen left the café, I warmed the soup stock and started making coffee. While it brewed, I got busy washing and then dicing vegetables. It was too early to immerse them in the warm broth, so I tossed them into an iron skillet and sautéed them in olive oil and garlic.

Knuckles rapped on the back door, making my arm jerk. Since when was I so jumpy? I rushed over to open the door. There was Sadie's forlorn face.

"*Gut* morning, Sadie."

"Am I late?" She pulled off her black sweater and hung it on a hook. She seemed as limp as her garment.

I glanced up at the clock. "*Nee.* You're right on time." I had nothing to apologize for, but I felt responsible for her misery. "Sadie, I feel terrible that Beatrice invited me to supper with Mark."

"No surprise she didn't include me." Sadie shrugged one shoulder. "She's never liked me."

"I'm not sure she likes me either, but she has something up her sleeve." I diced carrots as I spoke. "I want us to be honest with each other." I paused, hoping sage words would come to mind, but there was no way around the truth. "Mark asked me to the singing on Sunday. I'm sure it was Beatrice's idea. I think you and Mark are more suited to each other."

"But it's obvious he prefers you, Evie. I can't make him pursue me if his heart is with another woman." She glanced at my new shoes. "Love your Nikes. Where did they come from?"

"Stephen drove me to the outlet mall on Tuesday."

"I wonder if he has a crush on you too."

"*Nee*, he had to run another errand and was kind enough to give me a ride after I told him how much my feet hurt."

"I wouldn't sell yourself short, Evie. It seems all the men around here are flocking to get your attention."

If only she knew.

More rapping on the back door brought our conversation to an end.

Sadie grabbed a terry cloth rag. "I'll make sure the tables are clean and fill the salt and pepper shakers."

I opened the door to find Olivia looking pale and as downcast as Sadie. I'd never seen her without a grin on her face.

"Ta-da!" Olivia's exuberance seemed forced, her mouth forming a tight smile. Tendrils of flaxen hair escaped her *kapp*, its strings hanging behind her back. "My *bruder* was running late, so I talked my parents into letting me use their open buggy and bring the baked goods in myself." She deposited a box on the counter and then embraced me as if she were clinging to a life raft.

"I need to talk to you if you have time," she whispered when we finally parted. "If I don't speak to someone, I'll burst." Chewing her lower lip, she rubbed her puffy eyes.

"Whatever do you mean?"

Olivia wiped away a tear. "Keep your voice down. Would ya come out and help me carry in my baked goods?"

"Sure."

She tipped her head toward the door and stepped outside. I trailed her. "I'll confide in you only if you promise never to tell anyone."

"*Yah*, I promise." I couldn't imagine where she was headed.

"I may be leaving...with a man..." She buried her solemn face in her hands.

"Are you sure he's the right man for you?"

Her nod was barely perceptible. "*Yah*, but I best not tell you his name so you won't have to lie for me should someone ask."

I had to agree. I didn't want to have to fib to cover up her transgressions. Maybe she would change her mind.

She hefted up another container filled with baked goods from the back of her open buggy. "I promised my parents I wasn't seeing him anymore, so we've been meeting in secret in the middle of the night."

"Do they suspect anything?"

She looked over my shoulder, I assumed to make sure we were alone. "Not yet. But eventually we'll..."

"Get married?"

"Maybe. He hasn't asked me yet. But he says he loves me, so I'm sure we will."

"Sometimes men lie." Jake told me he'd adore me forever.

She must have noticed my distress "I'm sorry, Evie. I wish things were different with Jake. My guy has been upfront with me from the start. He's never wanted to join the church. He's been considering moving away and living in the *Englisch* world since he was a child. If he takes off, he said he'd take me with him."

"But not get married first?"

"It's not as if we don't know each other."

I was afraid to ask how well. I thought of Jake and was thankful we'd never gone beyond kissing. Kisses I would never forget. Not that we hadn't been tempted, but prudence and caution had prevailed.

I would not condemn Olivia's actions, but I hoped to influence her. Still, if I were in her position, I might have left the only life I'd ever known to be with Jake. If he'd asked me. Which he hadn't.

"Wait here." I deposited a box inside and then returned. "Liv, please promise you won't run off without saying goodbye first."

"I can't promise anything." She looked away. "I thought you of all people would understand."

"I do understand." All too well.

# Thirteen

Our many hungry customers kept me from fretting about Olivia's pitiful dilemma. I felt compassion for her because I knew what it was like to be in such a quandary. I'd always thought she was the prettiest and most vivacious young woman in the county, and I still did. In the past, many had speculated that she and Glenn Yoder would marry, and she would manage the café seamlessly. Now she would become the subject of gossip if she ran away with her young man. *Ach,* I hoped not.

But maybe she didn't care.

I was delighted at how well my soup turned out, thanks to Beatrice's stock. I felt guilty taking credit for its rich flavor, but I reminded myself I'd combined the ingredients. As my thoughts flitted like moths around a lightbulb, I wondered how and why the café had been visited during the night. I hadn't worked here long enough to understand the possible reasons, and I would have to let Stephen unravel that mystery. But what if he thought I'd been negligent and hadn't bothered to lock up? Surely he'd mention it to Glenn Yoder. Was my job in jeopardy?

Sadie kept her distance from me. She and I seemed to swim like two fish in a tank—in close proximity but never speaking to each other for more than a moment at a time. My heart went out to her. I knew what it was like to be rejected by the man I loved.

I cringed when Mark sauntered in for his coffee. Fortunately, we were neck-deep in customers. I asked Sadie to serve him. At first she ignored me, but a moment later she took him a mug.

Sipping his coffee, Mark tarried. He finally approached me and asked if I'd seen Heath.

"You haven't found him yet?"

"Not only that, but Glenn called Stephen. Glenn and Rose are extending their trip by another week. Rose's father is sicker than they'd thought. Glenn doesn't want to leave his *frau* and *dochder* behind to come home when he has Stephen here to manage things, plus many longtime employees like me." He spoke as if we were alone—as if Sadie were invisible. "Can you think of where Heath could be?"

"I heard barking in the night. Beatrice must have let him out."

"I'll go ask her. After you tell me you're coming to the singing with me." I should be thrilled to receive all this attention, even if walking into the singing would be awkward. But if I still loved Jake, I would be leading Mark on. *Duplicitous* is the word that came to mind, and I didn't want to be accused of one more false action. And I cared about Sadie's feelings too.

"Mark, I've decided to visit my parents on Sunday." As of this moment.

"I could drive you there." He seemed determined. "And then come get you for the singing."

My parents would be tickled if he did, but I said, "Please don't push me. People would think we're dating."

"Exactly what I wish to do."

Wanting to end the conversation, I glanced at the cash register and saw Beatrice attempting to use the machine. "Mark, I need to get back to work." I turned and retreated behind the counter.

"May I help the next person?" I smiled at an *Englisch* woman, who rattled off her order. I caught every item and rang it up. I congratulated myself on doing so well, but then I realized I was becoming prideful. I couldn't win.

After the lunch rush, I made a call to the phone in the shed between my family's home and our nearest neighbors. I left a message for *Mamm*, stating I wanted to fill her in on how well I was doing in person on Sunday. I assured myself my actions were those of a good daughter, but I mostly wanted to drive by Jake's farm, which was only half a mile from my parents'. I assumed many in our district were taking the Millers food or had stopped in to check on his father. I might see Jake one final time before I progressed into a relationship with another man.

Minutes later, Stephen sauntered into the café. "How are things going?" he asked me.

"Fine. I'm glad you came in because I have a question to ask. And a favor."

"Go ahead. Shoot."

"Sadie mentioned Glenn has a buggy and a mare."

"Yeah?"

"If Glenn is *Englisch*, why does he own a buggy?"

"He grew up Amish, and his parents gave him the buggy years ago. He says he keeps it for old time's sake, but I think he gets a kick out of taking it for a spin every so often. His wife, Rose, adores horses and riding in it."

I mustered up my courage. "Do you think I could borrow it on Sunday?"

Stephen glanced out the window. Thirty seconds passed. Maybe more. I sensed he was making a decision. "I could drive you in my pickup."

"Won't you be in church Sunday morning?"

"I could make an exception."

"I'd enjoy driving the buggy if it's all right."

"Well, now, I don't know. I'd better call and ask Glenn." He pulled his earlobe. "Say, can you even drive a buggy?"

"I've been driving one since the age of six, and I really miss it. I'll be fine unless Glenn's horse is a feisty stallion, like one my *dat* once owned."

"Just the opposite. Autumn is as sweet a mare as I've ever met. And she could sure use the exercise. Still, I'd better ask permission."

"Of course." I couldn't believe my good fortune. "I'll be very careful with her and avoid the highway."

"How about I meet you at the barn after work and introduce you two?"

"That would be wonderful. Thank you." I glanced over to see Beatrice was hovering near us, eavesdropping on our conversation.

"Has Heath shown up?" she asked. "He didn't eat his breakfast with the other two dogs."

Stephen tugged his ear. "Not yet. I called animal control and the local veterinarian, but no one's brought him in. I've asked several of my employees to put up lost dog signs. So far, no luck." He paused and then turned to me. "I'm going to search for him after you and I see Autumn. If you'd like to join me, I could use another set of eyes."

Again, I found Beatrice in close proximity. She must have heard his invitation.

# Fourteen

Stephen strode into the café near three. "Hey, good news, Eva. You may borrow the buggy. But Glenn would feel more comfortable if you demonstrated your abilities to me first."

"Okay, I'll take you for a ride. We can both look for Heath for an hour or so."

Beatrice closed in on us like a vulture. "I was planning to invite Eva over to dinner again. Ham and scalloped potatoes. Too much food for me to eat all by myself."

"Does that invitation include me?" Stephen's voice sounded jovial, as if restraining laughter.

"I was thinking just the two of us," she said.

"I understand." He gave me a wink. "Eva, do you still have time to hitch up the buggy? We could do it another day if you'd prefer."

"*Ach*, I want to meet Autumn today." I pivoted toward Beatrice. "Thank you for your kind invitation. How about tomorrow night?"

Beatrice's features hardened. "I'll have to wait and see."

Stephen and I walked around a greenhouse and into the small barn next to a chicken coop. He opened the barn's wide door to expose a gray buggy and an automobile, much to my surprise. Not that I assumed the Yoders didn't drive vehicles. Both of them must.

Stephen called Autumn, who trotted right over to him. I pulled a carrot I'd pilfered from the kitchen out of a pocket in my apron and gave it to the mare. She nibbled it and then swallowed the rest.

"Oh, you are a pretty girl. And you seem friendly too. *Gut.*"

Stephen pulled Glenn's gray buggy out of the small barn, and I hitched up the docile mare. So far, so good.

"She's gorgeous." Getting to know her, I stroked the roan mare's neck. "She needs grooming."

"After our ride. We'd better head out while there's daylight." Stephen beckoned me to get in and handed me the reins. As I climbed aboard, he jogged around to the passenger side. I realized he was testing my competence. If I couldn't climb in the buggy by myself, how would I manage?

At an easy pace, I navigated the buggy through farmland, passing homes, farms, and silos. Both Stephen and I called Heath's name and stopped several times to ask farmers and children if they'd seen the dog. After an hour, Stephen suggested we turn around.

A few blocks from the nursery I heard barking. "Wait. I hear a dog."

Stephen pointed. "There he is, tied to that porch. What the—"

"*Wunderbaar!*" I noticed a change in me. I'd never expected to be elated to see a dog, especially such a large and energetic one covered with mud.

"Pull into the driveway, Eva." The moment we stopped, Stephen vaulted out of the buggy and ran over to Heath, who seemed ecstatic, his tail wagging.

A middle-aged *Englisch* man dressed in jeans and mud-spattered work boots rounded the house, carrying a shotgun. "Hey, what you doing with that dog?"

Without hesitation, Stephen lumbered toward the man and said, "I could ask you the same question."

"That mutt killed one of my lambs." The man raised the rifle's barrel a few inches. "I should have shot it."

"I don't believe you." Stephen moved closer to the man. "Heath wouldn't hurt a flea."

"Tell that to my dead lamb." The man lifted the gun a few more inches. "Get off my property, and don't come back unless you have the cash to pay for my dead animal." The man lunged forward and poked Stephen's chest with the shotgun's muzzle. "Now, leave. You're trespassing."

Stephen held his ground. "I will as soon as you give me Heath." At the sound of his name, the dog started barking and yanking on the rope.

The *Englischer*'s face turned beet red. "He's my dog. His name is... Duke."

"Since when?" Stephen asked, a hand on one hip.

"Since I bought him as a pup." The *Englischer* poked Stephen again, but this time Stephen grabbed hold of the gun's muzzle, twisted it out of the man's hand, and flung it several yards away. The two men wrestled. Stephen maneuvered the man into a choke hold and held him like a vise. I'd never seen grown men fight. The Amish are nonresistant, a click beyond pacifists, who might march in a demonstration. Weren't Mennonites nonresistant too?

Half of me was terrified. The other half was fascinated.

Heath bared his teeth, his hackles raised. While the man struggled to get free, I ran over and untied the dog. Tail waving, Heath charged over to Stephen.

"Hey, stop that." The man grabbed for Heath. The dog sprang up and nipped him on the arm. "Ow!" The man's face contorted. "You've turned my own dog against me. I ought to call the police."

"You sure you want to do that? You would be charged with theft. This dog belongs to Glenn Yoder."

"Then what was he doing on my property in the middle of the night? He killed one of my lambs. Do you understand? My flock is my livelihood."

My heart was beating triple time. *Ach*, everything was happening so quickly that I'd forgotten to tether Autumn, who was grazing on weeds and grasses at the side of the road. I hurried over to her and grabbed the reins. Heath bounded after me and licked my hand. Then he jumped into the buggy.

The *Englisch* man shook his fist as Stephen backstepped toward the buggy.

"That dog bit me and killed one of my lambs. I'm calling animal control and the police."

The man trailed Stephen, who seemed unfazed.

Stephen came to a halt. "Where's your proof he killed the lamb? In fact, where is this dead animal?"

"You insinuating I'm lying?" He balled his fist.

Stephen seemed to grow in stature. He glanced my way. "You still driving, Eva? Better get in the buggy."

"*Yah*, but I wish we had your pickup to rely on." My face must have been white, drained of blood.

"You want me to drive?"

"*Nee*, I can manage." My hands shook as I hoisted myself into the buggy.

"Let's get out of here before that guy really goes ballistic." Stephen climbed in next to Heath. "One thing for sure, Eva. I can safely tell Glenn you know how to drive a buggy."

"But I forgot to tether Autumn."

"When you meet Glenn, you are welcome to relate that tidbit, but as far as I'm concerned, you did the best you could under the circumstances. He will be delighted to get his dog back."

As I steered Autumn toward the nursery, Stephen wrapped his left arm over the dog's back. "I wonder what brought him down here to begin with."

The same thought was weaving through my mind. "Do you think that man snuck into the café last night?"

"I can't imagine why he would. Unless he bears a grudge against Glenn for some reason."

"If he did, where did he get a key?" I looked out the back window to make sure he wasn't following us in a car or truck.

"That's a missing piece of the puzzle. In any case, I don't want to tangle with him again."

"He could have hurt you. I'm thankful you and Heath are okay."

I wanted to ask Stephen where he'd learned to fight so well, but he answered before I could speak.

"I grew up in foster care and on the streets in Philly until age thirteen. Then a Mennonite couple adopted me and brought me to New Holland."

"How about your parents?"

"My mother told me she didn't know who my father was. A one-night stand, and she never got his name or saw him again."

"Where does she live?"

"In the state penitentiary. I tried visiting her a few times, but it was no good. She wants nothing to do with me. I consider my adoptive parents my real parents." He swiped his mouth. "I bet they would not have approved of that tussle I just had."

"*Yah*, I suspect not if they're Mennonite. But he could have killed you."

He stroked Heath. "I never thought I'd have to defend myself again."

I noticed a buggy approaching, pulled by a black horse resembling Jake's father's standardbred. The driver, his chin cleanly shaven, wore a baseball hat and sat next to a young *Englisch* woman. As we neared, I pulled the reins to slow Autumn and take a good look at the driver. Was it Jake, or was my imagination tricking me?

As we passed each other, his gaze locked onto mine. Then, in an instant, he was gone.

# Fifteen

When Stephen and I returned to the nursery, Beatrice, Mark, and several other employees stood waiting for us. They gushed over Heath while Stephen and I were pummeled with questions. Stephen deflected their concerns and complimented me on my skill as a buggy driver.

"What's this?" Beatrice pointed out a drop of blood on the ground and a two-inch tear in Heath's back leg. "Looks as though Heath got caught in barbed wire."

"He may need stitches. I'd better run him to the veterinarian's office." Stephen clicked on Heath's leash. "I didn't notice under all that mud."

"You should call first to make sure they're still open," Beatrice said.

While Mark washed off Heath's leg, Stephen called the local vet, who told him to take the dog to the emergency veterinarian's office in Gordonville.

I unhitched Autumn and gave her the other carrot I'd stashed in my pocket. "Here you go, girl." She chomped into it.

I had thoroughly enjoyed driving her, and my confidence in my driving abilities had been confirmed. Still, visions of Stephen and that *Englisch* man fighting, Heath biting the man's arm, and then spotting Jake driving his *dat*'s buggy barraged my mind. More than ever I was determined to visit the Millers on Sunday to see him and to find out how his father was recovering. I figured my *mamm* had already dropped by to leave food and offer assurance.

Beatrice strutted over to me. "Looks as though you've had quite a time of it."

"Our ride was more than I'd expected." Because Stephen hadn't said anything, I wouldn't mention Stephen's scuffle with the *Englischer* or the man's accusations against Heath.

"I wonder why Heath ran away," Beatrice said. "He never has before."

"Maybe to chase the vandal?" Mark said. He unhitched the buggy.

Stephen said, "Or something as simple as following the scent of a female dog in heat."

Mark chortled and then swiped the smirk off his mouth.

I was grateful Stephen didn't invite me to go with him. I'd never hear the end of it from Beatrice.

I stepped into the barn to look after Autumn. I offered her fresh water and fed her a scoop of grain to compensate for all her exercise. She munched into it, and I searched for and found a currycomb. As I brushed her dusty coat, I felt the presence of another person in the barn. I whipped around, almost expecting to see Jake, of all absurd notions. But it was Mark who had followed me.

"Let me help you with that." He located another currycomb and started working on Amber's other side, his long arms far more proficient than mine.

I'd been enjoying the solitude, but I had to remain gracious. "*Denki*, Mark."

"Anytime." He looked at me over Autumn's withers. "I don't mean to be pushy, but is there something you don't like about me?"

"Not a thing."

"Other than my age? What difference would five years make? In fact, a younger husband can take care of you longer."

"Are you talking about marriage when we haven't even been out on a date? I'm not ready. Please don't rush me." I wondered if he found me attractive because I was evasive. Maybe the same reason I'd wanted to seek Jake's attention after he left.

A tangle of recollections snaked through my mind. Jake holding me in his arms as though he'd never let go. Our embraces in his buggy. But then my shock and bewilderment when I returned from Ohio to learn he'd gone away. I'd been tempted to hitch a ride or take the bus to New York to locate him. I'd held little dignity where Jake was concerned.

Fortunately, my parents suspected I was thinking about chasing him and stopped me. What kind of a man would marry a woman who'd grovel after him? Men were supposed to select their spouses, not the other way around.

Yet Jake told me he adored me, and I'd believed him.

My thoughts wandered to how the rumor I'd given birth to a child in Ohio had practically decimated me. According to the grapevine, my aunt and uncle had taken the child in and were raising it as their own. No way would I have abandoned my baby if I'd had one. In hindsight, maybe I shouldn't have thwarted Jake's more amorous advances. If I'd gotten pregnant, he might have married me. If not, I'd still have a child. Someone to love me more than anyone else in the world. Yet to deliberately raise a *boppli* without a father would be selfish.

Beatrice poked her head into the small barn. "How ya doing?" She seemed to feign a look of surprise. "Oh, I didn't notice you, Mark." Did she wish to be our chaperone?

"Stephen seemed to think you're a fine horsewoman, Eva," Beatrice said.

"I'm not as good as most." I continued my chore and tried not to get flustered.

I felt Beatrice's eyes assessing me. "My supper invitation still stands, Eva. You took off with Stephen too quickly to eat a meal at the end of your shift."

I was hungry, my stomach growling, but I was also exhausted.

"I have food in my cabin. But again, I thank you for your offer of hospitality."

"As you like." She humphed and left the barn.

The setting sun's peach-colored rays illuminated the dust motes in the air. I noticed again what a handsome man Mark was. I understood Sadie's attraction, but I felt more like his older sister. I wondered how he would have acted in Stephen's situation with the *Englisch* sheep farmer. Would Mark have turned the other cheek as a righteous Amish man should? Would he have retrieved Heath through gentle conversation?

# Sixteen

That night I awoke to a scuttling sound. A mouse in the roof space above the ceiling? As I drifted back to sleep, a tapping noise aroused me through the sheaves of slumber.

I imagined the intruder had returned to break in, but then I decided a perpetrator would try the door first. Maybe he'd found it locked and was about to throw a rock through the window.

Fully awake, I felt like a clock with a dead battery, its hands frozen in place. Until I heard rapping on the window. Pushing myself into action, I put on my bathrobe, grabbed the flashlight by my bed, and tiptoed to the window to see the silhouette of a man's face. I heard my name.

"Evie, it's me." Hearing Jake's voice sent a thrill through me.

"What are you doing here?" I moved closer and recognized his symmetrical face, illuminated by the main house's porch light. His blond hair was cut short—*Englisch*. His square jaw was indeed cleanly shaven.

"Please let me in." His voice sounded urgent.

"*Nee*, I can't. Someone will see us."

"*Nee*, they won't." His face pushed closer to the glass. "I walked in from the road without my flashlight on."

I'd waited an eternity for this moment, but I cautioned myself. I didn't break the rules anymore. And I didn't trust Jake.

"Please," he said. "I must talk to you."

I stood frozen for a minute, my mind a battleground of indecision. This might be my one chance to speak to him in private. "Okay, for five minutes."

Through the window, I scanned the big house, cloaked in darkness. Not a glimmer in Beatrice's bedroom. No barking. Maybe the veterinarian had given Heath a sedative. Still, usually Minnie yapped.

As I cinched my bathrobe, Jake stole around to the door. I unlocked it, turned the handle, and cracked it open. He slipped inside. Being this close to Jake was almost unbearable. I caught the scent of his skin and work clothes. A mishmash of conflicting memories bombarded my mind, making me dizzy.

I took another look at the big house, and then closed the door without making a sound. I hoped.

"How did you know I'd be here?"

"Olivia told me."

I wanted to throw myself into his arms, but I remained at a distance. "Why did you come?"

"To talk."

"About?"

"You. Me. Everything."

I was glad it was too dark for Jake to see my face or uncovered hair. A conflict of emotions flooded my chest, making it hard to breathe. "You shouldn't be here." I wanted to ask him about the woman I'd seen with him, but instead I said, "You sent me only two letters—with no return address—and left one phone message, but you didn't tell me why you left. All I knew was that you'd gone to New York, and you never said anything about your plans for ...us."

"I didn't include a return address because I didn't want my *dat* knowing where I was and trying to force me to come home. And then I heard you had a new beau and a child in Ohio."

"All lies. I never loved anyone but you. No baby. And even if I had one, why..."

I got the distinct feeling he was lying to me, so what was the use of talking about this now? I was tempted to cover my ears. "Are you married?"

"*Nee.* There's no one else. Never has been."

"Why should I believe anything you say?" My words bulleted out as a wave of antagonism surged through me.

"I'm being honest with you, Evie. I've never cared for anyone but you."

I warned myself not to be naive. "I heard you just moved back home because of your *dat*."

"*Yah.* My *mamm* knew how to reach me and called as soon as his accident happened and begged me to return. Not exactly an accident, because his mule is an ornery beast. *Dat* should've sold the ill-tempered animal years ago. He was in a coma in the trauma unit at the hospital." His words burbled like water from a hose. "When he finally woke up a couple days ago, he couldn't speak or hardly move. *Mamm* was frantic, but she demanded he be released this morning. She claimed *Dat*'s eyes were pleading with her to come home."

"I didn't know about his injury until Olivia told me, and then someone here said your *dat* was awake enough to be transported home. I'm very sorry. Truly, I am." I tried to imagine what it would feel like to lie unconscious in a blanket of clouds. Some days after Jake left, I'd wished I could. And never wake up. Depression and gloom had surrounded me like a shroud.

Jake shifted his weight. The floorboards creaked. "We thank the Lord he's still alive. No one thought he'd make it, yet alone wake up after five days. Not that he's completely aware."

"That doesn't explain what you're doing here right now, Jake." My voice cracked when I spoke his name. A tumult of emotions cavorted through my chest.

"I had to see you, Evie. That's all I know. Olivia told me you were still single and living here, starting a new life."

"Since you were in the area anyway, you thought you'd stop by?" Sarcasm snaked through my voice.

"Look, Evie, if you throw me out on my ear, I wouldn't blame you. I've been a coward." He moved closer, until I could feel his breath against my cheek. "I didn't light that barn on fire. But everything else said about me was true. I pushed all the boundaries during *rumspringa* and never repented. Two days after I sold my car, the young man who bought it—he was only sixteen—hit a telephone pole and died. I felt responsible. Well, I was responsible for his death. He didn't know how to drive worth a hoot. I shamed my parents. And my *dat* never let me forget it."

I had no answers for him.

He ran his fingers over his cropped hair. "I couldn't stand living at home anymore. Remember when my older *bruder* died? A few months after the barn fire. *Dat* never got over his death and took his anguish and wrath out on me. And he kept bringing up that barn fire and calling me a liar. *Dat* believed I was guilty and worked me like a beast of burden. So when my friend in New York told me about a job, I took it and went to live with him. I'd intended to return after a few months, but I couldn't face my father. Or you once I heard you were dating someone, and then that you'd had a baby." His voice sounded strangled. "I shouldn't have believed those rumors. I should have come back to see for myself," he said, his lips barely moving. "And courted you, if you'd have had me."

I continued to hold my swirling thoughts in. Part of me was glad to see Jake suffering as I had. Yes, his father had been domineering and strict, but Jake was blaming his *dat* for his skipping town? I should want Jake to leave, but I was still hooked into him as if I were a helpless minnow.

"Guess I'd better go before I cause any more trouble." He stepped toward the door. "I have a favor to ask." He massaged the back of his neck. "Would you stop by the farm and see *Dat*?"

"Why would he wish to see me?"

"*Mamm* said he's only murmured one word since he woke up. Your name. Eva."

"Maybe he believes I'm the cause of all your problems, and he hates me and wants to chew me out."

"I have no idea what he thinks, but *Mamm* thinks he believes you and I are getting married."

"What on earth? Where would he get that idea?"

"I don't know. His thinking's all *ferhoodled*."

"You want me to lie to him?"

"*Nee*, but at least see him. Please?"

"I'll have to think and pray about it." I hoped Bishop Harvey would stop in at the café and advise me. I already knew what he'd say—"Stay away from Jake Miller."

Jake paused at the door. "Was that you I saw driving a buggy with an *Englisch* man today?"

Seeing me with another man, he'd probably experienced a slice of jealousy and a sense of possession.

"That's why you came?" My voice rose in volume. "What I do is none of your business anymore."

I still wanted to ask about the *Englisch* woman in his *dat*'s buggy, but I wouldn't lower myself. I'd probably find out about her all too soon.

# Seventeen

I woke up the next morning with words in my head, spoken by a minister in my parents' district a couple of years ago—"One sin leads to another." I remembered his proclamation with clarity. He'd glanced my way, and then his gaze moved around the room. "None of us is without sin, but we must learn from our mistakes and sin no more." Then he read the Scripture about a woman who was nearly stoned for being an adulteress. *Ach*, he'd thought I'd committed adultery? That I'd been with a married man? Beatrice seemed to as well when she spoke to me about *The Scarlet Letter*.

But on that Sunday two years ago, sitting on the women's side of the neighbor's living room, I'd promised God I would turn my life around forever. Yet last night temptation had arrived to lure me back into its clutches.

With the morning light seeping through the cracks around the shade, I renewed my vow to submit to the teachings of the Bible and to the *Ordnung*, and I asked the Lord for forgiveness. Beatrice had requested I not allow a man in my cabin, and I'd agreed. Yet I'd been disobedient.

Once I showered and dressed, I made my way to the café. I could hear and smell spring in the air. Pairs of singing birds flittered past me, choosing future nesting locations, I assumed. I noticed a variety of unusual birdhouses in the nursery and surmised Rose had fabricated them. I'd heard she constructed them and was in the mail-order business when she and Glenn met.

I wondered what it would be like to have the freedom to create your own enterprise. In the districts in our area, a single woman could own a business, but the moment she married, it would be considered her husband's. I knew that idea was scriptural, as the married man was the head of the household. Still, it irked me that men made all the decisions. *Ach*, I wasn't ready to be baptized until I came to terms with the *Ordnung*. Maybe staying single was my best option. No, I wanted children.

As Sadie and I prepared to open the café, Beatrice breezed in. "Everything ready for opening?" she asked me.

"*Yah*. Olivia's brother delivered her baked goods, the bread arrived, Sadie has been slicing meat, and I made corn chowder."

Beatrice sampled the soup without enthusiasm. "What ingredients are in here?"

"Corn, chopped onion and celery, and chicken bouillon."

"No real chicken?" She rummaged through the refrigerator and extracted a couple of chicken breasts. "I'll dice some up right now." She put a pan on the stove top, turned on the burner, and drizzled in olive oil. "So much better with chicken." She cut into the poultry like a pro. "And next time use genuine chicken stock instead of bouillon. But this will be fine once I put in the chicken."

She scanned the dining area. "Don't forget to write the name of the soup on the chalkboard."

"I was just about to do that." Her suggestion was a good one, but it irritated me. I assured myself that once the Yoders got home with their baby, Beatrice would be too busy to come into the café. And it wouldn't hurt me to show gratitude for her suggestions.

"I appreciate your help," I said, but she didn't acknowledge my thanks.

An hour later I was delighted when *Mamm* arrived. She embraced me as only my mother could.

"How did you get here?" I asked.

"I caught a ride with a friend who's buying roses, so I only have twenty minutes." She looked tired—her skin chalky and her cheeks sleep creased. "I've missed you so."

"I've missed you too, *Mamm*. Didn't you get my phone message? I'm coming by to pay you a visit on Sunday."

"*Yah*, I got your message." She hesitated. "Of course, you know we always want to see you, but I think we should entertain you in the *daadi haus*, so please come to our little door."

"Seriously? I shouldn't use the back door to the kitchen like I usually do?"

"If you wouldn't mind."

"You can't eat in your own kitchen anymore?"

"We could, and we do sometimes." She worked her lower lip. "When invited."

"Why? What's going on?"

"Nothing." She sniffed. "Everything's as perfect as can be expected."

"So why the long face, *Mamm*?" I took her hand. "Tell me what's wrong."

"Nothing. Everything's fine."

"Then why are you so sad? You look *drauerich*."

"Your *dat* had looked forward to retiring, but things aren't working out as expected. Don't get me wrong. I'm not complaining."

I knew *Mamm* would reveal her thoughts in time. No use prodding her. Still, why hadn't she just called me?

*Mamm* scanned the room. "Is there a spot where we can speak in private?"

"Right over there." I directed her to a square table by the koi pond. The trickling waterfall would camouflage our conversation.

*Mamm* seated herself at a two-top. "You must have heard about Amos Miller, Jake's father."

I planted myself next to her. "*Yah*, I did. A terrible tragedy."

"I took Amos and Ruth a casserole yesterday." She shook her head in a way that told me she was holding back tears. "There's a bed set up in the living room. All the other furniture's shoved against the walls. There's hardly space to walk, but Ruth said that's how she wants it."

"Is he going to recover?"

"I don't know. Amos looked to be asleep—dead, really, the way his jaw was unhinged—but Ruth said he could hear us and encouraged me to speak to him. I said, 'Hello, Amos. It's Anna Lapp. I've come for a visit.' His lids cracked open, and he stared blankly." She let out a lengthy sigh. "I wonder if he'll ever wake up completely. Poor Ruth."

Now was my chance to be honest. "*Mamm*, Jake stopped by last night."

"I saw him, and I had a feeling he'd track you down. What did he want?"

"He asked me to visit his *dat*. Apparently, Amos's brain has gone haywire."

*Mamm* polished the table with her palm and nodded. "I'd better tell you right now if Jake didn't. The only word Amos has muttered is your name. I can't imagine why."

"That makes two of us. Unless he still bears resentment toward me and blames me for Jake's bad behavior."

"You call arson mere bad behavior?"

I leaned closer, against her arm, and spoke in her ear. "He and his *Englisch* friends didn't burn down that barn."

"How do you know? Because he told you?"

I still wasn't a hundred percent sure of anything. "I suppose they could have by mistake, but an upstanding man who was there that night told me otherwise. The barn's owner has long ago forgiven the arsonist, if there was one. And his new barn is twice as nice."

"You know, Eva, you've always been gullible. Even as a child."

Not the supportive words I'd hoped to hear. "I suppose you're right, *Mamm*. I do try to see the best in people." Not a true statement when it came to Beatrice and my sister-in-law, Marta. I needed to improve my attitude.

An *Englisch* couple sat down at the next table, each carrying a mug of coffee.

"This café isn't the best place for a private conversation." I wanted to change the subject. "When I stop by for a visit, we'll finish it." I stood. "Want some freshly brewed *kaffi*?"

"*Yah*, that would be nice. *Denki*."

I brought her coffee and a small pitcher of half-and-half. "I'll scramble up some fresh eggs if you like. The owners have several fine hens."

"*Denki*, but I already ate."

"Do you want to see my cabin?"

"Maybe next time. I stopped by there on the way here, so I've seen the outside. A woman named Beatrice gave me directions to the café."

"And an earful?" I heard annoyance in my voice.

"She was very pleasant. Do you have a problem with her?"

"Yes and no. The problem is most likely in my head. She's been helpful in her own way."

"*Yah*, she told me she was teaching you how to cook, something I should have done better."

"I just never enjoyed cooking as much as gardening and helping *Dat* in the barn. But I learned enough from you to read recipes and work in here."

"I must not have been much of a mother, or you wouldn't have strayed from the flock."

"That's not true. You were a fantastic mother. And I'm still living Amish."

Tension gathered at the corners of her eyes. "But not a church member."

"Didn't we talk about this before I left home? I thought you said this job was ideal."

"*Yah*, I thought you'd be working in the nursery with plants. But you seem to be doing fine here in the café." She stirred sugar and cream into her coffee until it was the color of milk chocolate.

"*Mamm*, are you okay?" I sat down again and appraised her haggard features.

"Just a little tired. Getting used to the changes at home. Nothing worth mentioning. Retirement is what your *dat* has wanted for years. And I have less housework, for sure."

I recalled *Mamm*'s diligent cleaning and food preparation. Not to mention her canning and meticulous quilting. She took great satisfaction in those activities.

"How are you getting along with Marta?"

"Fine as can be expected."

"I thought you and *Dat* were thrilled when she married Reuben." I'd never seen *Mamm* so pleased, making me feel like a failure for still being single.

"We were." *Mamm* added more sugar to her coffee. "She and I have different ways of doing things, is all, which is to be expected. I try not to give her too much advice, but, apparently, I do."

"But aren't you glad to have your grandchildren living under the same roof?"

"Of course. But Marta seems too strict." She covered her mouth for a moment. "*Ach*, I shouldn't have said anything. Your *dat* and I probably weren't strict enough. We looked the other way and spared the rod too often."

"And spoiled the child?" Meaning me.

"No use rehashing the past, Evie. You're a fine young woman, and I'm proud of you." She gulped a mouthful of coffee.

"*Mamm*, are you sure everything else is all right?"

"For the most part, *yah*." She swiveled in her chair to face me, as if shutting out the rest of the world. "If you talked to Jake, then you probably know he's working his *dat*'s fields until Amos gets better. If he ever does. *Ach*, Eva, I wonder if he will. Anyway, Jake is *Englisch* now. You'd best stay away from him."

"But Jake asked me to visit his *dat*, and I've decided to go on Sunday."

"Why on earth?"

Attempting to delay describing my guilty encounter, I took her half-empty mug to the carafe, refilled it, and then lowered myself next to her. "Like you and Jake both told me, Amos keeps asking for me."

"Sounds like a trick." *Mamm* stirred more sugar into her coffee, clanking the spoon against the mug. "Maybe you should have a deacon and a minister accompany you."

"That might frighten Amos, don't ya think?"

"Now, why would he be afraid? And how are you planning to get to their house—and ours too?"

"I have permission to use the nursery owner's buggy."

"It's a long drive."

"I was told the mare needs the exercise. I took her out yesterday, and it worked great. I enjoyed driving the buggy."

"But the traffic." She wrung her hands.

"I'll be extra careful and stay off the busy roads."

"I still say it's a bad idea." She shook her head. "No *gut* can come from it. None."

# Eighteen

On my afternoon break I decided to stroll back to my cabin. A mirror hung by the café's back door, but some would consider my checking my *kapp* a sign of vanity. Because it was.

I headed out the café's door and almost walked into Stephen.

"Have you seen Heath?" he asked, falling in step next to me. "He's missing again."

"No, I haven't seen him today."

"Wayne called to report two more lambs were killed at Bill Hastings's farm. Doesn't look good. If they spot Heath, they'll pick him up. Or worse." He advanced toward the big house, his stride purposeful. We slowed to allow *Englisch* customers to pass us from the other direction, and then we continued.

"Early this morning Heath begged to go out," he said. "When Beatrice called him minutes later and announced it was time for breakfast, he didn't come."

"Did you go looking for him?"

"I canvassed the nursery and then got in my pickup." He jammed his hands in his jeans pockets. "I even drove past the sheep farm where we found him before and called out his name. No sign of the dog or that sheep farmer. I decided it was best not to pay the creep another visit."

"Good idea, unless you have Wayne with you." I imagined another altercation and felt a shiver up my spine. "Perhaps Heath will come back on his own."

"I hope so."

"I know nothing about dogs, but maybe he needs to be tied up next time."

"If there is a next time."

Beatrice bustled after us from the café. "Please tell me you found Heath."

"Not yet," Stephen said.

"It's all my fault." A look of distress creased Beatrice's face. "I feel terrible for letting him loose."

"You had no way of knowing," Stephen said. "He never used to run off."

The black cat encircled her legs, but Beatrice paid the feline no heed. "I might lose my job. Then what will I do?"

Stephen moved toward the main house. "Glenn and Rose won't blame you."

"But, you see, I sold my home." She patted her chest. "Where would I live if I lose this job?"

"Let's not get ahead of ourselves." Reaching the back porch, Stephen supported her elbow as she ascended the steps. "For all we know, Heath will show up at any moment." His sentence came out more like a question than a statement.

Were the tales of dogs getting the taste of blood and turning feral true? I imagined Heath killing sheep—ripping out their throats. My body stiffened as my fear of dogs invaded me again, making me weak at the knees.

Stephen checked his wristwatch. "Eva, shouldn't you get to work?"

"Oh, dear." I spun on my heel and hastened back to the café, all the time thinking Beatrice wasn't the only woman who might lose her job. The moment I saw her, I should have returned to work.

Over the course of fifteen minutes, the café had filled with customers. I was stunned to see lovely and radiant Olivia standing behind the counter filling orders.

"No worries," she told me. "Everything's under control."

"Mostly tea and *kaffi* orders," Sadie said. "But I'm glad Liv stopped by."

Minutes later, all customers had seated themselves, leaving the three of us at the counter.

Sadie grabbed a damp rag and commenced cleaning the vacant tables, and then she refilled coffee mugs.

"Evie, I came by hoping you and I could share a word." Olivia and I stood side by side, her arm against mine.

She lowered her voice to a whisper in my ear. "I'm leaving tomorrow night and wanted to say goodbye."

My head whipped around to catch her expression. "Please tell me you're joking."

A smile fanned across her face.

"But you can't leave," I said.

"You want me to stay and end up like you? Losing the only man I'll ever love?"

My brain scavenged for ways to change her mind. "But who will do the baking?"

She chortled. "Come to my house today after work. I'll give you a lesson if you promise not to breathe a word about me and you-know-who."

"I don't even know who you-know-who is for sure." Maybe Olivia would come to her senses in the next twenty-four hours.

"I have a great idea." A grin widened her mouth. "My *schweschder* can do the baking. She helps me every day. *Yah*, we'll ask Emma. She's been begging our folks to let her work in the farmer's market, but they won't let her."

"No one can bake as well as you do." My arm slipped across her slim shoulders. "And I'd miss you too much."

"Shush. Keep your voice down." She turned toward me, her eyes sparkling as if she'd never enjoyed herself more. "In case Emma bags out on you, I'll give you my recipes. Ya don't need to be a brain surgeon to make whoopie pies. If that were true, I'd be in trouble."

"But I—"

"Evie, I've heard Beatrice can cook as well as any woman in the county. For an Italian, that is."

I recalled Beatrice's scrumptious spaghetti and meatballs and pie to rival even *Mamm*'s. "She's a marvelous cook."

"But asking her for help would be a humbling experience you'd rather not face?"

"*Yah.* A childish reaction, I know."

"I hear she's had a difficult life." Olivia's pert features turned melancholy, the corners of her mouth drooping. "Her parents arranged a marriage for her to a man she didn't love." She winced. "*Ach*, and they say he gambled and had ties to the Mafia and left her penniless. They say he was murdered. But you know how gossip is."

"Sounds doubtful. *Mamm*'s never mentioned a thing, and they grew up near each other."

"Well, think about it. Why would Beatrice need a job at her age? She's in her late sixties, don't ya think?"

"I wouldn't dare ask her."

"She sold her house last year. Where did the money go?" Olivia's eyes widened. "I've heard to pay off back taxes and her husband's debts. They say he was quite a handsome fellow who'd sing opera while doing chores and mowing the lawn. And a ladies' man."

I stared back at her in disbelief.

Olivia bumped her hip against mine. "But you know how gossip is."

"Do I ever. I've been a victim of the faceless viper." I lowered my volume. "I remember last year when one of the ministers admonished the congregation to refrain from gossiping. He glanced up and stared directly at me."

She shook her head. "Evie, he was admonishing the whole congregation. We're all guilty of it. The entire world doesn't orbit around you." Olivia's blunt words stung, but she was right. Hadn't we just been speculating about Beatrice?

She leaned closer. "Tongues will be wagging about me soon enough."

# Nineteen

Before turning in that night, I knocked on the big house's kitchen door and asked Beatrice to teach me how to make minestrone soup for the next day.

"I'd be delighted. In fact, I'll come help and bring homemade pasta."

"You make your own pasta from scratch?"

"*Certo!* Everything is better when you start from scratch. *Si? Mi dispiace*, but I forget sometimes. *Mio marito*—I mean, my husband—and I spoke Italian most of the time." She sighed.

I ventured into uncharted territory. "You must miss him."

Her eyes moistened. "You can't imagine if you've never been married. At first I resented him, but I grew to love and depend on him over the years."

"I'm sorry for your loss." Although heartbroken myself, I couldn't relate to her depth of sorrow.

That night I tossed in a sea of uncertainty, dreaming and wishing Jake would return. Knowing he shouldn't. Hoping to hear Heath's barking to be let in the main house. But nothing.

When would God answer my prayers? I'd prayed Jake wouldn't be incarcerated, and he hadn't been. I'd prayed his father wouldn't die, and so far, so good—although I dreaded seeing the semicomatose man. But my prayers for a happily-ever-after life floated out of my grasp like bubbles in the millpond where I played as a child.

The next morning I dragged myself to the café to find Beatrice already preparing the soup and singing along to what must be an Italian aria on the radio. "*O mio babbino caro ...*"

"Good morning," I said as I entered the kitchen. "You have a beautiful voice."

"You're too kind. I don't do Puccini justice." She turned off the radio. "The greatest composers were Italian." It occurred to me that her favorite music was the opposite of what we sang in church services. Fortunately, singings allowed voices to frolic up and down the octaves. I wondered if I could still sing as I did in school.

"A fine good morning to you, Eva. Or *buon giorno*, as they say in Italy."

I didn't resent her cheerfulness one bit. In fact, I was grateful she'd already warmed the chicken broth and chopped the vegetables, and was sautéing them in olive oil. Heavy on the garlic.

I peered around Beatrice and noticed a can of kidney beans. "Where did you learn to cook so well?" I asked.

"From *mia nona*—my grandmother." She turned to me and grinned, catching me off guard. "But maybe I'll write this down for you to put in your recipe book."

"I don't have one."

"Not even copies of your mama's favorite recipes?"

"No."

"Then I'll get you started. You'll need a cookbook and your favorites when you marry a good man. Not that Jake fellow."

"He's not so bad."

"No? Then why did he up and leave his family?"

"But he's back now."

"For how long? I must get over to his parents' house to see Amos and Ruth after Mass tomorrow. I'll ask Stephen to drive me."

I couldn't imagine a more awkward situation than arriving at the Millers' the same time Beatrice and Stephen did.

"You'd better make the coffee, Eva. You know how dark I like mine. The customers wouldn't like it."

"Yours was *gut* at dinner, but *yah*, okay." I started the coffee brewing—enough to fill the carafe and then some. I'd need all the caffeine I could get to perk myself up.

Sadie arrived in time to hear me say, "The whole dinner was *appeditlich*. Absolutely delicious."

"And the company? You're a fool if you don't snap up Mark before he loses interest. Although some men want what they can't have."

"Hello, Sadie." I heightened my volume to alter the trajectory of the conversation. Poor girl.

She produced a meager smile. "Hi, Evie and Beatrice." She inhaled. "It smells great in here."

"All Beatrice's doing."

Stephen sauntered in from the front door minutes later. "I wanted to let you know I'll be out for a while. Wayne called to say there's a dog running loose. He told me animal control is on the lookout. I may stop by that sheep farmer's again. Wayne said his name is Bill Hastings."

"Do you want me to go with you?" I asked.

"What? Who's going to run the café?" Beatrice clucked. "I think Stephen can handle this."

"You're right." But I worried about another altercation with the sheep farmer. "Maybe you should ride with Wayne," I told him.

His brows lowered, hooding his eyes. "Glenn called and said he'll come home early if Heath isn't found within the next twenty-four hours. But he doesn't want to leave his wife and baby. Not with his father-in-law so sick."

"What's wrong with him?"

"It's his heart. Surgery is scheduled for Monday."

# Twenty

A melancholy Saturday followed despite our many customers raving about the minestrone soup. Beatrice was delighted but took no credit.

Stephen finally returned. "False alarm." His shoulders slumped. "The dog running loose was a poodle mix. Fortunately, its owner caught up with it just as I got there. I helped her get the dog into her car."

"The poor woman must have been scared sick." Beatrice patted his back. "That was very kind of you."

He shrugged off her compliment. "So now we wait. I have a bad feeling about this."

He turned to me. "Be sure to lock the doors tonight."

"I have been."

"Well, fine, but give them one final tug to make sure."

He held me responsible for the break-in? I wanted to defend myself, but I clamped my lips together.

When I left for the day, I double-checked the back door and secured the front.

That night I heard an owl's hooting and the rustling of the tree branches in the breeze. And a branch snap. Jake had returned? I slipped into my coat, covered my head, grabbed my flashlight, and went out to investigate.

"Jake?" I whispered. No reply. The air was still, and the sky as black as a never-ending tunnel.

I considered rapping on the big house's back door to ask Beatrice for help, but she was most likely asleep. I imagined her coming to the door in her bathrobe and shaking her head at my cowardly reaction. Too many times I had succumbed to my fears, but not anymore. I'd prove to everyone, including myself, that I was brave.

Almost at the café, I saw a swoop of light in the interior through one glass wall. I tried the front door and found it unlocked. I tiptoed toward the kitchen and saw a man standing in front of the opened refrigerator.

In the darkness, I bumped into a chair. Its legs scraped against the floor.

"Who's there?" I said, trying to sound courageous.

The room lay silent.

I inched forward, turned on my flashlight, and pointed the beam over the counter. An *Englischer*—an older man—crouched in front of the refrigerator. He clutched a sandwich—sliced roast beef mashed between two pieces of bread.

"What are you doing in here?" I put heft into my voice, although he was maybe fifty and large enough to knock me over.

"Answer me," I said, and I stamped my foot for effect.

When he stood, he was indeed taller than I was by six inches. His shadowed face showed fear, the whites of his eyes glowing. "Please... please don't call the police," he said with a whimper. He reeked of hard liquor, like Reuben had once after partying with his friends when in *rumspringa*, sampling the evils of the *Englisch* world. Thankfully, meeting Marta had brought a halt to his tomfooleries.

"How did you get in?" I asked.

"When they were building this place, someone left a key in the door one night. I took it and made a copy the next day and then returned the original."

"But why?"

"I was hungry. I needed a place to sleep."

My eyes were becoming accustomed to the darkness. He was skinny. His cheeks were hollow and his thinning hair disheveled.

"Where do you live?"

"Nowhere in particular. Just down the road in a relative's basement or a barn if his wife gets mad at me. Please don't tell anyone. They'll toss me in the slammer."

"Don't you have other family?"

"No. I used to..."

Was he feeding me a bunch of malarkey? I didn't trust drunk strangers. No, I wouldn't be gullible no matter what he said. I mentally tallied my options, including calling the police. Or Stephen.

Keeping my distance, I put out my hand, palm up. "Give me the key." I figured Stephen could get the locks swapped out in the morning anyway.

The man dug through his wrinkled trousers pocket. "I must have dropped it."

"I don't believe you."

He fished in his jacket pockets. "Oh, here it is." He tossed the key on a table.

Sandwich in hand, he moved to the back door.

"Stop. What's your name?"

"Ralph. But please don't report me to the police. I can't stand being locked up."

No booze in jail, I figured. And he'd probably given me a phony name. "One more thing, Ralph. Have you seen a large brown Labrador retriever?"

"Uh—I don't think so."

# Twenty-One

Today was the day I would venture to Jake's parents' farm in Glenn's buggy to see Amos Miller. So I could arrive before Beatrice, I rushed through my shower and put on my teal-blue dress. With no time to obsess about my hair, I parted and covered my tresses with my *kapp* and used hairpins to anchor the white head covering. I thought of the verse from First Corinthians directing women to cover their heads when they pray. No doubt, I'd be praying on the way over. *Ach,* I should have prayed for the Lord's guidance before getting out of bed.

Through the cabin's window, I scanned the parking lot and was glad Stephen hadn't arrived yet to pick up Beatrice—if he were indeed coming.

Outside in the cool morning air, I found the buggy already rolled out of the barn and Autumn in the barn polishing off her breakfast. One of the men working here must tend to her food and water in the owners' absence. But who had brought out the buggy? Much as I appreciated the effort, I felt as though someone were orchestrating my day. I was under the impression only Stephen knew I was going home by way of this buggy and horse. Maybe he'd asked one of his crew to help me. Or maybe he'd stopped by himself before picking up Beatrice. Perhaps they were ahead of me. I felt my determination to see Amos wavering.

"Hey, Autumn." I knew better than to approach a horse from the rear without warning. She turned toward me, pricked her ears, and swiveled them my way. "Ready to go on an adventure, girl?"

Speaking to her in soothing tones, I led her outside and harnessed her to the buggy.

I climbed into the driver's seat and took up the reins. Autumn seemed relaxed. *Ach*, such a long trip in a buggy using the back roads instead of the highway. The poor mare would be exhausted at the end of the day. Yet Stephen said she needed exercise.

I would pass close by Jake's parents' farm on the way to see *Mamm* and *Dat*. I figured I should visit my parents' first, but I opted to visit them after. *Dat* had always said to tackle the hardest job first. Who was I kidding? I hoped to speak to Jake alone and find out what his plans were.

On a Sunday morning, with fewer cars and even buggies on the road, the trip passed more quickly than I'd imagined. I drove for several minutes behind an SUV, its occupants clicking photos of me until I took a sudden right to dodge them.

Finally, after zigging and zagging, I recognized the Millers' tall oak tree as I came upon their lane. I wondered how I'd be welcomed by Jake's *mamm*. Would Ruth lecture me or turn me away?

Entering their barnyard, I was surprised to see their barn and storage buildings freshly painted white, no doubt by neighbors when they'd heard Amos was in the hospital. The cornfield had been fertilized—I could smell the earthy aroma—and the coffee-colored soil newly turned.

"Whoa, girl." I pulled on the reins, and Jake stepped out of the barn and took hold of Autumn's bridle.

"I'll take care of your horse." He averted his eyes from mine. Not even a smile after all he'd said the other night.

"*Mamm*'s in the house." Jake angled his head toward the back stoop. If this was a prelude to my upcoming reception, I was tempted to head to my parents' right away. But I'd come this far, and Autumn needed water.

I knocked on the back door and waited several moments. As I was turning to vamoose, Ruth welcomed me with a hopeful smile. "Eva. Come on in. It's *gut* to see you." Her face was a road map of lines, and her mouth was white. She'd aged considerably since I'd last seen her. Poor woman. I had little doubt this transformation was from having her husband hanging on the brink between life and death.

She led me through a dark utility room and into the kitchen. She was wearing house slippers. I untied and kicked off my shoes and left them next to a pair of boots inside the kitchen door.

Ahead, an abundance of baskets filled with muffins, pies, Tupperware housing applesauce and canned peaches, and casseroles cluttered the table. "May I offer you anything?" she asked me. "*Ach*, our neighbors and church members have been generous, but it's more than we can ever consume."

"*Nee*, but *denki* for your kind offer."

"How about tea or *kaffi*?"

"Maybe later." I was on a mission of sorts and was determined to get it accomplished.

"Ready to see Amos?" She turned to me, her face as haggard as if all her life had been drained. "I should warn ya, he's awake, but in a half-dream state. But I was told at the hospital he can hear us. For some reason he's repeated your name over and over."

"Why would he want to see me? Does Amos blame me for Jake's going away?"

"I don't think so." She blinked, the whites of her eyes bloodshot. "I wanted to see you too, dear."

But why? Did she think Jake and I were getting married? Nothing made sense.

A hospital bed stood in the living room beyond the kitchen. Amos was a big man, but he was hardly visible under the blankets and quilts. All I could see was a pale, bearded face and closed eyes.

Ruth touched his arm. "Amos, look who's come to see us." He blinked his eyes open. When he noticed me, his face came alive. "Eva?" His voice was a mere sliver.

"*Yah*, it's me." I expected harsh words, but the corners of his mouth lifted a smidgen.

"Look! He moved his hand." Ruth sounded ecstatic.

Not knowing what to do, I placed my hand on his, the first time I'd ever been within six feet of him. His hand wavered, as if trying to grasp my fingers.

"You're the only person he's reacted to, Eva. Not even me, his *frau.*"

"Amos?" I said as his fingers went limp again. A moment later, he sank back to sleep.

"Please stay. Don't rush off," Ruth said.

"I don't understand."

"Amos thinks you've brought our Jake home, is what I'm guessing." Her face was drawn, her skin gray. "Eva, please talk Jake into staying. I can't run this farm by myself. Our *dochders* live in Indiana and have large families. Their husbands are busy managing their dairy farms. I'll have to sell."

"Is money the only reason?"

"*Nee.* I want our son back. I'm not strong enough to take care of Amos even with the community's help." She lowered her chin. "Now it's my turn to help someone in her time of troubles."

"What do you mean?"

"*Ach*, I shouldn't have said anything." She grimaced. "I'm a big blabbermouth."

I heard the heavy tread of a man's footsteps entering the room.

"*Denki* for coming, Evie." Jake spoke as if he hadn't seen me minutes ago. Maybe the whole Miller family had gone *ab im kopp*.

I was afraid to look at Jake, to be sucked into the vacuum of his deep-blue eyes.

"I was just leaving." I pivoted away from the bed.

Jake looked to his mother. "Has *Dat* improved? Did he speak to Eva?"

"Amos recognized her, I'm sure of it. But then he drifted back to sleep." She turned to me. "The doctor said Amos may do this for days. Or weeks. We're expecting a therapist to arrive tomorrow to help Amos recover his motor skills, if he ever does. A frontal lobe injury can change a man forever." Her lower lip quivered. "Will you come back, Eva?" Her words trembled as if she were restraining a sob.

"I can't. I work every day except Sunday."

Her fingers clammy, Ruth took my hand. "Then please come to supper after work."

"I don't want to cause Amos or you distress..."

"You won't, dear. I'll send Jake to fetch you." Her gaze fell to the floor. "He drives a car now. It's parked around behind a shed where no one can see it."

"*Nee*, I can't," I said. "And I must be leaving now to see my parents." I spun and walked right into an attractive late-teen *Englisch* girl. Her streaked, ash-blond hair cascaded over her shoulders. Her eyes were ringed with makeup that made her look like an owl.

Jake cleared his voice. "Evie, this is Brandy."

"Oh?" My gaze homed in on her prominent abdomen. She was dressed in leggings and a loose blouse, no doubt trying to camouflage the fact she was with child.

"Hi, there," Brandy said.

Despite my shock, I put my hand out to shake hers when she extended it.

"She's...she's a friend, Evie. Nothing more," Jake stammered.

I pivoted to Ruth and caught her look of distress. "So they claim," Ruth told me, her voice lacking conviction.

"It's true, Mrs. Miller," Brandy said. "I had a boyfriend, but he beat me up." She lifted her hair from her forehead to reveal an ugly yellowish-green bruise, and then she pulled up a shirtsleeve to reveal more bruises.

"Brandy told me her parents booted her out." Ruth moved closer. "I said she could stay with us if she'd help around the house and with Amos."

"She just showed up at your front door looking for work?" I heard derision in my voice.

"No, I came with Jake." Brandy rubbed her tummy as if she felt the unborn child moving.

"I have to leave." My mouth was so dry I could hardly speak. "My parents are waiting for me." I back-stepped toward the kitchen to find my shoes.

Jake shadowed me. "Evie, I'll walk you to your buggy."

"I can make it on my own, *denki*."

He paid me no heed. "Be right back, *Mamm*." He followed me through the utility room, with its washer and wringer and abundance of tools, and opened the door. At the bottom of the porch steps, he trotted to catch up with me and blocked my path.

"Please don't rush off." He took hold of my upper arms. "It's not what you think."

I wriggled out of his grasp. "Since when do you know what I think?" I sucked in a deep breath of air to clear my head and sharpen my senses. "That I'm dumb enough to believe she isn't carrying your *boppli*?"

"It's not mine, I promise. She wants to hide from her abusive boyfriend, so she hasn't told him where she is. She hasn't even told anyone in her family."

"Why didn't you mention her when you stopped by?"

"I was afraid you wouldn't come—or you would, and we'd have a scene just like this."

"In other words, your *mamm* needs my help? You hadn't come to see me?"

"Of course I wanted to speak to you. Everything I told you was and is true." He crossed his arms. "Please don't turn against me. Don't I have troubles enough?"

"I'd say you do." I strode into the barn to fetch Autumn, and then we hitched her to the buggy.

Jake took hold of the reins. "Wait, Evie. What happened to the compassionate girl I used to know?"

"Me? You killed her." I immediately regretted my mean-spirited declaration.

"Hey, I don't deserve such vicious words. You looked alive and well driving that buggy with an *Englisch* man the other day."

I was filled with shame. I'd accused Jake of emotional murder. What exactly had he done other than ditch me? I'd heard the term *walking wounded*. That's what I was.

"He's my boss at the nursery." I felt compelled to explain. "I came to visit your *dat*. And I feel sorry for Brandy." I took the reins from him and steered Autumn out of the barnyard.

# TWENTY-TWO

I fretted on the way to my parents' farm. My disappointment and uncertainty churned like a volcano ready to erupt. But it wasn't long before I saw our stately windmill, still used for pumping water. I admonished myself for wasting time thinking about Jake. My concern should be with Amos, even though he had always been overly strict and harsh with Jake, particularly after Jake's older brother died. Amos made no bones about it: His older son had always been his favorite and could do no wrong.

Entering my parents' barnyard felt comfortable. My tense arms relaxed until I saw Marta staring at me through the pane of the kitchen window.

I unhitched Autumn and tethered her next to the water trough. Then I skirted the house to the door of the *daadi haus*. It swung open before I could knock.

"Eva, *lieb*." *Mamm* clasped me in a warm embrace. *Dat* stood behind her awaiting his turn.

"*Gut* to see you, Evie." His bushy beard tickled my ear as he hugged me. "I know it was foolish to think we'd have you here with us forever, but the house isn't the same without you."

I looked around and noticed *Mamm* had done her best to decorate the smallish living area, with its woodstove and bookcase. The barren window ledge would be the perfect place for a potted flowering plant. The next time I visited, I would bring an African violet from the nursery to add color and life to my parents' new home.

"How do you like retirement?" I assessed *Dat's* face and saw no joy.

"I still help out when I can." His hand moved to his hip. "But it's time to let the next generation take charge. Reuben has big plans."

"Like what?"

His head shook as he spoke. "He wants to take out a mortgage and build a shop of some sort next to the barn."

"If our bishop allows it," *Mamm* said. "But you know he is elderly and suffers from gout. The poor man rarely leaves his home anymore."

I added my two cents. "If you don't want him to, say no."

*Mamm* wrung her hands. "As of last week, Reuben's name is on the title to the property. We have no say. And we wouldn't want to interfere anyway."

"But you have more wisdom, certainly. What does Reuben know about running a business?"

"It was Marta's idea."

I knew better than to make a negative comment, but I asked, "What kind of business?"

*Dat* tugged his beard. "We still don't know."

"So how's it going living with Marta?"

"I'm doing my best to keep out of her way," *Mamm* said. "I'm grateful to see our grandchildren, for sure, and I try not to interfere in the way she does things."

At that moment, Marta opened the door without knocking. She wore a shamrock-green dress and black apron, and her *kapp* appeared newly pressed. "Eva, what a pleasant surprise. I hope you'll all join us for the noon meal."

She normally didn't include my parents?

"Sure, that would be nice. I'm starving." I should have grabbed a snack earlier when visiting Amos, but seeing Jake with Brandy had soured my appetite.

"*Gut.* I'll set another place at the table." Marta whisked out of the room and left the door open.

*Mamm* hesitated. "Are ya going to visit Amos later?"

"I already did."

"Then you know what the poor man's going through. Not to mention their unusual houseguest."

"Brandy? *Yah*, I met her. Quite a shock. I must be the last person in the county who didn't know. I wish you would have told me, *Mamm*."

When we went into the main house for the noon meal, I was surprised to find Reuben sitting at the head of the kitchen table instead of *Dat*.

I turned to *Dat*, and he shrugged. "Marta's idea."

"Are you sure it's okay, *Dat*?" Reuben pushed his chair away from the table and stood. "I don't feel right about this. You should sit here."

"You're the head of the house now, son." *Dat* waved Reuben's concerns away. I'd never heard of such a thing, but I wouldn't interfere.

"I insist you sit here," Reuben said. I was pleased with his action as he helped relocate *Dat* to the head of the table, which meant the three children also stood.

"Come sit beside me." I patted the long bench on my side of the table, and Nancy and Mary Lou scooted in next to me. My eight-year-old nephew, Jesse, chose to sit next to Reuben, which was natural. Marta perched across the table from me.

*Dat* commenced the silent prayer, and we all bowed our heads. A minute later, he cleared his throat in his usual guttural way, indicating he was through.

Had I even prayed?

Suddenly, my mind was inundated with prayer requests when I hadn't even thought to thank God for my many gifts and triumphs. I was living by myself and able to sleep through the night—for the most part. I was running the café—as best I could. What would I pray for first and foremost?

*Mamm* worked her lower lip as she stared at the bountiful noon meal—an array of cold cuts and cheeses, pickled beets, salads, applesauce, and chocolate pie. All of Reuben's favorites. Marta knew how to treat her man right. No wonder she had my brother wrapped around her little finger.

I sighed as I envisioned myself keeping a husband happy. Why was I worrying about a scenario that might never happen?

During the meal, Marta was uncharacteristically chatty. She asked me about the café and what my duties were, and then she flattered me with compliments about my many new accomplishments.

"I hear you're thinking of starting a new business," I said.

Reuben narrowed his eyes. "Just thinking about it." He forked into the pickled beets. "Nothing's decided yet."

Marta spoke to me in a subdued voice. "If we open a business, we'll be needing to hire someone like you."

"That would be *wunderbaar*," *Mamm* said, her first words since sitting down at the table.

"But I have a job. I can't just up and quit without advance warning." I dabbed the corners of my mouth. "Anyway, I don't wish to quit. I'm doing fine at my job, and I like my little cabin."

"You'd desert your own family?" Marta's brows met in the center. I smiled in return. No use starting a confrontation with my sister-in-law. "We'd find a place for you to sleep," she said. "Our *dochders* have been asking for you, haven't you, girls? Wouldn't it be fun to have your *aendi* living here?"

"*Yah, yah!*" Each niece took an elbow and agreed. Nancy laid her head against my arm while Mary Lou gazed up at me with doe eyes. These charming girls might be the closest I ever came to children of my own.

Wheels in my head started gyrating. What if I were fired from the nursery? I had yet to meet the owner and his wife. If Beatrice unleashed complaints about me and told them I couldn't cook, I might find myself with nowhere to live.

# Twenty-Three

As I steered the buggy back to the nursery, I allowed Autumn to set a leisurely pace. My mind played a raucous game of badminton as I swung my racket aimlessly in the back of my mind.

A pickup tailgated me, so I pulled off to the side of the road to allow it to pass. The vehicle moved alongside of me, and I saw Stephen eyeing me through the window, past Beatrice. Her head pushed back against her headrest, she stared out the windshield.

Stephen pulled ahead on a wide strip, stopped his pickup, and jumped out. He came over to me. "How are you and Autumn doing?" He tugged a clean handkerchief out of his jeans pocket, reached over, and dabbed away a tear rolling down my cheek. I jerked. How humiliating. I never cried in public and hadn't known I was.

"Are you okay, Evie?"

"*Yah*, I was just visiting my parents..." I rubbed both cheeks. "I'm fine."

"I saw Autumn going so slowly I thought you might have some kind of trouble or she'd picked up a pebble."

"Is she limping?"

"No, I don't think so."

"I feel so silly." I forced the corners of my mouth to curve up. "I must have been daydreaming."

"Not a good habit with cars on the road. You really should pay more attention."

"I'm sorry. It won't happen again." I wondered if he'd let me borrow Autumn and the buggy ever again.

He must have heard anxiety grating in my voice. "Don't worry about it, Evie." He leaned closer. "Do you need help getting back to the nursery?"

"No. I'm fine." Obviously, I wasn't, but I straightened my back and gathered the reins, causing Autumn's head to jerk.

"Ruth said you stopped by to see Amos."

"*Yah*, so sad. Poor man. And poor Ruth. My heart goes out to her."

"Beatrice was terribly upset when she saw Amos. She told Ruth she'll be praying for his recovery." He glanced over to his pickup. "And we also saw Jake. And met Brandy." He paused. "That must have been awfully hard on you."

"Jake and Brandy claim the baby isn't his."

"I've walked in your shoes, Evie. I've played the fool before." Meaning he thought I was a fool? "Seems we all have been taken advantage of at some time." He rubbed his palms together. "Let's just get you back to the nursery in one piece, and we can talk more there."

"Wait. There is something I should have told you earlier. I found an *Englischer* in the café last night."

His features hardened. "Why didn't you call me right away? Or call the police?" His voice turned gruff. "Did you recognize him?"

"No. He said his name was Ralph, and that he used to work at the nursery. *Ach*, I should have called you, but he seemed harmless."

"What gave him the right to break into the café?"

"He didn't actually break in. He had a key."

"But he was stealing food, was he not?" Stephen gave his head a shake. "So now we know who's been coming into the café. I'll have the locks changed tomorrow. If he'd just come in and asked for a meal, we would've given it to him, but the man has a big drinking problem. He used to work for us... Never mind. I'll fill you in later as to why he was fired." He surveyed my face. "Do you think you're able to drive home?"

"*Yah*, Autumn and I will be fine. I'm so sorry about Ralph last night."

"No big deal. The man has problems."

I was fully alert now. The mare stood nibbling on grass and weeds at the side of the road. "Come on, girl." She grabbed a last mouthful of grass and raised her head, ready to proceed forward.

"I'm going to follow you."

"That's not necessary."

He gave me a stern look, but his voice was filled with compassion. "I want to make sure you get back safely, even if it takes us a few more minutes."

He cared for me beyond my being the café's manager?

When I reached the nursery, Autumn gathered momentum, aiming us toward the barn. I noticed Stephen veering toward the main house to let Beatrice out. *Gut.* The last thing I wanted was for her to hear him scolding me—not that I didn't deserve a verbal lashing for daydreaming while driving the buggy.

Minutes later, as I watered and fed the mare, Stephen entered the barn. "I called the locksmith. He answered even though it's Sunday. He said he'll stop by first thing in the morning. I'll give you new keys when the locks are swapped out. In a while I'll go home and get my sleeping bag and then spend the night in the café in case Ralph comes back." His no-nonsense expression reminded me of *Dat* when he was trying to drive home a point. "Please don't go in there alone."

"May I ask what Ralph did to get himself fired?"

"Besides being late almost every day? Glenn suspected he was stealing money from the till in the retail shop. One day, one of his employees saw Ralph's hand in the register. Glenn gave him a choice: He could quit, or Glenn would call the police and file charges. I thought that was generous of Glenn, don't you?"

"*Yah.* Stealing from your employer is like biting the hand that feeds you."

"I'm sure you never would, Eva. Glenn said you came with the highest of recommendations. Your former boss was disappointed to see you go."

I heaved a sigh of relief, but I still felt under Stephen's microscope. I wouldn't ask to borrow Autumn again until the owners got home. If Glenn didn't fire me then.

"I wonder where Ralph lives." Stephen scanned the wooded area behind the rows of mature trees at the rear of the nursery.

"He told me he lives with a relative. He must have arrived on foot."

"Most likely staying with a well-meaning family member who's only enabling his alcoholism." He glanced at me for an instant. "That could have been me if I hadn't come to my senses."

# Twenty-Four

That evening, as the sun lowered itself into a mattress of gloomy, gray clouds, I replayed the day in my head. I reminded myself visiting Amos was not a mistake. Our community relied upon one another's generosity, even if it meant my meeting up with Brandy.

"Your replacement carrying his child?" Olivia might say, jabbing me with her elbow.

My thoughts jumbled into one another until they were like a squiggly ball of tangled yarn after a couple of cats had batted it about. Alongside these chaotic thoughts galloped the memories of my parents sequestered in the little *daadi haus* as if they had no choice. No matter what *Dat* said, his working on the farm was what had kept him fit and healthy. He wasn't a man who enjoyed sitting around reading magazines and twiddling his thumbs. And what was going on with Reuben and Marta?

None of my business, I told myself. If I'd been paying more attention a couple of hours ago, Stephen wouldn't have seen me dillydallying in the buggy. I wondered how many tears I'd shed without even noticing. Pathetic.

A gentle rapping on the cabin's front door brought me out of my musings. In my befuddled state of mind, I was tempted not to answer.

"Evie?" I recognized Mark's voice.

"Just a moment." I glanced at myself in the mirror and cringed.

Maybe looking bedraggled would be a blessing and discourage his attentions. I wished I were attracted to him.

I turned the knob and opened the door. He was carrying a box of See's chocolates. "I thought I'd come by to see if you're up for a buggy ride." He handed me his gift.

"*Denki.*" I set it on the counter.

Mark looked so vulnerable and nervous that I couldn't help but smile to try to lessen his uneasiness.

"I just got home..." I covered my yawning mouth.

"Do ya have time to chat?"

I wanted to crawl into bed, but I couldn't voice my thoughts.

"Have ya had a bad day?" he said.

"A long one. And stressful."

"Have ya had your supper yet? I could take you to a restaurant somewhere close by."

"Yoo-hoo," Beatrice called from the back porch. "Remember, Evie, I'm planning to teach you how to make my chicken scaloppini. And you have tomorrow's soup to think about." She gave me an exaggerated wink I assumed was for my eyes only, as Mark had his back to her.

He shook his head in slow motion. "Tell her you're coming with me. You can cook with her tomorrow."

By the time I formulated an answer, Beatrice was only yards away.

"I'm sorry, Mark," I said. "I'd better stay here. I have lots to do."

"On the Lord's day of rest?"

"Maybe Sadie will go to the singing with you."

"Why on earth would you suggest her?"

"Just a thought."

"You know my mind better than I do?" He folded his arms across his chest. "If you have no interest in me, come out and say it."

Beatrice glided over to us. "Mark, would you like to stay for supper? I have plenty on hand."

Stephen trotted down the steps from the main house. "Does that invitation include me?"

"Of course. I already asked you."

"What are you doing here?" Mark asked him.

Stephen chuckled. "I could ask you the same question, although I think I know the answer."

Mark blushed, and then he shot Stephen a fierce glare.

"Stephen is planning to spend the night at the café," I told Mark. "A former employee with a key was in there stealing food last night. A man named Ralph."

"*Ach*." Mark nodded. "I remember him."

"I'm glad Stephen is staying," Beatrice said, "what with a vagrant sneaking into the café. Stephen told me all about it."

"I'd better go check the refrigerator to make sure there's enough food for tomorrow," I said. "I should have done it yesterday."

"I'll come with you," Stephen said. "Unless you're leaving with Mark."

I took in Mark's youthful features and saw a mixture of disappointment and indignation. "No, maybe another time." I hoped some pretty young woman would catch his fancy at the singing.

Stephen's cell phone chimed. He stepped away to answer. I listened to the ebb and flow of his tense voice. He finally returned. "That was Wayne." He stuffed the phone in his pocket. "There's a dead dog by the side of the road a few miles from here."

Beatrice crossed herself. "*Mio Dio*. Not our Heath, I pray."

"I'd better go check it out." Stephen dug his keys out of his jeans pocket. "I told Wayne I'd meet him to identify the animal."

"I want to come too," I said. "Sorry, Beatrice. I'll be right back." I had no appetite anyway. I scrambled after Stephen and ducked into the passenger side of his pickup. I buckled myself in as if I'd ridden in it a hundred times.

He started the engine. "Are you sure you want to come? Could be grisly."

"*Yah*." I was surprising myself. I didn't even like dogs, but I felt compelled to help.

Ten minutes later we neared Wayne's squad car at the side of the road. Wayne and another man stood speaking near the black outline of the dead animal. My heart sank, and my throat closed.

Stephen jolted to a halt behind Wayne's squad car and leaped out, only to return minutes later. He got back into the pickup and closed the door. "Poor beast was some kind of a Lab mix, but not our Heath."

Wayne sauntered over to the pickup, and Stephen lowered his window. "I need to tell you that another one of Bill Hastings's sheep was killed early this morning."

"Maybe I should drive back that way." Stephen jimmied his key into the ignition.

"Listen, Stephen, do us all a favor and let the police handle it. No telling what that man will do. I remember him from high school. Always a bully." Wayne's face was grim. "Please don't go back."

"Okay. I have troubles enough at the nursery. Eva found someone in the café last night."

Wayne's gaze scrutinized mine. "You did, Eva?"

"Yes. A disheveled fellow who said his name was Ralph."

"Remember that guy Glenn fired last year?" Stephen asked, and Wayne nodded.

"But Glenn never pressed charges, which makes it hard for me to do anything." Wayne rested his elbow on the window ledge. "He's a lush, but he seems harmless enough."

"You know who that must be?" Stephen slapped his forehead. "Ralph's last name is Hastings. He's Bill Hastings's brother."

"Yep, I was just thinking the same thing." Wayne spoke directly to me. "I'll keep an eye open and alert the rest of the crew. If he comes back, please call 9-1-1, Eva. If it's the same Ralph I know, he's never been violent, but you can't tell what a man will do when he's down on his luck and has had too much to drink."

"*Yah*, I'll be careful."

"I'll stay with her if she needs to go inside the café," Stephen said.

"*Denki*." I knew I'd be safe with him.

We entered the nursery's parking lot and rolled over to the main house. I was surprised to see Mark's horse and buggy still there.

"Beatrice must be feeding him supper." Stephen set the parking brake. "Looks as though you've found yourself a serious suitor, Evie."

I let out a weary sigh. My day had been like a roller coaster swerving off its tracks, and apparently the ride wasn't over yet. The back door opened, and Missy bounded out, followed by Minnie. As I exited the pickup, Minnie yapped and circled my feet, but Missy raced past us toward the café.

"Missy, come. Missy!" Stephen followed her, but he returned a few minutes later, saying she'd disappeared into the darkness.

"I wonder if she's following Heath's scent," Beatrice said as she and Mark both stepped onto the porch. "I've kept her in the house or on leash all day, although she tugged and tried to get away."

"It was my fault." Mark raked a hand through his hair. "She slipped right by me when I opened the door."

"Don't blame yourself." Beatrice's creased forehead betrayed her concern. "Missy was determined."

I was thankful she was being sympathetic with Mark, who seemed flustered, the way he ran his fingers around his shirt collar.

"Please come in, all of you." Beatrice had indeed been cooking. The kitchen's warm air was ambrosial with the scents of stewing chicken, garlic, oregano, and other tasty aromas I couldn't identify. But I still had no appetite.

The round table was set for four. Beatrice seated me between Mark and Stephen, and she landed across from me, nearest the stove.

Stephen led us in prayer, and then Beatrice served the meal. "What's wrong with everyone?" she asked when she saw us picking at our food." She put aside her fork. "I guess I'm not hungry either."

Stephen got to his feet. "Thanks so much, Beatrice, but I think I should check on the café for an unwelcome visitor and then zip home to fetch my sleeping bag." He took a leash.

"I'll come with you." I stood.

"Absolutely not," Beatrice said. "How can you possibly help if riff-raff is skulking around?"

"I should go with him to the café." Mark ramped up his volume and directed his words at me. "I do work here, even if it's Sunday."

"*Yah*, and so do I," I said with a snap. "I need to check the refrigerator to make sure Ralph didn't empty it."

"No one's even tried my dessert. I think you'll all agree my tiramisu is divine, if I do say so myself." Beatrice shook her head as we three made our way to the door. "Eva, please come back later and help me with the dishes."

"I will. And I'll try some of your tirami—your fancy dessert. I'm safer going to the café with an escort, don't you think?"

"I suppose. But please be careful."

"I'll walk her back," Mark said.

As we three neared the café, barking erupted. Missy galumphed over to us, her tail wagging. Behind her, Heath woofed and frolicked toward us, followed by Ralph, who squinted under Stephen's flashlight's beam.

"Heath! Good boy." Stephen patted his thigh, and the dog came to him. "Ralph, this had better be good."

"I—I was just bringing him home." Ralph slurred his words. I inhaled the bitter smell of liquor.

"You expect me to buy that?" Stephen clipped on Heath's leash. "You're drunk. I should call the police."

"No, please don't. I really was bringing the Yoders' dog back. He followed me home."

"Oh, yeah? When was that?"

"Uh...yesterday. Or a couple of days ago. I've always wanted a dog."

"And where exactly is home?"

"My brother Bill's basement, as long as I don't cause trouble." He wiped his nose on his shirtsleeve. "You see, his wife will kick me out. She hates me."

Stephen aimed his finger at Ralph. "Get out of here and don't return. If you do, I will take out a restraining order so you will be forbidden to set foot on this property again. I should press charges for stealing our food."

"But I'm broke. If you gave me my job back, I'd have money."

"Ralph, if you'd stay off the booze and..." He stepped closer, inspecting Ralph's eyes. "Are you on drugs too?"

"No. I swear. Nothing like that."

"As if I'd believe you." Stephen's mouth twisted. He put out his palm. "Give me the key."

"I don't have one."

"Give me a break. You made more than one copy." Stephen moved in on Ralph, who fished through his pocket and then flung a metal key at Stephen. Stephen caught it midair. "Get out of here."

As Ralph turned to skedaddle, Stephen grasped Heath's leash. "Apparently this dog has no sense of loyalty until Glenn and Rose return." Stephen fluffed the animal's coat. "Sure am glad to have you back, boy."

"Couldn't you give Ralph a second chance?" I asked Stephen once Ralph was gone. "God forgives us."

"When and if we repent. Only if Ralph attends AA, gets sober, and can prove it. For all we know, he's on drugs too. Those cost more, causing a man to do unthinkable things to support his addiction."

"I hear you used to booze it up," Mark said, and Stephen grimaced.

"You heard right. Almost ruined my life. It cost me the only woman I ever loved."

I wanted to ask him who this woman was, but I would have to bide my time until we were alone.

I moved toward the café. "Would this be a good time to inspect the kitchen?"

"Yes." Stephen pulled out his key ring, added the extra key, and unlocked the door. "I wonder how long Ralph has been coming in here and stuffing himself." Stephen turned to me. "You don't think Olivia knew about it, do you?"

"No. She never mentioned anything." About this man, anyway.

# Twenty-Five

I'd intended to crawl into bed, open my book, and concentrate on *A Room with a View* that evening, but Mark hung around as I helped clean Beatrice's kitchen. She'd already cleared the table, but the plates and dirty flatware were stacked in the sink.

"Everything all right at the café?" she asked me as I scrubbed.

"*Yah.*"

"You call running into an intruder okay?" Mark said. He'd told Beatrice about our encounter with Ralph as soon as we came in with Heath. I'd let her know Stephen left to pick up his sleeping bag and a few things from home before spending the night at the café.

Beatrice frowned, causing a crease between her brows. "I wonder how long he's been helping himself to food."

"My guess is ever since he was fired." I filled the sink with sudsy water even though the dishwasher yawned open.

"Probably since the café was built last fall," Mark said. "This guy has a drinking problem and can't be trusted." He sipped his coffee. "Stephen suffered from the same affliction."

He was bad-mouthing Stephen behind his back. I was tempted to defend Stephen, but I pretended I hadn't heard him. I hated gossip.

"I know nothing about that," Beatrice said. "But Stephen is a loyal and dependable employee. I can think of few men I trust more."

I rinsed the dishes and filed them in the drying rack, and Beatrice dried and put each one away. In no time the task was completed.

"Mark, I need to talk to Beatrice about tomorrow's soup."

"Go right ahead. I'll enjoy another cup of coffee." Apparently, he had no intentions of leaving until I did.

Beatrice seemed to be containing a smirk as she pressed her lips together. She brought down a cookbook from a shelf and opened it. "*Alora*, let's see what we can come up with."

Thirty minutes later, Beatrice yawned and told Mark and me she was tired. "I'll be in first thing in the morning, Eva," she assured me as she ushered us out the door. "Don't worry about a thing, but be sure to lock your door tonight."

As Mark walked me to my cabin, he said, "It's obvious Stephen has his eyes set on you. I certainly hope you don't feel the same way. He's not one of us."

"I realize that. But I nevertheless think very highly of him. And you're wrong if you think he has romantic feelings for me."

"Like you still have for Jake? I know you went to see him."

I was determined to end this conversation. "I paid a visit to his father, and I don't regret it." Even if I'd come face-to-face with Brandy.

"I don't see what you find so attractive about Jake to begin with." He ran his hands up his suspenders like a puffed-up rooster.

"Are you trying to tell me I'm not capable of making decisions for myself?"

"Hold on. The last thing I want to do is anger you. I'm trying to make sense of what you don't like about me."

"You mean that you are too young for me, and you are being judgmental?"

"I'm sorry if my honesty hurts your feelings, Evie, but you and I should start dating. I want to court you."

"What are you saying? We hardly know each other."

"I know that if I wait any longer, I'll never have a chance with you. I'd regret it the rest of my life." He drew so close I thought he was going to kiss me. "Tell me what I need to do to get your attention. Be a renegade like Jake? Is he the kind of man you want to father your children?"

"Please, Mark. Leave him out of this conversation." But my mind was writing its own narrative. Jake always loomed in my brain, forever out of reach.

"Fine, if you insist. But would you please come to the singing with me right now?"

He was beginning to annoy me with his persistence. How many times did I have to say no?

"Has no woman ever turned you down, Mark?"

"Not that I can think of. But no matter. You're the only one I want."

"As some sort of revenge against Jake?"

"*Nee*, I couldn't care less about him. I thought we weren't going to bring up his name again."

"Mark, please let me say good night to you, and we'll remain friends." Before I said something I couldn't take back.

"You'll regret this," were his parting words. Was he threatening me? No, this was just an inappropriate way to woo a woman that I chalked up to his youth. Once inside, I leaned against the door and let out a deep breath.

Ten minutes later a gentle rapping on my door made me jump. Mark had come back already? I swung the door open prepared for a verbal tussle and nearly walked into Jake, still dressed *Englisch*.

He pushed the door open wider and strode past me before I could say anything.

I peeked outside, and then I closed the door behind him. Fortunately, all the dogs were in the big house. I couldn't imagine Beatrice would let them out again tonight unless she accompanied them.

"How did you get here?" I asked him, recalling seeing him driving his *dat*'s buggy. But his mother also said he had an automobile.

"A car I borrowed from an *Englisch* friend in New York. Brandy's older *bruder*."

"Then why were you driving your *dat*'s buggy the other day?"

"I told you. Brandy said she'd always wanted to ride in a buggy."

Hearing Jake speak her name made me feel prickly inside, but I couldn't help being happy to see him. And both he and Brandy had assured me he wasn't the father of her baby. Yet I had to wonder if they were painting a facade for his *mamm*'s sake. And mine.

I tried to rid my mind of Brandy's image. "I didn't hear a car. How long have you been here?"

"Long enough." He widened his stance and tilted his head. "Long enough to see you have suitors coming out your ears. And here you were trying to make me feel guilty because I'm helping out one young woman in trouble."

"*Nee*, I wasn't. I was just surprised to meet her." My hands clamped on my hips. "I feel sorry for her, but shouldn't she be home with her parents?"

"She told you. They booted her out. It's a long story, but the bottom line is that I'm not the father. Do you believe me?"

"I want to."

I drifted into the kitchen area, and I leaned back on the lip of the sink. He placed a hand on either side, pinning me against it. "Are you ever going to forgive me, Evie?"

"You haven't asked for forgiveness."

"I thought— Well, I thought you'd given up on me." Light from the main house illuminated his face enough to see his manly features.

"I thought you'd completely forgotten me." I folded my arms across my chest. "And I see no evidence to the contrary or that you care about anyone but yourself, unless it's Brandy."

Outside, Millie yapped. I froze and put one hand to Jake's lips to hush him. He nibbled my fingers, but I turned away and stepped out of his reach. "Don't you dare," I whispered.

Minutes later, I heard Beatrice's voice fade as she closed her back door.

Jake said, "Come on. Let me take you to my folks' house for a little bit. My *mamm* begged me to fetch you."

"Pay a visit twice in one day? But it's so late."

"*Mamm* doesn't care. Anything to get *Dat* back."

"I'm not a doctor. What could I possibly accomplish?"

"So far no one has accomplished more than you have."

# Twenty-Six

"*Denki* for coming, Eva." Ruth fluttered toward me to bestow a hug. Never had I expected Jake's mother to show such affection.

"It wasn't easy." Jake removed his baseball cap and hung it on a peg in the kitchen next to Amos's straw hat. Jake and I both stepped out of our shoes. "But I finally convinced her to come."

If anyone had seen me get into his borrowed car, I was doomed. It was a beater in need of paint, but nonetheless, I was in a motorized vehicle alone with him.

"Amos is still in the hospital bed, but his head is propped up." Ruth's face glowed with childlike expectancy.

As I walked toward him, Amos lifted his chin the tiniest bit, and his eyes focused on me. "Eva..."

"Hello, Amos. How are you doing?" I had no idea what to do or say. The sheet and blanket covered him to his beard.

His lips moved, but he remained silent.

"He's trying to speak!" Excitement filled Ruth's voice. "Please, Eva, sit on the side of the bed."

I felt uncomfortable as I neared this man I barely knew. He'd never liked me as far as I could tell. Or maybe he never noticed me. I perched on the corner of the bed, near his feet. His gaze followed me. Hoping for encouragement or direction, I looked to Ruth. "What should I do?"

"How about seeing if he'll eat a couple of teaspoons of this?" She lifted a bowl of tomato soup and a spoon from a nearby table and handed them to me.

I stood and dipped the teaspoon into the soup for a small portion and then brought it to Amos's lips as Ruth tucked a towel under his chin. Fortunately, I had experience feeding my nieces.

When Amos noticed the spoon, he parted his lips and allowed me to serve him a mouthful, and then another. Ruth was nearly beside herself with excitement. "You have a way with him, Eva," she said, her voice giddy. "I couldn't get Amos to take even a taste before you got here."

Amos's hand jiggled. Ruth swooped to his side. "Look, the doctor said he might start moving on his own."

I wondered how she knew what Amos did or did not want. *Mamm* said she could always tell what my *dat* was thinking, but I had no clue as to what Jake thought about anything.

"You told me a therapist is coming tomorrow," I said. "In the meantime, I don't see how I can help Amos."

"I know my husband better than anyone does. He wants to see you, and your being here helps him. I'm sure of it."

My heart went out to her, but she was asking for the impossible.

Brandy descended the stairs wearing a smock over black tights. Ruth glanced at me. "She's really a very sweet girl. And she's been helping me out immensely. Doing the wash, helping me clean." She smiled as Brandy entered the room. "But I still think she should return to her parents. They must be worried sick, no matter what they said before."

Brandy's expression soured. "They don't love me, and they want me to put the baby up for adoption the moment it's born."

"Perhaps that's a good idea if you can't take care of it properly." Ruth's gray eyes were filled with compassion. "Mennonites in this area adopt. Occasionally, Amish do too."

Brandy's hands moved across her belly. "I could never have a stranger raise my baby."

"But how will you support it?" I asked. "Where will you live?"

"Maybe I could stay here as long as Ruth lets me. I'm a hard worker."

"But once you give birth, how can you do housekeeping, help with Amos, and take care of your baby all at the same time?"

"I'll have to find a way." Her long flaxen hair covered half her face like a veil.

Amos swallowed, drawing our attention to him.

"What is it, Amos?" Ruth sailed to his side.

I imagined Amos was frustrated, stuck in a lifeless body. Other than to pray for him, what could I do for this invalid?

Brandy disappeared into the kitchen and came back with a glass of water with a straw. She put the straw to his mouth, and he sucked.

"Thank you," Ruth said to her.

"No problem." Brandy turned to Jake. "Hey, can I use the car?"

"Sure." He dug out the key.

"No, wait a minute." I shot to my feet. "How will I get home?"

"Jake could use our buggy," Ruth said.

"That would take too long." I had to put an end to this craziness. "I should leave in five minutes."

"So soon?" Ruth said. "You just got here."

"But I have work early tomorrow."

"Evie, is it all right if we take Brandy with us?" Jake stepped closer to Brandy, as if they were best buddies.

"Hey, whatever works," Brandy said before I could answer.

"What's open this time of night that you want to go there so badly?" Jake asked Brandy. "Please don't say you're going to start smoking again,"

"Smoking is bad for the baby," Ruth said.

"No, I'll be good. I have an outrageous craving for ice cream. Is that so terrible?"

"And how about homemade dill pickles?" The corners of Ruth's mouth curved up.

"Now that you mention it, dill pickles sound fantabulous." She combed her fingers through her sumptuous tresses.

Ruth grinned. "Bring the ice cream home, and the pickles will be waiting. I mustn't act prideful, but I doubt you'll taste better anywhere in the county."

"Thank you, Mrs. Miller."

"You know we go by first names around here. Call me Ruth, dear." She slid her arm around the young woman's shoulders.

I was struck by the fact Brandy fit into this household better than I did. As if I were shrinking. I paused at Amos's bed out of courtesy and patted his hand. "Goodbye, Amos." I still wasn't sure he knew who I was.

"Goodbye, Eva," he murmured, much to my astonishment. "Come back soon. *Yah*?"

"Of course she will," Ruth said with enthusiasm. "In the meantime, you'll get better. We'll get you on your feet."

Amos's body seemed nearly lifeless, as if his brain had forgotten how to direct his limbs. From what Olivia told me and the article I'd read, I knew he might have to relearn how to walk—how to do everything.

# Twenty-Seven

When Jake opened the car's door, Brandy leaped in and sat in the center of the bench seat. I guessed I'd been so distracted I hadn't noticed the litter on the floor and the saccharine odor from an air-freshener dangling from the rearview mirror.

I scooted in next to Brandy and closed my door.

"I'm low on gas." Jake slammed his door. "I think there's a little twenty-four-hour store next to the gas station down on Route 30."

"Oh, I can hardly wait." Brandy wrapped her arms around her tummy. "Turn the heater up, Jakie, I'm freezing."

"Then why didn't you wear a jacket?"

His question inspired a giggle. "I was so excited about the ice cream I clean forgot. None of them fit anymore anyway."

"Seems like you act before thinking." Jake released the parking brake.

"I could say the same thing for you, Jake," barged out of her mouth.

"Can't argue with you there." Jake turned a knob on the dashboard. "This should warm us up."

As we drove out onto the road, I was happy to feel heat on my feet. Brandy and Jake chatted like siblings. But I couldn't help but wonder if they'd been intimately acquainted at one time. I finally scrounged up the courage to ask, "How do you two know each other?"

"Through my big brother." Brandy rotated her head to speak. "This is his car, but he got another DWI and lost his driver's license for six months. But he still won't let me use it. I can drive as well as Jake."

Jake chuckled. "If you say so. But you don't have a driver's license."

"You do?" I asked Jake, who nodded.

"I can still drive as well as you," Brandy said.

"But you can barely see over the steering wheel." Jake snorted a laugh.

She gave his shoulder a playful punch as a younger sister might. Still, I didn't completely buy the whole scenario.

"How old are you, Brandy?" My words sounded snarly.

The car fell silent for a moment except for the grumbling muffler and the sound of a truck passing in the opposite direction. "Brandy, how old are you?" I asked again, trying to sound less accusative.

"Seventeen. By the time the baby's born in two months, I'll be eighteen. Nice and legal."

"*Ach*, so young." I shouldn't pass judgment, as I'd loved Jake since age sixteen and had had a crush on him from afar for years earlier. Thankfully, he had not pressured me with his amorous actions. Maybe Brandy's boyfriend had forced himself on her.

Minutes later, Jake pulled into a gas station and stood outside pumping fuel into the tank. Because I had nothing to lose by being nosy, I pursued my questions. "Brandy, who's your baby's father?"

"A friend of one of my brothers." She inched away from me.

"Does he know you're pregnant?" It felt odd speaking of such personal matters, especially with someone I hardly knew.

"Yeah, but the only thing he offered me was money for an abortion. Nice guy, huh? And he said he'll deny the whole thing."

"They have DNA tests now." I'd read about it. "How old is he?"

"Twenty-five, not that I should believe anything he says. He's a rat."

Jake climbed back into the car carrying a brown paper bag. "Here's the ice cream."

Brandy clapped. "Goody. I can hardly wait." She grabbed the bag from him and peeked inside. "Three kinds? What did you get?"

"Strawberry, vanilla, and chocolate-chip cookie dough."

She leaned over and smooched his cheek. "You know my favorites, you sweetie pie."

I wondered if he still recalled my favorite. Apparently not.

"They were sold out of caramel swirl, Evie," he said, proving me wrong. He leaned forward to catch my gaze. "Well, did you think I'd forget your favorite ice cream? Or that you like half-and-half in your coffee?"

"Jake has the best memory of anyone I know." Brandy's voice rose in pitch.

"As I recall, he had a good memory in school."

"Jake's so smart, he got his GED in the blink of an eye." She snapped her fingers.

"Really, Jake?" I looked past her. "You got a GED?"

"*Yah*. I thought, why not?" He eased up on the gas. "Actually, I made a bet with Brandy's brother. He said he was smarter than I was because he'd gone through high school and all I had was eight grades."

"You showed him, didn't you?" Brandy slapped her knee. "Jake, please, please, please won't you just take me back to your parents' so this ice cream doesn't melt? I can't stand to wait another minute. I should have brought a spoon."

He chuckled. "Okay. If Evie doesn't mind."

"I guess not, if it'll only add a few minutes. But then I really do need to get back."

Brandy turned on the radio, and a raucous song I'd never heard before blasted out. Both she and Jake swayed to the heavy metal music and sang along.

"Turn that off." I felt myself being sucked into an evil domain, rubbing elbows with Satan.

Jake complied even with Brandy's moaning, "Hey, that's my favorite song. Party pooper."

He pulled a U-turn, causing an oncoming buggy to slow. The driver lifted a hand in a friendly gesture. I hoped he recognized Jake and not me. An Amish woman wearing a *kapp* in an automobile would be hard to ignore.

Minutes later, Jake cruised into his parents' barnyard. He came to an abrupt stop, opened his door, and got out. Brandy exited the car and scampered up the Millers' back steps, clutching the brown bag. She opened the unlocked door and bopped inside. Jake slid back onto the seat.

He was quiet for a moment. "Why don't we join her? Doesn't ice cream sound *gut*?"

"I don't have time. You promised to get me home right away."

"But maybe my *dat* will try some if you give it to him."

"Your *mamm* and Brandy can manage. Please don't pressure me." Although the image of Amos tasting the ice cream filled me with affection for the crusty older man. "Maybe he'll regain his strength."

"Or possibly slip deeper into his cocoon." Jake put the car in reverse. "Despite *Mamm*'s optimism, I doubt he'll ever get better." He rolled the car out of the barnyard. "Which makes me the worst son in the world for leaving him, *yah*? Maybe if I'd been here..."

"I feel terrible for your parents, but what about me? I thought we had something special." To put it mildly. "You abandoned all of us."

"Back then I thought you'd deserted me too." He gripped the wheel. "I wasn't thinking straight, only of myself."

Jake nosed the automobile back onto the road. Riding with him in the car felt all wrong. An *Englischer* and an Old Order Amish woman in a car together was like a dog and a cat sharing a food bowl. I was glad the streetlights were few and far between. Each seemed like a spotlight, especially when we passed a buggy. Jake proceeded past them as if he were meant to drive a motorized vehicle.

"Is this only a temporary stay?" I was afraid to hear his answer. "Or are you planning to live with your parents and join the church?"

"I haven't gotten that far. I'll probably stay at least long enough to find out if *Dat* makes it. He could croak, you know."

"What a horrible thing to say."

"Well, it's the truth."

"Says who?"

"The neurologist at the trauma center. He warned *Mamm* not to bring him home. But *Mamm* just crossed her arms and said, 'If he's going to die, I want him at the farm with me.'" Jake tapped the steering wheel as if replaying the rock song in his mind. "Even if he lives, he'll never be able to work again. Not like he did before."

"Meaning you'll stay?"

"*Yah.* If he can't work the farm, what would happen to *Mamm*? She can't keep the farm going or even do her chores if she's tending to his needs. Maybe Brandy will stay and help her for room and board."

I wondered if he and Brandy had already agreed upon a scheme.

"With a *boppli,* Brandy will need help herself."

"Let's leave Brandy out of this discussion, Evie. You'd be my real motivation for staying. If you'd take me for your husband over all your other suitors." He pulled off to the side and rolled to a stop. "But you don't seem to care for me anymore."

I still adored Jake with all my heart. But trusting him was another subject. He'd believed all the gossip about me. And now he'd just proposed and then retracted the invitation? Despite his many attributes, he was as unstable as ever.

He turned toward me and said, "If you won't wed me, I might marry Brandy to give her child a father. No child should grow up without one."

"What? You'd marry a woman you don't even love?" A searing pain stretched from my throat to my stomach.

"Well, you won't marry me, will you?" he said, his voice turning acidic.

"How could I marry an *Englischer*, Jake? You're not even Amish anymore."

"And you are? If you ask me, you've used me as an excuse to not join the church."

"How dare you? You think I'd forsake *Gott* for you?"

As we neared the nursery, the sky turned dark. We passed a buggy coming from the other direction. Mark was driving and had a young lady nestled at his side. Was it Olivia?" It was hard to tell in Jake's headlamps. No, it was her younger sister, Emma, almost Olivia's spitting image. She was giggling and clinging to Mark's arm. His gaze zeroed in on me, and his jaw dropped. His arms straightened, and his torso lifted from his seat, but he offered no salutation. He'd gone to the singing after all and found himself a date. Not necessarily a date, but a girl to escort home. He wasn't moping over me. Which was good.

Maybe Mark would keep what he saw to himself. But Emma would tell Olivia, and then the whole county would hear about me. Again.

Wait. Olivia said she was leaving with her boyfriend last night. Why was Emma at a singing if her sister ran off? Didn't she care? Or maybe Olivia changed her mind. I didn't know how to find out without risking getting her into more trouble.

"Better drop me off somewhere," I told Jake as we closed in on the nursery.

"*Nee*, I can't leave you alone."

I recalled Ralph and decided I did want an escort after all. The man could be prowling around and harbor a grudge against me.

"Jake, maybe you could park in that used car lot and walk with me the rest of the way. It looks closed." The interior lights of the brick one-story building had been dimmed, leaving only a few exterior lamps.

He slapped the turn indicator. "Okay. This clunker will fit right in."

"When I saw you driving Brandy the other day, you looked in your element," I said.

He shot me a look of skepticism. "You mean because I was using the buggy? No sooner did we get here than she started pestering me to give her a ride in ours."

"And how did it feel driving the horse?"

"What are you getting at?"

"Could you ever live without a car again?"

"I doubt it. But I'll need to return this one to Jeff and then take the bus or train back—if I return. Or buy another. I was earning good money up there. And I've been saving it. When I go, you should come with me. We could take a side trip to Niagara Falls."

"Or Florida?"

"Isn't that the wrong direction?"

"*Yah*, but really, if you could go anywhere, where would you pick?" I knew we were playing in the Land of Make-Believe, as we had as teens. "I'd choose Italy." I could hardly believe what I'd declared. "I'm reading a novel Beatrice lent me."

He chuckled. "That's more than a bit out of the way."

"Then how about the Grand Canyon?"

"It's out of the way too, but maybe someday we could go there. You never know." He shot me a fleeting glance. "You could help me drive."

I guffawed. "I don't have a clue how to drive a car, and you know it."

"Well, then, let's change that right now." Jake came to a halt in the far end of the car lot, next to a squat building with a sign that said *Auto Parts*. All customers and staff had left hours ago, I assured myself.

He swiveled in his seat to speak to me. "Have you never driven a car? Not even once?"

"*Nee*. Never."

"Not even in your running-around time?"

Technically, I still was in *rumspringa* because I hadn't yet committed to a lifetime as a church member. "I'm not capable of driving an automobile."

"I bet you're more capable than you know. Why don't you give it a try?" His voice was tinged with amusement. Or maybe he was teasing all in fun. In any case, I'd ignore him.

"I might." I angled my head toward him and raised an eyebrow. "Sometime. When I'm *gut* and ready. Not when you're badgering me."

"Come on, Evie. Seize the moment." He opened his door and got out. "Sit here." He beckoned me to slide behind the steering wheel.

Like a ninny I obeyed. "I shouldn't." I scanned around to see if anyone was watching.

He chortled. "This may be your last chance if you're serious about getting baptized." He was taunting me. "Come on, don't be a scaredy-cat. There's nothing to it. You can drive a buggy, can't you?"

"But our mare understands what I tell her. And she obeys."

"Same with this car. More people die in horse-related accidents than in cars."

"I don't believe that for a minute. Who told you such a ridiculous thing?"

"An *Englisch* friend looked it up on the Internet on his iPhone."

"And you believe everything you hear?"

"At least I'm willing to take a risk, unlike you."

My fingers rose to touch the steering wheel. It was wrapped with leather and felt secure in my hands. I knew I was doing wrong, but being alone with Jake in the first place was wrong.

In a burst of bravado, I was ready to spread my wings. To prove myself mistaken. Maybe I was my own worst enemy. "Okay, but don't say I didn't warn you."

I reached down and turned the key. A screeching metallic sound erupted.

"Whoa, slow down. The engine's already running." Jake closed my door, jogged around the car, and jumped into the passenger seat. "Do you know where the gas pedal and brakes are?"

"*Yah*, I've watched you."

"The car's in park, so..." The headlamps shone against a brick wall into the empty store.

"I know." I was pleased I could release the parking brake and maneuver the transmission into reverse easily. Maybe driving wasn't so difficult after all.

I pressed my foot on the gas pedal. The car rocketed backward into something large and metal. We stopped short, my head bobbing forward. "*Ach*. I'm afraid to look."

Jake gawked over his shoulder. "You had the car in reverse."

"*Yah*, I couldn't go forward, now could I?"

"But you didn't check over your shoulder to see if anything was behind us."

"What could possibly be behind us?" My head whipped around to see uniformed Wayne, his scowl illuminated in the car lot's overhead lights, inspecting the damage I'd done to his squad car.

# Twenty-Eight

"Okay, both of you. Get out." Wayne wrenched open my door. "Not even wearing a seat belt, young lady?"

My hand moved to my waist. "Oh, sorry. I didn't think to."

"Looks like you weren't thinking of much." As I clambered to my feet, he said, "I won't even ask to see your driver's license, Eva Lapp. That's your name, isn't it?" He was all business, his features bunched as he looked across the hood at Jake. "How about you, Jake? I don't suppose you have a driver's license."

"Yes, I do, as a matter of fact." He pulled out his wallet and extracted his license. "I was driving tonight—for the most part—not Evie. And this is private property, not a public road."

"Yeah, but not your property, right?" Wayne scanned his dented squad car and grimaced. "How am I going to explain this to my sergeant?"

Out of the corner of my eye, I saw a white pickup ease into the lot, and then noticed Stephen. Scowling, he paused for a moment before getting out and heading over to Wayne without glancing my way.

"What brings you out this time of night?" Wayne asked him.

"I'm on my way to the nursery." Stephen's features were stamped with disapproval. "I called Beatrice to make sure the dogs were in, and now I'm going to spend the night in the café in case Ralph comes back. We can't be sure how many keys he had made, and we can't get the locks changed until tomorrow morning."

Stephen finally looked me in the face for a moment, shook his head, and then turned away.

I shivered as the evening breeze picked up velocity.

"I was doing the driving." Jake stepped between Wayne and me.

"Listen, don't try to feed me any garbage. I know what I saw." Wayne looked me up and down. "That's the last time I'll park behind an Amish woman driving a car. It all happened before I could get out of her way." He surveyed the dent again. "I suppose it could be worse. But I'll be the laughingstock at the station."

"I'll take the rap for it," Jake said. "I deserve to. I coaxed her into trying something she didn't want to do."

Stephen moved in on us. "She had no business driving without proper instruction, which I would have been glad to give her if that's what she wanted."

Wayne inspected Jake's driver's license. "Looks okay, but I'll have to check for outstanding warrants." Perspiration glistened on his face. "Any proof of ownership in the car?"

"I didn't steal it, if that's what you mean." Jake got back into the car and rifled through the glove box. "The owner's certificate must be in here."

A crooked smirk on his face, Wayne stood with his arms crossed. "You mean the license plate certificate? At least the tabs are current."

"I'll give you a ride home," Stephen told me.

Jake must have heard him because he poked his head out and said, "No, you won't. I'm taking Evie home."

Wayne neared Jake and sniffed the air. "I should give you a Breathalyzer test, Jake. Have you been drinking? Smoking dope?"

"No, no, none of that." Jake waved him away.

Wayne grabbed hold of Jake's arm. "Unless I see a little more cooperation and respect, you're spending the night in jail."

"Come on, Evie," Stephen said, "I'll drop you off at the cabin."

"But Beatrice will see us."

"So? I have every reason to be there. I'm making sure you get home safely."

Wayne and Jake were arguing, so I turned away from them and pretended I couldn't hear their jagged words. I climbed into the pickup's cab.

The accident was my blunder, and I should stay and pay the consequences, not Jake. "It was my fault," I told Stephen. "Jake's trying to protect me."

"So he put you behind the wheel without teaching you how to drive first? Some protection."

Stephen steered his pickup onto the road. "What are you doing hanging out with him?" He gripped the wheel. "Yeah, yeah, I know his father's ill, but don't let Jake sucker you in."

Minutes later, we were entering the nursery's expansive parking lot. Stephen pulled to a halt near the retail shop and left the engine idling.

"I only wish..." I felt like a failure.

"What? That you could learn to drive?"

"*Yah*, that might have been my one and only opportunity, and I blew it." My world felt topsy-turvy. "I'll never have another chance."

"I can help you learn to drive if you really want to." Stephen turned to face me and inspected my expression. "But no pressure if you say no." His voice was assuring but not pushy. With him I felt confident.

"*Yah*, I do want to try—as long as you don't let me run into anything."

"There's not much to hit in this huge parking lot." He gave me a methodical lesson on which pedals did what, and then he adjusted the mirrors and the steering wheel. We switched places. "Buckle in and take a moment to look around. Now, go easy, okay? We're in no hurry."

"*Yah*, okay." I tapped the gas pedal so lightly the vehicle crept a few feet and then stopped.

"You can give it more gas, Evie."

I pressed harder and the pickup gained momentum.

"Turn the steering wheel to the right." His hand grasped onto it to help me rotate the wheel. "And you can try going a little faster."

My foot punched the gas pedal, spinning the rear wheels out on the gravel. It felt like ice-skating on the pond in winter.

"Ease up on the gas." He reached over to take the wheel as my foot jammed on the brakes. "It's all or nothing with you," he said. "Have you never heard of the saying 'moderation in all things'?"

I thought I was going to cry, but instead giggles erupted from my mouth. Stephen chortled too until the cab was bursting with laughter. Tears of hilarity sprang to my eyes. His eyes were brimming too.

Without thinking, I collapsed into his arms. As quickly as our laughter started, it subsided. His face was inches from mine. He bent his head closer, and his lips brushed against my cheek. A gentle and sweet kiss, but a kiss nevertheless. I wanted to kiss him back, to sink into his embrace, but sanity took hold. I pushed away and leaned against the cab's door.

Stephen straightened his back. "I'm sorry. I shouldn't have done that. Please forgive me."

I sat in silence for several moments, pondering my actions. I wanted to drive an automobile. I was tempted to kiss Stephen, and I still might.

"I must ask you to forgive me," I said. "You could lose your job."

"For kissing you?" The backs of his fingertips directed stray hairs behind my ears.

"Isn't there a rule about fraternizing with the employees?"

"I don't think so. Or against falling in love with one. Several Amish couples working here have later become wedded."

"But they were both Amish, *yah*?"

"Yes, they were." He took hold of one of my *kapp*'s strings and twirled it between two fingers. "And I'm not. You know I'm attracted to you, don't you?"

I stared back at him in disbelief.

"It doesn't seem you're in a rush to become baptized."

"I promised my parents I would. I was planning to, but now I don't know."

He flicked the string behind my back. "Are you waiting for Jake to make up his mind before you do? You could wait forever for him and never be wed." The truth of his words stung.

"When I drove Beatrice over to the Millers' and met Brandy, it was plain to see she dotes on Jake." He expelled a lengthy sigh. "And no, I don't believe Jake's story about not being the father. I expect she'll give birth to a towheaded baby—blond like both parents."

The image had entered my mind earlier tonight, but I'd tried to brush it away like a cobweb that wouldn't let go. I pictured Jake cradling the baby in his arms and felt a flood of grief saturate my heart.

"Wouldn't Ruth and Amos be thrilled to have Jake and their new grandchild living with them?" Stephen brought me back to the present. "I'm sorry. I don't mean to make you sad. But sometimes facing the truth is for the best, even if painful."

"Then why does Amos ask for me?" I recalled Amos's shriveled lips mouthing my name.

"The man's mind is all messed up. His memory's shot?"

"No one knows for sure."

"It's time to move on, Evie. Even if Amos remembers you, what does that have to do with Jake? Has he been faithful to you?" Stephen's words felt like a needed slap in the face to bring me back to reality.

My hand moved to the nape of my neck. "*Nee.* Out of sight, out of mind. And he believed the rumors about me without even verifying them." I felt salty moisture pushing behind my eyes, but I held it in. I was done crying over Jake Miller.

# Twenty-Nine

The sun was fully up, the light threading itself past the window shades and making a slit of gold color along the left side of my single bed. Promises of a beautiful day, but I felt in a benumbed state, slow and doltish. I pushed to a sitting position and propelled myself out of bed. I needed to scramble.

As I entered the café, my mood spiraled upward upon hearing Beatrice singing an Italian song in the kitchen. Stephen and his sleeping bag must already be gone.

"Hope you don't mind that I started the soup." She grinned over her shoulder. "I know we talked about a different soup yesterday, but I couldn't sleep. So I got out my grandmother's cookbook and found a family recipe that's out of this world. *Molto deliciosa.*"

I inhaled the aroma of browning sausage. "What are you making?"

"*Zuppa Toscana.*"

"*Ach*, that sausage smells so good."

"That's because it's Italian." She stirred her concoction of sausage, diced onions, garlic, and crushed red peppers. "Would you please wash and slice these potatoes for when I need them?"

"Of course. Anything you say." Her good mood was infectious—exactly what I needed after a confused and sleepless night.

"I'll add chicken stock and heavy cream later." She kissed the air for effect. "Our customers will rave about it, I promise. You know, ten percent of the population in Lancaster County is of Italian descent. But Amish customers will love this soup too."

"That's news to me. I hadn't heard that statistic." I wondered if she were teasing me. "Are you sure?"

"*Certo*—absolutely. Why, I wouldn't be surprised if Stephen Troyer weren't of Italian descent."

"But he's Mennonite, and his last name isn't Italian."

Her belly shook as she chuckled. "Stephen took his adoptive parents' last name. He told me once he'd never met his father. I'd say he's at least half Italian with that striking profile."

"Really? You think he's handsome?"

"What woman wouldn't? But I'm afraid he's too young for me." She smirked. "It's a shame he's not Amish, Eva." She raised her brows, as if she'd been watching Stephen and me out the window last night. The dogs had no doubt heard Stephen's truck and our voices and had awakened her.

Reliving spending time with Stephen last night, I couldn't remember when I had last laughed so hard or experienced so much fun. Later, when he walked me to my cabin, in my wild, impetuous mood, I might have kissed him on the lips if he'd tried. He'd lingered longer than seemed necessary. The electrical current zinging between us was not my imagination.

Urgent rapping on the back door ended my musings. I scuttled to open the door and found Olivia's brother carrying her baked goods in a cardboard box. He set the box down hard and swung around to face me. "Have you seen Liv? Has she called you here?"

"She stopped by a couple of days ago." I recalled my promise to her and now wished she hadn't confided in me.

Her brother's bearded face was stern, his eyes growing small. "If you know where she is, Eva, please tell me. Our parents are frantic."

"I don't know where she is." That was the truth. "I'm sorry I can't help you. I know she has a boyfriend, but I've never met him."

He pinched between his eyes. "Did you encourage her to leave us?"

"Absolutely not! I never would." The fact I might never see my dear cousin again filled me with despair. I didn't have many women friends.

He expelled a weighty breath. "I'd best be on my way or I'll be late to work."

"Wait a minute." I sniffed in the aroma of the baked goods. "Who did the baking this morning?" I didn't want to let on that Olivia told me she'd have Emma bake.

"Our younger *schweschder*, Emma."

I wouldn't mention seeing Emma in Mark's buggy last night, although I doubted anyone in her family would disapprove of Mark. Still, Amish couples liked to keep their dating habits confidential. "I hear she's a fine cook. I'll be delighted to try her whoopie pies today."

He tossed me a blank look as if he weren't listening. "My hunch is she knows where Olivia is, but Emma refuses to say a word. If she stops by later or calls here, please ask her, will ya?"

"Well, I don't know. I'd better stay out of it. I need Emma's help with the baked goods."

His upper lip lifted into a snarl, but thankfully he didn't state his opinion.

After he left, I told Beatrice and Sadie we had a new baker for now. "Olivia's away." Fortunately, neither of the women asked where Olivia had gone. I'd fibbed enough for one day.

Ten minutes later, Emma called from her family's phone shanty and asked if her baking was up to Olivia's caliber.

"Are ya happy with my whoopie pies?" Her voice sounded exuberant, not like a young woman whose older sister had run away from home, which puzzled me.

"Beatrice and I were going to sample one as soon as they arrived, but then we got too busy. I'm sure they'll be as delicious as Olivia's. She said you're a fine cook."

"She did? I'm so happy to hear that. Does this mean I'm hired?"

"*Yah*, Emma, you're hired for a week to start, to produce our baked desserts. Can I count on you?" I imagined she was basking in her accolades.

"*Yah*, as long as my parents don't nix the idea. But so far they're happy with the arrangement because I won't be working in a store with tourists." She seemed a regular little chatterbox, not the little sister treading in Olivia's shadow. I imagined spending time with Mark yesterday evening had boosted Emma's ego. She'd probably been the envy of every young woman at the singing last night. But I wasn't the least bit sorry I hadn't attended.

"Will your *bruder* keep delivering the baked goods?" I asked.

"He said he would. If not, I'll just have to find another man. Maybe Mark, who works for the nursery. You know which man I mean, right?"

"*Yah*. In fact, I can see him out the café's window." Fortunately, he didn't glance my way as he passed by pushing an empty wheelbarrow.

Minutes later, Stephen strolled in. "Everything okay?"

"*Yah*." I lowered my eyes in embarrassment. I assumed he felt the same way, as if we both regretted crossing the invisible boundary of propriety.

Only Beatrice seemed at ease and said, "Don't keep us in suspense. Did Ralph return to the café last night?"

"No. And Wayne's men staked out Bill Hastings's place, but they didn't see him there either." Stephen finally glanced my way. "The bottom line is the police have pronounced Heath innocent. They think coyotes have been killing the man's sheep."

"Hurray!" I never thought I'd care for a canine. "Does Glenn know?"

"Yep, I texted him right away. There's a three-hour difference, so I didn't want to call and wake him."

"I'm so happy." Beatrice butterfly-clapped her hands. "May I let him run out during the day?"

"Well, better wait on that." Stephen glanced at me out of the corner of his eye, making me wonder if he knew I was still afraid of Heath at a stratum so deep I couldn't shake it.

Stephen helped himself to coffee. "The locksmith should be here soon." He aimed his voice at me. "I don't want you ever coming in here again and finding you're not alone." He paused. "No more acts of heroism, okay?"

Sunlight danced off Beatrice's gold hoop earrings. "When Glenn and Rose return, everything will be back to normal."

"I hope so." Stephen sent me a furtive glance I couldn't interpret.

I figured nothing would ever be normal again. Jake was possibly planning to marry Brandy—maybe more to spite me than to give her baby a father—and I might not join the church so I could explore a relationship with Stephen. If he were even interested.

Sadie arrived twenty minutes late, which wasn't like her. When I met her at the back door, she looked bewildered, her posture slumped.

"Don't waste any more of your time hoping for Mark," she whispered. "He's just stringing you along." She wrestled off her jacket and hung it on a hook. "I saw him last night at the singing, all lovey-dovey with Emma, Olivia's little *schweschder*. Then they both hopped in his buggy, laughing and joking as if they'd never been so happy."

I wrapped an arm around her shoulders. "I'm sorry, Sadie." I couldn't tell her under what circumstances I'd also seen the couple. Or that I was glad to be free of Mark's attentions.

We joined Stephen and Beatrice in the kitchen. Beatrice placed a chocolate whoopie pie on a plate and sliced it into quarters, its frothy filling bulging out. "Let's sample one of these." She grinned as she wiped the knife on her finger and tasted the filling. Then her mouth puckered, and she spit into her palm and dumped its contents into the garbage. Coughing, she poured a glass of water and gulped it down. "We have a problem."

"What?" I nibbled a bite, but my mouth refused to swallow the offensive taste. I washed it down with a mouthful of coffee.

Sadie burst into a ripple of laughter. "What are you doing? Playing a joke?"

"I wish." I sipped more coffee.

"Here, give me some." Stephen's large hand scooped up a morsel, which he plunked in his mouth. His face contorted. He turned away and spit his bite into the garbage too. "This is terrible." He poured some water and cleansed his mouth.

Sadie shook her head and giggled. "I'm not eating any. Is it rat poison?"

"Tastes like it." Stephen swigged more water.

Beatrice shook her head. "I wonder if she used salt instead of sugar. We certainly can't serve these to the customers."

"Evie, call Olivia right away," Stephen said.

I hated to be the bearer of bad news when Stephen had so much else to deal with. "Her brother says she's away. Her younger sister, Emma, cooked these."

"Why didn't Olivia warn us?" Stephen said. "We'll have to buy some at a local bakery."

"All is not lost. I can easily bake corn bread and bran muffins." Beatrice brought out a cookbook of Amish favorites. "Let's see, I'm pretty sure we have most of the ingredients for whoopie pies. Flour, baking powder, vanilla, unsalted butter, milk, brown sugar, eggs, confectioner's sugar, and vanilla." She jotted down several words on a piece of paper and handed the slip to Stephen.

"While you're out, please pick up some Marshmallow Fluff and Dutch-processed cocoa powder. Don't worry. The local grocery store employees will know what they are. I can make whoopie pies this afternoon." She seemed unruffled. "They may not taste as good as Olivia's, but I can cook anything using a recipe. So can Eva. She'll help me."

I stiffened. "But I've never made whoopie pies in my life."

Beatrice shot me a grin. "There's a first time for everything, no?"

"But I'll be busy—"

"Then we'll cook them after supper. Time to experiment with new things. Like driving a car?"

"Oh." So she'd seen me driving Stephen's pickup. I wondered how long she'd watched us.

# Thirty

I dreaded having to call Emma and tell her the bad news. Fortunately, she was near their phone shanty—perhaps hoping to hear from Mark?—and answered on the third ring.

"*Gut* morning." Emma was all giggles until I told her about our assessment of her whoopie pies. Like the flip of a switch, she flew into a rage. "You're just jealous 'cause Mark likes me now!"

I held the receiver away from my ear to lessen her volume. So Olivia had told her about Mark's interest in me. Well, I figured hurt feelings about the pies were spurring her on, but she needed to know the truth.

"*Nee*, I'm not. Emma, maybe you got the ingredients mixed up." I couldn't win. I was either telling her I had no interest in the man of her dreams or that she was a lousy cook.

Without saying goodbye, she hung up on me with a resonating clunk.

"Anything else you ladies need?" Stephen asked before he left. "I'm taking Heath with me just to get the poor dog out of the house."

"Good idea." Beatrice was already gathering ingredients for corn bread, bran muffins, and whoopie pies. "Everything will be okay. My soup will be so good today, and for this morning, we'll have the whoopie pies you're bringing back."

"What would we do without you, Bea?"

"Now, now. You'd be fine." She glanced at me. "You have Eva."

I was bamboozled by her statement.

Later in the morning, Mark strolled into the café, but he barely glanced my way—only long enough to avoid walking right into me. Sadie sashayed over to him with a mug of coffee. He thanked her. Scanning the glass case, he said, "Where are Emma's baked goods?"

"Still in a box right here." Sadie's grin was too wide to conceal her delight. "Come taste a whoopie pie, Mark." The cardboard box sat on the counter. She placed a whoopie pie on a plate.

"*Denki.*" He brought it to his mouth and sank his teeth into the cocoa-colored dough, only to sputter. "*Ach*, this is *greislich*." He washed it down with a couple swallows of coffee. "How can this be?"

Sadie mashed her lips together, but her eyes remained bright. "Maybe she doesn't cook as well as Olivia."

I stepped in. "We're not sure what went wrong, but we can't serve those. Stephen drove out to buy some for today. This afternoon or evening, Beatrice and I will bake more."

"I have work to do." Mark lumbered off wearing a surly expression. An idea took shape in my mind, but I'd keep it to myself until I spoke to Stephen.

An hour later, he returned with the Marshmallow Fluff and Dutch-process cocoa powder and handed the bag to me. He had a dozen whoopie pies too.

I turned to Sadie. "Would you like to lend a hand in the baking?"

"*Yah*, I would. My *mamm* says I bake as well as she does. Not that I should brag." Her blush permeated her translucent skin.

"Stephen, Sadie wants to help us cook too. Would you mind?"

"Not one bit," Beatrice said to me before Stephen could answer. She bustled over to retrieve the bag.

"Glad to have her help," he said. "But then we really must hire someone else to bus the tables."

"I can stay late, seeing as I've nothing else to do." Sadie moved to his side. "I won't even make you pay me."

"Thanks for your kind offer," Stephen said, "but as long as you're working, you'll earn a wage. I'll ask around the nursery and see if anyone's sister wants to come in and work here. In fact, doesn't Mark have a couple of sisters?"

"Susie, but she has her hands full already with laundry." Shaking my head once, I silenced myself. "I mean, I'd rather you didn't hire her, if at all possible."

Understanding seemed to dawn. "All right. Whatever you say."

"I know someone," Beatrice said. "A fine young woman from church who mentioned she needs a part-time job. She's worked in fast-food places in the past."

"Please ask her to come in for an interview with me and Evie, who is the café's manager, after all," Stephen said.

"Thank you, I will." Beatrice glanced to the ceiling for a moment. "What should we do with Emma's whoopie pies?"

"Dump them in with the food recycle if you think the hogs will eat them. Better save a couple in case she or her brother come back demanding proof." He aimed his voice at me. "Call her, will you, Evie?"

"*Ach*, I already did, and our conversation didn't go well. She hung up on me." I hoped Stephen wouldn't take it as an indication that I couldn't manage our staff.

"Women." Stephen slapped his thigh. "Sorry, ladies, but sometimes I just don't understand you. Why take everything so personally?"

I wanted to tell him I didn't understand men either. But he was correct. At least about me. I took most everything personally, often for no tangible reason. Another hurdle to surmount, I decided.

Beatrice was right about her soup. Customers came back for seconds, and we served her fresh-out-of-the oven corn bread and bran muffins with raisins, as well as buttered toast and the whoopie pies Stephen bought. Fortunately, the crowd thinned out quickly, and

Sadie and I could clear the tables and fill the dishwasher in a timely fashion.

Beatrice swabbed the cooking counter and brought out ingredients. Here I was twenty-nine, and I had never baked a whoopie pie.

She turned to me. "Always preheat the oven. This recipe calls for 400 degrees. We're going to make a double batch, so we should get out the baking sheets ahead of time and grease them to make sure we have enough. Otherwise, I have plenty of pans in the house."

Beatrice asked Sadie to combine the sugar, oil, and eggs in a large mixing bowl and beat until creamy. "Then stir in flour, dry cocoa, and a teaspoon of salt." Beatrice scanned the recipe. "Come on, Evie, I want you to also mix the ingredients for the cookies."

With trepidation, I brought out a stainless steel bowl and followed the directions as she read them aloud. "Stir until thoroughly mixed." She spoke over my shoulder. "No lumps, mind you."

When I finished mixing, she steered me to the baking sheets and handed me a teaspoon. Moments later, I was dropping rounded teaspoons of the mixture onto the greased sheet. "They'll need to bake for eight to ten minutes." She held the recipe out so I could see it. "Says here, we mustn't let them overbake. Then they'll need to cool completely before cutting them in half. That will give us plenty of time to make the filling. I give that chore to you, Evie."

"But I'm your boss at the café. And I give Sadie that job."

Beatrice raised an eyebrow. "Evie, it's time you learned your way around a kitchen. Whatever you make has to be better than Emma's."

"*Yah*," Sadie chimed in. "*Ach*, hers was the worst ever."

An hour later, as Beatrice and I assembled the whoopie pies to be served the next day, Stephen ambled in.

"Well, the locks to the café are changed. How goes the battle?" he asked, handing both Beatrice and me our new keys. "Smells good in here."

"We were just about to sample our first one." Beatrice placed a complete whoopie pie on a plate with flourish. As she cut it, I prayed all our labor had produced a good result.

She put the plate out for Stephen to sample it. He took his time, probably recalling the appalling pie he'd eaten earlier. He cut into it again until his portion was the size of a grape. Finally, he closed his eyes and plunked the morsel into his mouth. His eyes flew open, and a grin spread across his face. "Why, this is fabulous!"

Beatrice took a bite and swallowed. "Simply delicious."

I paused as Sadie pronounced it the best she'd ever eaten. All eyes turned to me.

Stephen held out the plate. "Come on, Evie, you can't serve customers what you won't eat yourself."

As I bit into the whoopie pie, my taste buds sprang to life. The chocolate cookie was delectable, and the creamy filling luscious, far superior than I'd hoped for. "I can't believe it. As good as Olivia's. I'm sure Sadie or I could reproduce them, especially with Beatrice standing by." I felt a burden lift from my shoulders and my stomach relax.

But Olivia's disappearance and the whoopie pies were just a couple of my problems. Other challenges loomed on the horizon—of that I was sure.

In uniform, Wayne marched into the café. "Pardon me, folks, but I need to speak to Stephen."

Stephen stepped toward him and then said, "You've got to be kidding."

"Wish I was. Please check for Glenn's big male Lab, will you?"

Stephen turned to Beatrice. "Is Heath in the house?"

She nodded. "As far as I know. I checked on him a couple of hours ago. And Mark walked him on leash earlier."

"Hold on. I'll go look for myself." Stephen seemed to bristle inside.

Like following the Pied Piper, Wayne, Beatrice, and I trailed after Stephen toward the house. We could barely keep up. As we neared the house, I expected to hear Heath's woofing, but when I looked through the glass-paned kitchen door window, Missy stood inside, her tail wagging. She let out a gentle woof, and Minnie yapped with excitement.

Stephen opened the door. "Heath?" He turned to Beatrice. "Why wasn't this door locked?"

"We never lock it during the day. Just at night."

"Why on earth not?" Wayne's voice boomed.

Growing up in a house where the doors were never bolted, I wasn't at all surprised. "Who would enter a home with three dogs?"

Wayne's mouth contorted. "Obviously, someone who isn't the least bit afraid of them." He sounded as surly as a German shepherd. "I need to get over to Bill's house pronto."

"I'll come with you," Stephen said.

"No, you don't. This is official police business."

"Then I'll follow you. If Heath's there, he'll come when I call. I'm the only one he obeys other than his owner."

"I'm not giving you permission to follow me, but I won't stop you. But, please, Stephen, let me do all the talking. Got that?"

"Yep. Other than to call for Heath, I'll keep silent."

"I'm coming too," I said. Much as I feared a repeat of our last encounter with the sheepherder, I was bound and determined to accompany Stephen. "Sadie can close the café without me, can't she?"

"Yes, not a problem," Beatrice said. "I'll go back and make sure the place is prepped and ready for the morning."

Wayne's patrol car tore out of the nursery's parking lot. I ran after Stephen and climbed into the pickup's passenger seat as he was igniting the engine. "What do you think you're doing?" he snapped.

"The same as you." My heart racing, I clipped on my seat belt.

When we reached the sheep farmer's property, Bill must have

heard the vehicles arriving. He swaggered out onto the porch. Wayne got out of his squad car and headed to the house.

We pulled up next to Wayne's car. As Wayne neared the house, Bill yelled at him and shook his fist, but I couldn't understand his words. Just as well, as I assumed he was pelting Wayne with profanities.

Wayne stood at the bottom of the steps, putting him at a disadvantage, although I noticed he wore a firearm.

"I wonder if we're too late." Stephen cut the engine.

"Please, Stephen. Whatever happens, keep your temper in check." Half of me was glued to the seat, but my hand reached for the door's handle.

He exited his pickup. I got out slowly, not wanting to stir up further turmoil. I reminded myself I didn't even like dogs, but I'd be distraught if anything bad happened to Heath. I imagined the dog in the pasture attacking a lamb and Bill with his shotgun. My lungs felt as though they were collapsing.

Stephen sauntered over next to Wayne. Stephen pressed his lips together and remained silent. I guessed he was using herculean strength to keep himself under control.

"How should I know?" Bill's words rippled with rage. "Probably killed another of my prize sheep and took off."

"Calm down, Bill," Wayne said, patting the air. "We'll get this all straightened out."

"What about Ralph?" Stephen asked Wayne. "Where is he?"

Bill sneered. "No clue. I'm not my brother's keeper."

Stephen called for Heath and then rounded the house and proceeded toward the basement door at the bottom of a flight of cement stairs.

"Hey, hold on, let me handle this." Wayne sprinted to reach the basement first, and I followed to watch. He knocked on the door, using the side of his hand.

Silence.

"Open up, Ralph, or I'm coming in." Wayne tried the doorknob and found it unlocked. With his hand on his weapon, he shouldered the door open.

"If I know him, Ralph went out on a binge last night and is sleeping it off somewhere," Bill said.

"Your brother's been raiding our café," Stephen said.

"No way. Got proof?"

"I was an eyewitness." My voice came out tinny. "He had a key—"

Wayne raised his hand to silence me. "Better let me do the talking." He turned to Bill. "You sure you have another dead sheep?"

Bill winced as another squad car pulled up and two officers got out. Wayne motioned them around the back of the house. "We'll go check." He turned to Stephen. "You can come with us, but I want Eva to wait here in case there's any trouble."

Bill followed them. Impatiently, I sat on the front steps for a few minutes. The gray paint was chipped and pealing. One of the steps looked to have dry rot at the end. The whole house needed to be painted. As I inspected the disrepair, a woman cast a shadow in the window. Clad in a bubblegum-pink chenille bathrobe, she finally cracked the door.

"Hello. I'm Eva Lapp." I tried to appear composed.

A cigarette hung from her lower lip. "I'm Bill's—er, wife." She cinched her robe and leaned through the doorway. "Don't pay no attention to Billy. I didn't hear nothing last night or this morning."

"What about Ralph? Do you know where he is?"

"I haven't seen that bum since yesterday, and good riddance."

"Did he have a dog with him?"

"He don't own no dog." She hacked but didn't remove the cigarette.

"Do you know where he might be?" I was determined to pump her well dry for information.

She exhaled a puff of smoke. "Bill thinks Ralph often goes to a barn to sleep it off. Because he comes back with a hangover and covered with hay."

"The one that got burnt down years ago and then rebuilt?"

"I wouldn't know. Ralph could be anywhere. One thing we got plenty of around here is barns."

Male voices expanded in volume as all the men except Bill returned, grumbling to each other.

"Well?" I stood. "I'm almost afraid to ask what you found."

"Nothing. One lamb is missing, according to Bill, and no sign of Heath." Stephen moved closer. "My hunch is a pack of coyotes dragged the lamb away."

"*Ach*, that's sad." Thankfully, I hadn't seen a lamb's mangled carcass.

"Yep. If any of his story is true."

"What about Ralph?" I looked to the front door, but Bill's wife—or whatever her relationship to him was—had retreated into the house, leaving a trace of cigarette smoke as a witness to her presence. I assumed living with Bill was no picnic, but who was I to judge?

"I spoke to a woman who said she hadn't seen him."

"Bill's wife?" Wayne asked. I figured he knew all the local gossip, so no need to fill him in on the couple's questionable living arrangement.

"She said she hasn't seen Ralph since yesterday," I said. "And that he might be sleeping in a barn somewhere."

Bill finally came around the corner of the house, but Stephen ignored him and aimed his words at Wayne. "So now we have a case of theft."

"No way to prove Ralph stole Glenn's dog." Wayne stood akimbo. "Our trip was a waste of time."

Stephen folded his arms. "I think Ralph broke into Glenn's house and stole his dog. I want to press charges."

"How you gonna prove that?" Bill's tone was belligerent. "Any witnesses?"

On the drive back to the nursery, Stephen lowered his window and called Heath's name. The sun was setting, the sky draining of color. When we finally arrived, I was surprised to find Jake's borrowed car parked near my little abode.

# Thirty-One

"What's he doing here?" Stephen's pent-up anger seemed to inflate the air pressure in the pickup's cab.

I recognized the silhouette of Jake's profile in the dim light, but I didn't respond. I had no idea why he was here, but the sight of him sent a tingling buzz through me. *Ach*, I couldn't help myself.

When Stephen turned off his engine, he made no move to get out or stop me. "Call me if Heath returns. Please tell Beatrice I'm still looking for him. Goodbye, Eva." His farewell sounded final. Like the end of an era. I watched as he pulled away.

As I turned toward Jake's car, he opened his door. He wore clean *Englisch* clothes and looked as though he'd just stepped out of the shower. His bangs hung longer, or maybe that was just me wishing he was intentionally growing them. He approached me slowly as I walked to the cabin.

"Wait up, my love."

I whirled around. "Is this some kind of cruel joke? You said you might marry Brandy."

"*Nee*, I want to spend my life with you." He took hold of my elbow, but I jerked out of his grasp.

I cautioned myself to stay strong. "I don't know what to believe, Jake." A dreadful thought flooded my brain. "Is Amos worse? Did your *mamm* send you here?"

"Just one minute." Jake's handsome face transformed to a mask of indignation. "What about Stephen? Were you two just out on a date? Are you infatuated with him?"

If I claimed I wasn't attracted to Stephen, I'd be lying. "None of your business."

"I'd say it is. Don't you still have feelings for me? I adore you."

"But you told me you're marrying Brandy."

"A rash and foolish remark I regret. Although my heart goes out to her and her unborn child."

"*Yah*, mine does too." I wished I could assist her without forever losing Jake.

"There's something you could do to help me right now, Jake. As a friend."

"Yeah? What is it?" His blue eyes darkened, conveying distrust.

"Remember the barn that burned down?"

He ran his fingers through his bangs and then let them flop back across his forehead. "How could I ever forget?"

"Would you take me there?"

"To the barn? Right now? Are you *ab im kopp*?"

"*Nee*, I'm not crazy. I just—" I wasn't ready to share my hunch with him or anyone. "Please, will you take me?"

He paused, as if weighing his options. "*Yah*, okay. In the car or on foot?"

"It's close enough to walk, don't you think? And quieter."

"But why go there? I heard just a couple of mares are living in that barn now. And the owner's stallion. Jeremiah Schmucker refuses to give up the horse even though it's unruly."

"The farmer doesn't own dairy cows anymore?" I recalled his two dozen black-and-white Holsteins, but that was more than seven years ago.

"Jeremiah grew too old to milk the herd and had no sons to help him," Jake said. "As it turns out, we rebuilt that barn for nothing."

"You rebuilt it because it needed rebuilding. And I want to see it."

"Evie, you don't know how close I came to being charged for arson.

I could be behind bars." He shivered for effect. "Some people still think I'm guilty. I've changed my mind. I don't want to get anywhere near that place." He jingled the keys in his pocket, making me think he was about to take off.

"Jake, I'm walking over to the barn by myself if you won't accompany me." I lifted my chin and headed off in that direction.

All was quiet. I didn't see Beatrice peering out the window, and I hoped she hadn't noticed us. An idea took shape. I marched over to the back porch, climbed the steps, and rapped on the door. Missy and Minnie barked, and Beatrice appeared to let me in.

"I'm going for a short walk, and I would like to take Missy with me."

"Have you ever walked a dog in your life?" Beatrice's voice got lost amid the barking. "On leash, I assume."

"*Yah*. Would you please clip one on her? She needs to go out every evening anyway, doesn't she?"

"Yes, but why now?" She glanced over to Jake and greeted him with an unenthusiastic nod. "What's going on in that noggin of yours?"

"She might pick up Heath's scent," I said. "Please? I'll take good care of her."

"You'd better." Beatrice's words came out a threat. "Here, take this." She handed me a flashlight.

Missy's body sprang to life when Beatrice snapped on the leather leash and I took hold of it. Her tail beat against my leg. She nearly tugged me off my feet as she pranced down the porch steps.

I jerked on the leash and lowered my voice as I'd heard Stephen do when the dogs became rambunctious. "Missy, if you want to come, you must behave." She looked up at me, her ears perked, as if she understood I was the boss. For now, anyway.

I sensed Beatrice watching as I ushered Missy across the road and onto a path toward the barn. I heard Jake's footsteps behind us, praise the Lord. He walked ahead and opened the gate to a low fence. "I hope you know what you're doing." He closed it behind us.

Missy's tail wagged with expectancy, and she pawed the ground. She dragged harder on the leash the closer to the barn we got. She barked. Two woofs emanated from the depths of the dark barn.

"Heath, are you in there?" I called, but the air turned silent. Missy tugged on the leash, and it slipped from my hand. Jake leaned down to retrieve it, but he was too late.

# Thirty-Two

By the time Jake and I caught up with Missy, she was at the barn and sniffing under the door. I couldn't get it open. "Jake, help me."

"Are you sure you want to go in there?"

"*Yah*, we have to now."

He shouldered it open. Exuberant Heath came barreling out.

Jake said, "Good boy!"

As the two dogs danced in jubilation at our feet, the barn remained quiet except for the sound of horses shifting in their stalls. Jake clicked on the small flashlight he always carried with him and stepped inside. He shone the light's beam around the interior and located one Holstein—an old gal, in my estimation—two mares, and the stallion, his ears flicking back and forth and his tail swishing. The horse held his head high, closed his mouth, and snorted, reminding me of *Dat*'s gelding when he thought he was in danger.

"Maybe the dogs are spooking him," I said.

"Sniff the air," Jake said.

I inhaled. "Cigarette smoke?" We both turned our flashlights to the hayloft above.

"No one would be stupid enough to smoke up there." I hoped not, anyway. "A hayloft is a tinderbox waiting for a spark."

Heath let out a throaty growl that made the hairs on my arm

prickle. But I was grateful for his protective instincts. Maybe having a big dog around was a good idea after all.

"Who's up there?" Jake placed his foot on the wooden ladder rung. "Show yourself or I'm climbing up to find out for myself."

"Be careful, Jake."

I hoped no one was there, but the floorboards in the loft creaked. Bits of hay floated down like feathers.

"Ralph?" I called. "Is that you?"

"What of it?" Ralph's words were garbled and sloppy. "I sleep here all the time, and the Amish owner has never complained."

Jake scaled another rung. "He would if he knew you smoked."

Ralph belched an expletive. "You stupid idiot, you made me spill my whiskey."

"*Ach*, that's almost as flammable as lighter fluid!" Jake scrambled up the ladder as Ralph revealed himself, arms extended.

"I'll show you." Ralph rushed at Jake, who teetered, but regained his balance and brushed past him.

"Look, your cigarette butt started a fire!" Jake's voice emanated panic. I could hear him trying to stamp out the flames, without success. He leaned over and tossed me his cell phone. "Call 9-1-1!"

From the hayloft, crackling erupted. "Go down," Jake told Ralph. "Hurry." But Ralph ignored him.

"Please come down, Jake," I said. "I can't get the phone to work." I wanted him safe, and maybe Ralph would follow him.

Jake scaled the ladder as nimble as a cat. He snatched the phone and pressed some buttons. "Barn fire at the Schmuckers', across the road from Yoder's Nursery."

The stallion pawed the ground, his head raised and his nostrils flared. Ears back and the whites of their eyes enlarging, the mares snorted and kicked against their stalls.

The crackling, burning straw gained momentum, sounding like an oncoming locomotive.

"Evie, let the mares and cow out." Jake ran to the stallion and opened his stall. The horse reared up and refused to leave. The mares had much the same reaction. I was flabbergasted that they wanted to stay in their stalls.

I pulled off my sweater and covered one of the frantic mare's heads. I felt a metal shoe gouge into my leg—but no time to look. I led the blinded mare out of the barn, and the other followed. Both galloped into the descending darkness.

As Jake struggled with the stallion, I unclipped and led the bawling cow outside, but I had nowhere to tie her. "Shoo!" I clapped my hands and she trotted away, disappearing into the field.

The sky lit up from the flames. The heat increased.

I ran back into the barn in time to see snarling Heath dash into the stall and nip at the stallion's legs, further enraging the horse. When the stallion turned to bite Heath, Jake shoved the horse's rump. The frantic animal left the stall, but then it paused. Heath stood with bared teeth and blocked the stallion from returning.

"Come out of there!" I yelled to Heath. He ran to me. I dashed over to close the stall's gate.

A thunderous noise above reminded me of a jet flying too low. Flames leaped and danced. Sparks flew. The heat grew unbearable.

Jake grabbed a rope halter and maneuvered it onto the stallion's head. He seized control of the frantic horse and forced it out of the barn, and then gave its rump a whack. It bolted into the darkness.

The multiplying flames were hypnotizing me. I tried to breathe, to fill my lungs. I gulped for air and put my hand in front of my face to ward off the heat.

"Come out, Evie." Jake grasped my hand and pulled me to safety.

A moment later, the blazing loft collapsed, as loud as a stick of exploding dynamite. I thought my eardrums would burst.

"Thank you, Lord," I said, knowing no one but God could hear me.

Sirens screamed in the distance, traveling our way. The whole barn was a blistering furnace, illuminating the sky.

Three fire trucks careened to the farm—two stopped in the barnyard, and one screeched to a halt in the lane from the road, spewing up gravel. Several dozen firemen—both *Englisch* and Amish clad in gear and helmets—descended upon the scene like an orchestrated team. I'd heard most firefighters in the county were volunteers, but each brave man was well trained. Minutes later, water gushed from the trucks' hoses, fighting to subdue the crackling flames consuming the blackened timbers. Hissing like serpents filled the air, the black flames raging, refusing to submit. Sparks rained down.

Cars stopped by the side of the road. *Ach,* I wondered if one belonged to a reporter. If not now, soon enough. Amish neighbors—men dressed in black, wearing hats, rubber muck boots, and leather gloves—arrived on foot or in buggies. Several offered to help locate and care for the missing horses.

Police cars, their blue lights flashing, crunched to a halt at the side of the road.

The smoke continued to billow, and the gushing water sent steam into the sky. Finally, the smoke turned gray. The uniformed fire chief wearing a badge and carrying a clipboard approached us. "This your barn?" He appeared to be in his midfifties.

"No. It belongs to the Amish farmer here, Jeremiah Schmucker." Jake pointed to the small clapboard house. A woman stood on the porch, crying with her husband's arm around her shoulder. Other Amish and *Englisch* had gathered. Knowing the Amish community, women were already preparing food and gathering supplies for the family and workers who would arrive to clear away cartloads of debris and ruined timber, preparing for the upcoming barn raising.

"Hey, you look familiar." A uniformed fireman stopped. "You Jake Miller?"

I knew where he was headed with his line of questioning. "We came looking for our dog," I said.

Heath and Missy were milling nearby, sniffing the tall grasses. I wished they could talk.

"Aren't these Glenn Yoder's Labs?" the fire chief asked.

The smoldering wet ashes made me cough. "*Yah*, they are." I cleared my throat. "We think Ralph Hastings stole Heath, and we came looking for him."

"Oh, yeah? Then where's Ralph?"

"Dear *Gott*, what happened to him?" My words burbled out. "He was up in the hayloft drinking whiskey and smoking when we came in." My mind spun with the gruesome possibility he'd fainted from smoke inhalation and burned to death. "He tried to push Jake off the hayloft. That's the last time I saw him."

"You mean there was an altercation?" The man started writing on a tablet. "The two men were fighting?"

"Not really," Jake said. "Evie and I smelled cigarette smoke coming from the hayloft, and then Ralph started swearing and yelled that he'd tipped his bottle of whiskey over. When I climbed the ladder, Ralph rushed at me, but he was so snookered he missed his chance to push me off the loft. Then I saw the hay had caught fire, and I lost sight of Ralph. I tried to stomp out the flames, but I was too late. Sparks had started flying."

"Jake tossed me his cell phone to call 9-1-1. I couldn't get it to work, so he came down and made the call." My hands cupped my cheeks. "The fire spread so quickly that all we could think about was freeing the livestock." I was proud of Jake's courage and thoughtfulness. Other men might have turned tail and run rather than risk their lives to save the frantic horses.

The fire chief called to several firemen. "Did you find anyone in there?"

Their faces grim, they shook their heads. "The next shift had better sift through the debris in the morning when it cools down. And call for the arson squad. This barn didn't torch itself."

I bent to snatch up Missy's leash. "May I take the dogs home now? I'm afraid Heath might wander off."

"This woman is innocent of any wrongdoing." Jake had tied some twine around Heath's neck to serve as a leash and made a loop at the end. He handed it to me.

"*Yah*, you can ask Officer Wayne Grady or review his reports," I said. "And Stephen Troyer might still be looking for Ralph and Heath."

"Okay, but I'll need a signed statement from you. Can you come by the office tomorrow?"

"I have to work in the nursery's café all day."

"Okay. Someone will stop by the café."

I turned my face away as a photographer got out of his sedan and took pictures of the barn.

Stephen's pickup zoomed to an abrupt stop at the side of the road. He jumped out. "Evie, what on earth happened?"

"Missy needed a walk, and it occurred to me she might lead me to Heath. Which she did."

Stephen glared at Jake, who stood answering questions. I heard Ralph's name tossed about, speculation on his whereabouts, and the words *smoking in the loft*.

"Can you prove Ralph was here?" the fire chief asked.

"I saw him," I said, but Jake frowned.

"She did nothing wrong," Jake said.

The chief stepped closer. "I'll do my job if you don't mind. Weren't you involved with a barn burning here a few years back? Did you arrive with the intention of burning this barn down too?"

Jake didn't look away, but he clamped his lips together.

"He came because I asked him for help." A blue-white flash told me my photo had just been taken. "He was never charged or found guilty." Another flash, but I couldn't run away.

To my surprise, Stephen stepped in. "Jake didn't burn the first barn down. I was with him that night and can attest to that. My guess is someone noticed his car parked outside earlier that night and reported it. The barn was still standing when he and I and a few buddies took off."

The fire chief's expression turned severe, his eyes bulging. "Why didn't you speak up? Maybe you *were* the guilty party."

"Absolutely not." Stephen stood tall and looked the man in the eyes. "Just a friendly card game and a couple bottles of beer, and then we went home. No kerosene lanterns, no smoking, no matches."

"But that was then and this is now. Were you Jake's witness today?"

"No, I can't vouch for him. We haven't been friends for years. But everything Evie said about Ralph is true. He's been breaking into the nursery's café and stealing food. Then he upped the ante and took Glenn Yoder's dog right out of the man's house."

"Any witnesses?"

"No." Stephen swiped his mouth.

The fire chief stepped closer, his gaze intense. "Can this Amish woman be trusted?"

"Yes, but after tonight I have to wonder about her common sense. She was with Jake Miller." Stephen's lips formed a grim line.

"Maybe I should take her down to the station."

"No need," Stephen said. "Her name's Eva Lapp, and she won't run off. I'll keep an eye on her. She lives and works at the nursery and reports directly to me until Glenn Yoder returns."

The officer looked over to Jake. "Would she take off with Jake? What's to keep him here?"

Jake must have heard his name. He spun around. "I'm not running away. After I help rebuild this barn, I have to care for my ailing father and his farm."

"You'd better not leave town, or I'll issue a warrant for your arrest."

"The fire was an accident, and I wasn't responsible. Nor was Evie. If she hadn't insisted on coming over here to look for Heath, the Schmuckers' horses, cow, and Heath could have been lost."

"Let's get something straight." The chief narrowed one eye. "If you two hadn't been poking around on private property, this barn might not have caught fire. For all we know, Ralph may have slept in here a hundred times." The corners of his mouth drew back. "No matter, really, as the owner probably won't press charges. What's with these Amish?" he asked the air.

"Forgiveness," Stephen said, for which I was grateful.

"But they carry it too far when they stop us from doing our job." The police chief glanced over to the Schmuckers' residence. "I need to get a statement from the owner."

The crowd watched the smoke and smoldering fire. It wasn't long before slow-moving cars and buggies caused a traffic jam. A truck honked, frightening a buggy horse into rearing. Wayne, in his sleek squad car, sped up and came to a stop at the side of the road. He got out and positioned himself in the center of the lanes. "Nothing to see," he said as he motioned cars to continue. "Keep moving."

"Isn't that Eva Lapp?" a woman said from her buggy to her female passenger. I recoiled and pretended I couldn't hear her stringent voice. "She's the one who had a baby—"

I should be used to malicious gossip, but I'd suddenly heard enough. Like a cork popping off a bottle of sparkling apple cider, I twirled around, rage oozing out my pores. "None of that story is true!"

The two women stared back in silent surprise. The driver prompted her horse to move forward.

"May I be of help?" Bishop Harvey asked me, seeming to appear out of nowhere.

I wanted to sink to the ground and ooze into a puddle. "I'm sorry I lost my temper. I wish I could apologize to those women, but I don't see the buggy anymore through all that traffic."

The bishop's voice sounded kinder than I expected. "It's not easy turning the other cheek seventy times seven times, is it?" He stroked his beard.

"But surely it is for you," I said.

"*Nee*. I'm human, just like everyone." I might have missed his smile if his upper lip hadn't been shaven. "You're a *gut* girl, Eva. Why don't you settle down and join the church?"

"I'm still thinking about it."

"A lifetime commitment should not be made on a whim. But consider your other choices carefully."

I watched both Amish and *Englisch* men help the firemen contain the fire. Jake was arguing with a fireman, their voices rough, reminding me of the dogs that used to menace me on the way to school when I was a girl. I bet those mongrels wouldn't have bothered me with Heath and Missy there to protect me. I glanced down at the two Labs and was pleased to see them sitting at my side, gazing up, waiting to escort me home.

# Thirty-Three

During the sleepless night, images of the fire assaulted my mind. The flames and hoses spewing water jostled and competed with one another. Somehow, though, I managed not to dream about Ralph and his possible demise.

The next morning, sunshine illuminated the cabin as I dressed for work in a daze. My clumsy hands pricked me twice with straight pins while fastening on my apron, which still reeked of smoke. I wriggled into my sweater, which also carried the noxious odor. When I opened the front door, a cloud of stinky, damp air drifting from the decimated barn bombarded me. But the sun shone brightly, no doubt drying the water the firemen had provided.

The night before, I'd left without saying goodbye to Jake, nor had he come over to fill me in. For all I knew, he'd spent the night in jail and was awaiting trial for arson. I'd vouched for him, but who would believe me? And I wasn't up in the hayloft when the fire started. I couldn't see Ralph for more than a moment, or the flames igniting.

"Evie, wait." As I walked toward the café, Stephen sauntered up behind me with Heath and Missy on leash. Their bodies wriggled with excitement. "Beatrice asked me to walk these two and then lock them in the house."

"Maybe there's no need to lock the back door anymore if Ralph is gone."

"His death would be a blessing in some ways." He gave himself a mock slap in the face. "No, what am I saying? At AA I've seen far worse cases turn their lives around."

I peeked toward the burned-out barn and heard the whirring of machinery and voices.

"Want to go over and have a look?" Stephen asked.

"I don't know. I might be running late." Times like this, I wished I could wear a wristwatch. "I need to get to work."

He glanced down at his watch. "No, there's plenty of time. I bet you have an extra twenty minutes. Beatrice just told me she's making the soup today as well as an extra vat to take over to the workers later. And Sadie will be in soon."

"Okay." I couldn't pass up the opportunity. As we neared the barn, the stench increased. Both Amish and *Englisch* men waited for the arson inspector's signal to begin filling the trucks with rubble and debris. The ground was muddy, the trucks' humongous wheels sinking into it. *Ach*, what a mess.

I saw Jake waiting along with the other men, but he either didn't notice us or was ignoring me because I was with Stephen.

"Do you suppose Ralph could have escaped?" I asked Stephen. "The fire ignited so quickly. I can't imagine how he could have gotten out."

"Especially if he was smashed."

We passed a weary-looking fireman. "Pardon me," Stephen said to him. "Any human remains found in the debris?"

The man shook his head. "Not that I've heard. The investigation is still going on."

Stephen glanced down at me. "Are you sure Ralph was drunk?"

I buttoned my sweater and stuffed my icy fingers in my apron pockets. "He was cursing up a storm and griped that he'd tipped over his bottle of whiskey. That's one reason Jake hurried up to the loft so quickly. He said whiskey is flammable, almost as bad as lighter fluid."

"I don't know about that, but it sounds like Ralph was on a binge."

He turned to watch Jake, who took notice of us but didn't say hello. "You still love him, don't you, Evie?"

"Yes. No. I don't know anything anymore."

"I'd never do anything to hurt you, but I get why you're steering clear of me," Stephen said. "I'm not Amish."

"Would you consider joining the church?" I asked, already surmising the answer.

He paused for a moment. "At this stage in my life I doubt it. Not that I don't respect the Amish greatly and embrace their biblical faith. But I couldn't follow the *Ordnung*, especially when it comes to driving."

"I figured you'd say that." Yet I felt a ripple of disappointment.

"I don't see you rushing to join. What's keeping you? Waiting on Jake?" His hand moved to brush a stray hair off my cheek. "Evie, you can do better than Jake Miller. I heard the police took him down to the station last night for questioning. If a death occurred in that fire, the law will insist on an inquest."

"But I told the fire chief what happened."

"Some women will say just about anything to protect a man they care about. They probably took your statement with a grain of salt if they know of your long history with Jake."

We paused as Heath sniffed a clump of grass.

Stephen turned to me and said, "In the meantime, a man like me is falling in love with you."

My head whipped around to catch his countenance. Years ago I'd heard a romantic song in an *Englisch* restaurant Jake took me to several times. The music was playing in the background, and that particular song—"The Look of Love"—stuck with me. Now it circled in my brain.

Stephen wore an expression of love right now—the way his gaze took me in and his mouth softened.

Our eyes locked until I forced myself to look away. "What happened to your former girlfriend?"

"Joni couldn't take my drinking. She gave me an ultimatum, but I kept on boozing it up until she dumped me. Which I deserved. Her courageous act may have saved my life."

"Would you two get back together?"

"No, she and I are history. She moved on to another man months later and married him. They're expecting a child."

"Do you miss her?"

"At first I held one giant pity party, but not anymore. Certainly not since I met you."

Our eyes locked again. Warmth and tenderness filled my heart. I didn't know what to say. I trusted Stephen. I'd never seen him flirt or heard him distort the truth. He was courageous and kind. A righteous man. But not Amish.

Heath broke the silence with a woof as a buggy conveying half a dozen men and a yappy mixed-breed pulled to a stop. The men hopped out and the buggy took off—with the little mutt, thank goodness.

Over by the Schmuckers' home, Amish women were setting up card tables and bringing out paper and Styrofoam cups, carafes of coffee and juice, and donuts and other baked goods, preparing to serve the firemen and all the other volunteers the forenoon snack around nine.

"These women probably either stayed up half the night cooking or stopped by a bakery on the way here," I said, glad to change the subject.

"I admire how the Amish community sticks together and takes care of outsiders too."

Stephen lifted a hand and waved at Bishop Harvey. "Good, Harvey's here. He has a wealth of knowledge about building barns stored in his head. Several of the older Amish men will also be invaluable. I bet they've already calculated an order for the lumberyard."

"I wish I could stay and help," I said, lagging.

"You'll be busy feeding our customers today, Evie. Come back later. These men will be here all day, if not into the night, unless they need to go home to milk. I'd be surprised if the new barn got started before a couple of days goes by, especially if the arson inspector takes much longer. It's just now getting light. Anyway, a solid foundation is essential to everything in life, don't you think?"

His question spiked into me. I speculated if he were hinting at Jake and me as a couple.

As the sky brightened, a line of both Amish men in broadcloth trousers and *Englisch* men wearing jeans formed in front of the tables. Men sipped coffee, gobbled up the donuts, and chatted about the forthcoming barn building.

I wondered if Jake would get coffee, but he continued to stare at the barn.

"Eva." I recognized my father's voice.

I twirled around. "*Dat*! You came all this way?"

"*Yah*, we wouldn't miss it. Just left one of your *mamm*'s breakfast casseroles on a table by the house." He wore his straw hat and a black work jacket.

"But how did you know?"

"We could see the orange sky and heard the sirens all the way from our house." He waved at several bearded friends. "Nothing like a barn fire to bring the community together."

I noticed Amish women greeting *Mamm*, who deposited plastic containers on a table amid a growing accumulation of food and then trudged our way.

"How did you get here so early?" I asked her.

"I rose at three thirty to cook breakfast for the workers. Fortunately, we had plenty of eggs on hand. Several neighbors hired a van, and we all chipped in." She gave me a hug. "When we heard you were in the barn at the time, we were beyond thrilled to find you were all right." She gave me another hug. "Praise *Gott*."

Bishop Harvey ambled over to us. " 'Tis a shame tragedy is a catalyst that encourages unity. But 'all things work together for good to them that love God,' *yah*?"

I recognized *Mamm*'s favorite verse from the Bible, Romans 8:28. She'd certainly recited it enough times, even when I saw nothing good in a situation.

"But a man may have died in the fire, and this couple lost their barn," I told him.

The bishop spoke without hesitation. "Then it was *Gott*'s will." I'd heard that explanation for death and tragedy my whole life, but I still didn't understand or quite believe it. How could the fire and Ralph's demise possibly be God's will? How could my living as a spinster be God's will?

*Dat* sounded upbeat. "I already heard neighbors corralled the horses and the cow and are putting them up in their barns."

"Well, I'll be." Stephen watched Ralph's brother, Bill, zoom up in his pickup.

"Now what?" I said. "Do you think he's heard about Ralph?"

"No doubt," Stephen said. "He could probably smell the smoke from his home, and surely he heard the sirens last night."

My parents went back to the Schmuckers' house as Bill vaulted out of his vehicle and tromped over to a police officer. Bill's arms moved erratically, his gestures jerky. The officer seemed to be trying to calm him down, but to no avail. Bill spotted Stephen and pointed at him.

"Look out, Evie," Stephen said. "Here comes trouble."

Heath's hackles raised as Bill plodded over to us and jabbed Stephen in the chest with his index finger. "That dog killed another one of my sheep last night."

"That's impossible." I wedged myself between the two men. "Heath was with me or in the main house all night. I don't know what's killing your sheep, but it's not our dog. He was in this barn when it caught fire and kept the farmer's stallion from trampling my friend."

The police officer strode over. "Hey, Bill. What's going on?"

"You know about my sheep? I lost another one last night."

"Sorry to hear that, but can't you see we have our hands full here?" The officer's face grew solemn, the corners of his mouth angling down. "Bill, we tried to find you last night, but you weren't home. Do you know where Ralph is?"

"Me and the wife were out well past midnight. My brother's probably in my basement sleeping off a hangover. Why?"

"We have witnesses who claim Ralph was here last night. His cigarette may have started this fire."

Bill seemed to shrink in stature. "If he did, maybe this will knock some sense into him. Nothing I've said or done has made a whit of difference."

"No one's seen him since the hayloft went up in flames. I hate to be the one to tell you, but your brother may have died last night in the fire."

"I don't believe you." Bill closed his eyes. "No way is my brother dead."

The officer persisted. "Would you please call home and ask your wife to check on him? Unless you want to drive home and do it yourself."

"Listen, buddy, I don't have to do what you say." Bill's face was ghostly pale.

"If you'd rather I sent a couple of my officers over there, I will. This is official police business."

"Okay, okay. Don't get all bent out of shape." Bill opened his cell phone, did whatever was necessary to place the call, and said, "Hey, sugar. Would you do me a big favor?" He turned his back for a few minutes, and then he rotated to face the police officer. "My wife checked. Ralph ain't there, but that's nothing new. He don't show up sometimes, even for days at a time." Bill winced as he surveyed the trucks filled with charred wreckage. A veil of sadness seemed to cover his ornery features. "Are you trying to tell me Ralph was responsible for this fire? I don't believe it." He pointed at Stephen and me. "I'd bet you anything one of them is the arsonist."

Two more flatbed trucks arrived to haul off rubble. Their tires sank into the muddy slush, but the vehicles didn't slow until they'd reached a hard surface.

Dozens more Amish and *Englisch* men, some wearing tool belts, appeared and seemed eager to join the cleanup project. The trucks' rumbling engines and the men's chatter drowned out Bill's tirade. Stephen slipped his hand under my elbow and steered me toward the nursery. The dogs kept their gazes fixed on Bill as they trailed Stephen.

"Let's get back to make sure everything's running as it should be." He kept a tight grip on the dogs' leashes.

I caught *Mamm*'s attention and waved goodbye, assuming she and *Dat* would realize I had to get back to the café. I planned to introduce myself to the Schmuckers later—if they'd speak to me once they found out my involvement with the fire.

Stephen allowed the dogs to pull on their leashes. "We may be swamped with business with all these cars. The drivers might wander into the café with empty stomachs and demand a meal. We'll probably have a bare-bones staff if most of the men at the nursery want to help build the new barn. I'll pay them their usual salary."

"Did Beatrice mention what kind of soup she's making today?"

"No, but I bet it's another one of her mother's favorite recipes from the old country." He slowed his pace. "I'm glad you two get along. At first, I was concerned. She can be a bit stubborn."

"*Yah*, me too. But she and I have become friends." I hoped. When the Yoders returned, Beatrice might have nothing to do with me. She'd be too busy taking care of their little girl to help out in the café.

I felt anxious about meeting Glenn, my real boss, the man with the final say as to whether I'd remain here. And his wife, Rose. Wives could influence their husbands. For better or for worse.

# Thirty-Four

Stephen was right about the café's business being brisk. I was grateful for Beatrice's help. She prepared three kinds of soup, both in expectation of a large crowd and to share later with the workers across the street.

"No sign of Mark," Sadie said. "He must be helping with the barn raising, assuming they were able to get started."

Later that morning, Wayne slogged in, his eyes puffy. I breezed over to him with a mug of coffee. "Have you been up all night?"

"No. My wife insisted I come home and sleep a few hours and at least have some breakfast." His hand reached out. "But I'll take that coffee. Thanks."

"On the house. Anything new happening over at the barn?"

"Yeah. The arson inspector finished his work."

"Any sign of Ralph?"

"Nope. So far, no human remains, cremated or otherwise. An officer went to Bill's house to let him know. I hope he contacts us if Ralph shows up."

I sank into a chair with relief, but I had no idea how Ralph got out of that burning loft. "Could the inspectors have been mistaken?"

"Between you and me, I wondered the same thing. But it's unlikely."

"Anything else you can tell me?"

"Men are contemplating whether to replace the barn's foundation. The concrete isn't that old, and it may be salvageable. Not that I know much about barn building. Bishop Harvey is the expert. He, along with several other men with experience, will decide."

He flattened his palms together. "Say, mind if I give you some advice? If you see Ralph's brother, Bill, again, steer clear of him. A family of hotheads. I told Bill two days ago I suspected coyotes were responsible for killing his lambs, but he wouldn't believe me. He still kept blaming the Yoders' Lab. I warned him he should bring his sheep in at night and advised him to buy himself a herding dog to protect his flock, but he paid no heed."

He scanned the area, I assumed to make sure no one was listening in. "About the unpleasant dent in my squad car—I didn't press charges against you. Jake paid for the damages, and what prosecutor in the county would take you to court?"

"Jake paid?" How sweet. Why hadn't he told me so I could thank him?

"Stephen offered to pay too, but Jake beat him to it. That's a first. Two men offering to pay for a dent neither made." He stroked his chin. "You certainly are a popular girl."

"*Ach*, no I'm not."

"Could have fooled me." He swallowed his remaining coffee, handed me his empty cup, and left.

I told Sadie and Beatrice the good news about Ralph.

An hour later a late-teen *Englisch* girl strolled into the café carrying a job application. She found me and said, "Are you Eva Lapp? Stephen Troyer sent me to speak to you."

She placed the application in my hands. As I scanned it, I pondered how much handwriting said about a person. Hers was precisely neat, and her cursive letters were even. Annie Romano wore a dress made from a small floral-patterned fabric, making me think she was Mennonite. But she had no head covering and an Italian last name. I assumed she attended Stephen's church, which could be liberal as far as dress. According to her application, she'd worked at three fast-food places in the past. At the bottom, Stephen had written, *You have my approval to hire Annie if you like her.*

"When can you start?" I asked, thinking how much I wanted to zip out the door and check on the barn's demise. And to see if Jake was still there. I hated that I cared so much, but I couldn't shake my curiosity.

"Anytime." Annie's short, curly brown hair framed her face. "I'd be thrilled to spend the day in such a cool café." She surveyed the case full of food and then watched the koi swimming in graceful arcs in the pond for a moment.

I folded the application. "How about today? Right now."

"Yes, okay. The place I worked at closed last week, so I'm free as a bird."

Ten years my junior, she looked free as a bird in her flowered dress and her rosy, blemish-free cheeks.

I introduced Annie to Beatrice and Sadie. Beatrice's grin stretched wide, and she whispered. "Good for you, Annie."

"You two know each other?"

"Remember I told you about the young woman from my church?" Beatrice's smile was wry. "Is there a problem?"

"Not at all. Just caught me off guard."

I gave Annie a tour of our kitchen and then showed her where we stored the folded white aprons. She tied one on and got busy clearing tables and washing dishes as if it were second nature to her.

"I dare not leave the active café until three," I told Beatrice.

"Go ahead." Beatrice practically shooed me out the door. "We are more than capable of serving our customers. Stephen is coming any minute to take the extra soup across the street. Plus, I made several dozen extra sandwiches."

As if on cue, Stephen appeared at our back door looking disheveled, soot smudging his cheeks and clothes and mud caking his boots.

"I figured I'd better not come in the café's front door looking like this." He used a paper towel to wipe his face. "No use getting myself too cleaned up since I'm going back into the mess. Wayne told you Ralph Hastings may have escaped that fire in the barn, right?"

We all nodded, but his glance seemed to slide past mine, making me wonder if he regretted his ardent profession of affection. No, when Beatrice inserted a ladle and set a lid on the metal vat of soup, I saw he was watching me with the same expression he'd had earlier. But he said nothing. With Beatrice close at hand, we'd have to wait to continue our discussion.

Stephen lifted the heavy vat from the stove top and stepped toward the back door.

"Wait a minute," Beatrice said. "I also made a tray of ham-and-cheese sandwiches. Why doesn't Eva carry them?"

"That would be great." I tried to tame the anticipation in my voice.

Beatrice led me back to the refrigerator to retrieve a tray mountained with sandwiches sliced diagonally and covered with plastic wrap. She dipped her chin. "Sorry, Eva. I should have asked your permission first to make sure it was okay. But when I saw Stephen earlier, he said making sandwiches was a good idea since we had plenty of bread, cheese, and ham."

"Of course it's okay." I lifted the heavy tray. "I wish I'd thought of it first."

# Thirty-Five

When Stephen and I crossed the road, I caught sight of the demolished barn. My heart sank in on itself, as if I were attending a funeral. A mammoth yellow backhoe belching diesel exhaust pushed debris into heaps off to the side. Another filled a truck with blackened scraps of timber and roofing. Dozens of men, some wearing straw hats, others baseball caps and dressed *Englisch*, helped in the cleanup. But no Jake. He must have gone home to check on his parents and their farm.

I followed Stephen to the tables set up for food. He placed the soup vat on several newspapers to keep the metal from melting the plastic tablecloth. I set our sandwiches down next to fruit, breads, and deviled eggs. Another table housed coffee, juice, and water.

"I'm going to stay here," Stephen said. "I put Mark in charge of the nursery this afternoon." Stephen strode over to speak to Harvey and two other older men, who all seemed to be coordinating the effort.

As I scanned the crowd for Jake, an aged Amish woman said, "You're Eva Lapp. I'm Hannah. My husband and I own this farm." Her hair was as snowy white as her *kapp*. I steeled myself as I waited for her to unleash her indignation, but instead she shook my hand.

"Hannah, I feel terrible if in any way I caused this catastrophe."

"It doesn't sound as though you did. And even if you had, we wouldn't hold it against you. In the end, *Gott* will do the judging, *yah*?" She put out Styrofoam bowls and plastic spoons to use for the soup and a pot of beef stew sitting on a trivet.

"*Yah*, but—"

"We're grateful to you for saving our horses and Daisy, our one remaining cow." Her gaze lifted to the blue sky. "And we're grateful for this beautiful sunny day. The mud may dry and grow firm by tomorrow. Bishop Harvey thinks the barn's floor is *gut* enough to keep and so does the fire chief. A gift from *Gott* as we just replaced it six years ago. Or was it seven? When you get to my age, the years all blend together." Her weary face divulged no animosity. "And we're grateful for the mostly volunteer fire department, brave *Englisch* and Amish men who risked their lives. The Lord blessed us with no injuries."

I wondered how I'd react if I were in her shoes.

"Last fire we lost our calves and two horses," she said. "It was a bitter disappointment for my husband. But he'd already decided he wanted out of the dairy business."

"You never found out how the fire started?"

"No matter. We asked the police to give up their search for the arsonist."

Jake sauntered over to us. "Hannah."

"You two know each other?" I asked.

"*Yah*." Hannah put out more paper napkins. "Jake came to us after the first fire to offer assistance as needed. He was of most help rebuilding that old barn better than it had been for years. We'd let the farm decline and were thinking about replacing the leaking roof. Fortunately, we waited."

"It's *gut* to see you again, Hannah." Jake wore a tool belt and a baseball cap with *Phillies* written on it.

"You too. We've missed seeing you."

In other words, Jake had made peace with the Schmuckers while I'd held on to the past.

After Hannah returned to help with the food tables, Jake spoke to me. "Could you come home with me later?" He gave me a slow smile.

Several heads turned.

"Shush," I said. "Keep your voice down if you speak to me in public."

"But *Dat* keeps asking for you. I promise I'll take you home when you want to go. And no more ice cream runs."

"Won't Brandy mind?"

"No worries there." He took my hand right out in public, in front of all those people, but I pulled it away.

"Sometimes I say and do the stupidest things." Jake repositioned his baseball cap. "Although I'm afraid the father of her child will track her down. Or maybe he's glad to be rid of her. My *mamm* says she can stay with us, but I told her I'd have to make sure you don't mind."

"Why would I mind?" No need for him to answer. I'd been judgmental, what I'd accused others of. "Your *mamm* is generous to offer her a safe haven."

"Well?" Jake said. "May I take you to visit my *dat* later? I parked the car a block away." He tilted his head. "I'll come by and walk you to it."

"Keeping up this charade is ridiculous. Everyone knows about your borrowed car and that you and I have spent time alone together."

"In that case, I'll drive by to fetch you."

The backhoes quieted, and the drivers jumped out. Dozens of men set down shovels and rakes, removed their gloves, and spoke as brothers. The tide of workers formed two lines at the food tables. I moved to help the women serve them.

As *Mamm* and I poured coffee into Styrofoam cups and offered bottled water donated by a local grocery store, the men mounded their plates with food, accepted bowls of soup and stew, and then plopped down on benches, fold-up chairs, or the ground—upon grassy spots not water soaked.

Stephen waited in the line farthest away from me, making me wonder if he now regretted saying he was falling in love with me after seeing me with Jake.

Bishop Harvey came through the line last.

As the men polished off pies, cookies, and cakes, I thought of Olivia's marvelous desserts and missed my friend. I followed the women into the house to help clean. The sink was chock-full of crusty pots and pans, which I scrubbed as another woman about my age dried. The air was melodious with female chatter and merriment. Even Hannah engaged in cheerful conversation, saying she was grateful their barn had been built so far away from the house. Twice their home had gone unscathed.

She meandered around the kitchen and made sure everyone had been introduced. "Thank you very much," she told each individual. I wondered if all these women were aware of my connection with the fire. If so, they kept poker faces and treated me warmly. "Hope ta see ya at church on Sunday," one said to me as she prepared to leave.

"We'll be holding it in my house," another chimed in.

"I might keep attending in my parents' district," I said. Thankfully, neither woman asked if I was baptized yet. I needed to make new friends. I thought of Olivia once more, and a river of sadness sluiced through my chest. I might never see my cousin—my only confidant—again. I silently prayed for her safety, that the man she loved would treat her like the splendid young woman she was. But I knew men could be fickle. I wondered if they'd gotten married, but maybe he'd taken advantage of her innocence. Or had that time long ago passed by?

After four hours, we were again serving the hardworking men a light supper. They scarfed up the sandwiches Beatrice had assembled, and canned fruit and applesauce, followed by cookies and fruit-filled tarts.

The uniformed fire chief cruised by the barn for another inspection. After meticulous scrutiny, he pronounced the barn's floor still sound enough to build on. Finding all in order, he moseyed over to the food tables, chomped into a sandwich, and then chatted with the men, comparing various barn fires over the years.

As the azure-blue sky faded, *Mamm* and *Dat* gathered with their neighbors to board a hired passenger van. I ran over to say goodbye.

When I returned to Hannah's kitchen ten minutes later, most of the women had gone home to look after their children and prepare more food for the next day.

Our soup vat sat empty—a good sign. Beatrice would be pleased. I told Hannah I'd take it to the café to be cleaned. I needed to make a sweep through the café anyway to make sure all was prepared for the morning.

I tried to leave unobserved, but to no avail. News of the barn fire had traveled across the county and brought motorists and buggies to this seldom-used road. My arms wrapped around the vat, I initiated my crossing, but a car stopped in my path. I tried to walk behind it, but it backed up, and then rolled forward again. I was about to ask one of the men for assistance, when Olivia popped her head up. "Yoo-hoo!" She giggled like a teenager through the opened window.

Attempting to see who sat behind the steering wheel, I lowered my head. But the man angled his face away from me and raced away until the the car was out of sight.

# Thirty-Six

"Psst. Evie." I recognized Jake's voice as I returned to the cabin after scrubbing out the soup vat in the café's kitchen.

Jake hustled around me to the front door and blocked my way. "Hey, did you forget about me?"

As if I could. "I don't want to be seen leaving with an *Englisch* man, not after meeting those nice women at Hannah's. And Bishop Harvey's still here. Surely he'd see." Not to mention Stephen. *Ach*, he and I could never be wed. Although I was yet to be baptized so I wouldn't be shunned from the church...

"I could offer Harvey a ride home," Jake said.

"Please don't."

"Why not? Today I didn't see his buggy—an easy one to recognize. Someone must have dropped him off this morning." Jake took my fingertips and guided me toward the road. "Come on. My parents will be so disappointed if you don't come. I promised to bring you."

"Why did you do that without my agreeing first?" I withdrew my hand.

With audacity, he strode over to the barn. I followed, but I stopped short of joining him when he found Harvey. The two men chatted in what seemed to be an amicable conversation, and then they strode toward me. Harvey raised a hand to greet me—the opposite of what I'd expected.

"I thank you for the ride, Jake, but don't take this as an indication I approve of your driving a car," Harvey said.

"*Yah*, I understand. *Denki* for coming to see *Dat* first. Unless you'd rather go straight home?"

"*Nee*, I look forward to seeing your parents. I should have visited Amos days ago."

Minutes later, Jake had us in the sedan and was chauffeuring us to his family home. I insisted on sitting in the backseat, behind Harvey. Harvey removed his black hat and placed it on his lap.

"A visit from you will bless my parents greatly." Jake turned on the headlights. "I have to warn you not to expect too much from my *dat*. Sometimes he falls asleep even when someone's speaking to him."

"I won't take it personally." Harvey chortled. "Many a man has nodded off during one of my sermons."

I held in my laughter, but Jake guffawed. "They were probably just overly tired."

Harvey cleared his throat. "Speaking of church, I'm concerned that you two aren't yet baptized. How about you, Eva?"

I squirmed as he tried to peer over his shoulder at me. "I'm waiting..." Jake must have turned up the heat because I was sweltering.

"To see if Jake wants to marry you?"

Humiliated, I felt as if my mouth were clogged with oatmeal.

"Eva, if he doesn't join the church, then you'd leave your family and community and live in the *Englisch* world with him?"

"I might." There, I'd stated the truth.

"You might leave us? If you had children, how would you want them raised? Without your parents and community close by?"

Jake fingered the steering wheel, making me think he was as nervous as I was.

"Jake, are you planning to marry Eva?"

"*Yah*." Jake stared straight ahead, searching for traffic or maybe to avoid Harvey's intense eyes. "If she'll have me."

I sat forward, scooted to the middle of the seat, and spoke in his ear. "But you said you might marry Brandy."

"I told you. I didn't mean it."

Harvey's words turned harsh. "You'd joke about the holy sacrament of marriage, Jake?"

"You see, my friend's little *schweschder* is pregnant." Jake swerved to pass a slow-moving buggy. "I'm not the father, but I told Evie if she wouldn't marry me, then I'd marry the girl to give her child a father. I admit I said it out of spite, because Evie's the only girl I've ever loved. I only brought Brandy to Lancaster County to protect her from her abusive boyfriend."

"Shouldn't the girl go back home?" Harvey said.

"Her parents kicked her out. And her boyfriend wants her to have an abortion even at this late date. She's due to give birth in a couple of months."

"*Ach*, the world is a grievous place." Harvey slouched. "Jake, what's stopping you from joining the church and courting Eva properly? Your *Englisch* haircut and fancy clothes?"

Jake tossed his baseball cap into the backseat.

"This your car?" Harvey swiveled in his seat to face Jake.

"No." Jake stared out the windshield at an oncoming buggy. "I borrowed it so I could come see my *dat* in a hurry. I have to return it."

"But you did own a car at one time, did you not? The lad who bought it drove into a telephone pole and died, *yah*?"

After a moment of silence, a tear rolled down Jake's cheek. I'd never seen him cry. He wiped it away with the back of his hand. "If only I hadn't sold him that car, Lester would still be alive."

"Maybe. Only *Gott* knows the future. Lester might have bought a different vehicle and done the exact same thing." Harvey's voice was somber, as if recalling the funeral. "If you feel you sinned, repent and attempt to sin no more. Our Lord is quick to forgive."

The car was a tomb of silence for several minutes. I knew we were all sinners. I needed to forgive Jake and all others who might have hurt me through their gossip. Ignoring them hadn't healed my pain or resentment.

"Okay, *yah*. I want to be baptized and marry Evie." Jake slowed as we neared his parents' farm.

"Not so quick," Harvey said. "I caution you not to take the baptism classes until you've given it careful thought. This last week back with your parents, I've noticed a new stability in you, but you must prove it's permanent before I or any minister baptizes you."

He craned his neck to speak to me, but I moved closer to the window. "Same goes for you, Eva. You seem insecure. As if what others think of you is all-important."

He had me pegged. I sank into my seat and wished I could vanish into the upholstery.

"But marrying Jake won't fix anything unless your faith in *Gott* matures. His opinion is the most important."

Jake stopped the car and turned off the engine, but he didn't remove the key. "So if I'm stable and Evie's faith matures, we can be baptized?"

"We'll see. You're both teetering on the fence, but I'll allow you to take classes if you're serious. After you've finished, we'll speak again. And then possibly of marriage if you two are set on it."

"*Ach*, so long to wait. And in the meantime?"

"In the meantime, you work your father's farm, and you both weigh the pros and cons. Too many young people dive into marriage. After the initial infatuation fades and the babies arrive, the couples come to the deacons and ministers with their complaints." He placed his black hat atop his head. "Now, shall we visit your parents?"

When we exited the car, I was the last one out. The bishop and I followed Jake up the back steps, through the utility room, and into the kitchen. Ruth welcomed us with an ample grin. "What a wonderful surprise. We're so honored, Harvey, and it's *gut* to see you, Evie."

"Hi there, everyone." Brandy sashayed into the kitchen looking ready to burst, her abdomen extended even more than the last time I'd seen her. Wearing a long smock and leggings, she shook Harvey's hand as naturally as could be. She had more moxie than I did. I couldn't imagine being in her situation and acting so blasé. I'd hide out in Oregon or travel to Italy and stay in a quaint *pensione* in Florence for six months. Reading *A Room with a View* was having a bad influence on me. I could book passage on an ocean liner across the Pacific and into the Mediterranean Sea.

No, even if I were unmarried and pregnant, I wouldn't leave. Jake needed to support his parents, and I needed to prove I was stable. We'd stay here.

I'd best keep my thoughts to myself or the bishop would never baptize either of us.

"Brandy, I'd like you to meet Bishop Harvey," Ruth said.

"My goodness. A real bishop? Did you come over to give me a lecture?"

"Nah. He didn't even know you existed until ten minutes ago," Jake said. "He's here to visit my father."

"Nice to meet you, Brandy." Harvey's glance slid over to Ruth. "Where is Amos?"

"In the living room. We weren't expecting company..."

I figured she was trying to warn Harvey of Amos's wretched condition. We straggled into the living room toward his bed. A propane lamp illuminated the space and cast a yellow-white light across Amos's gaunt face, giving him a ghostly appearance. The head of his bed was raised, and his wiry beard lay off the side of his pillow.

"Amos, look who's come to see ya." Ruth lay her hand on his arm, and he blinked his eyes open and caught sight of me.

"Eva." His voice was faint, a mere whisper.

"Look," Ruth said, "Bishop Harvey's come by specially to pay you a call." But Amos kept his gaze glued to me.

"Eva."

Wanting to defer to Harvey, I paused for a minute. Then I went to Amos's side and greeted him. "You look *gut*, Amos. You must be eating."

"*Yah*, he is." Ruth stood at my side.

"We mush his food and feed him little bites," Brandy said. "I'll be an expert by the time my baby's a toddler."

Ruth sidled up next to her. "Brandy's been such a fine, *gut* help."

"We're helping each other." Brandy rested her head on Ruth's shoulder. "I wish I'd had a mother like her."

"I hope we're not breaking the *Ordnung*," Ruth said to Harvey. "Brandy has nowhere else to go."

"Is that true?" Harvey asked, the full force of his attention on Brandy.

"Yes. My parents are in the middle of an ugly divorce and turned their anger on me. They told me to leave and never come back." She stroked her abdomen. "Not that I have any right to blame them."

"Are there homes for unwed mothers where you're from?" he said.

"But couldn't we keep her here?" Ruth took Brandy's hand. "She keeps me company. I was planning to ask a midwife to stop by next week."

"*Yah*, go ahead. Maybe a *boppli* will comfort Amos. Have you spoken to your deacon about it?"

"Not yet. He's been sick with a head cold and didn't want to infect Amos by coming over. I don't think Deacon Samuel knows anything about Brandy yet. I didn't myself until Jake showed up. *Ach*, I hope Bishop Jonathon and our ministers don't want me to turn Brandy out."

"I'll speak to them on your behalf," Harvey said. "Jonathon is a fair man, although more conservative than I am."

"Brandy has been a great help to me, yet the only thing Amos seems to care about is Eva." Ruth's head pivoted toward me. "But the doctors said he may not remember any of this time period when he recovers."

"If he recovers," Jake said, bringing us back to harsh reality.

# Thirty-Seven

Chauffeuring Harvey to his home, Jake remained quiet. He and Harvey sat in the front, and I sat in the back. I snuggled under a lap blanket to ward off a case of the shivers.

I speculated as to where Jake's thoughts lay. On his near comatose father, who might never regain strength? On his stated decision to join the church and marry me? If we had to wait too long to get married, might both of us change our minds?

Or was Jake still struggling between two monumental choices—staying *Englisch* or being baptized—and not sure which one was right for him?

A buggy passed us coming from the other direction. I wondered if the metal clanking of the horse's hooves sounded to Jake like chiming bells or keys to a prison cell where he'd serve a lifetime sentence. I was still unclear myself. Did I want to live under the stringent laws of the *Ordnung* for the rest of my life if neither Jake nor Stephen was at my side?

"On the right." Harvey pointed to an imposing stone home. Behind it stood a white barn, several outbuildings, and three silos.

"Your house is elegant," I said.

Harvey pointed to a smaller home attached to the corner of the stone house. "Ever since my wife's death two years ago, I've considered moving into the *daadi haus*, but I still have four *dochders* living at home. One adult son runs the dairy farm."

"This is a beautiful farm."

"Much too large for one man. I have my plate full as bishop, and I was grateful my son took over the milking business."

Jake drove around the house and rolled to a stop near the back steps to a wraparound porch.

He unhooked his seat belt, but Harvey stayed put. "We have a bishop's meeting next month. Both your names have come up many times over the last five or so years. Some of the other bishops may insist on a six-month waiting period after you're baptized before you can marry."

My hand covered my mouth. I hadn't been paranoid when I thought others were talking about me. "Do all the bishops in the county think I had a child out of wedlock?" I sounded like a squawking hen.

"*Nee.* Your *aendi*'s deacon in Ohio wrote us and explained the situation. We knew you were innocent of that."

"You knew, but you never told anyone?" They should have defended me.

"Your sin has been avoiding joining the church because you were pining over Jake." He turned in his seat to face me. "Let's say Jake had married another woman, and you knew he was never coming back. Would you or would you not have joined the church?"

I felt as if I were on the witness stand under oath. "I'm not sure."

Jake shot me a snarly look. "But I didn't marry. Evie and I are both free and will join the church."

"Not so fast. I want to hear from Eva's lips that she will be obedient for life. When I'm satisfied with both of your commitments, we'll speak again."

I'd waited years and years for this opportunity, but did I really want it?

Harvey smoothed his beard. "Anything else you two wish to ask? If not, I'll say farewell. My *dochders* are expecting me." He got out of the car and positioned his hat atop his head as he waited for me to get in the front seat.

"*Denki* for taking me to see Amos," he told Jake before shutting my door.

Jake sat gripping the steering wheel. "Why did you have to say you weren't sure?" Jake's voice reminded me of a serrated knife cutting into a block of ice.

"You mean, be honest? Are you being honest with me? Will you be content living on an Amish farm without electronic gizmos and a cell phone?"

"My cell phone summoned the fire department. That fire could have spread to the house."

"*Yah*, I was there. But once you're baptized, you'll have to give it up, unless your parents' deacon, ministers, *and* bishop suddenly turn ultraliberal." I watched him work his lower lip. "Well, your bishop isn't, is he? Not according to Harvey. To the best of my knowledge, your parents have a phone shanty like mine do."

I stared into his eyes until he looked away and then piloted the car back onto the road.

"It all comes down to trust, doesn't it?" I savored the heat blowing through the vent.

"Are you trying to say you don't trust me?" He jammed on the brakes to avoid hitting a deer darting across the road. The seat belt restrained me from flying forward, praise the Lord. A car honked. Jake muttered to the driver behind us and moved us forward.

"Maybe Harvey's right about us waiting," I said.

"You mean forever?" He took a hard right without using his turn indicator. The car behind us belted out an extended honk but fortunately remained going straight.

"Please slow down. You'll get a speeding ticket."

"Driving instructions coming from a woman who backed into a police car? You'd never make it in the *Englisch* world."

I realized I hadn't thanked him for paying to have the squad car repaired, but I was too frazzled to do it now. If I opened my mouth, what might fly out? Something ugly, no doubt. Something final.

He crunched into the nursery's parking lot and stopped in the middle. "Good night, then," he said.

I let myself out and he sped away, his tires spitting up gravel.

My ears filled with white noise. I covered them. I stood frozen, my mind replaying the last half hour in fast-forward. I expected Jake to return to his senses—to hang a U-turn and come back to apologize. But he didn't. Maybe I didn't really know him. Bishop Harvey was right about my not rushing into marriage with Jake.

I lurched when a man cleared his throat. I turned to see Mark.

"You and lover boy having a quarrel?" Sarcasm snaked through his voice. *Ach*, he'd seen Jake drop me off like a sack of fertilizer.

"Hi, Mark. What are you doing here so late?" I pretended I hadn't heard his cynical comment.

"With such a low staff and fewer workers expected tomorrow, I needed to make sure all the nursery cash registers had been rung up and emptied, among other things. Stephen asked me to be in charge. He took off an hour ago."

"I'm sure you're doing a fine job." I felt like a bug under the magnified glass of his disapproving scrutiny.

"You could have had me, you know." Mark's hands ran up and down his suspenders.

"Mark, you're a fine young man." And arrogant, so it would seem. "But I didn't wish to lead you on when I cared for another."

"Don't think I'm going to come groveling after you now. I saw what just happened."

I felt mortified, but I decided I was done acting the guilty party. "I wouldn't expect you to." Or want it.

"What would Bishop Harvey say if he saw you alone in a car with Jake?" Behind his benevolent youthful facade, Mark was apparently also judgmental.

I stayed my voice, and forced my demeanor to act unscathed. I wanted to defend myself and rant about Jake's uncouth behavior, but there was no need to gossip about myself and make matters worse.

How I longed to be alone and have a good cry. I turned away from him. "I'm headed to the café to make sure we're ready to open in the morning. And that the doors are locked properly."

"You haven't done that yet?"

"*Yah*, I did, but I want to double-check." I shivered. "I've got to go." I hurried to the cabin to grab my warm coat as Mark walked away. As I reached my door, Beatrice opened hers.

"I'm going to check on the café," I said before she could speak.

"Eva, would you do me a huge favor and take Heath with you? Not only should you be careful with Ralph on the loose, but Heath is restless and keeps pacing. Stephen told me not to let him run free. He might sneak down to the sheep farm." She cinched her chenille bathrobe. "Here. I'll put him on leash."

Beatrice clipped on Heath's leash and held it out. "Please? Otherwise I'll have to go outside dressed like this."

Heath sat at her side until she transferred the leash to my hand. In a burst of energy, he bounded from the porch, pulling me off my feet.

"Heath!" Beatrice stepped out onto the porch. "You behave, you naughty dog."

I knelt and then struggled to my feet as Heath continued tugging. I had the oddest notion he was beckoning me to follow him. Now I wished Mark hadn't left, even if he chided me. Or Stephen. And Jake was long gone. Jake had shown me he didn't really love me. I needed to accept the truth.

I allowed Heath to lead me to the café. He whimpered. "No dogs allowed inside," I told him as I tied the leash to a post by the door. I slid in the key, unlocked the door, and cracked it.

An arm wearing a wool shirt slid around my neck, cutting off my air supply. I struggled as a man walked me inside and closed the door behind us. As he exhaled, the warm, foul odor of alcohol made me gag.

He loosened his grip enough for me to see grubby *Englisch* clothes. "Ralph?" I gasped for air and coughed.

"Yeah. It's me, honey."

"How did you get away from the fire?" My voice was raspy.

"A window in the loft in the nick of time, not that you really care." He loosened his choke hold, but I was still his captive. No one would hear me scream if I could even get the sound out.

As my heart beat triple time, I admonished myself to remain calm. "I'm glad you're okay. Really, I am."

"Oh, yeah? Then let's you and me have a little fun." His grin exposed crooked yellow teeth. "How's about a little smooch?"

"*Nee*, I can't." I recoiled as he turned me toward him. He pulled off my *kapp* and tossed it to the floor.

"Too good for me? I hate you Amish. Always think you're too good for the rest of us. When I was young, I had the biggest crush on an Amish girl..." His words were garbled. "She wouldn't even give me a second look, like I was beneath her. You're all like that."

Outside, Heath barked, a muffled sound as if he were in a fish tank, confirming that no one would hear our voices. I prayed in my head to the Lord to save me.

The door blew open, and Heath barged in, followed by Jake.

His hackles raised, the dog growled and bared his teeth.

Jake stopped dead in his tracks. "Hey, Ralph. You're okay." Jake seemed to be containing seething anger.

"No thanks to you." Ralph's words were slurred. Heath rushed forward, menacing Ralph.

"Get that mutt away from me." Ralph reached out, grabbed a butcher knife off the counter, and held the blade to my neck. "Jake, control that animal or your girlfriend is dead meat." The words bulleted into my brain, exploding. I wondered if I'd be in the newspaper again—in the obituaries. I thought of my parents.

Heath rushed over and bit Ralph's ankle. Ralph yowled, his knife-wielding arm swinging out. "Get that dog away from me!"

Jake sprinted over and yanked me out of Ralph's hold.

With agility, Jake kicked the knife out of Ralph's hand and allowed Heath to corner the man while he called 9-1-1.

"I'm going to tell the police you lit the barn on fire," Ralph said in slurred words. "I'll tell them what really happened. How I barely got out with my life when you trapped me up in the loft."

"You're drunk." Jake pulled out a chair. "Sit down and shut up."

Ralph thudded onto the chair and bent at the waist until his head rested on his hands.

Jake turned to me. "Are you okay, Evie?"

"Just shaken up." My legs trembled.

Hackles raised, the dog kept his gaze latched onto Ralph.

"Evie, sorry about the way I acted," Jake said. "Like a jerk."

"I'm glad you came back." I was still trembling. "*Denki.*"

By the time two officers arrived, Ralph had sobered up enough to give them an earful about how Jake and I had burned down the barn across the road and how we'd attempted to kill him just now. "Tried to slash me with a knife." He pointed toward Heath. "Sicced that dog on me."

Jake crossed his arms and shook his head. "No way."

I stepped forward. "I'm the manager of the café. Ralph grabbed me when I opened the door, and then he held a knife to my neck. The fire chief will want to question him about that barn fire."

"They tried to burn me alive" were Ralph's last words as an officer escorted him to his squad car.

I took Heath's leash from Jake. Heath knew I belonged here, and I trusted him. I wished I possessed complete trust in Jake.

# Thirty-Eight

The next morning the rumble of diesel engines woke me. My clock by the bed declared it was six o'clock. I arose and peeked out the window to see clear skies. The sunrise was turning the world golden. Soon its glorious warmth would dry the mud left over from the fire hoses.

I hoped last night's ghastly scene at the nursery would evaporate from my thoughts. My muddled mind flipped through the events as if reading a book. Jake leaving me in the parking lot, Mark's negative remarks, meeting up with Ralph—who wanted to kiss me of all disgusting things. Then he threatened to kill me. I abhorred violence, but I could have been a victim of his drunken wrath.

Jake had returned and saved me. Or would Ralph have eventually stumbled out the back door with Heath nipping his heels? My mind was muddled.

I wasn't ready to see Jake yet. I imagined the many activities I'd missed as I'd waited for his return. Years and years of my life wasted as if walking on a treadmill going nowhere. But I would not miss at least some of the barn raising on his account. He might not even show up.

I hurried to get dressed, shrugged on a black sweater, and trotted across the road. A flatbed truck carrying newly milled timber rolled into the Schmuckers' driveway and parked near two others. The lumber's fragrance replaced the smoky stench like a promise of rebirth. A new start.

I shivered in the chilly morning air, even with my sweater and the sunshine. I should have worn a coat, but there was no time to get one now, not when I needed to hustle to the café soon. I had a job to do too.

Hannah came bustling over to tell me that, after much consulting and planning last night, several older men with experience in barn raisings had ordered the wood. They'd prayed, conferred, and chosen the team captains.

By the house, the tables were still set up. A woman I'd met yesterday scrubbed the vinyl tablecloths as several others set out cups, paper plates, and napkins. Both Amish and *Englisch* women appeared with boxes of donuts and muffins.

A steady stream of buggies, cars, and vans arrived like a river of plenty. Amish men, including *Dat* and my brother, Reuben, and boys wearing straw hats; *Englisch* men dressed in T-shirts and sporting baseball caps; men of every size and shape. Most wore tool belts, ready for the task and grinning with expectation. They swarmed to unload the oak timbers and sheets of metal from the flatbed trucks.

The air was soon buzzing as saws cut into the sturdiest logs to be used for beams.

Men heaved the six-by-six beams and posts into place. The first wall was assembled on the ground. With heavy ropes fastened to either side, men surged together, pulled it up, and attached it to the foundation, securing the first wall with massive bolts and nails, hammers banging.

Other walls were soon constructed and put in place. More women arrived with food for the forenoon break at nine.

I spotted Jake, wearing a black T-shirt, jeans, and a baseball cap. The world came to a halt. All noises melded together, and the backs of my knees grew weak. I stood gawking like a pitiful teenager, admiring his agility as he climbed the tallest ladder and then pounded nails with sculpted biceps.

"Evie?" Stephen stood at my side. He wore denim overalls, a plaid shirt, and a tool belt. "You coming to work today at the café?" he asked, and chuckled.

"Oh, dear. What time is it?"

He glanced at his watch. "Only seven. Still early enough to start the soup. Most customers will come over here to watch the barn raising. But they may want coffee and a snack or lunch after a bit."

"I'm so sorry." Like a moth to a flame, my gaze returned to Jake. Below him I recognized Bishop Harvey, working alongside a man half his age whose wife might be among the women and praying for his safety.

I watched Jake move with ease and wondered if he adored danger and the thrill of uncertainty. Would he always be drawn to the perilous? And dream of escape? No wonder Harvey wanted us to wait.

And yet here stood Stephen, a stable man of integrity who had already faced his demons. He was humble and put others' needs before himself. I peered at his ruggedly handsome face. My, he was tall and his shoulders wide. In the morning sunlight, I noticed flecks of bronze in his hazel-brown eyes. And this man had professed he loved me.

What was I doing musing over two men at once? *Ach*, Stephen was a Mennonite. An *Englischer*. Suddenly, I hated the word.

I imagined a tranquil life with Stephen. Living with all the modern conveniences I'd been taught were wrong because they dispersed the Amish community. Leaving the *Ordnung* behind and following only the teachings of the Bible. I wondered what attending Stephen's church would be like and if I should visit it some Sunday.

When he noticed I was gazing up at him, the corners of his mouth lifted. He shot me an intense look. "Evie, I apologize if I came on too strong, but everything I told you is true. I'd like to pursue a relationship with you. A permanent relationship. Will you give it some thought?"

"*Yah.*" How could I not? Had he just proposed marriage, or had I misinterpreted his words?

Two *Englisch* men dressed for a day of labor strode past us.

"I'd better get to work." Stephen's glance followed them. "See you later."

"Okay." I stared at his departing form as he joined the builders. Much as I wanted to continue watching the barn raising, I forced myself to stride to the café and unlock the front door.

As I entered the café, last night's living nightmare came to mind. The officer said Ralph would spend the night in jail. Did I want to press charges and bear witness against him in court? No. It was not the Amish way. Yet did I want to follow those stringent rules anymore?

On the kitchen counter sat a large can of cannellini beans—I'd never heard of them before—serving as a paperweight for a recipe for Tuscan vegetable soup written in Beatrice's bold hand. *The chicken broth is in the refrigerator*, she'd scrawled at the bottom. *It's facile*. Which I hoped meant "easy."

She came in an hour later and helped prepare for opening. "I needed to walk the dogs." She winked. "And watch the spectacle across the street." She made coffee as Sadie and Annie filled the food cases.

A few hours later, the café swelled with hungry customers, all talking about the skilled and brave men constructing the new barn. I figured the workers were resting and enjoying their noontime meal. Mark stopped by and reported the project was going well.

"Any injuries?" I couldn't help asking.

"Only one young fellow missed the nail and smacked his thumb." Mark's voice was upbeat and friendly. "Poor guy, with so many spectators."

I set aside our differences and offered him a pumpkin whoopie pie, which he savored. "The best I've ever tasted. Who cooked this?"

"Meet our new chef." I hurried over to Sadie, linked arms with her, and took her in tow. Her cheeks turning pink, she lagged behind me until we'd reached Mark.

"You cooked these?" he asked.

"*Yah.*" She poured him a mug of coffee.

"Are all your baked goods this delicious?" he asked her.

She gazed up at him through her eyelashes. "You'll have to try them and tell me."

It was as if Mark had noticed her existence for the first time. They fell into conversation, and I backstepped. Minutes later, he asked Sadie if she wanted to accompany him to watch the barn raising. She asked me for permission, and I assured her we would be fine, what with Annie's abilities working the cash register. Next week, when Beatrice went back to work for the Yoders, keeping their house and babysitting full-time, I'd be all set.

Mark and Sadie were gone for more than an hour. Sadie returned glowing. I was happy for her and prayed Mark would ask her to a singing, even though my cousin Emma would no doubt be disappointed.

"Evie, dear." *Mamm* waited at the end of the line to place an order. With so many in the café, I'd missed her entrance. Plus Marta's. My sister-in-law wore an olive-green dress that echoed her eyes. Her perfectly pressed *kapp* was tied under her chin.

"Is it always this busy?" Marta canvassed the café, especially the glass case filled with baked goods.

"*Nee*, this is unusual because of the barn raising. But we do a *gut* business all in all."

"Do you have time to sit with us?" *Mamm* motioned to an empty table.

"*Yah*, unless more people come in."

"Hello," Beatrice said to *Mamm*, and then she placed her hand on my shoulder. "People are hurrying through their meals to return to the barn raising. You have time for a break, Eva. I'll let you know if we get in trouble."

I sat facing the door, just in case we were barraged again. Or in case Jake came in, although I knew he wouldn't. In fact, I didn't want him to, especially in front of *Mamm* and Marta.

*Mamm* tasted her soup as soon as Sadie delivered their orders. "This is delicious, Evie. Nothing like we make at home, though. Different spices."

"Beatrice gave me the recipe and a can of beans. She's been a blessing to me." I never thought I'd sing her praises.

"*Wunderbadr.*" Marta sat tall. "This place won't miss you when you come and work for Reuben and me at our new business."

*Mamm* nibbled her blueberry muffin and kept her attention on the koi pond.

"I have a job, Marta. Right here."

"But Reuben and I have decided to open a wholesale bakery. Plus have a roadside stand when the weather warms. Maybe sell touristy gifts too."

I doubted Reuben had anything to do with the idea. "Who would do the baking?" I asked.

"You, your *mamm*, and I will." Marta slathered a muffin with butter. "And hire a young woman the way you have once we get busy. My *dochders* will help after school and on the weekends, after they do their chores and their homework." She sent *Mamm* a furtive glance. "Your *mamm* offered to help out."

"You did?" *Mamm* had mentioned she looked forward to quilting more, her lifelong passion she'd mostly set aside until *Dat* retired.

*Mamm* refolded her napkin. "*Yah*, I said I'd help them, but I never said you'd be quitting this job, *dochder*."

"Evie wouldn't choose to work for strangers over her own family, would she?" Marta contorted her mouth.

For all I knew, the Yoders would fire me when they got home. I might need a job. But not working for Marta. *Ach.*

"How will Evie meet her future special man working at our home?" *Mamm* asked.

"At our roadside stand or delivering baked goods to restaurants." Marta scanned the thinning crowd. "This place is too far away from home for delivery unless we hired a driver. And too many *Englischers*." She wrinkled her nose.

Harvey wandered in with Stephen. He raised a hand in greeting and then sat at a nearby table while Sadie brought the two men coffee.

"Isn't that Bishop Harvey?" *Mamm* asked. "Such a fine man. I don't suppose you'll join his church district?"

"We've discussed it."

"*Yah?*" *Mamm*'s grin stretched from ear to ear, her smile lines deepening. "Maybe I should go over there and speak to him."

"*Nee!*" I blurted out. "Another time would be better when he's not so tired. He's worked on the new barn since sunup. I'm glad to see him resting."

"He appears a kindly sort." Marta watched Harvey shake an Amish man's hand. "I've never met him."

I was horrified by what she might say to him. As she stood, so did Harvey and Stephen. They exited the café before she could pounce on them.

"Perhaps you'll meet him later this afternoon," *Mamm* said. "Before we give *Dat* and Reuben a ride home."

"I bet they'll both be fatigued, but they'll still have chores to do." Marta settled in her seat and finished her sandwich. "I can't say I'm crazy about this soup." She puckered her lips. "I hope I haven't offended you, Eva."

"Not in the slightest." I smoothed my hand over the table's cracked surface.

Wayne came into the café and made a beeline toward me. I introduced him to *Mamm* and Marta.

"Evie, can we speak later?" Wayne looked imposing in his uniform, wearing a firearm. "I'd like to get your take on something."

"Of course." I sent him what I hoped was an angelic, innocent smile. "I'll be here or maybe watching the barn raising."

"What's this about, Officer?" Marta asked.

"Sorry, ma'am. Police business I can't discuss. Nothing urgent." I was thankful he didn't divulge any further information about my involvement with the fire or mention my encounter with Ralph the night before. I'd never appreciated Wayne more. Not everything about the *Englisch* world was bad. What would we Amish do without them? I had many questions for Harvey.

Sadie cleared away *Mamm*'s and Marta's dishes, including Marta's uneaten soup, while Beatrice brought them coffee.

"*Ach*, this *kaffi* is too strong." Marta seemed to have a complaint for everything, but I knew she'd led a sheltered life. If anything, I was too worldly. I offered her hot water to dilute the coffee, along with cream and sugar, but she declined.

"Ruth appreciates your visits, Evie," *Mamm* told me.

"Everyone in the county's talking about how Amos keeps repeating your name," Marta said.

I wanted to plug my ears. "He's in a half-dream state and doesn't know what he's saying."

"Even so, don't you think it's strange he's so fixated on you and not that *Englisch* girl who moved in? She must be Jake's doing."

"How about some dessert?" I wanted to change the subject.

*Mamm* smiled, but Marta said, "*Nee*, we'll find something across the road." She stood and spoke to *Mamm*. "Come on. Let's go see what our husbands are doing. We should be giving the other women a break."

As I helped *Mamm* to her feet, Beatrice spoke in my ear. "If you wish to escort them across the road, go ahead. My best guess is we'll be slow the rest of the afternoon. And I have two young ladies to do the cleanup."

Marta frowned. "Aren't you her boss?" she said to me when Beatrice was out of earshot. "You should be telling her what to do."

"First I want to see your cabin," *Mamm* said. "The inside this time."

"*Yah*, I wish to see it too." I figured Marta wanted to see if I'd made my bed. I wondered if I had.

On the way out, I paused to ask Beatrice, "Do you want me to let the dogs out?"

"No, thanks. Stephen said he would."

I led *Mamm* and Marta to my cabin, unlocked the door, and was pleased to see I'd remembered to make the bed and wipe the counters clean.

"Why, this is very nice." *Mamm* circumnavigated the room.

"No electricity?" Marta inspected the lamps.

"The woman who lived here before me was Amish. All appliances were installed according to the *Ordnung*."

"No telephone either?"

"*Nee.*" I heard annoyance in my voice.

"Still, it looks fancy."

"Not to me." *Mamm* came to my rescue. "Evie's quilt complements this room perfectly. I'm so glad. I'm happy for you, dearest *dochder*."

On our way out of the cabin, the three dogs barked and yipped from inside the main house.

"*Ach*, I don't know how you can tolerate that racket." Marta cringed with drama for my sake, I supposed.

"They're guarding the house in the owners' absence."

Marta's hands clamped on her hips. "Apparently, you're not afraid of anything. Going off on your own. Living in this cabin all by yourself."

If she only knew the fears I still harbored. But I was overcoming them one by one. Besides, she didn't mind my leaving until she decided I should help with a new business.

We left the cabin. Hearing the banging of hammers and saw blades gripping into lumber, I steered them toward the barn raising, and we crossed the road.

"They've come a long way so quickly." *Mamm* scanned the industrious men, installing siding while others roofed. "Where's your *dat*, Evie? I hope not atop a ladder or on the roof."

I made a conscious effort not to look for Jake or Stephen among the laborers so Marta wouldn't catch me gawking at them. And so they wouldn't see me and wave.

"There he is." *Mamm* finally located *Dat*—not on a roof or ladder, praise the Lord.

"We should have been helping the women instead of sitting in the café being waited on," Marta said.

"*Nee*, I enjoyed the café." *Mamm* linked her arm in mine. "And I'm delighted with Eva's accomplishments."

Minutes later, she and Marta traipsed off to assist the other women clean up and prepare more coffee. Was I turning paranoid, or did all the women's heads rotate my way? Most likely *Mamm* had mentioned me.

"Eva?" I cringed when I recognized Wayne's voice. The women's attention still was directed at me, as well as half of the men's.

I composed my features and turned to Wayne. "Is this a good time to talk?" he asked.

"*Ach*, with everyone watching?"

"It's here or down at the station."

A flock of cackling starlings landed in a nearby tree. I hoped they'd distracted the women, but I noticed they were still watching me. Their heads tipped together as they spoke.

"Is there a problem?" I asked Wayne.

"I hate to be the bearer of bad news, but Ralph woke up ornery and ready for a fight. He claims you lured him into the café, which I find hard to believe. And yet he has his rights. Did you have a witness?"

"No, other than a dog."

"On top of that, he wants to sue you and Jake for slander. He said he was nowhere near this barn the night it burned."

"But his brother's wife said he wasn't home."

"Well, we're not sure they're legally married, and Bill changed his story too. He says Ralph told him he was going to a friend's to play poker that night. Those games can be all-nighters."

"But none of that is true."

"At this point, it's your word against theirs, unless the arson investigator found any traces of Ralph's tobacco or whiskey bottle. We won't have his report for a few days yet. To make matters worse, Bill called animal control and launched a complaint against the Yoders' dog."

"But Heath was protecting us."

"Still, we can't have vicious dogs running loose."

"He's not vicious."

"Bill said the dog bit him on the arm last week. Apparently, Stephen witnessed that attack. I doubt he'd lie under oath. Plus, Bill said he tackled him."

"Bill Hastings pointed a shotgun at Stephen and threatened to use it."

"Hey, you don't have to convince me. Stephen has an excellent reputation. Can't say the same for Jake. Bill says he's planning to sue Jake if he continues to accuse Ralph of starting the fire. Those Hastings brothers stick together."

"I was there..." No use talking about it now with an audience. "I'd best head back to work."

"Hey, Evie." Jake strolled over to us. I felt a pull so deep I had to remind myself Stephen and a multitude were watching us, sizing up our relationship. More fodder for gossip.

"Hi, Wayne," Jake said.

Wayne nodded in return.

A moment later Stephen joined us. "Something going on I should know about?"

"Bill and Ralph are on a rampage," Wayne said. "They've filed complaints against you, Evie, and Jake. Even Glenn's dog."

Stephen wiped his sweaty forehead with a handkerchief. "I'd better call Glenn and let him know. He may want us to use his attorney."

"I'm not paying Glenn's attorney five hundred dollars an hour for him to defend me against some lamebrain false accusation," Jake said. "If I hadn't shown up last night, who knows what would have happened to Evie?"

I recalled the feel of Ralph's arm around my neck and trembled at the narrowness of my escape. Jake had rescued me.

"What exactly were you doing there, Jake?" Wayne's demeanor turned rigid, his knees locked.

"Yeah, I'd like to know the same thing." Stephen jutted out his chin.

"I wanted to speak to Evie about visiting my *dat*." Thankfully, Jake didn't elaborate further.

"You don't have permission to enter the nursery after hours." Stephen folded his arms across his chest. "I'm tempted to take out a restraining order to keep you off the property permanently."

The muscles on Jake's jawline twitched. "Can he do that?" he asked Wayne.

"Well, I don't know. Glenn could."

"I'll suggest it to Glenn next time I talk to him." Stephen's voice was terse, his words clipped.

"Have you spoken to Glenn recently?" Wayne asked Stephen.

"We keep in touch. But I've kept the conversations lighthearted. Glenn's father-in-law may only have days to live. Glenn has worries enough, and his wife and daughter need him." He rubbed his chin. "In retrospect, it was a mistake to hold anything back. But my guess is Beatrice speaks to Rose daily."

"You'd better give him the full scoop today." Wayne's gaze turned to the road as a pickup cruised to a halt. "This problem isn't going away by itself."

# Thirty-Nine

"Please tell me that isn't Bill Hastings." Stephen angled his body away from Wayne.

"That's Ralph's brother?" Jake asked, watching Bill exit his vehicle and tromp toward us.

My hand at my throat, I wanted to escape. To bolt across the road, hide in my cabin, and lock the door. No, I still wouldn't be safe. And a cowardly act would make me seem guilty of crimes I hadn't committed.

Bill tromped over to us. "Well, now ain't this handy?" Bill reminded me of *Dat*'s bull when riled. He turned to Wayne. "I hope you've filled these lowlifes in. How Ralph and I won't tolerate their insults and accusations anymore. Someone's gonna pay." He glanced at the barn out of the corner of his eye. Half the men had stopped working and stared back at him.

Bishop Harvey climbed down a ladder and strode over to us. He put out his hand to shake Bill's. "Hello, I'm Harvey."

Bill seemed reluctant to shake his hand. "Yeah, I know who you are. Someone told me you're an Amish bishop, which means nothing to me. Don't expect me to kneel down and kiss your ring."

Harvey smiled. "I don't even wear a wedding ring, so no problems there. And no one has ever bowed down to me. Although I might be able to help out if you'd accept my input."

"Nah. How could you possibly help? I know how you Amish

think. Forgive and forget. Well, the people in this county won't forget what's been said about my brother and me. And I sure won't forget the Yoders' dog biting me. He could have rabies, for all I know."

"He's been vaccinated," Stephen said, but Bill ignored him.

"But the dog bit me, right? I still think it killed some of my lambs. And now Ralph has been accused of burning a barn and accosting a young woman. He had to spend the night in jail."

I mashed my lips together to keep silent. Ralph had attacked me and might have killed me if Jake hadn't shown up and let Heath in.

Harvey seemed to be pondering as he stroked his beard. "Perhaps you could go speak to your own minister, Bill."

"Look, you're not my bishop, so don't bother preaching to me." Bill snorted a laugh. "I gave up that phony-bologna Bible business years ago. The only part I remember is an eye for an eye."

"Did ya never hear 'Love your neighbor as yourself'?" Harvey's voice remained calm.

"Oh, you mean like God does? Don't make me gag. Those platitudes mean nothing."

"Has no one ever forgiven you when you didn't deserve it?" Harvey asked.

"That's a trick question, isn't it?" Bill blinked. "God died the day my mother did. I was six years old."

Harvey rubbed his palms together. I figured he was weighing his words. "Did your father remarry?"

"No. And he never forgave Ralph and me for nothing. When he came home snookered, we used to hide out in the barn."

"Where is he now?"

"Not in heaven, that's for sure." Bill swiped his nose with his cuff. "One snowy night when I'd just turned eighteen, Dad's car skidded off the road and down an embankment. He was barely holding on according to the only witness, an Amish man, who didn't have a cell phone to call 9-1-1. By the time the medics finally arrived, it was too late."

"I'm sorry for your loss," Harvey said. "Losing both of your parents must have been very difficult."

Bill's mouth twisted. "If that Amish guy had owned a cell phone and a car, our father might have made it. You Amish are all screwed up."

Harvey stood in silence for a moment. "God's ways are difficult to understand."

"That makes you pretty dumb. I mean, you only went to the eighth grade and haven't even been to divinity school, and yet you claim to be a bishop."

"Many would agree with you." I imagined Harvey had plenty on his mind, but he didn't defend himself.

"Hey, Bill. This isn't the time or place," Wayne said.

Bill clenched his fists.

"Don't make this situation worse." Wayne raised his hand to chest level, as if ready to ward off a punch.

"How are you with a hammer?" Harvey asked Bill. "We could use another hand on this barn."

"Yeah, right. As if I'd help out an Amish farmer."

"Well, there's coffee and food over there. You're welcome to a snack."

"Look, I don't want anything from you because then you'd think I owed you."

"I'm surprised no one helped feed you when your father died," Harvey said.

"A few neighbors brought food over, and we ate it only because we were hungry. Our father always said, 'Don't take nothing from no one. There's always a catch.'"

Despite everything, my heart went out to this wounded man. Not that I trusted him. Not that his circumstances gave him the right to hurt others. But still, I felt pity for him. I knew I had been gullible much of my life, but he trusted no one. I had to ask myself if I had become guilty of the same trait.

I walked over to the food table and returned with napkins and a paper plate supporting several donuts and other baked goods. "May I tempt anyone?"

Wayne's hand flew out to snag a sugar-covered donut. "I couldn't refuse a lady." He bit into it and then grabbed a napkin as the creamy filling dripped down his chin.

"How about you, Bill?"

I could tell Bill was wavering by the way he shifted his weight back and forth, but he shook his head. "I haven't been working. You'll all take this as a sign I won't press charges."

"No, we won't. There's coffee over there too."

Apparently, Bill couldn't resist the chocolate donut. He reached out to take it. "Yeah, well, this doesn't change anything." He chomped a mouthful. "Where's the coffee?"

I pointed to the cups on the table, and he sauntered off to fetch some. I noticed his shoulders had relaxed and his gait turned easy.

The clanging of hammers resumed. The chatter of men working on the barn started up again.

"Good work, Eva." Wayne tidied his mouth, wadded up the napkin, and stuffed it into his jacket pocket. "I thought I was going to be in the middle of a fistfight. I would have hated to give up that donut before I finished it."

"A temporary lull in the storm." Stephen kicked a pebble. "But I agree with Wayne. Evie calmed the turbulent waters." He sent me a smile.

"Don't get any ideas," Jake said. "She and I are going to get married."

Harvey's eyebrows lifted. "Are you sure you wish to speak of private matters in public?"

I waited to see a sign of contrition on Jake's face, but his features seethed with frustration. Finally, he turned to face Harvey and then me, and said, "You're right. I apologize. Lots of work yet to do here, but I need to return home to my *dat*."

He pivoted and marched back to the barn, which was nearing

completion—on the outside, anyway. Over my shoulder I watched Jake's departing form and felt more confused than ever.

I tracked down my parents and found them preparing to leave, their buggy all hitched.

*Dat*'s eyes brightened when he saw me. If we'd been *Englisch*, I know he would have hugged me and told me he loved me in front of everyone.

"Your *mamm* says you're doing a fine job at the café," he told me. "But then you've always been capable at whatever you've pursued."

"To be honest, I still can't cook very well."

"But you're learning, I assume."

"*Yah*, I'm getting better."

"No thanks to me," *Mamm* said. "I wasn't a very *gut* teacher."

"You're the best *mamm* in the world," I said. "And I told you before, I liked being in the barn with *Dat*."

Again, *Dat*'s eyes lit up with delight.

"You did well working at Zook's Fabrics," Marta said. She was reporting positively about me? "And from what I saw today, you run the café seamlessly. I think you'd be bored silly baking at home, even if you ran the roadside stand." The hem of her dress fluttered in the breeze as she swayed back and forth. "Anyway, our plans have changed. I've spoken to several women in the last few hours who are looking for places to sell their quilts. Your mother was one of them. I've admired her quilts but didn't think she'd wish to sell them." She rubbed her belly. "I've been stupid to miss such a great opportunity. Your *mamm* can babysit and quilt at the same time."

My brother and Marta were having another baby? I didn't dare ask.

"Anyway, I'm sorry for being such a ninny," she told me. "Reuben made it clear he doesn't want a bakery business, but I wouldn't listen.

Raising our children and keeping the farm going is more important. Not to mention obeying my husband. Reuben told me to apologize to you and I am. I was acting selfishly and bossy. I'm sorry."

"No need to apologize." And yet I savored her words. She put out her hand to shake mine, but I hugged her instead. I felt my fondness for her expanding.

At that moment Reuben strode over to us, looking beat. "Someone just offered me a ride home, and I think I'd better accept it. I've so much to do yet today. Maybe if I leave now, I'll be done by the time you get home."

"You go ahead and don't worry about us," Marta said.

"*Yah,* I'll do the driving," *Dat* said. He looked tired, too, but a good kind of tired.

"See ya later." Reuben strode off and met up with Jake, of all people. What on earth?

Before leaving, *Dat* spoke in my ear, claiming my attention. "I know you're not a little girl anymore, but I don't want you going over to the café at night alone," he said.

So he'd heard the whole story. That probably meant everyone in the county had.

# Forty

Beatrice and Heath accompanied me to the café to check the place over before turning in.

"Stephen's orders," Beatrice had said.

"*Yah*, he already told me to not walk there alone. As well as my *dat*."

"Do you want to sleep in the big house with me tonight?" Her question caught me by surprise. My head swung around to see her serious expression.

"That big old house has a guest room Rose's sister and husband use when they visit. It has a nice, comfy queen-sized bed." Beatrice watched me lock the café and double-check the door.

"Thanks for the kind offer, but I'm content in the cabin with all my things." Including my book. The heroine had returned to Great Britain and the story lagged, but I wanted to finish it.

"Do you miss Italy?" I asked her.

"Often. But I remind myself my relatives came here for a purpose. This is where I belong. Are you thinking you'd like to visit Italy?"

"It sounds so beautiful."

"So is Lancaster County. If it's a change of scenery you're seeking, maybe there's somewhere closer by. You're not thinking of leaving the café, are you?"

"No, I just got started. Oh, I don't know what I want. I thought I did growing up, but now I'm conflicted."

"Everyone goes through that. Particularly unmarried women your age. Well, even if they're married." She patted her cheek, as if deep in thought. "Or were married..."

I imagined she was thinking of her deceased husband.

"I wasn't in love with my husband when we married," she said. "Maybe not for the first five years. First impressions can be wrong, don't you think?"

"Yes." I recalled meeting Beatrice and not liking her one bit, but I'd been wrong about her. "Life is so confusing sometimes."

"Are you talking about Jake? Or Stephen? I couldn't help but notice Stephen is infatuated with you."

"*Yah*, those two men, and about joining the church."

"Sometimes I find my answers in the Bible. Proverbs 3:5 says, 'Trust in the Lord with all thine heart; and lean not unto thine own understanding.'"

"Hey, are you the one who put the Bible by my bed?"

She smirked. "Guilty as charged."

"Thanks. I've been reading it. I want to trust God, but when I pray, he doesn't tell me what I should do." I thought about all the nights I'd lain in bed praying the Lord would bring Jake home. But would that have solved all my problems?

"And then there's the *Ordnung*," I said. "So many rules that make little sense when you think about it."

"You should talk to Bishop Harvey about that. The Catholic church isn't perfect either, but don't tell anyone I said so." She winked. "I'm glad you came here. At first I had my doubts, but I was wrong. You're a fine, hard-working girl." She grinned when I winced. "Yes, you're a girl compared to me. But I'm the one who acted immaturely."

I recalled how judgmental I'd been. "*Ach*, I'm certainly less than perfect." No need to hurt her feelings by telling her my initial reaction.

"Aren't we all?" She hugged me. A real hug. And I hugged her back.

"Now, about tonight," she said, releasing me. "You want Heath to stay with you?"

"Better not. If he ran off—oh my, what an uproar." I recalled my first night here. "Do you think Minnie would stay with me? She'd bark if someone were prowling around."

"Are you hoping Jake will come see you?"

"No, and if he does—if anyone does—I'll simply refuse to open the door so Minnie can't escape." I was in no mood to see Jake even though he'd been kind enough to give my brother a ride home. "But I do want to visit Amos again one day."

"I'll ask Stephen to drive us over there after work tomorrow. If he's free. Would that be okay?"

"*Yah*, I'd appreciate it. Amos could die before I say goodbye."

"I'll make something to take Ruth. That poor woman." She tilted her head. "Whether you call Jake and tell him we're coming with Stephen is up to you. But I don't want those two men arguing in front of Amos and Ruth."

"I think we're better off just showing up." At least I was.

"Did I mention I've known Amos all my life? Ruth too. My parents rented a small house between their childhood homes. Stop me if I'm repeating myself."

"Did Amos and Ruth love each other way back then?"

"*Smitten* is a better word. They used to meet secretly in our small apple orchard..."

"Sounds romantic."

"Yes, it was. But over the years Amos's heart grew bitter. I saw less of him, so I don't know the cause of his anger."

"But you lived right next door to him."

"Well, Amos went to his Amish one-room school and my parents insisted I go to Catholic school. I got a good education, even if one nun hated me." She gave the back of her hand a fake swat with her first two fingers. "Can you believe I've held on to that grudge so long?"

"Maybe she was mean to everyone."

"It didn't seem that way. She probably wanted what was best for me, but I was a strong-willed adolescent. That's why my parents arranged my marriage, even though I loved another young man."

Her dismal reality struck me like a slap on my face. "I'm so sorry." What else could I offer her? "Is the other man still around? Not that it's any of my business."

"We actually eloped, but my parents caught up with us and had the marriage annulled. And then they forced me into an arranged marriage I didn't want. Of course, after that, my boyfriend gave up on me. He still lives in these parts."

"Was it Amos?"

"No." She grinned and wagged her head. "You've been reading too many romance novels."

"Was he not Catholic?" I knew I was being nosy, but my curiosity was riled up.

"Yes, he was Catholic, but from a poor family. After my parents had our marriage annulled, he joined the military so he could go to college, where he met his wife. All that seems a lifetime ago." She expelled a lengthy breath.

"Do you ever run into him?"

"Occasionally, but we don't do more than say hi and then go our separate ways."

"Why are you so dead set against Jake?"

"I'm not, but I found the way he's treated his parents disgraceful. Not to mention leaving you dangling on a string. You can do better."

"He says he wants to marry me." Speaking the words made me feel helpless and immature, as if I were still being manipulated. "He may even join the church. But Harvey told us the bishops would have to wait until they see a real commitment."

"And what do you want?"

"Me?" My mind floundered for an intelligent response. "I want Minnie to keep me company tonight."

"Okay. Maybe dogs really are a woman's best friend."

# Forty-One

With Minnie on leash, I coaxed her into my cabin with a small plastic bag Beatrice had filled with chopped ham. I knew I was both Rose and Beatrice's surrogate, a temporary owner for the night, but I got the feeling the terrier liked me even without the tidbits. At this moment I needed all the friends I could get.

I slipped into my nightgown and then between the chilly sheets. As I opened my book, Minnie hopped on the end of the bed as if she knew she had a job. I probably interpreted too much from her actions, but I appreciated her company.

My lids drooping before I got started, I shut the book and set it aside. The two younger lovers in the novel didn't resemble Jake and me. And yet every love story made me think of him.

I dozed off and awoke when Minnie expelled a low growl. I assured myself a raccoon was rummaging around near my door. But Minnie jumped off the bed and yapped.

A knock-knock-knock on the door made her bark. I put on my bathrobe and tiptoed to the door to hear my cousin Olivia's voice. "Evie, it's me. Please let me in."

Much as I wanted to see her, I said, "I can't. I promised Beatrice I wouldn't open this door to anyone."

"Please let me come in, Evie. Am I not your cousin and best friend anymore?"

"I could lose my job." But I couldn't ignore her plaintive voice. I cracked the door enough to see she'd cut her hair and was dressed *Englisch*.

I scooped up Minnie so she wouldn't escape. "What are you doing here, Liv?" Not a warm welcome, but I was in shock, plus I feared I was jeopardizing my livelihood. Yet she wasn't a stranger or even a man, so what could Beatrice complain about?

Olivia squeezed her way inside. I closed the door behind her and set Minnie on the floor.

"What do you think?" Olivia twirled and fluffed her fingers through her short, highlighted hair. "Like it? I just step out of the shower, shake my head, and it's dry. Then I add a little hair product that smells so good." She was dressed in jeans and a purple knit jacket. And she was also wearing perfume.

"What have you done to your beautiful hair?" I sounded judgmental and critical, everything I abhorred.

"I donated it to a charity in Florida that makes wigs for children who go bald for whatever reason. 'Locks of Love.' Isn't that cool?"

"But your hair. You cut your beautiful hair."

"That's what my boyfriend said. He was not pleased because he thinks I should have gotten paid for it."

"Money is not my issue, Liv. It's against the *Ordnung*. Women must never cut their hair. In the Bible, it says a woman's hair is her glory, doesn't it? And you pierced your ears?"

She fingered her silver earrings. "Aren't they darling?"

She still looked cute, but like another person without her hair parted in the middle and covered with a *kapp*.

"Who cut and colored your hair?" I asked.

"A girl I met who works in a beauty salon."

"A beautician styled it that way, all spiky and uneven?"

"I asked her to highlight it with lavender too, and I love it." Gazing at her image in my mirror, she flashed a smile at herself. "When the beautician told everyone at the salon where my hair was being donated, all the other women clapped."

I supposed Olivia had performed a generous act, but I couldn't support it.

She fluffed her coif. "Don't worry so much. It'll grow back. I thought you'd be proud of me."

"Have your parents seen it?"

"*Ach*, you should have heard my *mamm* when she came into the restaurant where I'm working. Plus, I was carrying a tray of alcoholic beverages."

"You've started drinking too?" I must have sounded as flabbergasted as her mother had been.

"No, just carrying them to customers. Part of my job." Her voice turned sour. "I thought of all my friends, surely you wouldn't condemn me. But you're as bad as all the rest."

"I'm just surprised." To put it mildly.

"No, you're judging me. And here I thought I'd invite you to visit me where we're living in New Holland."

"An apartment?"

"Yes. In an old woman's basement. You want to come see it right now? I borrowed her car in exchange for going to the supermarket for groceries."

"I don't think I should."

"Because?" Olivia asked with a snarl in her voice.

"It's too late, and it's too far away. I have to get up early. And I'm taking care of Minnie." The dog perked her ears and wagged her stubby tail at the sound of her name.

"Jake could drive you another time. Or I'll come fetch you in a friend's car."

"You know how to drive?"

"Yes, I have for years. So come on right now. It'll be fun. Aren't you bored in this little cabin with no TV?"

"Liv, I don't want to be caught in the middle." I was curious, but I was already labeled a deceiver. "I don't want to have to fib if someone asks about you. It's better I don't know anything."

"At least come by the place where I work someday. My shift runs from afternoon to evening."

I recalled Stephen's disclosing he avoided places that served liquor. "I'd better not."

"What happened to my adventuresome cousin I always looked up to?"

"I got too old to live in the land of uncertainty."

"But nothing in life is for certain, Evie. I could get killed driving home tonight."

"*Ach*, don't even say that, Liv."

"No worries. I bet I drive as well as Jake." She stepped closer and asked, "Is this the beginning of the end of our friendship?"

"I don't want it to be." But I also felt our bond disintegrating.

"You'll only talk to me if I leave Butch and move home? *Ach*, I told you his name." She slumped down in the recliner. "I might as well tell you. We're thinking of moving to Philly soon."

"But why?"

"Butch landed a better job. And he has friends there. He says living in Lancaster County is a drag."

"But what will you do? Where will you live?"

"We haven't figured that out yet. Philadelphia isn't so far away. You can still visit us. Take the bus."

"Are you sure you want to move to a big city?" I felt a gulf opening between us.

"Why not? It'll be exciting. Come with us."

"And leave my new job? No way."

She sprang to her feet. "This was my job."

"*Yah*, I know. What are you saying? That you'll want it back if you don't like living *Englisch*?"

"I might if something goes wrong with me and Butch. And working in *Englisch* restaurants is no fun. Did you know Glenn and I have been friends for years and years? In fact, the café's design was my idea, koi pond and all."

"But I'm all settled in. I love working and living here."

"But what would I do if I decided to come home and my parents wouldn't let me in the house looking like this? Plus, I'd have nowhere to work."

"I wish you'd thought of all that before you cut your hair." Although I felt sorry for her, I would not let her bamboozle me.

"I can't believe you'd turn on me, your own flesh and blood."

"Likewise, Olivia." I felt tears pressing at the backs of my eyes, but I stood tall, shoulders erect. "We'd still buy your baked goods if needed. We have a lovely girl doing the baking here now, but you never know. She may eventually get married."

Olivia glowered. "Don't worry about my darkening your door ever again. If I have business with this nursery, I'll go directly to the owner."

She spun away without saying goodbye and slammed the door behind her. I figured wounded feelings were guiding her tongue, but I felt a searing pain, as though a limb had been severed.

At sunup, Minnie groaned and sniffed the air.

"I should have brought you breakfast, little one," I told her.

I checked out the window and saw lights illuminating the main house's kitchen. I freshened up and dove into clothes. By this time, Minnie was pawing at the door and whining to get out. When I snapped on her leash and opened the door, she tugged me outside. After relieving herself, she dragged me to the main house's door just as Beatrice opened it.

"*Buongiorno, ragazze,*" she said. "Good morning, girls. Come in."

Minnie yipped as Missy and Heath sniffed her over, no doubt detecting trace aromas of ham. Beatrice filled the dogs' three food dishes, and their jaws chomped into the kibble with gusto, as if they hadn't eaten for weeks.

"How about some coffee?" Beatrice asked me. Before I could answer, she was filling a cup. "If it's too strong, I have cream or milk." She set out a small carton of cream.

"This is perfect." I dribbled in some cream and delighted in the roasted, bitter taste. "I was glad to have Minnie with me last night."

"Yes, she's a good little watchdog."

"She would have let me know if a prowler was lurking about."

"*Che strano*—how strange—my bedroom window was open. And I thought I heard a woman's voice."

"I did have an uninvited female visitor, but I promised not to tell anyone."

Beatrice wagged her finger. "Never mind fretting. I recognized Olivia's voice right away. And I got a look at her hair."

I envisioned Beatrice tiptoeing down to the kitchen to watch and straining to listen to our conversation.

"It sounded as though you were arguing. I've never heard Olivia raise her voice."

"Me neither." I covered my blabbing mouth. I was tempted to tell her everything. That Olivia had threatened to steal my job if she needed it, and probably live in my cabin. Beatrice might know what Glenn's reaction would be. I was aching to tell her all about Olivia's threats, but I mustn't become a gossip like those who had plagued me.

"Her hairdo was atrocious." Beatrice pulled out a hairpin and adjusted her bun. "Hideous. Why would a lovely young woman do such a thing?"

"She said it was for a good cause, but I've promised not to speak of it." I sipped my coffee to keep myself from tattling more. "I mustn't gossip."

"Telling the truth isn't gossiping."

"It seems a fine line." I had to hold my ground.

She reinserted the hairpin. "I certainly hope you weren't arguing over a man."

"No, although don't men creep into most every conversation?" I needed to steer our discussion in a different direction. "I was very careful to keep Minnie inside."

"That's good, but I don't think our little Minnie would run off. She misses Rose too much."

I felt the air leaking out of my balloon. The fact that Minnie was devoted to Rose while the pooch barely knew me made me feel deflated. Well, what did I expect? I reminded myself I didn't even like dogs. Not most of them, anyway. But I did love my cousin Olivia. And I'd thought she loved me.

The rest of the day whizzed by like a roller-coaster ride at a carnival, with twists and turns on rough tracks.

Our bread delivery was late. "Sorry, folks. Transmission problems," Scott said. "I had to swap out vans. And no rye bread today."

I tried to support him. "I'm sure it couldn't be helped." And yet my confidence in motorized vehicles had diminished.

Minutes later, three *Englisch* women brought five youngsters under school age into the café. The unruly children fussed and squirmed and ran around swiping saltshakers off the tables, but the women paid no attention. When the children became fascinated with the koi in the pond, I gave them a little bit of food to sprinkle on the water's surface. But the oldest child grabbed the container and tossed the contents into the fountain.

The flashy six-inch fish, tame and hungry, slammed to the surface and gobbled up the pellets. The children were fascinated and delighted but then turned surly again when I told them that's all the fish food I could give them. "We can't feed them too much at a time," I tried to explain, but I was met with frowns and the stomping of feet. Even their mothers glared at me.

Stephen and Mark chose that moment to enter the café. I was sorely tempted to tell them this situation was not my fault. Those youngsters were misbehaving and should know better. But this statement would conflict with the notion that the customer was always right.

As I brought out crayons and paper to entertain the children, one of the boys tripped and knocked over a potted palm. The four-foot-tall tree plummeted to the floor, and its dirt scattered everywhere.

The boy yowled, and one of the women rushed over to console him. But she didn't offer to clean up the mess or pay for the palm. She glowered at me as if I could've prevented the accident.

"This place isn't child friendly," she said to her friends in a huff. "Let's go somewhere else." The remaining women jolted to their feet and gathered their belongings. The other customers all gave one another a knowing look, as if the children's unruly behavior had interfered with their peaceful interlude.

Broom and dustpan in hand, Beatrice came up behind me as the women were leaving, children in tow. "Whatever you do, don't tell them to come back again soon."

I tried to take the broom, but she insisted she'd get assistance repotting the palm.

"Here, Beatrice, let me help you." Mark stepped forward and took hold of the broom. Behind him trailed a younger Amish laborer, already scooping up the palm and the debris.

"Thanks, Mark," Beatrice said.

Mark aimed his words at me. "This café may be open to the public, but you don't have to put up with such hooligans."

"It wasn't Eva's fault," Beatrice said. "Was she ever instructed on how to handle situations like this?"

"Should we put up a sign saying, *No obnoxious, out-of-control children allowed*?" Stephen gave Mark's shoulder a slap.

"Not such a bad idea." Beatrice chortled into her hand.

Minutes after the floor was swept and mopped, a customer dropped a ceramic mug full of coffee, its contents and shards scattering across the newly cleaned surface. This was apparently going to be a trying day.

"Maybe God is warning me not to go to the Millers' tonight," I whispered to Beatrice.

"Don't be silly." Beatrice grabbed a mop and commenced gathering the broken pieces into a pile. "We have accidents and mishaps every other day. If you want the Lord's protection and guidance, ask for it."

She was right. Just a couple of days ago, Sadie had spilled a bottle of olive oil, and I didn't bat an eye. My own apprehension was the catalyst for my anxiety.

As the day and customers waned, Beatrice, Stephen, and I stood outside the café's front door to enjoy the fresh air, alive with the aromas of spring blooms. And for privacy.

"Are you still driving us over to the Millers' tonight?" Beatrice asked Stephen.

"Yes, I'll stick around after work. There's always something to keep me occupied. You two let me know when you're ready."

Several hours later, getting into Stephen's pickup, I encouraged Beatrice to sit in the center of the bench seat. But she refused, saying the pickup was too hard to climb into and then scoot all the way to the middle.

Minutes later, I was sandwiched between Stephen and Beatrice, and we were on the road. A chiming sound repeated itself.

Stephen leaned in front of me to speak to Beatrice. "Please fasten your seat belt."

"Sorry." She clipped it on and then spoke past me to Stephen. "Thanks so much for this ride. I hope you behave yourself."

"You mean if Jake antagonizes me?" His face was too close to mine for comfort.

"I doubt he will, but yes," she said. "That's exactly what I mean."

Stephen let out a resounding breath. "I promise to ignore Jake if he's there. Let's hope he isn't. Or he's busy with chores."

"Thank you." Beatrice folded her hands in her lap. "Ruth and Amos don't need hostile conversations."

On the drive over, I pondered how much I cared for Amos and Ruth, as if they were family. No matter if Jake deserted them and me, I would continue to visit. If Brandy didn't mind and make a fuss. She might be a hindrance, to say the least. Or maybe a blessing to them.

"I hope Jake doesn't think you're running after him," Beatrice told me. In front of Stephen, no less. I was mortified.

He turned to me. "I'm not chauffeuring Evie all the way over there so she can flaunt herself at Jake." Stephen lowered his mouth toward my ear. "Let me share a little secret. Men are most intrigued by what they can't have."

Chasing after Jake had never worked in the past, that was the truth. I looked up to see what Stephen was getting at, but he changed the subject. "I heard some women in the retail shop talking about Olivia. Guess one of them saw her at the grocery store last night. According to this woman—and she's a good customer—Olivia's hair is lopped short and styled in an unsightly way. The woman said she couldn't believe the total transformation. She claimed she spoke to Olivia, who seemed pleased as punch with herself, as she put it."

Beatrice remained silent and stared out the window as we passed a buggy. I imagined the wheels in her head were churning and whirling like the buggy's, but she kept her thoughts to herself.

Stephen asked me, "Have you seen Liv recently?"

I felt like a rabbit trapped in a snare. I'd either have to lie or gossip. "She's not living at home anymore, as must be obvious now. If she were, she'd be baking for us." I inched closer to Beatrice.

"Never mind," he said. "It's none of my business. But I do worry about her."

"*Yah*, me too."

# Forty-Two

Stephen pulled into the Millers' barnyard and then helped Beatrice and me out of the pickup. The field looked plowed and the mules were grazing, as well as the buggy horse. I saw no sign of Jake's car, but it was probably hidden somewhere.

Stephen, Beatrice, and I climbed the back steps, and I knocked. When Ruth opened the door, her face was red and her clothes disheveled.

"Thank goodness you're here. Come help me." We followed her to the living room to find Amos lounging on a recliner.

"How wonderful!" I moved to his side with Beatrice close behind.

"How long has he been mobile?" Beatrice asked.

"Just today. He tried and tried to get out of bed until finally Brandy and I helped him." She motioned with her hand. "But I'm not strong enough to get him back to bed."

"Couldn't Brandy help you?"

"*Nee.* Jake took her to the hospital to have her baby." Her moves erratic, Ruth's words marbled out. "He tried calling the midwife, but she couldn't come. She was busy delivering twins." Her hands covered her cheeks. "*Ach*, Brandy was screaming that she was going to die from the pain. 'Take me to the hospital! Something's wrong.' So Jake scooped her up, and they left in his car."

"She's having her baby?" My question sounded stupid, even to me.

"*Yah*, *yah*, the *boppli*." Ruth's voice quavered. "Two months early."

"Why didn't he call 9-1-1?" Beatrice said.

"I don't know. Everything happened so quickly."

"Eva, is that you?" Amos struggled to get to his feet without success.

"*Yah*, it's me." I hurried to his side.

"*Denki* for bringing our Jake home," he muttered.

"But he came back for you, Amos."

"That's what I told him," Ruth said, "but he won't believe me." She glanced into my eyes. "Maybe Amos is right, but no use starting an argument. I'd do anything to see my husband and son reunited."

"You want Amos back in bed?" Beatrice asked Ruth.

"*Yah.* I didn't dare try to manage by myself."

Beatrice held Amos in place. "Stephen, please get over here and help me, will you?"

"Sure." Stephen hastened around to the other side of the recliner, slid his arm around Amos's back, and hefted him to his feet with ease. "Want me to carry him all the way?"

"No. Since you're here, let's see how steady Amos actually is." Beatrice grasped Amos's other arm and steered him toward the bed. "Are you strong enough to walk back?"

"*Yah*, I can do it." His legs wobbled, and his spine bent. I could see Stephen was bearing most of Amos's weight.

"Maybe this is a bad idea." Ruth stood by the mattress, her arms extended, ready to ease his descent. "Take care that he doesn't fall."

"I can easily lift him," Stephen said.

"*Nee.*" Amos's voice turned pugnacious. "I'm fine."

Eventually, after mincing to the bed, Amos tumbled onto the mattress. Stephen straightened Amos's legs. Ruth pulled up his covers.

"Thank you." Moisture gathered at the corners of Ruth's eyes. "I don't know what I would have done."

"Don't worry. Jake will be back," I said.

Ruth pursed her lips.

"Won't he?"

We all stood like statues until Stephen brought out his cell phone. "Do you know his number?"

Ruth shook her head, and I said, "I don't know either."

"He never told you?" Stephen asked me, incredulous.

"I knew his old number, but that was years ago."

"I'll call the hospital in Lancaster." I could tell by his compressed expression Stephen was irked. "But I don't know Brandy's last name."

"She said it was Mallory," Ruth said, "but I don't know if that's true. She was trying to conceal her identity, and I never asked again. Jake would know as he's friends with Brandy's older brother."

"I'll try the hospital, but I doubt I'll get anywhere." As a courtesy to Ruth, Stephen stepped outside with the phone. When he returned, his face was pinched. "No Brandy Mallory in their delivery unit. I spoke to someone at the desk and asked if a Jake Miller was there. The attendant wanted to know if Jake was the father." Stephen glanced to me. "I told her I didn't know, but that he'd driven her there."

"Now what?" Beatrice asked. "I'm not in the mood for waiting around for Jake to show up. And I'm sure Stephen has better things to do."

"As a matter of fact, I need to be somewhere." Stephen glanced at the clock on the mantel. "Yep. I'm running late."

"Eva, don't leave." Amos's voice was just above a whisper. "I need you here."

"*Yah*, so do I." Ruth grasped my elbow. "How will I manage by myself?"

I was conflicted. I didn't want to leave Amos and Ruth, but what could I do? "Have you no neighbors or relatives to help?" I asked.

"*Nee.* Over the years Amos scared them off."

"What happened to him to make him so fierce?" I knew about his flaws from Jake, but to look at him now in his weakness—a shell of his former self—filled me with compassion. I imagined Ruth was indeed afraid. How could she lift him or turn him? What if he decided to get up again on his own and fell?

"For reasons I still don't understand, Amos never treated our sons equally," Ruth said. Her words echoed off the wall. "He doted on our first son, Michael. Treated him like royalty but was always on Jake's case for every little thing. Even when he was a toddler. Amos used to say, 'Spare the rod, spoil the child.'"

"Which is biblical," Beatrice said, "if done with love."

"But Amos couldn't control his temper with Jake." Ruth wrung her hands.

"Yes, I remember," Beatrice said.

"Then disappointments mounted up." Ruth spoke to me as if Amos couldn't hear, when in fact she stood mere feet away from him. "One by one. First, our daughters moved to the Midwest with their new husbands, so we rarely see our grandchildren." Her hand covered her heart. "Our grandchildren hardly know us anymore. Just their other grandparents, who never ask us to visit. And they won't accept our invitations." Lines of stress bracketed her mouth. "And then Michael died. Finally, when Jake turned sixteen and said he didn't want to farm, it was like a dagger in Amos's heart. It was his pride, ya see, that his remaining son would wish to desert him. Amos was mortified.

"Our deacon and minister encouraged Amos to lure Jake back with kindness, but Amos became cruel. Belittled him is what he did, punishing him until eventually Jake ran away as fast as he could."

Beatrice stepped closer. "Ruth, we have women at church who might help you and Amos."

"But we're Amish," I said. "I can't believe no one would help you."

"When Amos was injured, half a dozen young men came to work the farm until Jake arrived. And women brought food and helped me with the cleaning, for which I am grateful. But they never visited Amos in the hospital or asked about him. Only our deacon and one minister visited."

Beatrice walked over to her and wrapped an arm around Ruth's shoulders. My admiration for Beatrice grew as I watched her kindness. "I hate to have to leave you, Ruth."

"If you want to spend the night here, I'll pick you up in the morning," Stephen said.

"Really. You'd do that?" Ruth said, looking first to Stephen and then to Beatrice.

Beatrice nodded. "I will if Stephen and Eva will go in the house and let the dogs out."

"Maybe I'm the one who should stay here," I said, but I was met with scowls of displeasure.

"You want Jake to come and find you moping over him?" Beatrice asked. I knew she was right. Enough of my waiting for Jake to maybe show up.

"I can sleep on the couch right here," Beatrice said.

"Okay. I'll go back to the nursery now if Stephen has the time to drive me." Stephen nodded, and I moved to Amos's bedside and took his hand, feeling paper-thin skin. "I need to leave, Amos, but Beatrice will stay and help Ruth. Please don't get out of bed without their assistance, okay?"

"But I want you, Eva."

"Why?" Ruth said. "I don't understand." She turned to me. "I wonder if Amos even knows. The doctor said he might not recall any of this time when he's trying to get back on his feet."

*If he does,* I thought.

# Forty-Three

Before leaving the Millers', Stephen checked the phone shanty and found no messages left from Jake—or anyone.

"Wait up." I was surprised when Beatrice fished a cell phone out of her purse. "I'll call Stephen if we hear from Jake or need help. I usually leave my phone off, but I'll keep it on tonight. Eva, won't you please spend the night in the main house so I can get in touch with you if I need to? Plus, the dogs..."

"*Yah*, okay. If Stephen will let me in. I'll sleep on the couch."

"But we have plenty of beds upstairs. The guest room's all made up, not to mention my room on the third floor."

"No. Better I find a blanket and camp out on the sofa."

Stephen scratched his scalp in a way that told me he wanted nothing to do with the conversation about where I slept, but he agreed to lend me a key to the house.

On the way to the nursery, I kept my eyes peeled to oncoming traffic, hoping to see Jake's vehicle. But I didn't recognize it, not that Jake would drive this route. Stephen and I traveled in silence for ten minutes, until I saw the Yoder's Nursery sign.

"Thanks for bringing me home." I glanced over to face him. He kept his vision on the road. His features were stern, his lips drawn tight.

"I couldn't just leave you there, now could I?" He cruised into the nursery's parking lot, around the house, and stopped at the cabin.

"I'm sorry if I've made you late."

"You haven't. I was going to visit a friend, but I called when I was outside and said I couldn't make it."

"An excuse to leave the Millers'?" I wondered if it was a guy or female friend.

"Yep." He stopped near my cabin's front door. "First, go in and get everything you need while I let the dogs out. I don't want you shuttling between the cabin and the house during the night, you hear me?" He switched off the engine but made no move to exit the vehicle. "We'll get you situated in the house and make sure the doors are locked before I leave. I'll write down Beatrice's and my numbers on a piece of paper and place them on the kitchen table by the phone. If anything comes up, call me first. Not much Beatrice can do other than worry."

"Okay."

"You have your key?"

I reached into my pocket. "Right here." I hopped out of the pickup, proceeded into the cabin, and packed my toiletries, nightgown, slippers, and bathrobe in a brown paper grocery bag. And a scarf. At the last moment, I scooped up my book, although I doubted I could concentrate on reading. On the other hand, I might lie awake all night with skittering thoughts disturbing my slumber.

I told myself I could handle anything, but I felt adrenaline pumping in my veins. What was I afraid of? Sleeping in the big house with all its electric appliances? Getting a call in the middle of the night from Jake, saying the baby had died? Or that the child was indeed his, and he was moving away? No, Jake wouldn't desert his invalid father and helpless mother and deprive them of a grandchild. Or would he? Jake and I had never talked about having children. *Ach*, so much we never discussed.

Stephen was standing on the main house's back porch and watching the dogs when I stepped outside. I locked my door behind me. The dogs flounced over to me, and I felt a fondness for each one. I knew they would protect me from any harm and warn me if they smelled smoke. The barn fire still raged in the back of my mind when I let it. I liked to think Ralph had unwittingly set that fire, but I had no way of knowing what he might do to harm me. Not after he'd put that knife to my neck.

My arms encircled the bag as I climbed the porch steps. "I hope Harvey doesn't disapprove of my spending the night here." I figured he would object to this whole scenario, which was bound to get back to him.

"Don't Amish sometimes stay in motels when traveling?" Stephen opened the door to the kitchen. The dogs scampered inside.

"*Yah*, I guess they do if on a long trip. I've even heard they watch TV occasionally."

"No TV in this house, so no worries there." He examined my face. "What's got you worried?"

"Is my anxiety that obvious? *Ach*, I wouldn't know where to begin."

His phone buzzed. When he answered it, I gathered he was speaking to Beatrice. He told her he'd pick her up in the morning at six and then stuffed his phone into a pocket.

"Well?" I tried to keep my voice sounding calm, to no avail.

"Brandy had a baby girl in Jake's car. He ushered them to the hospital, where he called Brandy's oldest brother, Jeff. He's coming from New York to pick up Brandy and her baby as soon as he can." His eyes got glassy.

"What's wrong? Is the baby okay?"

"Yes, and as it turns out, not premature and perfectly healthy." He blinked. "Brandy named her Eva Ruth."

"She named her baby after me and Ruth?"

"According to Jake, she said you two never judged her."

My thoughts hurtled back to Jake and Brandy and the new baby. "Stephen, did Beatrice tell you what the baby's last name is?"

"You mean Miller? She didn't say. The fact you're even wondering tells me you don't trust or believe Jake. If I were you, I wouldn't either."

"*Ach*, I want to see the baby." But I couldn't tonight. Maybe ever.

"Jake might take a photo on his phone and show you," Stephen said, as if trying to console me.

"Is he staying at the hospital?"

"For a while, but he promised to be home by the time I pick up Beatrice." He backstepped a few feet. "Are you going to be okay alone in this big house?"

"I'm not alone. I have three canine companions to keep me company."

"Just the same, please call me if you need anything. Any sign of Ralph, dial 9-1-1. Promise?" So he was worried about Ralph.

"*Yah*." The thought of Ralph showing up made the hairs on my arms prickle.

"Evie, don't open the door to anyone until I come in tomorrow. I'll call and ask Wayne or whichever officer is on duty tonight to cruise through the nursery parking lot a few times. So don't worry if you see a patrol car."

"*Yah*, okay. I'll be fine."

"Beatrice said blankets, sheets, pillows, and clean towels are in the hall linen closet upstairs. You want me to help you find them?"

"I bet I can on my own."

"Nah." He headed to the stairs. "Better follow me up there and have a look around. Get the lay of the land, as they say."

I trailed him up the wide wooden staircase. Off to the right I saw another set of stairs that must lead up to Beatrice's quarters.

"Are you sure you don't want to sleep in this cushy guest room?" Stephen pushed a door open and flicked on a ceiling light to expose a four-poster queen-sized bed, draped by a vibrant nine-patch quilt and wearing a pleated dust ruffle around its perimeter. I moved closer to see the quilt's exquisite hand stitching and thought of my humble *mamm*, who was equally skilled but would never admit it.

The room's windows were framed with flamboyant flowered

curtains, and the floor was covered with a plush carpet. Another door led to a bathroom. I was surely being tempted.

"Want to see the master bedroom?" Stephen asked.

"Oh, no. Not without one of the Yoders here. Or at least Beatrice." I envisioned this scene through Bishop Harvey's eyes. He wouldn't approve. Nor would Beatrice.

"The master bedroom and bath is next door, and then another room for Emmy. You should come and take a look. It's quite a beautiful space."

"I'd better not." Although my curiosity was piqued.

Downstairs, Heath let out a throaty woof, followed by Minnie's yapping.

"The dogs are restless, probably because they're waiting for Beatrice." Stephen glanced out a window into the parking lot. "I have an idea. You sleep in this guest room, and I'll sleep on the couch."

"What if someone's at the door?" I felt anxious being alone with Stephen. Being in this house, period.

"We aren't doing anything wrong. I'll go check." Yet his gaze landed on mine longer than necessary, until I turned away.

An instant later, Stephen left the room and stood at the top of the stairs. "I'd better go see what the problem is."

I considered my options as I listened to his feet patter down the staircase. If I wasn't guilty of anything, why was I hiding in the guest room? But I decided to stay upstairs as Stephen had asked. I tiptoed down the hall, passing an aged painting of a brown-eyed girl and a pony. I peeked into the master bedroom and saw a king-sized bed covered by an exquisite Double Wedding Ring quilt. Paintings and ornaments adorned the bedroom. I saw wall plugs, telling me everything was electric. I shouldn't be here.

Near the bed stood a cradle. Rose and Glenn must sleep with their little Emmy near them until she grew old enough to sleep in a crib. I thought that if I ever had a child, I'd do the same thing. I'd heard of babies ceasing to breathe during the night. Sudden infant death syndrome, it was called. *Ach*, that would be more heartbreaking than dying barren.

I imagined Brandy cradling her newborn right now and felt a warm wave of tenderness. Eva was her first name. I'd never had a baby named after me, or at least with me in mind. I was determined to be an outstanding woman if a little girl was named after me, even if she was *Englisch*.

I heard men's voices in the kitchen and then the back door closing. Feeling a pang of guilt, I scurried back to the guest room.

I recognized Stephen's feet ascending the stairs. He poked his head in. "Wayne just dropped by to see how everything is going. I told him you're sleeping up here, and I'm going to sack out in the living room."

"No, we can't do that."

"Wayne agreed it's best you aren't out in the cabin in case Ralph shows up." Stephen said. "Or in this house alone."

"But I can't live in fear of Ralph forever—"

"Being prudent for one night isn't such a bad idea." He massaged the back of his neck. "You can trust me, Evie. I won't come upstairs during the night. Between me and the dogs downstairs, you'll be safe. And with my pickup parked out back, I can't imagine anyone would be dumb enough to try breaking in."

I descended the stairs to collect my belongings from the kitchen. When I returned, Stephen stood at the second-floor hall closet, gathering a blanket and pillow.

"I just spoke to Beatrice on the phone," he said, "who told me this arrangement is fine and that she should have thought of it herself." He tilted his head. "I won't come back upstairs unless you call me. Please do if you need anything. That's why I'm here." Then he turned away and trotted down the stairs.

In the guest room, I changed into my nightgown and bathrobe. A painting with an ornate gold frame of Venice caught my eye. I wondered if Rose's aunt, sister, or Beatrice had given it to the Yoders as a wedding present or if it were on loan from Beatrice. I'd seen photos of the intriguing city built on islands, the exquisite ancient architecture, and men guiding gondolas through the canals. Wouldn't I adore riding in a long, slender boat, perhaps listening to the gondolier singing opera at the same time?

I wondered if Beatrice had ever visited Venice. Would I rather go to Florence? Or would I prefer living a humdrum life in Lancaster County with a husband and children? And my parents close by. Most likely I'd choose the husband and at least one child. But at what cost? Did I have a choice? Olivia had wanted out and might skip town. I missed my cousin, but I understood I might never see her again. She could move to California, for all I knew. She'd always complained about our frigid winters.

What about Stephen? If I continued to work in the café, I'd see him every day. We'd most likely grow closer unless he fell in love with someone else. He was not a man many women could resist. Maybe if his old flame heard he was sober, she'd want him back. I wondered if he still hoped she would, even though she was married and had a child. If he dreamed of her at night. Or did he dream of me?

I took off my *kapp*, removed my hairpins, and allowed my tresses to cascade down over my shoulders. No makeup to remove, just me.

Under the overhead light fixture, my hair glinted with hints of copper and gold. I looked stunning, catching myself off guard. All my life, I'd been saving the sight of my hair for my future husband. Only Jake had seen it once when I'd allowed him a chance. I wasn't supposed to, but he'd talked me into removing my *kapp*. His fingers had combed through my hair, awakening all my senses. At least I hadn't succumbed to his amorous advances as Brandy had to her boyfriend's.

I glanced at the clicking clock on the nightstand and admonished myself to go to sleep. It was past midnight. I pulled back the covers. The bed stood high, higher than any bed I'd ever slept in. I needed to climb to reach the surface. I slipped between the satiny sheets and sank into the softest of pillows and mattresses. Did all *Englischers* live with this luxury? My hunch was Rose had embellished this room for her sister, who must adore antiques. I thought about the term *a woman's touch* and longed to own a home of my own someday. I'd want a garden, of course, and trees growing around it. And a view.

A barking commotion erupted from downstairs. I heard knuckles thrumming on the kitchen door, and then Stephen speaking, followed by Jake. Their jagged voices were as loud as the dogs'. I stood at the top of the stairs until my patience ran out. I returned to the guest room and found a camel-colored woolen coat in the closet. I stuffed my arms into the sleeves and buttoned the front, and then I covered my head with my scarf.

I padded down the stairs and found the two men yelling at each other.

"You and Evie are sleeping together?" Jake's face twisted with anger.

"Buddy, you're on private property," Stephen said. "How dare you force your way in here!"

Jake caught sight of me. "Then it's true? You and Stephen are together alone in this house?"

"How dare you accuse me of anything?" My hands planted themselves on my hips.

"Jake, what are you doing here?" Stephen took hold of Heath's collar as the dog lunged toward Jake, who seemed unconcerned.

"I came to see Evie. On the way, I spotted Ralph skulking around by the new barn. When I went to Evie's cabin, she didn't answer her door. Naturally, I was worried about her."

"Didn't Beatrice tell you I was sleeping in the main house?" I said. "Not that I owe you an explanation. You're the one who has some explaining to do."

"Yeah, I'd say so. Are you a father now?" Stephen let go of Heath.

Jake kneed Heath to keep him from jumping on him. "None of your business. Get off my case, and keep away from my girl." He turned to leave. "I'm going over to see what Ralph is up to before he burns down that new barn."

"Maybe he's just going in there to sleep," I said. "Shouldn't you call the police?" If Ralph were Amish, I wouldn't suggest such a thing. "Please let Wayne handle it, or whoever's on duty."

Both men narrowed their eyes at me.

"No straw to use as a bed." Jake yanked the door open.

"You don't know that. If he's drunk enough, he won't care." Stephen dove into his jacket. "He might have a blanket or sleeping bag he keeps stashed somewhere. I'd better come with you." Stephen zipped up his jacket, grabbed a flashlight, and clipped on Heath's leash.

"Evie, keep the doors locked," he said before disappearing into the darkness with Jake and the dog.

# Forty-Four

When had I ever felt more helpless? I double bolted the door. Missy and Minnie stood side by side, both peering through the door's glass panes. I was happy to have them here with me, but I felt utterly baffled. How could two men, who despised each other, go off as a search party to locate Ralph? My only option was to wait around to find out what happened. No, I wouldn't do it.

I called 9-1-1. "Is Wayne working tonight?"

"Is this an emergency, ma'am?" The female operator's voice was terse.

"It might be if no one comes to help. Stephen Troyer asked Wayne or whoever is on duty tonight to cruise through the Yoder Nursery."

"There's a problem?"

"Someone said they saw Ralph Hastings near the Schmuckers' newly built barn."

"I can see by your telephone number that you're calling from Glenn Yoder's home."

She could view that information on her end of the call?

"Yes, this is Eva Lapp, an employee and a guest in the house tonight. Beatrice Valenti gave me permission to stay here."

"Remain on the line, will you, ma'am?"

I pressed the receiver to my ear and waited. Missy and Minnie both whined and pawed at the door.

A bullet's twang spun through the air.

The image of a man sprawled on the road with a gunshot wound in his chest made me woozy. Jake or Stephen? "Please, Lord, protect them."

I should have prayed before they left the house. I should've called 9-1-1 before they left. All those should-haves meant nothing now.

I blurted out, "I just heard a gun go off from the direction of Jeremiah and Hannah Schmuckers'. Please send someone right away!"

No reply. I was on hold, speaking to a dead line.

Finally, the operator returned, and I repeated myself. "I heard a gunshot."

"You sure of that? Not just a car backfiring?"

"I grew up on a farm, and I know what a gunshot sounds like." My mouth flooded with a rusty taste.

"Wayne's in the area, ma'am. I'll send him right over there. In the meantime, stay in the house."

But I had to go out and see what was going on even if I received a reprimand. If Jake or Stephen were wounded or lay dying, I needed to offer my comfort.

I was already wearing a coat and my head was covered. I stepped into a pair of what must be Beatrice's clogs and fetched the house key where I left it on the windowsill. Minnie and Missy were looking up at me expectantly.

"You two *hunds* better stay home and defend the house." I found a flashlight and headed out the door. *Ach*, how could this be happening? I couldn't stand it if Jake or Stephen had been shot. Or Heath. Or even Ralph. All my life I'd been taught to be nonresistant, to never take another person's life. Only the Lord Almighty made those decisions.

I stepped outside and locked the door. Chill evening air surrounded me, and I shivered. As I made my way to the barn, I saw the flashing blue light of a police car. I heard the muffled sound of men arguing. I crept closer, hoping to be unnoticed, but Stephen stepped out in front of me.

"What on earth are you doing here?" Though Heath was trying to get free, Stephen gripped the leash firmly.

"I heard a gunshot. Was anyone hurt?" Obviously not Stephen, leaving Jake. But no, I saw him up ahead, raising a hand and motioning me to keep away.

"Wayne was on his way to cruise through the nursery's parking lot when Ralph came out of the barn brandishing his gun. Ralph shot at him." Stephen moved between Ralph and me, blocking my view.

I peeked around him to see Ralph standing on shaky legs, his limp arm holding a gun at his side, the barrel tipped down. Judging by his face, illuminated by Wayne's headlights, he hadn't shaved or changed his clothes for days.

His posture rigid, Jake inched toward me. "Evie, be careful. Ralph blasted a hole in the side of the vehicle, but he missed Wayne, praise God."

In a swift movement, Wayne pulled out his firearm, held it with both hands, and aimed it at Ralph. "Give me that gun, you knucklehead." Moments passed. "Come on, Ralph. Don't make me shoot you."

"Okay. Okay." Ralph tossed his weapon a few feet away.

"Where'd you get the gun?" Wayne roughly cuffed Ralph and checked his pockets.

"It was my dad's." His words were once again garbled. "Hey, I didn't mean anything. I was just trying to scare you away."

"Are you crazy? You could have killed me." Wayne frisked Ralph and then shoved him into the back of his squad car and slammed the door. Wayne turned to Stephen. "I'm glad he missed me, but I'll never hear the end of it back at the station. The car just got out of the body shop...thanks to Eva."

My cheeks filled with heat. Why had I let Jake talk me into that immature stunt? Because I'd been in search of adventure. Well, this was more adventure than I'd anticipated or ever wanted to experience again.

"I'm glad you're okay, Wayne." I turned to Stephen and Jake. "You too, of course."

Both men sent me aggravated expressions. But I noticed fear lurking in the depths of their eyes.

Buggies and cars slowed or stopped by the side of the road. Wayne holstered his gun and waved them on. "No barn fires tonight, folks. Nothing to see here."

He turned toward us. "I'll be right back. I'd better have a look around." Flashlight in hand, Wayne entered the barn.

Mark piloted his buggy to the side of the road. He disembarked and secured his horse to a railing. I shrank back as his gaze assessed the situation, including me in my *Englisch* coat and scarf.

"What brings you out so late, Mark?" Jake asked him. "Paying a visit on Evie?"

Jake frowned at me.

"You got it all wrong." The corners of Mark's mouth lifted into a smug grin. "*Nee*, I'm seeing someone. Eva and I have never been more than friends."

"Whom are you seeing?"

"None of your business." I guessed he'd paid a call on Sadie.

Mark turned to Stephen. "What's going on?"

"Looks like Ralph was planning to spend the night in the barn again. The idiot shot a hole in Wayne's squad car."

"Praise the Lord he missed Wayne," I said, but no one acknowledged me except Heath, who snuffled and licked my hand.

Wayne lumbered out of the barn and over to us. "I didn't find any evidence of planned arson. Although Ralph had a Bic lighter in his pocket along with cigarettes and a flask." He glanced over at his squad car. "I'll take him into the station. This time he's in a little more trouble. If he weren't such a lousy shot, I could be dead."

Minutes later, Wayne jetted off down the road toward town. My heart was full of thankfulness, but I could tell Jake and Stephen were both angry. At Ralph, me, or each other?

Stephen spoke to Jake. "Hadn't you better mosey on home and take care of your parents and new baby?"

"The baby is not mine, but she's a darling little *boppli*."

I moved closer. "Did you really deliver her? Right in your car?"

"I didn't have much choice. The baby came so quickly, there was nothing I could do but help Brandy as best I was able. I'm glad I had that towel and a blanket in the backseat. I drove her to the hospital, and the ER staff took over. They said it was fine I hadn't cut the umbilical cord. No hurry there."

"Were you afraid?" I asked.

"*Yah*, but I remembered all the calves I'd helped my *dat* deliver. I told myself I could do it, even though Brandy was writhing in pain." He looked as though he might cry, but straightened himself and stood tall. "She said she wants me to be her godfather."

"Oh yeah?" Stephen said. "Sure you're not the baby's father?"

"Yes, I'm sure. If I must submit to a DNA test to prove I'm not the child's father, I will."

"Not such a bad idea," Stephen said.

"I don't like your insinuations." Jake crossed his arms.

"What color hair does she have?" I asked. An innocent enough question. Yet I knew I was testing him.

The corners of Jake's mouth twitched back. "Black, and a lot of it. And skin the color of milk chocolate. Isn't that proof enough?"

"If you say so," Stephen said.

"I do say so." Jake's gaze focused on me. "Don't turn against me because Stephen's attempting to make me look like a liar." His voice came out a growl that got Heath barking.

I stared back into his indignant face.

Stephen chortled, further enraging Jake. As Stephen pivoted toward the house, Heath tugged, causing Stephen's elbow to knock into Jake's arm.

"Is that what you want?" Jake's expression grew fierce, his eyes bulging. "You want to steal my girl?"

"Hey, fellas, trying to make a spectacle of yourself?" Mark strode over to us.

Both Jake and Stephen stiffened, as if they'd forgotten Mark was there. They gave each other another contentious glare and moved apart.

"I can understand your frustration," Mark said, "but control your tempers." A buggy rolled by, and Mark lifted a hand and then watched the buggy recede into the darkness. For the youngest man present, he was acting the most maturely.

"Jake has no business coming to the nursery." Stephen folded his arms across his chest. "Who does he think he is?"

"Under the circumstances, I doubt you'll get anywhere with that," Jake said.

"Jake, why don't you go home where you're needed?" I said. "I can take care of myself."

Jake and Stephen both shot me a look of disapproval, as if a reminder I should have stayed in the house.

"Jake, please go home," I said. "I want to keep my job at the nursery. Don't make big troubles for me."

Jake kicked a rock, sending it spinning across the road. "*Yah*, okay. I'll leave. I'll go home and tell my *mamm* you're spending the night in the house with Stephen. Then let's see what she thinks of you, Miss Goody-Goody."

Jake stalked off in a huff without bidding me farewell.

"I'm headed home, Stephen." Mark's gaze skimmed past me. "Unless you want me to stay for any reason."

"Thanks for the offer," Stephen said, "but you might as well get home and get some rest. We have a busy day ahead of us."

Mark gathered up his reins and climbed into his buggy. I truly hoped he was courting Sadie on the sly, but I could keep their secret.

Stephen and I waited for several cars to cruise past us, and then we crossed the road with Heath tugging on his leash toward the nursery.

Stephen's pace slowed. "Maybe I shouldn't sleep in the main house tonight after all. I'm thinking of your reputation, Evie."

I lagged behind him. "In that case, maybe I should just sleep in my cabin. Ralph isn't a threat. Not tonight, anyway."

We approached the back door to the main house. I did want to sleep in that plush bedroom just once in my life.

Stephen fished his keys out of his pocket. "No, you stay here with the three dogs. It's all arranged with Beatrice. I'll give her a call and let her know our plan." He wrangled the key into the lock. "Please promise to call me if anything happens. Anything at all. And don't open the door to anyone, including Jake. He can wait another day to see you."

"*Yah*, okay. I'll open the door only if you or Beatrice come back."

"I'm going to make a quick walk-through of the house to make sure no one entered while we were over at the barn."

Stephen still wore his jacket. I got the feeling he was delaying his departure as he paced through the entire interior. I even heard him climb the second set of stairs to Beatrice's room. Once he was back on the first floor, he rechecked the dead bolt on the front door and finally returned to the kitchen.

"Evie, that guest room you're in has a phone right by the bed."

"Okay. I hadn't noticed." Were phones in the house becoming second nature to me now? I'd been so dazzled by all the frivolous items in the room I hadn't spotted it. I knew I was being sucked into the *Englisch* world. I might as well have been a dust ball being swept by a whisk broom. In the future, could I be satisfied living without its tantalizing amenities?

The moment Stephen left, I double bolted the kitchen door. Surely I would be safe tonight.

I mounted the staircase to the second floor still wearing the coat. Standing in the guestroom, I hugged myself. Never had I felt more luxurious fabric. Even the pockets were lined with satin. As I reluctantly removed the garment and hung it up in the closet, I glanced at its label. The cloth was half wool and half alpaca. *Ach*, I would never be permitted by the *Ordnung* to own such an extravagant coat.

Despite my determination to banish Jake from my mind tonight, my thoughts looped back to him. I envisioned his delivering Brandy's baby and felt admiration for him. He was a capable man when he wanted to be. But the truth was, I had no control over his behavior. What would life be like living with an unstable man, as opposed to a conscientious man who had overcome his demon—alcohol—like Stephen? Who wasn't Amish.

Where would I find my answer?

# Forty-Five

The next morning, crows outside my window woke me. For a moment I didn't know where I was. Rays of light shone through the flowered curtains, illuminating the room with vibrant hues of plum and cerise. I was tempted to jump up and watch the sunrise, but I enjoyed my snuggly nest too much. I looked forward to having this time to myself.

My thoughts meandered as they wished. I decided when I finally built my dream house it would have a room with a view the way the home I grew up in did. My view had been of a cornfield and gently rolling hills and farms behind it for as far as the eye could see. But I should be content with my cabin for now.

Perhaps sleeping in this *Englisch* bed was akin to sinking into quicksand—soft and cushy but deadly. Never had I experienced such luxury. Would I ever be satisfied again sleeping on a bumpy old single mattress? I pulled the silky sheets up around my face.

I'd tried several new adventures recently.

After my one abysmal attempt at driving, would I ever give it another try? The answer was maybe I would. I figured I could handle driving with lessons from a real instructor. When I recalled everything I'd learned since working in the fabric store and then the café, I assured myself I could conquer anything. And I could learn to live without Jake.

Barking and yapping erupted from the kitchen, followed by the voices of Stephen and Beatrice. I'd meant to be dressed when they arrived, and now I needed to hurry.

I leaped from the bed. "I'll be there in a minute," I yelled down to the kitchen.

In the bathroom, I washed my face, but before I could get fully dressed, Beatrice knocked at my door. I opened it, and she said, "Yoo-hoo. Sleeping in?"

"*Ach*, I neglected to set the alarm clock." I parted my hair and pulled it back into a bun. "Truth is, that bed is so comfortable I didn't want to leave it."

"Not content with your single bed in the cabin anymore?" Her question startled me.

"Of course. I'm fine." But I was already questioning my statement as I envisioned tonight in the cabin.

Beatrice tilted her head. "I have to wonder about you. You've blamed Jake for everything. Is he really the reason you haven't gotten baptized?"

"*Ach*, I don't know anymore."

"When Jake got home last night, he told us all about Brandy's baby. How exciting is that? She named the little girl after you and Ruth. But mostly after you, Eva, according to Jake. I got the distinct impression he wants a child of his own now."

I turned to her to assess her open expression. "But will he marry an Amish or an *Englisch* woman?"

"That is yet to be seen."

"He didn't say anything to you?"

"Maybe his parents will have more influence than you think. I was watching him out the window this morning, and he looked content plowing the field with the mules."

"But would he rather have been plowing with motorized machinery?"

"That I cannot answer." Beatrice drew up her shoulders "He let slip he feels inadequate as a farmer compared to his father. Probably because Amos often ridiculed him in the past. But it seems as if Jake wants to stick around and learn."

"I almost forgot to ask how Amos is doing."

"He's plopped on the easy chair again. I'm glad I stayed to help Ruth. She really can't lift him by herself, and despite my extra pounds I'm strong. They could have both fallen."

"I don't understand why someone from the Amish community hasn't come to her aid, even if Amos has been rude to them in the past. So what? Are we not admonished to love our neighbor?"

"Good questions for Harvey if he comes into the café today." She sent me a wry grin. "Have you noticed he's been hanging around the nursery more than usual?" All the lines in her face curved up. "You know he's a widower, don't you? His daughters cook for him and keep house, but his eldest son and his wife also live in the area and are hoping Harvey will remarry. Don't be surprised if Harvey invites you over for supper in the near future to meet his family. He's hinted he plans to."

"Are you serious? He's never said a thing." I caught sight of myself in the mirror and saw a woman wearing an expression of shock, her mouth gaping open.

Beatrice said, "Why would he if he knows you're pining over Jake?" She straightened the bed. "I've known Harvey for a long time, and he's a fine man who wouldn't pressure you if you adored someone else. But he might have become enamored with you in spite of himself. He might think you and Jake make an unlikely couple and will give up on each other."

Astonished as I was, I spent a moment contemplating Harvey. He was a fine man and well established in the community. If I married a bishop, surely others would respect me, and gossip would be laid aside. Maybe. I supposed rumors would continue to circulate one way or another.

If and when Harvey came in today, I might accept his invitation should he ask me. Or maybe Beatrice had her facts all mixed up.

I was glad Stephen wasn't there when we went downstairs for breakfast.

Later, as I prepared soup in the café, a tentative rapping on the back door snagged my attention. With all the crazy circumstances of the last week gyrating through my brain, I hesitated.

"Who is it?" I spokc through thc door.

"Olivia."

Deplorable scenarios came to mind, but when I opened the door, I found her dressed Amish, a *kapp* covering her head. "What happened?" floundered out of my mouth.

"I moved home, to my real home with my parents. Thankfully, they forgave me and let me come in as long as I don't do anything idiotic again." She draped her arms around my neck and said, "*Ach*, irresponsible is the only word for the way I've been acting."

I pulled her into the kitchen and repeated my question. "What happened?"

"Other than scraping my landlady's fender in the supermarket parking lot on the way home?"

"*Ach*, you didn't." My desire to drive a car again evaporated like dew under the blazing sun.

"The car was nothing compared to what Butch did to me." She blotted her eyes with the corner of her apron. "When I got home last night, he was gone."

"You mean just not home yet?"

"*Nee.* All his belongings were gone too. He'd scribbled out a note saying he wasn't coming back. No forwarding address. He left me with the rent, that dirty rat."

"I'm so sorry. At least your parents let you come home. And I'm delighted to have you back, my dear cousin and best friend. I thought I'd lost you forever." Now I was the woman with tears seeping out of her eyes.

"But just look at me. I'm a freak. Thank goodness the beautician left enough bangs to part them in the middle, but they won't stay in place unless I plaster them with hair gel and use bobby pins. I might have to hide out at home for six months." Her eyes were pink and swollen. "Can you ever forgive me, Evie? I'm so sorry for the mean-spirited things I said to you. And I was leading you into temptation. *Ach*, I've been such a fool."

"In a few weeks it won't seem so bad. You still know how to cook like a master chef."

"Here's something I didn't tell you," she said. "You may have heard that someone was vandalizing the nursery a while back. Last week, Butch admitted to doing it because he thought Glenn Yoder was coming on to me, when in fact he never did, not once. Glenn and I are like siblings."

"What gives?" Sadie said as she entered the back door. "Is that you, Olivia?"

"Well, of course it is." I knew Sadie wasn't fooled, and I didn't appreciate her making fun of Olivia. Then it occurred to me Sadie thought Olivia was coming in here to work this morning.

Olivia must have picked up the same vibes. "Don't you two worry about my trying to steal either of your jobs. I'm officially grounded, except my parents let me come today to apologize to Evie in person."

"But you can still cook better than I do," Sadie said.

Olivia fiddled with miscreant bangs slipping out beneath her *kapp*. "I heard your baking is excellent."

"It is," I said. "As long as Sadie wishes to bake, we'll buy her pastries."

Sadie's gaze slid away from mine. "If I didn't have to bake so many whoopie pies, it wouldn't break my heart one bit. I've been seeing someone..."

Olivia giggled, sounding like the girl I'd once known. "You have a suitor?"

"I'd rather not say. But I'm staying up later these days."

"To meet someone?" Olivia's eyes brightened, and her voice rose an octave. "Anyone I know?"

Although I was dying to hear Sadie's answers, I stepped in to interfere. "Now, Olivia, you know better than to pry."

"I know better than to do a lot of things, but it doesn't seem to stop me. *Ach*, I still acted like a blockhead." She looked to me, her face turning solemn. "Are you getting baptized soon?"

"Maybe."

"You and I can take the classes together and get baptized at the same time."

"That would be fun if it works out." We clasped each other for a quick embrace, and then she was gone. I never did ask how she'd arrived, but I decided it was best I didn't know.

# Forty-Six

The next morning, Harvey was one of our first patrons. "Eva, may I have a word with you?"

"Of course. What can I do for you?" I assumed he'd heard about last night's altercation and about my sleeping in the Yoders' house.

"I have a busy day ahead," he told me, "but I wanted to get in here early to ask you to come over for supper this evening to meet my family."

"Are you sure? Couldn't we speak here?"

"*Nee.* My *dochders* wish to meet you." He patted his beard the way *Dat* did when he was pondering a weighty subject. The two men must be near the same age.

"*Ach*, have you told them about me?" I served him coffee. "Or have they heard the rumors and want to check me out for themselves?"

"Nothing like that. I mentioned I've been coming in here..."

I couldn't face more disapproval. He must have recognized hesitance in my demeanor.

"Please. They begged me to bring you home." He sipped a mouthful. "So I suggested tonight. If you're free."

"I have no other plans. In fact, I was hoping you'd come in so I could talk to you about baptism classes."

His smile lines deepened. "That's *wunderbaar* news. Do you wish to become baptized in this district or your parents'? Although their bishop has been ailing with gout."

"What do you think? I now live in this district, but would it be awkward for me to get baptized in one of your church services?"

He settled himself at a nearby table and beckoned me to sit across from him. "To answer your question, not at all. But if you prefer that one of the other ministers baptizes you, I can arrange that. I only want what's best for you."

I was touched by his kindness and consideration.

"Give it some thought during the course of the day," he said.

"You said I'd have to wait—"

"Or show me that you truly want to join the church with all your heart. Getting baptized is like marriage. It's a lifetime commitment. Are you ready to pledge yourself to obey the teachings of the Bible and the *Ordnung*?"

"*Yah.*" I would erase the Yoders' guest room and the extravagant coat from my memory. I was done dabbling with the *Englisch* world. *Ach*, I was done with nonsense about driving a car and reading *Englisch* books that lured me to another continent.

He leaned closer to me, and I felt the force of his gaze. "I'll come by at six o'clock and pick you up. We can discuss it more on the way to my home." He looked right into my eyes as if trying to read my thoughts. Or connect with me? Maybe he'd always gazed at me with intensity, but I hadn't noticed earlier. Maybe I'd been intimidated or been glancing away because I thought he was judging me.

"Oh."

"Eva, you seem reluctant to join us for supper."

"It's just... You caught me off guard."

"Tell you what. I'll come earlier. If you've changed your mind, we'll discuss your baptism. In any case, please don't go to any trouble. Our suppers are casual. My *dochders* will be wearing their everyday clothes. Come just as you're dressed today."

I stuck out one foot, and he smiled down at my Nikes.

"Those shoes are fine. Well, not for your baptism. But as I said, suppers are casual in our home. We usually kick off our shoes when we enter the house."

I saw my reflection in his spectacles and wondered how he viewed me. I hoped as another daughter and not a convenient surrogate mother to his children? *Ach*, he couldn't harbor ardor in his heart, making him wish to kiss me with that huge beard. I could barely see his lips. But if Jake got baptized and we married, he'd be required to wear a beard too. For the rest of his life.

Harvey glanced up at the wall clock above the cash register and got to his feet. Our few *Englisch* customers watched him, and yet none dared bring out a camera. The man commanded respect.

"See you, Eva." He replaced his black hat and pushed in his chair.

"All right."

Minutes later, as Beatrice and I stood behind the counter, her face beamed as she arranged muffins on a plate and set it on a tray for Sadie to deliver to a table. I tapped my elbow against hers. "Did you put that supper invitation into Harvey's head?"

"I can't insert a random idea into a man's brain that isn't already percolating. He brought up the subject. And apparently you didn't discourage him."

My mind filled with apprehension. "How many children does he have again?"

"One married son with young children of his own, who lives in a small house near Harvey. Two of his four daughters are in *rumspringa* and of marrying age, and two are still in school and in need of a woman's guidance. A ready-made family."

Reality struck. "What have I gone and done? I don't want to marry him and be a grandma yet or raise another woman's children."

"Sounds fun to me." Beatrice cut a dill pickle in half and laid it on a plate as a garnish.

I lowered my volume. "But I want to have my own children."

"I never could. Not for lack of trying." For the first time I saw Beatrice blush, but I pretended not to notice. "Maybe Harvey's girls don't want their father to be lonely. Or they simply want to meet you. At least be courteous enough to go."

That afternoon, a lanky *Englisch* man strode into the café asking for me. "If you're Eva Lapp, I've brought someone to see you," he said as I strolled out to greet him.

I couldn't imagine who he was. I scanned the room and asked, "Where?"

"Out in the parking lot in my car."

After all the uncertainty in my life over the last couple of weeks, I wondered if I should summon Stephen or someone else to accompany me. I held my ground and asked, "Who are you?"

"Jeff Mallory. Brandy's oldest brother."

"*Ach*, is there something wrong with Brandy?"

"Nope, but she insisted I drive by here on the way out of town to say goodbye. And show you her newborn."

"Really? Oh, yes! I'd love to see her baby."

Following Jeff, I traipsed across the parking lot to his sedan. Its engine was running. Brandy lowered her window for a minute and waved. "Hey, Eva! Come and meet little Eva."

In a car seat in the back slept a precious baby swaddled in pink blankets. I rounded the car and got in the backseat to get a closer view.

"*Ach*, she's perfectly beautiful." Taking in her angelic features, I inhaled the sweet, unique fragrance only a baby could produce and yearned for one of my own. "But shouldn't you two still be in the hospital?"

"The doctor says I must have gotten my dates mixed up because your namesake appears to have arrived exactly on time. I never was good at math or watching the calendar."

"That's a lame excuse for getting pregnant," Jeff said. "Didn't anyone ever teach you the facts of life?"

I ignored the siblings' squabble. "You're so beautiful," I told my namesake. "I've never had a baby named after me. I can't tell you how thrilled I am." My hands naturally reached out to straighten her knit hat and fluff the blankets around her neck. More than anything, I wanted to rock my own baby in my arms. "I'd better not wake her up," I said with hesitancy, because I was dying to. "She looks so peaceful."

Brandy spoke to me over her shoulder. "She's got a full tummy, so I hope she sleeps the whole way home. Maybe we can come back next month. Or you can visit us. Jake could drive you."

"Where will you be living?" I asked.

"At our oldest sister's," Jeff said, buckling his seat belt. "Cindy's been lamenting that her four kids—ages twelve to nineteen—are growing up too quickly. One's away at college, leaving a spare bedroom. Their house is a rambler that goes on forever. Plenty of room and a built-in babysitter."

"Cindy kept her crib and all her kids' clothing for when she's a grandma. She's spending today getting everything ready for us."

"She's real excited," Jeff said. "Says she can't wait."

I imagined Brandy's little one crying in the middle of the night and wondered how long her enthusiasm would last.

"Is she married?"

"Oh, yeah," Brandy said. "Her husband's a big old teddy bear. He said he don't mind. The more the merrier. He'll go along with the program as long as his wife's happy."

I gave little Eva one last looking over. "Brandy, please keep in touch." I dreaded shortening the visit, but I didn't want the baby to get cold. And Jeff seemed ready to leave.

"Of course," Brandy said.

"Please wait just a moment. I got out, dashed into the retail store, and grabbed a piece of stationery and an envelope. Coming around to Brandy's window I handed her the paper. "You can write me at this address. The café's telephone number is printed on here too. And please do call me anytime."

"Absolutely."

"And send me a photo, okay?"

"I thought Amish can't have photographs."

"She's not Amish, now is she?"

"No. I assure you, neither of her parents is Amish."

I stood for a few minutes, watching them leave the parking lot. I wanted to help Brandy, but maybe I'd done all I could. I tried to recall the baby's sweet scent, but already the aroma was being replaced by the exhaust of a nearby SUV, its back hatch full of shrubs.

When I returned to the café, the phone was ringing. Sadie swiped up the receiver and then held it out to me.

"A call for you, Evie. I think it's Jake," she whispered as she handed it to me.

"Did you see little Eva?" Jake asked me the instant I answered.

"Yes. She's adorable." I missed her already.

"The most beautiful baby I've ever seen," he said. "But then we haven't seen ours yet."

"Ours? You mean yours and mine?"

"You don't hope to marry Stephen, do you, Evie?"

"*Nee*, I suppose not."

"*Gut*, because you and I should get married and start our own family immediately. I can't wait. How about you?"

"Hold on. You mean get baptized first, don't you?"

"I don't want to wait six or more months the way Bishop Harvey insists. He isn't even a bishop in my district. Let's get married by a justice of the peace tonight and then get baptized later." His voice was exuberant, full of self-assurance.

"Are you sure we can do that?" I'd never heard of it. And did I really want to embark on a merry-go-round marriage?

"Why not?" he asked.

"For one thing, I'm going to Bishop Harvey's house for supper later today."

"What? Are you pulling my leg?"

"*Nee*. He wants me to meet his family."

"You know what that means, don't you?" Jake sputtered. "He wants to court you. Right under my nose, that dear, kindly bishop is trying to steal you away."

"I have no idea what he wants. I think his *dochders* talked him into the invitation."

"But finally, we can be together. Forever. And live right here with my parents, who already love you like their own *dochder*."

"I'll think about it. But not this evening because I have other plans."

"I forbid you to go."

"Ha, that's a laugh. You are not my husband, nor my minister, deacon, or bishop, and you have no say over how I spend my time or with whom."

"But Harvey's an old man. Probably too old to have or want more children. He's a fine man, but no doubt set in his ways. And you're too young to throw in the towel."

I wasn't going to make things easy for Jake anymore. I cupped my mouth with my hand. "Jake, if you really want to marry me so much, you'll have to wait."

"Please promise me you won't commit yourself to Harvey or Stephen. I know you won't because you don't love either of them. Am I right?"

Sadie was emptying the cases and storing the leftover food in the refrigerator. She rolled her eyes at me.

"Jake, I need to get back to work. I told Sadie she could leave early."

"If you don't promise me, I'm going to drive over there right now." I could hear exasperation expanding Jake's voice, like bubbles rising to the surface.

Two *Englisch* couples entered carrying bags from the retail shop, followed by two Amish women.

"Customers are arriving, and it's almost three," I told Jake. "I need to show them how to serve themselves coffee and tea. And how to pay." My patience with his demands were vaporizing like drops of water in a hot skillet. "Please don't come here" were my final words to him.

The two Amish women were already pouring themselves tea and leaving money, while Beatrice gave the *Englisch* couple directions as they begged for pastries. She broke down and sold them each a muffin. Then she covered the glass case from view.

"When will I learn to say no in a way that people believe me?" I asked Beatrice as she and I finally closed the café's kitchen. Sadie and Annie bustled around straightening and washing.

"I could have put Harvey's dinner invitation off for a week, and I should have." Stress was invading me.

She glanced back at me and batted her eyes. "So what are you going to do?"

"I can't not go with Harvey when he comes to fetch me."

"Why not? Tell him you have a headache."

"Not so far from the truth. My temples are pounding. But I can't lie to a bishop."

"Then tell him the truth. You've changed your mind. Women do that all the time."

"Not to a bishop, they don't. I couldn't."

"He's only asked you to come for supper. Maybe his daughters really do want to meet you, and it means nothing more."

"Then why haven't they come in here to the café? Doesn't everyone in the county know where I work and every detail of my life?" The image of me on the front of the newspaper flitted through my mind.

She scrutinized my eyes. "I see no happiness on your face. Do you not care for Harvey at all?"

"*Yah*, as a friend, and I respect him as a mentor and spiritual leader. But he's as old as my *dat*."

"About my age, probably." She clucked. "You said you were going to his house for supper, so go already. Otherwise you'll never know."

"He told me not to dress up."

"Suddenly you care how you look?"

"*Ach*, none of my *kapps* are pressed, and I don't have an iron. Mark's sister Susie was going to help me out, but I didn't think to ask her today."

"We have an iron in the laundry room in the basement."

"But I assume it's electric."

"I wonder how Edna used to press her *kapps*. Who knows? A non-electric one might be waiting for you down there. Or I'll press one for you myself. Now, are you satisfied? You're not headed to a church service or a wedding."

"You're right. Maybe I should look like a slob. He'll be disappointed and his *dochders* will disapprove."

"In other words, they'd be making up your mind for you. Honestly, Eva, you need to make your own choices and stop relying on other people's opinions. I speak from experience." She glanced to the ceiling, as if remembering the past. "You're not the only one who's been the subject of gossip and ridicule. I was miserable in high school. Bottom line, I was chubby and never thought anyone would date me. But then I met my soul mate, who said he adored me exactly as I was. So when he asked me to elope, I said sure.

"As you can imagine, when my parents' attorney annulled my marriage, I was devastated and again the subject of gossip." She expelled a sigh and her shoulders rounded. "Everywhere I went, heads turned. I was so embarrassed and belittled that I allowed my parents to force me to marry a man I didn't even know, let alone love."

"But it all turned out for the best, *yah*?"

"Eventually. Although I've often wondered what would've happened if I'd simply refused to obey my parents. How different my life would be if I'd stayed married to..."

"Will you tell me his name?" I asked.

"I'd better not, as he could stop by."

"Seriously? He'd come here?"

She shrugged, but her face brightened up, and she looked ten years younger. "We attended a small high school, so many have kept in touch, especially with our quarterly newspaper." She nibbled her lower lip. "In it I read his wife passed away last year. Of course, I was sad to hear of her death, and yet surprised and pleased when he contacted me and said he wanted to get together. For old time's sake."

"Well? What did you say?"

"I said yes, but he told me he'd be out of town on business for several weeks. I didn't tell you about that when we talked about him before, but that was more than a month ago. I haven't heard from him. It would have probably come to nothing anyway."

The image of Beatrice in a wedding gown sent me for a loop. Would she remarry before I married for the first time?

"Now you know my secret. Please promise not to tell anyone as I don't want to be the subject of more ridicule if he never shows up. I only told you my story because I wanted you to know I can empathize with you." She removed her apron and tossed it into our laundry hamper. "Now I'll go down to the basement and look through our irons."

"I have a clean *kapp* in the cabin."

"If you don't mind my going in there, I'll get it," she said.

"Of course I don't mind if it's not too much trouble."

She stared out through the glass. "Oh my. Looks as though you have another visitor."

Harvey sauntered through the café's front door as Sadie and Annie slipped out before the end of their shifts. His grin expanded when he saw me.

"Hello, Harvey. I wasn't expecting you this early." I flattened my apron, but no use in trying to improve my appearance after a day's work. I was wiped out and must look it.

"I was wondering if we could stroll through the nursery," he said. "I'm looking for a gift. Is it true you sell flowering plants in the greenhouses?"

"*Yah*, so many beautiful flowers and shrubs, but I know little about them. I can get someone to help you."

"But it's you I came to see."

"Why?" I blurted out.

"To get to know you better." I must have looked startled because he added, "And talk about your baptism. Classes will start soon."

"Would Olivia Beiler be allowed to take them with me?"

"She is welcome, although her parents are in the same district as yours, and they've graciously taken her back to live with them. I was most thankful to hear she's returned to the fold. The *Englisch* world tempted the poor girl away. I heard she cut her hair for what she thought was a generous act, but that's the least of her transgressions. She has much confessing and repenting to do."

"Maybe I should join in that district too." But I didn't plan to move home unless I lost this job. My life was a whirlwind of uncertainties.

"That would be a long drive."

I noticed a man walking by lugging a potted rosebush, budding but not blooming. I kept expecting Jake to barge in and make a scene. If he did, Harvey might never let him join the church, and then what? I decided the sooner Harvey and I left, the better.

"I should go back to my cabin and change my clothes for supper," I said.

"No need, really. You look perfect as you are."

"But at least a clean apron. And Beatrice has kindly offered to iron a clean *kapp*."

"No need to change a thing, Eva. That is, if you decide to come home with me for supper."

"*Yah*, I accept your invitation."

"As I said, by the end of the day everyone will be dressed casually."

"Even on a Saturday evening?" I didn't buy his story. "If you have *dochders* in *rumspringa*, they might be all spruced up to go out with their friends or beaus."

"They'd better not, as this get-together was their idea." He cleared his throat. "And I agreed it was a *gut* one."

Through the glass wall, I saw a young Amish fellow pushing a wheelbarrow.

"You have a wistful expression on your face," Harvey said.

"In truth, I'd rather be working out in the nursery than in here." I thought he might quote a proverb about learning to be content where God plants you. But he smiled back as though he found me delightful.

"Many young women would envy you. For instance, one of my *dochders* loves to cook more than anything."

"Is she looking for a job?" Maybe one of his daughters had an ulterior motive for meeting me. "She could fill out an application in case one of my girls quits." I would not be surprised if Sadie and Mark announced their intention to wed, or if Annie found a higher-paying job or enrolled in school. Or if we got plain old too busy, which I supposed was an oxymoron.

"I'll let her know," he said. "I hope my invitation hasn't made you anxious."

I realized I was wrapping my *kapp*'s string around my index finger. Tighter and tighter, until my fingertip ached. I tried to appear nonchalant as I released my digit. "*Ach*, I guess I am nervous. Am I in some kind of trouble?" Maybe Harvey had heard about my driving Jake's automobile and backing into Wayne's patrol car. "Is that why you wish to speak to me?"

"Not in the slightest." He rested his chin on his knuckles. "I'm extending a welcome to you to our district, and I hope you'll feel comfortable attending church in the future. Tomorrow is a non-preaching Sunday. Maybe you'd feel more comfortable meeting my family during the day."

"I might go to church with my parents tomorrow if I can borrow the mare and buggy. I should have thought to ask Stephen earlier in the day."

The phone in the kitchen jangled. I ignored the intrusion, but the ringing continued relentlessly. It finally fell silent.

As Harvey and I entered the nearest greenhouse, he read the sign aloud. "Tropical Plants. Sounds interesting." The air was warm and moist. We were embraced with the ambrosia of gardenias.

"I could spend my whole day in here. When I take a break, I often wander through the greenhouses." I took a leap of courage and asked, "Did your wife enjoy gardening?"

"*Yah*, very much. She could name each flower and bush in her garden."

"That is my goal, someday. For now, I only know the more common varieties." We strolled past pots of African violets and orchids.

"Plus she grew pumpkins, cucumbers, and gourds. Not a space left open."

In a bold moment I asked, "Do you miss her?"

"*Yah*, I do." His upper lip trembled, but he steadied it. "I'm grateful for my children and grandchildren, but they don't take the place of a spouse. A man gets lonely." I waited for him to expound, to elaborate, but he said nothing.

"Do you think one woman can take the place of another?" The greenhouse turned silent. What was I thinking, asking such a personal question of a bishop? I imagined he had helped many widows survive the loss of their spouses. Even after some gruesome tragedies.

"Her death was *Gott*'s will. If the Lord selects another spouse for me, I must obey." His eyes turned jovial. "Or puts one in my path and allows me to do the selecting."

"Even if you don't love her?"

"What makes you think I wouldn't love her, or at least find her attractive?"

To give myself something to do, I picked up an African violet and removed a broken leaf and shriveled flower. "I'd like one of these for my parents' window."

"Then I shall purchase it for you. I told you I was looking for a gift."

I was left speechless as I weighed the implications.

"When you come over to our house, you can see the flower garden, although it's not in bloom yet." He was changing the subject, perhaps for the best. "Of course, you'll have to wait a few months to see the bounteous blooms. My *dochders* have started weeding it, but there's much to be done. They want to keep it beautiful in their *mamm*'s honor."

"I can imagine so." Always, she would come first.

"In truth, our marriage got off to a rocky start. I don't know what I was expecting. That somehow she'd read my mind and fulfill all my wishes." He gazed across the length of the greenhouse. "Almost immediately we were awaiting our first child, and my wife was sick day and night. My *mamm* assured me morning sickness is common, but I grew to resent her and the baby, who was born with colic. And then another child arrived right on its heels." His beard wagged as he shook his head.

"My wife and I were both shocked and saddened when someone nominated me for minister and I was chosen by lot. In the blink of an eye, I had two full-time jobs. That was in your parents' district, but it was bursting, beyond capacity with more than two hundred people. We had to split. That was when you were so young you wouldn't have remembered me anyway. And then, after the split, much to our disappointment and horror, the Lord chose me to replace the elderly bishop with heart problems. I know now we were being selfish, but my wife and I both cried that day." One side of his mouth curved into a smile. "I remember the looks of relief on the other men's faces. Their pats of condolence on my back."

We were skirting the issue, but I didn't dare come right out and ask him what his plans were. Was he set on remarrying in the near future? Marrying season was in the fall and winter, after the crops had been harvested. But I'd heard widowers could marry anytime.

Huffing and puffing, Beatrice bustled into the greenhouse. "*Caro Dio.* Bad news, Eva." She held up my drooping *kapp*. "I turned the iron on too warm and scorched your *kapp*." She inhaled another breath. "But worse than that, Jake called to say Amos fell."

"How bad a fall?" Harvey asked.

"Did he lose consciousness?" I said, not knowing what her answer would mean.

"I didn't think to ask questions like that, silly me," Beatrice said. "But Ruth is frantic."

"Did you actually speak to her or to Jake?" I had to wonder if this was a ruse to keep me from going to Harvey's.

"Jake called me, but he passed his phone to Ruth, who said Amos had been determined to walk to the kitchen, where he lost his balance and fell against the counter."

"Where are they now?" Harvey asked.

"In the Lancaster County Hospital emergency room. He's getting x-rayed as soon as possible." Beatrice held my ruined *kapp* as if it were a wounded bird.

"I'd better go and see for myself," Harvey said. "Since I've been to see them once, I'm sure they expect to see me there. I've heard their own bishop is still housebound."

"By buggy?" Beatrice asked. "It's too far from here."

"No, I'll hire a driver. May I use a phone, Beatrice?"

"Sure, come with me to the house. I'd like to join you if you don't mind. Ruth and I go way back."

"*Yah*, I know you do."

"I'll come too." In my inner ear I could hear Amos calling my name.

"No need." Harvey's expression grew complex, his eyes narrowing. "Beatrice and I can handle this."

I set the African violet back down amongst the other potted plants. "But if Amos is dying, I want to say goodbye to him."

"Eva has been the only one he wants to see," Beatrice said. "I can testify to that." She channeled her words to me. "But I have to wonder if you're only going to see Jake."

"I'm going there for me. I won't be dissuaded by what others think. Just like you said, Beatrice."

She readjusted her bun and reset a hairpin. "Stephen would probably drive us, but there's only room for two passengers."

"We can't rely on him for everything." I recalled the many times he'd helped me out. "If you don't want me to go, I'll find my own ride. There's a Mennonite driver's card in the café. I'll call him."

"I have his card in the house too, and I need to let the dogs out while we wait."

"We could all use him," Harvey said. "I'll pay the fare. I'll put my horse in the barn."

I got the feeling he wanted to be in charge, so I agreed.

# Forty-Seven

An hour later, our van neared the hospital's handsome facade and slowed to a halt. Harvey insisted on paying the driver, including a tip for his speedy arrival to the nursery.

I was surprised to see so many cars coming and going. Plain and *Englisch* people milled in the foyer as we entered. Groups clustered, and individuals waited at the reception desks.

I strode in as a couple was leaving a receptionist behind the counter and asked the woman if we could see Amos and Ruth Miller.

"Are you a relative?" She surveyed my *kapp*.

"No, but we were asked to come by relatives."

Harvey stepped forward, and she immediately deferred to him. "Good to see you, Bishop Harvey."

"How are you, Gladys?"

"It's been a busy day. Whom are you here to see?"

"Amos Miller."

She glanced at her computer screen. "He's in the ER. The waiting room's right through there."

"Thanks. I know where it is." Harvey led Beatrice and me down a corridor and then into a large waiting room. My guess was he'd been here often. Only a few chairs were empty. I saw several Amish people I didn't recognize huddled like zombies—vacuous eyes and melancholy conversations.

"There's Jake," Beatrice said, pointing across the room. "Sitting in the chair near the fish tank."

His back was stooped, and his face was propped in his hands. Harvey proceeded over to him. "Jake."

Jake jerked at the sound of Harvey's voice, as if he'd been deep in thought or prayer.

"We're here to support you and Ruth. How is your *dat*?"

"He's still alive." Jake looked to be in agony—drained of all energy. I felt like rushing over to embrace him, but I restrained myself. Comforting and counsel were Harvey's domains. Nothing I'd done in the past had made a whit of difference.

Beatrice and I found seats and waited for maybe an hour. Time moved in slow motion. It appeared as if Harvey and Jake were praying.

I started to get up, but Beatrice patted my knee. "We shouldn't interrupt them." She sent me a dubious smile. "It looks as though all your worries about tonight's supper were for naught."

"*Ach*, do you think his daughters are waiting for us?"

"No, he called their phone shanty. One of them was close by and answered. I'm sure this family is used to his comings and goings, always serving others."

"Being married to a man of God would have its challenges." I thought about Harvey's deceased wife. Did it take a terminal disease to garner his full attention?

"Some women enjoy the stature of being married to a bishop or minister, but I've heard few desire that privilege. When a man gets baptized, he promises to serve if chosen by lot—God, that is."

"Meaning that if Jake got baptized, he'd have to make that commitment to be available too?"

"Yes, but only married men in excellent standing with the church can be nominated by a secret ballot. No offense to Jake, but I can't see that happening with him. Although age will temper a man the way heat does metal."

"Could a man nominate himself?"

"Possibly, but I doubt many do. I'm the wrong person to ask. Harvey's the expert, not me."

She glanced across the room as Ruth came out of a door and shuffled toward Jake and Harvey. Beatrice and I stood and joined them.

"It's all my fault." Ruth's voice quavered. "I never should have brought him home from the trauma unit so early to begin with. The doctors warned me not to." She looked at Jake. "And Jake told me to call if I needed him."

"I should've been checking on him more often," he said, his voice flat. "I knew you might need me." Moisture glazed his eyes.

"I couldn't ask for your help while you were busy working in the field."

"The past is behind us," Harvey said. "No use punishing yourself about it. You did what you thought was best."

Beatrice touched Ruth's arm. "How is Amos? What's going on?"

"He's having X-rays. I wanted to be in the room with him, but the technician told me to wait out here. Someone will come and get me."

"Is he awake?" I asked.

Ruth slipped an arm around my shoulders. "*Yah*, praise the Lord. I was afraid he was slipping away from us again, but he came around as soon as he was in Jake's car. He was in terrible pain. I should've called for an ambulance. I didn't know what to do. Anyway, Jake drove us here."

"It looks as though you and Jake have handled the situation well," Beatrice said. "You're here now, and that's all that matters."

"For the moment." Jake's posture sagged, his neck bent. "Now we wait. Not my best personality trait, as you know."

"Each of us is flawed," Harvey said. "They that wait upon the Lord shall renew their strength."

I wondered if Harvey was referring to me. Waiting for others was all I seemed to do.

While speaking in hushed tones, Harvey steered Jake back to the two empty chairs, and the men sat down. Their heads tipped together as they conversed and prayed.

Beatrice stepped out of the waiting room to use her phone. When she returned, she told me Stephen was coming to get her. "I called to explain the situation so he could take care of the dogs, and he offered to drop by the hospital to fetch me. You, too, if you need a ride."

I tallied up my other options. "Absolutely, yes."

"Stephen has become the son I never had," Beatrice said. "Not that I'd wish to take the place of his adoptive parents, who love him dearly."

A nurse carrying a clipboard appeared and glided over to Ruth. "Are you Mrs. Miller?"

"Ruth, the nurse is talking to you," Beatrice said.

"Oh?"

"The doctor wants to speak to you now," the nurse said.

Ruth looked over to Jake, who rose to his feet and joined her.

"The nurse's serious expression gives me the impression she's about to report bad news," I said to Harvey. "What if Amos dies?"

"Amos has always been a strong man," he said. "Perhaps too strong for his own *gut*. But now he must rely on *Gott* and others to care for him."

Twenty minutes later, Jake plodded back into the waiting room. "You can come in and visit him now if you wish. I should warn you he's not doing well. He has a fractured rib, which causes outrageous pain. They've given him enough medication to practically knock him out."

As we followed Jake, the smell of disinfectant grew.

A doctor and Ruth met us at Amos's door before allowing us entrance. "Falling after a head injury is not that uncommon." The bald man glanced to Ruth. "I explained this to Mrs. Miller when she insisted on taking her husband home so soon. Today, my advice is to keep him here for several days until he stabilizes."

Ruth let out a sigh of relief. "*Yah*, that sounds like a good idea."

"You might want to consider a convalescent center." The doctor ran his hand over his head.

"Run by *Englischers*? No, he wouldn't like that. No offense meant, Doctor. We certainly appreciate your care."

He bobbed his head as if he'd heard that sentiment before and was not offended. "There's a Mennonite nursing home not too far away," he said as we moved inside.

"We can't afford the cost. And he might think we've given up on him and don't love him anymore." Ruth stroked Amos's feet through his blanket. The doctor left, but a nurse stayed behind.

"How will Ruth and you get along if you take him home?" I asked Jake.

"No idea."

"Maybe you can hire a young woman to live in and help," said Beatrice. "How about Mark's little sister, Susie?"

"Or Olivia," I said. "If she's willing and her parents will consent. Maybe for a couple of weeks, anyway. If a bishop supported the idea, her parents would be more apt to agree."

Harvey's beard moved up and down as he spoke. "That's a wonderful idea. Olivia must stop thinking only of herself, and she should volunteer to help others in times of hardship. Not that Jake won't assist, am I correct?"

"*Yah*, of course I will," Jake said.

An unnerving thought slithered through my mind. Did Harvey hope Jake and Olivia would fall in love and leave me in the lurch? Well, not in the lurch with Harvey there to mend my broken heart. Would a man of God do such a devious thing? I liked to think not, and yet he seemed to be pursuing me.

"The doctor said I should go home," Ruth said, "but I can't leave Amos. If he comes around and I'm not here, he'll be frightened."

"We'll take good care of your husband," the nurse said. "You should go home and rest."

"*Mamm*, I'll drive you," Jake said. "I need to take care of the livestock."

"*Nee*, I'm staying here. There's nothing anyone can do to dissuade me."

"All right. Eva? Beatrice? I'll take you home."

"No need," Beatrice told him. "Stephen is on his way."

Jake frowned and turned to Harvey. "I can drive you home if you'd like."

"My horse and buggy are at the nursery. I would appreciate a ride there," Harvey said. "You and I have much to speak about."

"That's the truth."

"When will you talk to Olivia about helping *Mamm*?" Jake asked.

Harvey examined the wall clock. "Too late tonight, but I'll go to their church service or their home tomorrow morning to confer with them. I'll leave a message on the phone in their shanty." He glanced to me. "You mentioned you might attend your parents' service. If so, I might see you there."

"I'll have to wait and see how I'm feeling in the morning."

After my wishy-washy answer, Harvey gave me a sour expression.

# Forty-Eight

I awoke the next morning when my arm dangled over the edge of my bed and knocked the clock off the nightstand. Some sort of nightmare, I guessed as I reached down to retrieve the clock. Stephen was in my dream. That much I recalled.

My eyes focused on the clock's hands. Already eight? I'd overslept. I needed to put on my soup of the day but couldn't remember what I was preparing.

Then it struck me. Today was Sunday, the Lord's day of rest.

I envisioned my go-to-church attire—my white organza apron and my periwinkle blue dress—still at my parents' home, which seemed in another county at this moment of blurriness.

I wondered if Harvey would indeed attend my parents' church service. I couldn't imagine what he and Jake had spoken about on the way home last night. Had Harvey talked Jake into attending the service with him? That question alone should have made me spring to my feet, but the cabin's air was cold and clammy, and my nose felt clogged. Had I picked up a virus in the waiting room of the hospital? I could tell I was trying to talk myself into being sick so I wouldn't have to get up.

But then I sneezed, and sneezed again several times. I reached for a tissue and dabbed my nose. Probably an allergy, I told myself. Dust had always made me sneeze, and I hadn't scrubbed my living quarters since I moved in.

I sneezed twice more and then coughed. I had a perfectly good excuse to skip church today, but I felt guilt invading me as if I were a sponge in a puddle. I scurried over to the sink, filled up the kettle, and turned on the gas burner. I was thankful I'd brought *Mamm*'s homemade herbal remedy tea, which seemed to fix everything, especially colds. I'd hunker out in my little cabin all morning. No one would notice. Beatrice had probably already left for church, but I wouldn't even peek out the window lest she be there waiting for a ride from a friend.

I turned on my small space heater and climbed back into bed. I opened the Bible and decided to have my own church service with just myself and God. I sighed, as I knew I was disobeying the *Ordnung* this very moment. Or maybe not. Maybe God wanted me to spend this morning at home contemplating his Word and praying for Amos.

Then it occurred to me that I hadn't heard the dogs today. Usually by now they were out and at least one of them had barked a few times and loped up on my porch. Odd. I hadn't heard the main house's back door open and close or a car's engine idling. Maybe Beatrice was doing the same thing I was. Although she was consistent when it came to attending church.

*Ach,* last evening had been exhausting. I thought of Amos in the hospital bed, barely breathing. When he did, he must experience excruciating pain with a fractured rib. Hadn't the poor man suffered enough? Or was he being taught a lesson like Job was? He was completely dependent upon Ruth and Jake. And God. Although I couldn't remember ever seeing him at a church service when I was growing up. He would've been my parents' age and would've sat near my father and brother on the men's side.

I allowed my thoughts to meander into a fairy-tale world. I imagined Jake's and my wedding day. We would exchange vows and promise to love and obey. No worries about kissing him in front of the congregation as it was *verboten* during a church service.

The water kettle screeched. I made myself tea and returned to bed. As I watched the steam rising off the surface of the liquid, I tried to imagine myself married to Jake.

Earlier this morning Jake and Harvey might have returned to the hospital to check on Amos and Ruth, who must be exhausted. No way around it, I was uncomfortable with Jake and Harvey spending time together. I wondered if visiting a sick man was considered work on this day of rest. No, Jesus had healed a lame man on the Sabbath.

I left the warmth of my bed, washed my face, and dressed. I had the oddest inclination to wear *Englisch* clothes so I'd blend in with the customers here at the nursery. Just for once, I didn't want to stand out. But I didn't own any and knew better than to attempt such an ill-conceived stunt.

I asked myself what I'd like to do more than anything. My inner response was to stroll around the nursery and pretend I worked with the plants. The business didn't open until noon on Sunday. And certainly no Amish would be working today. I'd have the whole place to myself.

Dressed and my head covered with a scarf, I laced on my Nikes and scuttled out the door. I rounded the big house and almost walked right into Beatrice, whose arms sprang up in surprise.

"Are you trying to give me a heart attack?" she squawked.

"Me? How about you?"

"Looks as though both of us had the same idea." She fingered the cross at her neck. "We're playing hooky." The dogs gamboled over to us. "Although I needed to let the dogs out."

"I didn't mean to sleep in. But since I did, I spent time in bed reading the Bible." *Ach,* I sounded self-righteous.

"Well, I spent my time in prayer."

We both fell into laughter like schoolgirls. Then we turned serious when I asked if she'd heard word about Amos.

"Over the phone. I felt as though I were swimming upstream trying to track him down in that hospital," she said. "I finally reached the nurses' station outside his room. I told the nurse I was his sister-in-law, although I think she caught my lie. Nevertheless, she said he was in stable condition and that Ruth was on a cot, deep in slumber. The nurse said, 'Best not to wake her.'"

"Praise *Gott* he's still alive."

"Maybe we can visit later and give Ruth support." She lowered her gaze. "In the meantime, we're both skipping church."

"This is a nonpreaching Sunday in this district," I threw in to save face.

"I thought you were going to your parents' church service today."

"*Ach*, I slept in. And I forgot to ask Stephen's permission to use the buggy again."

"Want me to call Stephen for you?"

"No, he's probably at church. And it's too late to travel all that way by buggy." Even though the nursery was devoid of customers and employees, I spoke in her ear. "Jake wants me to marry him before a justice of the peace and then get baptized later if we can."

"And you said?"

"I'm sorely tempted." I felt like a hose spewing its contents. I pressed my lips together lest I divulged too much, when in fact I didn't know the answer.

Both she and I could make a mad dash and get to our destinations. But neither of us hurried. I needed someone to speak to. Not *Mamm*, not this time, and certainly not Olivia at this point.

We strolled along together toward the house's grand front porch, with the dogs weaving between us. They clambered up the steps and snuffled around the swing.

Birds tittered and squirrels chattered on the branches of the maple tree, catching our attention.

"Look at the tiny new growth." Beatrice tipped her head back. "The tree is still alive."

"A sign from God?" I wondered aloud.

"According to Stephen, the arborist said we'll have to wait and see."

"*Ach*, always waiting." I watched a squirrel balancing at the tip of a branch.

Beatrice let out a wistful sigh. "Sometimes when I'm caught in indecision, I write down the pros and cons." She stroked Missy's satiny forehead as the dog rubbed her muzzle against Beatrice's skirt. "After I pray, of course."

"My mind must have done that all night, as I barely slept." I yawned. "For all I know, Jake has changed his mind by now. Most important should be Amos's health and Ruth's well-being."

"My best guess is that both Ruth and Amos wish Jake to be baptized and to marry you."

"But if Olivia moves in with them, everything could change. She's far more attractive than I am, with a lively and outgoing personality. And she can cook too." Jake could easily choose Olivia over me. With them living in the same house, how simple it would be.

"Eva, have you never turned your problems over to God and then let them go? As it's written in Proverbs: 'Trust in the LORD with all thine heart; and lean not unto thine own understanding.'"

"*Ach*, I keep forgetting to do that."

Beatrice and I strolled across the path leading to the greenhouses. The sun warmed the earth and leaves, still damp with dew. Rhododendrons and rosebushes bulged with the heady aroma of impending growth. I noticed hanging baskets, soon to hold a rainbow of colors. Birds tweeted up and down the scale, filling the air with harmonies.

The dogs snuffled the ground with intensity. I'd heard canines can detect smells hundreds of times better than we humans can. My hunch was they were hoping to catch the trace aroma of their owners. No matter how long I lived here, I might always be an outsider.

I wondered if Beatrice's lost love would show up today. Unlikely on a Sunday morning. He would assume she was at church. But maybe this afternoon? She must have been thinking the same thing because her hair had been combed with care, and she wore a paisley shirt and a long flowing skirt.

"I know I'm being nosy, but do you think your friend might stop by?" I asked.

She shrugged one plump shoulder. "No way of knowing. The best thing I can do is put him out of my head." Her hand moved toward a greenhouse door. She handed me Heath's leash as she opened it. "Shall we go into a greenhouse before the customers arrive? It's always so nice and warm in there, not to mention the aromas of the plants."

As I followed her, we both stopped short at the sight of Bill Hastings. He was examining a small azalea bush, its pink buds ready to bloom. Heath's hackles raised, and his ears drew back.

"What are you doing in here?" My voice came out with force and authority. "The nursery isn't open yet." I wanted to tell him he was not welcome in any case.

"I wish to buy these for my wife. I wasn't planning to steal them, I promise." He set the pot back down on the ground amid the other plants. "Will the Yoders not take my money anymore?" He extracted a wallet from his pocket and brought out two twenty-dollar bills. "Is this enough?" He handed the money to me.

I checked the price of the azalea. "This should more than cover it. But I don't have change."

"Keep the change after all the trouble we've caused you." He glanced at Heath, who'd gone back to sniffing around the plants. Yet the dog's presence gave me a feeling of assurance.

"Go ahead and take the azalea with you," Beatrice said. "I'll leave the money at the front cash register later. Better get out of here before Stephen arrives."

"Actually, I spoke to Stephen when he stopped by our house yesterday. At first I thought he was coming to get on my case, but believe it or not, he said he wanted to apologize, that he'd acted badly and wished he could take back his words and actions." Bill slipped his wallet into his jeans pocket. "I was totally blown away, but I found myself apologizing to him too. And we shook hands. After that, he shared some of his own story, and it seems we have a lot in common."

I thought Bill had treated Stephen brutally, not to mention making false accusations against Heath and demanding the dog be shot. But both Beatrice and I listened, absorbing his story and trying to visualize the scene.

"And about Ralph's burning down the barn?" Bill said. "When we were kids, we never played with matches. I can't believe Ralph did it. Not on purpose anyway. His drinking dominates his life and makes him act like an idiot. He has blackouts, when he can't remember anything. If I could only get him to go to AA. That's something else Stephen and I spoke about. Stephen assured me there's hope for Ralph, and he even promised to pray for him. Can you believe it? I thought Stephen would despise me forever." He picked up the pot. "I wonder how a man ever gets past his childhood disappointments."

"It sounds as if you've made a good first step." Beatrice spoke as if she bore no grudge toward him, as if Bill were any old customer. "We all have a heavenly Father watching over us."

"I don't buy into all that religious rigmarole."

"Oh, I see." She ran her tongue across her upper lip. "Say, not that you've asked for my suggestions, but there's a group called Al-Anon for people whose lives are affected by someone else's drinking. An Al-Anon group uses one of our church's meeting rooms a couple of times a week, but you don't need to be Catholic or any religion to attend it. They meet all over the place."

"Anyone I might know go to them?"

"All is kept strictly confidential, so I have no idea." She deadheaded a flower in his pot and flicked it aside. "Take those flowers home, and tell your woman you love her. You'll find her sweeter too."

I was impressed with Beatrice's forthrightness. And Stephen's brave and generous act made me appreciate him all the more. No wonder Glenn trusted him with his business. It seemed I was the only one in a whirlpool of indecision.

Watching Bill leave, thoughts ping-ponged in my brain. If I married Jake in the near future, I'd have to quit this job and move into his parents' home, leaving the café without a manager. If I married Stephen, I could continue to work here, but I'd live as an *Englischer*, apart from my parents and extended family

As Beatrice and I exited the greenhouse, I heard a melodious, "Yoo-hoo, Bea, over here." The *Englisch* woman wore a quaint little hat that matched her yellow flowered scarf and beige suit.

"Did you forget about me?" She scuffled over to us wearing high heels. "I called and called, but when you didn't answer, I was worried."

Beatrice's hands cupped her cheeks. "I forgot. Oh dear, I'm sorry." She turned to include me. "Viola, I'd like you to meet Eva, who manages the café here." Beatrice took Viola's hand and put it in mine. Her nails were polished mauve.

"I've made you late for Mass," Beatrice said.

Viola squinted down at her diminutive wristwatch. "Only a few minutes. Grab a coat and let's be on our way. Otherwise, you'll have to go to confession before you can take communion again."

Beatrice turned to me. "I haven't even fed the dogs yet."

"Don't worry about it," I said. "I'll take care of everything if you leave the back door unlocked."

Beatrice passed me a key. "Better take this." She went into the house and then reemerged wearing a long jacket. Her girlish grin made her look younger. A minute later, Beatrice eased into Viola's aged boat of a sedan, and they puttered out of the parking lot.

# Forty-Nine

After feeding the ravenous dogs, I left them in the main house. Enjoying my solitude, I skirted the house and the café and made my way to the barn to say hello to Autumn. When she noticed me, her ears stood up tall as a welcome. She bent her head in my direction and made a soft nickering sound. Had she grown fond of me, or was she expecting a treat? I wished I'd brought a carrot, but I could offer her only a scratch where her neck met her withers, a spot she couldn't reach herself.

Her head jerked, and her ears swiveled back. I heard the sound of hooves as the bishop's buggy rolled to a stop. Harvey sat for a moment watching me, as if planning what to say.

"Hello." I smiled and tried to look at ease.

"*Wie gehts*?" He got out of his buggy.

"I'm okay, but I overslept. I woke up sneezing and thought I was coming down with a cold. I figured I should avoid people so I wouldn't spread germs. But my *mamm*'s herbal tea seems to have knocked it out."

"Where's your *kapp*?"

My hands flew up to cover my hair. I was relieved to feel the scarf, shabby as it was. "*Ach*, my *kapps* need pressing." My excuse sounded lame even to me.

"Go back to your cabin and collect a wrinkled *kapp*. We'll take it to my house. One of my *dochders* will heat up the iron."

"Would that not be considered asking her to work on the Sabbath?"

One brow raised as he looked down on me, the way I guessed he conveyed to his daughters they were being silly. "We can't have you spending the rest of the day looking like that. Now come along, and I'll take you to meet my family."

He must have noticed my reluctance because he said, "Don't worry. I'm a cautious driver. You'll get back here safely."

I couldn't refuse his offer. After all, Harvey was a bishop, not a casual friend. I dashed to my cabin to find the cleanest *kapp* that wasn't too badly creased. In fact, when I set it on my head, it looked halfway decent. But not good enough to be escorted around the county by a bishop.

He took my hand and helped me climb into his buggy. "Since it's a visiting Sunday in this district, is there anyone else you wish to see?"

"Eventually, I'd like to check on how Amos is doing. But I could use a phone to call the hospital."

"Later we can arrange that. I spoke to Olivia's parents this morning about her helping Ruth and Amos when he gets back home. They promised to pray about it and let us know."

"Oh, *gut*. I'm glad."

I'd never felt more ill at ease in a buggy. All other Amish drivers craned their necks to see who was perched next to Harvey. He seemed as relaxed as ever and raised a hand to everyone who waved. I endeavored to wear an expression of tranquillity, as if I didn't notice them.

What had been a gentle breeze gained velocity, tossing the treetops. I looked up to the sky and saw clouds scudding by. It was times like these that I wished I read the weather report in the newspaper or listened to a weatherman on a radio. But nothing to be done about the weather now that I was on my way to Harvey's. *Ach*, how easily he'd maneuvered me into his buggy. Or was he simply showing an act of kindness to one of his flock?

When we finally arrived at his home, I was again impressed by its stature and regal architecture. My first thought was that an *Englisch* man had constructed it. A wealthy man.

"How long has this home been in your family?" I asked.

"During the Great Depression, my grandfather purchased it from a man who was deep in debt. My family removed all the electrical wiring, but we kept everything else pretty much as it was except for the fancy curtains and such. I hope you like it."

"If the inside's anything like the outside, I know I will." I couldn't hide my awe.

I received a grin in answer to my remark. As Harvey pulled into the barnyard, a young woman—a fair-haired slip of a school-age girl—scurried down the back steps to greet us. She was indeed dressed casually, and she was barefoot.

"This is my youngest *dochder*, Linda." Harvey seemed to brim with satisfaction. "Come and meet Eva," he said to her.

Her eyes lifted, but not up enough to meet mine.

"Happy to meet you," I said. She seemed to be mouthing words in return.

"Don't be shy, Linda," Harvey said to her, but she glanced away. I immediately felt a fondness for her, a warming in my chest. What a dear young teen.

She took hold of her father's hand, and he patted it before letting go. "Be a *gut* girl and show Eva into the kitchen."

"*Kumm rei*— No, I mean, please, come this way," she told me. I got the distinct feeling she'd practiced this phrase. I wondered if the girls spoke only *Deitsch* at home, as I had as a child.

Just inside the kitchen stood willowy Naomi, Linda's older sister, who also appeared a bit disheveled, much to my surprise. She shook my hand when Harvey announced her name. "Glad ta meet ya."

"I'm happy to meet you too." I wondered which girl took after her *mamm* because they were as different as night and day.

Out of the corner of my eye, I gave Harvey a looking over. Hard to tell what color hair he had as a younger man. "Grizzled" is how

I'd describe it now. But he had good posture, and he carried an air of confidence and vigor.

Rapping knuckles on the back door brought Harvey's daughters to open it. "*Mammi!*" they said in unison, enthusiastically welcoming their grandmother. The round-faced, plumpish woman bustled past me carrying a cake pan covered with tinfoil.

"You brought my favorite cake?" Naomi asked.

"*Yah.* Chocolate with brown sugar frosting. Go ahead and cut it, and then help yourself."

"*Denki!*" Naomi took the pan from her grandma and headed for a rectangular table covered with a red-and-white gingham cloth.

I glanced out the window and saw several buggies and Amish people making their way to the back porch. As they entered the kitchen, Harvey welcomed them by first names.

A woman carrying a Tupperware container entered. "We saw you out in the buggy," she said. "May we come in?"

"Of course, Abigail. *Gut* to see you. Come in." Harvey took the container from her and set it on the table.

"I brought muffins. We had them in the buggy..." Her face flushed.

"*Denki* for bringing them. We are now officially prepared to entertain today."

Abigail's husband removed his hat and placed it on a peg as if he'd been in this room many times. He shook Harvey's hand, but his gaze was planted on me. Before he could get in a word, more people strolled into the kitchen, several carrying food items. Soon, the kitchen table was a smorgasbord of scrumptious-looking tarts, whoopie pies, cakes, and candies.

In twenty minutes the room was filled with chatter and laughter. I shook many hands and recognized some of the women I'd met at the Schmuckers' home during the barn raising. I also saw several of my parents' neighbors, people I'd seen on Sundays before the district split. I'd only seen them since if they came into the fabric store.

They barraged me with questions about the nursery and the café.

"*Ach*, you're really the manager?" one woman about my age asked. Several declared they would hire a passenger van and visit the café.

"I can't imagine our food is better than what you brought." I nibbled on a chocolate brownie.

"In that case, we'll each bring you our favorite recipe," one woman said, and they all agreed. But could they bring me a recipe for a new beginning? How much easier my life would be if I fell head over heels in love with Harvey. But there was no buzz of attraction between us.

"*Denki*. I'm overwhelmed by your generosity." I polished off the brownie.

They continued to ask about the café, but I surmised their real questions circumnavigated Harvey's and my friendship.

This was a visiting Sunday, so I shouldn't have been surprised people were calling upon their neighbors. But they might have been headed to see relatives and changed their destination the moment they saw Harvey's buggy on the road with me perched next to him. Curiosity was natural, and in this county they could be Harvey's relatives or lifelong friends.

Harvey's daughters brought out plates, flatware, and paper napkins for the growing crowd. Several men gave me a double look and then chatted with Harvey in a way that made me feel as if I were on display. I doubted he'd been talking about me, but others probably had. Well, I knew they'd been gabbing about me for years. I was the wanton woman who'd conceived a child out of wedlock. I was Jake Miller's girlfriend on the side when he wasn't out-of-state living as an *Englischer*. I bet they thought Jake had only come home so he could inherit the farm and be rich if Amos died. And they might be right, for all I knew.

I was *ferhoodled* when moments later Jake entered, dressed Amish. He removed his hat and shook Harvey's hand. "I hope you don't mind my stopping by like this," Jake said. "*Mamm* spent the night at the hospital and won't leave. I offered to take her with me to church, but she doesn't want to leave my *dat* for more than a minute."

"I can imagine she's beyond exhausted." Harvey scanned Jake's attire. "You went to church without her?"

"*Yah.*"

"Driving an automobile?"

"*Nee,* I brought out my parents' buggy horse. That poor animal was dying to get out of the barn."

"That's the only reason you drove their buggy?"

"I didn't wish to be disrespectful." Jake held his hat by its brim. "Since I plan to be baptized, I'll return the car to my friend in New York today and take a bus back home. Before church, I stopped by Eva's parents', who were expecting her. Finally, they gave up." He glanced to me and said, "They were worried but supposed you'd made other plans. And, apparently, they were correct. I intended to drive over to the nursery, but I noticed every buggy coming from the other direction turning into Harvey's lane."

I needed to speak up for myself. "Coming here was a spur-of-the-moment decision. Harvey invited me." But no one seemed to hear me.

"Did you attend church by yourself, Jake?" Harvey asked.

"*Yah.* It was most enjoyable to see my old friends."

"And what was the message?"

"Minister Stephen spoke about the prodigal son from the book of Luke. After, I asked him if the ministers had decided it would be a good topic since I was there. But he said no. They went upstairs to pray about it before I arrived. But he was pleased I'd attended. He didn't even make a wisecrack about my short hair."

Jake gazed into Harvey's face as if waiting for the bishop to reprimand him, but Harvey said, "I'm glad you attended church and that you went to the trouble of getting your parents' horse out. You're moving in the right direction, for sure."

Several other men nodded. "*Gut* for you, Jake," one said. "Our heavenly Father is always willing to take us back into his arms."

Harvey's daughters snuck glances at Jake the whole time he was there. One offered him muffins and squares of cake in what seemed to be a coquettish manner, which initiated a frown from Harvey.

"If you don't mind, I'll eat this later." Jake scooped up a muffin and wrapped it in a paper napkin.

"I must be on my way," he told Harvey, as if I weren't even standing there. Which was the proper etiquette because Harvey was the host, but it made me feel invisible and sad. Jake's glance glided right past mine as he moved toward the back door.

"Wait." The word flew out of my mouth and hung in the air. The room went silent, conversations halting, all eyes turning to me. I wasn't invisible after all.

"Are you going to the hospital to see your *dat*?"

"*Yah.*" Jake glanced toward the back door as an Amish couple strolled in, full of cheer.

"Eva," Harvey said, "I'll take you later."

"And leave your family and company?" I couldn't bring myself to look into his face.

"But you haven't met my son and his family. Later, I'll rent a van, and several of us can escort you."

I knew my parents would be horrified, but I said, "*Denki* for your kind offer, but Ruth and Amos need me now."

"You'd drive all the way to the hospital in Jake's buggy? Or in his car?"

Jake stood tall and faced Harvey. "You are welcome to accompany us in the car if you'd like to see my *dat*. But then I'm leaving town to return the car."

Harvey tugged on his beard as he fixed his gaze upon him. "I'll come with you since you so kindly asked. And to make sure that car goes back to its *Englisch* owner."

One woman covered her mouth with her hand as if in shock over his response.

"You're leaving us?" his *mamm* asked.

"*Yah, Mamm.* Would you step in for me and be the hostess? What's mine is yours."

The lines on her creased face deepened. "I wish my *dochder* were still alive to see this." Her statement hinted she was his former wife's mother.

Harvey cracked a forlorn smile. "Being married to a bishop was a hardship for her, that's for sure. I should have thought to visit Amos and Ruth myself, first thing this morning."

# FIFTY

Several women said goodbye to me as I ducked my head and followed Harvey and Jake outside. I felt a splat of rain on my forehead.

"Grab one of those coats in the utility room," Harvey told me.

"*Denki.*" I went back inside and took hold of a black hooded raincoat.

To say riding back to Jake's parents' farm in their buggy was awkward was an understatement. Several teenage boys had already unharnessed Harvey's horse and led it into his barn soon after we'd arrived, as well as most of the other horses. Only Jake's buggy stood close to the house, the horse tethered to a nearby post as if Jake had not meant to spend much time there anyway. I wondered if his showing up at Harvey's at all would be considered a rude, brash, in-your-face move. He was braver than I was.

I could only imagine the conversations about us in Harvey's house now, but I felt sure I should visit Amos and comfort Ruth. Or maybe her daughters and friends had finally come to support her. Either way, I found myself hunched in the backseat of the buggy. Before I'd slipped inside behind Jake, I'd seen how Harvey's face wore a serious mask. But as the rainfall accelerated, my guess was he'd soon be happy to ride in an automobile.

"As I said before, my accepting this ride in no way means I approve of Jake driving cars." Harvey glanced over his shoulder to include me.

"If you'd rather I drove this buggy all that way, I can," Jake said. "But a storm is brewing."

"*Nee*, your horse is obviously fatigued and needs to be watered and fed. Have you forgotten how to take care of your animals?"

"Actually, I have feed in the back and will be in no short supply of water this afternoon."

"Never mind. Let's get to your parents' home, make the switch, and get on with it."

By thc time we reached the Millers' farm, the rain was sheeting down. Jake hopped out of the buggy, unhitched the horse, and escorted the animal into the barn. Several minutes later, he returned, unlocked the car, and we all dove in, with me in the backseat.

"I'm tempted to ask you to drive me home," Harvey said.

"As you like." Jake started the engine.

"*Nee*. We've come this far." Harvey buckled his seat belt. "I might as well accept your hospitality, such as it is."

"Harvey, I don't mind driving you back home. It will take but a few minutes."

"Just go. My family is used to my erratic hours. When people like your parents need comfort, I should help them even if they are in a different district. Their bishop is in no condition to do so."

Jake switched on the windshield wipers as the storm increased. Although it was only early afternoon, the sky turned elephant gray. Streams were forming on the sides of the road. Vehicles approaching from the other direction splashed blinding arcs of moisture on the windshield.

We passed several buggies. My heart went out to the drenched horses and the buggies' occupants. I started to tell Jake that Olivia's parents told Harvey they might let her come help his parents, but then I decided to let Harvey bring it up.

Jake slowed the car and spoke to Harvey. "My guess is you're fixing to marry Eva. Am I right?"

"That's a presumptuous question."

"Well, then, I'll discuss it for the both of us. You want to marry Eva, and I don't blame you." Jake's eyes caught mine in the rearview mirror. "My opinion is she should marry you and put her past behind her. I'll never live up to her expectations."

I leaned forward and saw Harvey crossing his legs at the ankles and then uncrossing them. "As you well know, a couple must decide these private matters between themselves."

Jake slowed behind a semi, thus avoiding a spray of water. "You are a fine man, and I truly respect you, Harvey. But if you don't snap up this opportunity, you're acting the fool."

"Hey, don't I have any say in this?" My hands gripped Jake's seatback in front of me. "For one thing, Harvey hasn't asked me to marry him."

"And if he did?" Jake shot back.

"I'd tell him another man owned my heart." There, I'd said it.

"Rubbish." Harvey bulleted his words at me. "You've been reading too many *Englisch* romance novels, haven't you?"

"How do you know?"

"Beatrice said she lent you one." Harvey tugged his beard.

"How and why did that subject matter come up?"

"She was going on and on about her beloved Italy. How much she missed it. Then she let slip you wished you could visit after reading a borrowed book."

Jake let up on the gas. "If you go, Evie, take me with you."

"Don't be preposterous," Harvey said. "Of course she's not crossing the Atlantic on a jet. Flying in an aircraft is *verboten*."

"What about taking a cruise ship?" Jake's singsongy voice told me he was taunting Harvey, whose upper lip lifted into a snarl.

"Do you or do you not wish to become baptized and marry Eva?" Harvey said.

"*Yah*, I do. But could we not take a trip as a honeymoon? Or even go somewhere special before then?"

"Before you get married?" Harvey's raspy voice flooded the car's interior.

"We could go to a justice of the peace," Jake said. "I asked Eva to go to one with me yesterday before it dawned on me we needed a marriage license first. Maybe tomorrow, before my *dat* returns home."

If Jake were trying to exacerbate Harvey's ire, he was doing a fine job.

"I could never allow such a thing," Harvey said.

"But tell me this," Jake persisted. "If Eva and I married outside the church, could we later become baptized?"

"I've heard of such cases, but why would a couple choose to do such a thing? In my opinion, you're being obstinate and thoughtless."

As the men spoke, I envisioned traveling to Italy. But wasn't the view of the barn and fields at sunset from Jake's kitchen as beautiful as any I'd ever seen? I guessed we could always hop on a train sometime and visit the rest of the country, as others had.

Harvey turned in his seat to speak to Jake. "Why are you suggesting such a preposterous idea?"

"Because I don't want you to marry Eva, and I don't want to wait to marry her. You have control over when we get baptized, but we are not helpless."

Harvey craned his head to speak to me. "You would actually consider marrying this reprobate of a man in a courthouse?"

"Would it not be legal?" I asked.

"*Yah*, it would be legal, but not obedient." His eyes narrowed. "Don't you wish to obey *Gott*? Aren't you the girl who's tried to break loose from the rumors encumbering her like lead weights? How can you expect the Lord's forgiveness when you disobey him?"

"Ask for compassion?" I said. "Forgive all others who've harmed me?"

"Are you implying I'm harming you now when all I'm trying to do is help you?" Harvey's mouth twisted.

"But, Harvey," Jake said, "I have yet to see any indication that you love her."

I held my breath as Jake took a sharp turn onto a side road.

"I love everyone in the district." Harvey was stalling, as far as I could tell.

"But do you love Eva above all other women? You're lonely, as any widower who adored his wife would be." Jake seemed to have us driving in circles.

Harvey's face sank into his opened hands. "You can't imagine how lonely I've been."

I felt like weeping when I heard the tremor in his voice. I, too, knew loneliness.

"*Yah*, I can relate," Jake said. "But Evie will never take your *frau*'s place."

"I know that." Harvey pinched between his eyes. "No one could ever replace my dearest wife. But eventually—maybe when my girls marry—I might wed a widow. I can't imagine the solitude once my *dochders* leave home."

Jake slapped the turn indicator. "One way or another, I will marry Evie, and sooner rather than later. Either at the county courthouse or during a church service, which means both Evie and I must be baptized in the near future. We can't wait until the crops are harvested in the fall and the celery has grown in her *mamm*'s garden. We'll pick up celery at the supermarket."

Jake pulled to a halt and caught my eyes in the rearview mirror. "Do you agree, Evie?"

"*Yah*, I do. I can't wait that long either, not after all these years."

"*Ach*, what are we doing here?" Harvey looked up at his own house. Jake had driven him back home without our noticing.

Harvey's mother-in-law opened the door and waved.

"Where to now?" I asked Jake after Harvey had gotten out.

"To visit my parents, to announce the *gut* news. And then to yours."

# Epilogue

***Two years later***

Eva Miller stood at the kitchen sink gazing out the window at the most beautiful view on earth. Her loving husband, Jake, cradled and bounced their six-month-old son. Their collie—Jake's engagement gift to her instead of a clock—circled Jake and licked the child's bare feet, generating giggles of laughter. Beyond them stretched their cornfields.

Next to the house, Eva's flower garden thrived, blooming in a riot of color, a pleasant view for Ruth and Amos from the *daadi haus*, where they now resided. Amos's thinking was still a bit fuzzy, but he was growing stronger every day. Both he and Ruth had been ecstatic to add Eva to the family.

Eva's smile widened as she recalled how quickly the bishops had convened for a special meeting once Harvey told them Jake and Eva planned to obtain a marriage license at the Lancaster County courthouse, even if that required Eva to get a photo ID. The bishops agreed it was best for Jake and Eva to marry in the church, which required the couple to be baptized immediately. Harvey bent the rules, but not without reluctance. He warned Jake he intended to keep a close watch on him. Eva told Harvey she would too.

Eva's *mamm* provided them a home wedding, much to her *mamm*'s delight. Upon hearing the news, Marta flew into action and orchestrated the festive celebration. Olivia Beiler, again the manager of the café after helping Ruth with Amos for a time, took charge of the menu and food preparation. Three hundred people squeezed into Eva's parents' home. Two sittings were required to accommodate the hungry crowd after the ceremony. A few *Englischers*, such as Stephen, his new girlfriend, and Beatrice, were welcome guests.

Bishop Harvey officiated at the ceremony. His eyes glistened with genuine happiness as he pronounced Jake and Eva husband and wife. There was hardly a dry eye in the house. Ruth and Amos dabbed their eyes repeatedly, not to mention Eva's parents and even Marta.

As to their honeymoon, Jake and Eva didn't travel to Italy but rather ventured to the historic Italian Market in Philadelphia, which Beatrice said was the closest thing to it without leaving the state. Hiring a driver of Italian heritage to take them there was her wedding present. Jake and Eva enjoyed meandering through the grocery and cheese stores, bakeries, gift shops, and restaurants that left Jake's breath smelling too much of garlic for Eva's taste. Yet his kisses remained sweeter than ever.

Eva figured she and Jake would continue to be the subject of rumors. But she was determined to forgive those who'd gossiped about her—no doubt a lifelong challenge she was committed to overcome. She'd learned she couldn't change others, only her response to them.

Forgiveness came easier to her now.

# Discussion Questions

1. How did false rumors alter the course of Eva's life? Do you have empathy for her, or do you think she should have acted differently? Could she have prevented the rumors?
2. Have you ever been the subject of gossip? How did it feel or alter your life? Do you know of a way to move beyond rumors?
3. Why do you think people gossip? Do you find yourself gossiping even when not meaning to? I think we've all been guilty of this. What's the remedy?
4. Do you think Eva can truly forgive those who have maligned her? Does a person need to ask for forgiveness for you to bestow it? How is forgiveness healing and strengthening for the individual granting it?
5. Do you think Eva's plan to begin anew—starting from scratch—was a good one? Was she brave or foolhardy to embark into the unknown? In your opinion, did she marry the right man?
6. Who is your favorite character and why? What element of his or her personality or behavior do you relate to?
7. Do you like Beatrice? How and why does her attitude toward Eva change as the novel progresses? How do you think Beatrice overcame her own difficult situations?
8. As you've come to know someone, have they surprised you in a good or bad way? Did Olivia's behavior shock you? Were you surprised that once she repented, she was forgiven and accepted by the Amish church?

9. Most of us have seen actors awake from a coma in a movie or on TV, but did you know the Hollywood portrayals of instant recovery are for the most part false?
10. Do you think Stephen's apology to Bill was warranted? How did both men benefit? Sometimes an apology is met with anger, but how can it bless the person bestowing it?

# Acknowledgments

Thank you, dear readers, for choosing to read my book. I am indebted to each one of you. Much time, rescarch, and effort went into writing and publishing it for your enjoyment.

Humongous thanks to all the fabulous folks at Harvest House Publishers, foremost Kim Moore. My gratitude to each person at Harvest House who helped craft it, and to the sales team. Thank you to my excellent editor, Jean Kavich Bloom.

Thanks to talented Amish author Linda Byler for her encouragement and fact verification. Thank you to friends Sam and Susie Lapp in Lancaster County, Pennsylvania; Amish Quilter Emma Stoltzfus of ES Quilts; and many other Amish who have helped me but prefer to remain anonymous. Thank you, friend Herb Scrivener, owner of Zook's Fabrics in Intercourse, Pennsylvania.

Others who have helped me are Rudy DeLaurentus, president of the Lancaster Italian Cultural Society; Jamie at the Quarryville Fire Station, Lancaster County; and Allegra Johnson, adult services librarian at Lancaster Public Library.

Thank you to Linda, for describing her remarkable journey through a two-week coma.

Many thanks to my dear cousin Alex McBrien, who saved her family's horses and her father's Arabian stallion and prized Black Angus bull from a horrific barn fire and kindly described the chaotic scene to me.

I'm grateful for my faithful writing/critique group: Kathleen Kohler, Roberta Kehle, Judy Bodmer, Thornton Ford, Paul Malm, and Peyton Burkhart.

Always, I'm thankful for my stupendous literary agent, Chip MacGregor.

# About the Author

**Kate Lloyd** is a novelist, a mother of two sons, and a passionate observer of human relationships. A native of Baltimore, she often spends time with family and friends in Lancaster County, Pennsylvania, the inspiration for her bestselling books in the Legacy of Lancaster Trilogy, and *A Letter from Lancaster County*. She has Mennonite relatives in Lancaster County and is a member of the Lancaster County Mennonite Historical Society. Kate studied art, photography, and Italian in college. She's worked a variety of jobs, including restaurateur, both as sole proprietor and manager. Kate and her husband live in the Pacific Northwest.

Kate loves connecting with her readers. Please feel free to visit her at:

Website: www.katelloyd.com

Facebook: https://www.facebook.com/katelloydbooks

Twitter: @KateLloydAuthor,
https://twitter.com/KateLloydAuthor

Pinterest: Kate Lloyd,
https://www.pinterest.com/katelloydauthor

HARVEST HOUSE PUBLISHERS
EUGENE, OREGON